D1600082

FICTION

They drew her back before they dared attempt to raise her.

# The Works of Guy de Maupassant

VOLUME V

## UNE VIE

AND OTHER STORIES

*ILLUSTRATED*

BIGELOW, BROWN & CO., Inc.
NEW YORK

# CONTENTS

|  | PAGE |
|---|---|
| A Woman's Life (Une Vie) | 1 |
| Hautot Senior and Hautot Junior | 268 |
| Little Louise Roqué | 287 |
| Mother and Daughter | 335 |
| A Passion | 341 |
| No Quarter | 352 |
| The Impolite Sex | 361 |
| Woman's Wiles | 369 |
| A Night in Spring | 378 |
| The Jewels | 385 |
| A Coward | 395 |

# INTRODUCTION

## By Edmund Gosse

THE most robust and masculine of recent French novelists is a typical Norman, sprung from an ancient noble family, originally of Lorraine, but long settled in the Pays de Caux. The traveler from England towards Paris, soon after leaving Dieppe, sees on his left hand, immediately beyond the station of St. Aubin, a handsome sixteenth-century house, the Château de Miromesnil, on a hill above the railway. Here, surrounded by the relics of his warlike and courtly ancestors, Henri René Albert Guy de Maupassant was born on the 5th of August, 1850. He was early associated with the great Norman master of fiction, Gustave Flaubert, who perceived his genius and enthusiastically undertook the training of his intelligence. Through 1870 and 1871 the young man served in the war as a common soldier. He was somewhat slow in taking up the profession of letters, and was thirty years of age before he became in any degree distinguished. In 1879 the Troisième Théâtre Français produced a short play of his, *Histoire du Vieux Temps* (An Old-World Story), gracefully written in rhyme, but showing no very remarkable aptitude for the stage.

It was in 1880 that De Maupassant was suddenly made famous by two published volumes. The one was a volume of Verses (*Des Vers*), twenty pieces, most of them of a narrative character, extremely brilliant in execution, and audacious in tone. One of these, slightly exceeding its fellows in crudity, was threatened with a prosecution in law as an outrage upon manners, and the fortune of the volume was secured. The early poems of De Maupassant like those of Paul Bourget, are not without sterling merit as poetry, but their main interest is that they reflect the characteristics of their author's mind. Such pieces as " Fin-d'Amour," and " Au Bord de l'Eau," in the 1880 volume, are simply short stories told in verse, instead of in prose. In this same year, Guy de Maupassant, who had thrown in his lot with the Naturalist Novelists, contributed a short tale to the volume called *Les Soirées de Médan,* to which Zola, Huysmans, Hennique, Céard and Paul Alexis also affixed their names. He was less known than any of these men, yet it was his story, *Boule de Suif* (Lump of Suet, or Ball of Fat), which ensured the success of the book. This episode of the war, treated with cynicism, tenderness, humor and pathos mingled in quite a new manner, revealed a fresh genius for the art of narrative. There was an instant demand for more short stories from the same pen, and it was soon discovered that the fecundity and resource of the new writer were as extraordinary as the charm of his style and the objective force of his vision.

It is unnecessary to recount here the names of even the chief of De Maupassant's stories. If we judge them merely by their vivacity, richness and variety, they are the best short tales which have been produced anywhere during the same years. But it is impossible not to admit that they have grave faults, which exclude them from all possible recommendation to young and ingenuous readers. No bibliography of them can be attempted, the publishers of M. Guy de Maupassant having reprinted his lesser stories so frequently, and with such infinite varieties of arrangement, that the positive sequence of these little masterpieces has been hopelessly confused. Three stories in particular, however, may be mentioned, *La Maison Tellier*, 1881; *Les Sœurs Rondoli*, 1884, and *Miss Harriett*, 1885, because the collections which originally bore these names were pre-eminently successful in drawing the attention of the critics to the author's work.

It was not until he had won a very great reputation as a short story-teller, that De Maupassant attempted a long novel. He published only six single volume stories, all of which are included in the present edition. The first was *Une Vie* (A Life), 1883, a very careful study of Norman manners, highly finished in the manner of Flaubert, whom he has styled " that irreproachable master whom I admire above all others." In certain directions, I do not think that De Maupassant has surpassed *Une Vie*, in fidelity to nature, in a Dutch exactitude of portraiture, in a certain distinction of tone; it was the history of an unhappy gentlewoman, doomed throughout life to be deceived, impoverished, disdained and overwhelmed. *Bel-Ami*, 1885, which succeeded this quiet and Quaker-colored book, was a much more vivid novel, an extremely vigorous picture of the rise in social prominence of a penniless fellow in Paris, without a brain or a heart, who depends wholly upon his impudence and his good looks. After 1885 De Maupassant published four novels — *Mont-Oriol*, 1887; *Pierre et Jean*, 1888; *Fort comme la Mort* (As Strong as Death, or The Ruling Passion), 1889; and *Nôtre Cœur* (Our Heart), 1890.

Of these six remarkable books, the *Pierre et Jean* is certainly the most finished and the most agreeable. In *Mont-Oriol*, a beautiful landscape of Auvergne mountain and bath enshrines a singularly pessimistic rendering of the adage " He loved and he rode away." Few of the author's thoughtful admirers will admit that in *Fort comme la Mort* he has done justice to his powers. In *Nôtre Cœur* he has taken up one of the psychological problems which have hitherto lain in the undisputed province of M. Bourget, and has shown how difficult it is in the musky atmosphere of fashionable Paris for two hearts to recover the Mayday freshness of their impulses, the spontaneous flow of their illusions; he displays himself here in a new light, less brutal than of old, more delicate and analytical. With regard to *Pierre et Jean*, it would be difficult to find words wherewith to describe it and its relation to the best English fiction more just or more felicitous than those in which Mr. Henry James welcomed its first appearance:—" *Pierre et Jean* is, so far as my judgment goes, a faultless production. . . . It is the best of M. de Maupassant's novels, mainly because M. de Maupassant has never before been so clever. It is a pleasure to see a mature talent able to renew itself, strike another note, and appear still young. . . . The author's choice of a *milieu*, moreover, will serve to English readers as an example of how much more democratic contemporary French fiction is than that of his own country. The greater part of it — almost all the work of Zola and of Daudet, the list of Flaubert's novels, and the best of those of the brothers De Goncourt — treat of that vast, dim section of society, which, lying between those luxurious walks on

whose behalf there are easy suppositions and that darkness of misery which, in addition to being picturesque,
brings philanthropy also to the writer's aid, constitutes
really, in extent and expressiveness, the substance of
every nation. In England, where the fashion of fiction
still sets mainly to the country-house and the hunting-
field, and yet more novels are published than anywhere
else in the world, that thick twilight of mediocrity of
condition has been little explored. May it yield tri-
umphs in the years to come!"

The great merit of M. de Maupassant as a writer is
his frank and masculine directness. He sees life
clearly, and he undertakes to describe it as he sees it, in
concise and vigorous language. He is a realist, yet
without the gloominess of Zola, over whom he claims
one great advantage, that of possessing a rich sense of
humor, and a large share of the old Gallic wit. His
pessimism, indeed, is inexorable, and he pushes the misfortune, or more often the degradation, of his characters to its extreme logical conclusion. Yet, even in his
saddest stories, the general design is rarely sordid.
For a long while he was almost exclusively concerned
with impressions of Normandy; a little later he became
one of the many painters of Paris. Then he traveled
widely, in the south of Europe, in Africa; wherever he
went he took with him a quick and sensitive eye for the
aspects of nature, and his descriptive passages, which
are never pushed to a tiresome excess of length, are
often faultlessly vivid. He attempted, with a good
deal of cleverness, to analyze character, but his real
power seems to lie in describing, in a sober style and
with a virile impartiality, the superficial aspects of
action and intrigue.

# UNE VIE

## (A WOMAN'S LIFE)

### I

J EANNE, having finished her packing, went to the window, but it had not stopped raining.

All night long the downpour had pattered against the roofs and the window-panes. The low, heavy clouds seemed as though they had burst, and were emptying themselves on the world, to reduce it to a pulp and melt it as though it were a sugar-loaf. A hot wind swept by in gusts; the murmur of the overflowing gutters filled the empty streets, and the houses, like sponges, absorbed the moisture which, penetrating to the interior, made the walls wet from cellar to attic.

Jeanne, who had left the convent the day before, free at last and ready for all the happiness of a life of which she had dreamed for so long, feared that her father would hesitate about starting if the weather did not clear up, and, for the hundredth time since the morning, she studied the horizon.

Looking round, she saw that she had forgotten to put her almanac in her traveling bag. She took from the wall the little card which bore in the center of a design, the date of the current year 1819 in gilt letters, and crossed out with a pencil the first four columns, drawing a line through each saint's name till she came to the second of May, the day she had left the convent.

A voice outside the door called: " Jeannette! "

Jeanne answered: " Come in, papa." And her father appeared.

The Baron Simon-Jecques Le Perthuis des Vauds was a gentleman of the old school, eccentric and good-hearted. An enthusiastic follower of Jean-Jacques Rousseau, he had a loving tenderness for all nature; for the fields, the woods, and for animals. An aristocrat by birth, he hated '93 by instinct; but of a philosophical temperament and liberal by education, he loathed tyranny with an inoffensive and declamatory hatred. The strongest, and at the same time the weakest, trait in his character was his generosity; a generosity which had not enough arms to caress, to give, to embrace; the generosity of a creator which was utterly devoid of system, and to which he gave way with no attempt to resist his impulses, as though part of his will were paralyzed; it was a want of energy, and almost amounted to a vice.

A man of theories, he had thought out a whole plan of education for his daughter, wishing to make her happy and good, straightforward and affectionate. Till she was twelve years old she had stayed at home; then, in spite of her mother's tears, she was sent to the Sacred Heart Convent. He had kept her strictly immured there, totally ignorant of worldly things, for he wished her to return to him, at the age of seventeen, innocent, that he might himself immerse her in a sort of bath of rational poetry; and, in the fields, surrounded by the fertile earth, he meant to instruct her, and enlighten her by the sight of the serene laws of life, the innocent loves and the simple tenderness of the animals.

And now she was leaving the convent, radiant and brimful of happiness, ready for every joy and for all the charming adventures that, in the idle moments of her days and during the long nights, she had already pictured to herself.

She looked like a portrait by Veronese, with her shining, fair hair, which looked as though it had given part of its color to her skin, the creamy skin of a high-born girl, hardly tinted with pink and shaded by a soft velvety down, which could just be seen when she was kissed by a sun-ray. Her eyes were blue, an opaque blue, like the eyes of a Dutch china figure. On her left nostril was a little mole, another on the right side of her chin, where curled a few hairs so much like the color of the skin that they could hardly be seen. She was tall, with a well-developed chest and supple waist. Her clear voice sometimes sounded too shrill, but her merry laugh made everyone around her feel happy. She had a way of frequently putting both hands to her forehead, as though to smooth her hair.

She ran to her father, put her arms around his neck and kissed him.

" Well, are we going to start? " she asked.

He smiled, shook back his white hair, which he wore rather long, and pointing towards the window:

" How can you think of traveling in such weather? " he said.

Then she pleaded coaxingly and affectionately, " Oh, papa, please do let us start. It will be fine in the afternoon."

" But your mother will never consent to it."

" Oh, yes, I promise you she shall; I will answer for her."

" Well, if you can persuade your mother, I am quite willing to start."

She hastened towards the baroness's room, for she
had looked forward to this day with great impatience.
Since she had entered the convent she had not left
Rouen, as her father would allow no distracting pleasures before the age he had fixed. Only twice had she
been taken to Paris for a fortnight, but that was another town, and she longed for the country. Now she
was going to spend the summer on their estate, Les
Peuples, in an old family château built on the cliff near
Yport; and she was looking forward to the boundless
happiness of a free life beside the waves. And then
it was understood that the manor was to be given to
her, and that she was to live there always when she was
married; and the rain which had been falling incessantly since the night before was the first real grief of
her life.

In three minutes she came running out of her mother's room, crying:

" Papa! papa! Mamma is quite willing. Tell them
to harness the horses."

The rain had not given over in the least, in fact, it
was coming down still faster when the landau came
round to the door. Jeanne was ready to jump in
when the baroness came down the stairs, supported on
one side by her husband, and on the other by a tall
maid, whose frame was as strong and as well-knit as a
boy's. She was a Normandy girl from Caux, and
looked at least twenty years old, though she really
was scarcely eighteen. In the baron's family she was
treated somewhat like a second daughter, for she was
Jeanne's foster-sister. She was named Rosalie, and her
principal duty consisted in aiding her mistress to walk,
for, within the last few years, the baroness had attained

an enormous size, owing to an hypertrophy of the heart, of which she was always complaining.

Breathing very hard, the baroness reached the steps of the old hotel; there she stopped to look at the court-yard where the water was streaming down, and murmured:

" Really, it is not prudent."

Her husband answered with a smile:

" It was you who wished it, Madame Adélaïde."

She bore the pompous name of Adélaïde, and he always prefaced it by " Madame " with a certain little look of mock-respect.

She began to move forward again, and with difficulty got into the carriage, all the springs of which bent under her weight. The baron sat by her side, and Jeanne and Rosalie took their places with their backs to the horses. Ludivine, the cook, brought a bundle of rugs, which were thrown over their knees, and two baskets, which were pushed under their legs; then she climbed up beside old Simon and enveloped herself in a great rug, which covered her entirely. The concierge and his wife came to shut the gate and wish them good-bye, and after some parting instructions about the baggage, which was to follow in a cart, the carriage started.

Old Simon, the coachman, with his head held down and his back bent under the rain, could hardly be seen in his three-caped coat; and the moaning wind rattled against the windows and swept the rain along the road.

The horses trotted briskly down to the quay, passed the row of big ships, whose masts and yards and ropes stood out against the gray sky like bare trees, and entered the long Boulevard du Mont Riboudet. Soon they reached the country, and from time to time the outline of a weeping-willow, with its branches hanging in a corpse-like inertness, could be vaguely seen through the watery mist. The horses' shoes clattered on the road; and the four wheels made regular rings of mud.

Inside the carriage they were silent; their spirits seemed damped, like the earth. The baroness leaned back, rested her head against the cushions, and closed her eyes. The baron looked out mournfully at the monotonous, wet fields, and Rosalie, with a parcel on her knees, sat musing in the animal-like way in which the lower classes indulge. But Jeanne felt herself revive under this warm rain like a plant which is put into the open air after being shut up in a dark closet; and the greatness of her joy seemed to prevent any sadness reaching her heart. Although she did not speak, she wanted to sing and to put her hand outside and drink the water with which it would be filled; and the desolate look of the country only added to the enjoyment she felt at being carried along so swiftly, and at feeling herself sheltered in the midst of this deluge.

Under the ceaseless rain a cloud of steam rose from the backs of the two horses.

The baroness gradually fell asleep; her face, surrounded by six stiff curls, sank lower and lower, though it was partly sustained by the three big waves of her neck, the last curves of which lost themselves in the amplitude of her chest. Her head, raised by each respiration, as regularly sank again; her cheeks puffed out, and from her half-opened lips issued a deep snore. Her husband leaned over towards her and softly placed in her hands, crossed on her ample lap, a leather pocket-book. The touch awoke her, and she looked at the object in her lap with the stupefied look of one suddenly aroused from sleep. The pocket-book fell and opened, and the gold and bank-notes it contained were scattered all over the carriage. That woke her up altogether, and the light-heartedness of her daughter found vent in a burst of laughter.

The baron picked up the money and placed it on her knees.

"There, my dear," he said. "That is all that is left of the farm at Eletot. I have sold it to pay for the doing up of Les Peuples as we shall live there so much now."

She counted the six thousand, four hundred francs, and put them quietly into her pocket.

It was the ninth farm that they had sold out of the thirty-one left them by their parents; but they still had about twenty thousand livres a year coming in from property which, well-managed, would have easily brought in thirty thousand francs. As they lived quietly, this income would have been amply sufficient for them, if their lavish generosity had not constantly exhausted their supplies. It drained their money from them as the sun draws water from a swamp. The gold melted, vanished, disappeared. How? No one knew. One of them was always saying: "I don't know how it is, but I have spent a hundred francs to-day, and I haven't anything to show for it."

To give was one of the great joys of their existence, and they perfectly understood each other on this point in a way that was at once grand and touching.

Jeanne asked: "Is my château looking beautiful now?"

"You will see, my child," answered the baron, gaily.

Little by little the violence of the storm diminished; soon there was nothing more than a sort of mist, a very fine drizzling rain. The arch of the clouds seemed to get higher and lighter; and suddenly a long oblique sunbeam fell on the fields. Through the break in the clouds a streak of blue sky could be seen, and then the rift got bigger as though a veil were being drawn back, and a beautiful sky of a pure deep blue spread itself out over the world. There was a fresh mild breeze like a happy sigh from the earth, and from the gardens and woods came now and again the merry song of a bird drying his wings.

The evening was drawing in; everyone inside the carriage, except Jeanne, was asleep. Twice they had stopped at an inn, to rest the horses and give them water and corn. The sun had set, and in the distance the bells were ringing; in a little village the lamps were being lighted, and the sky was studded with stars. Sometimes the lights of a homestead could be seen, their rays piercing the darkness; and, all at once among the fir-trees, behind a hill, the large, red, sleepy moon arose.

It was so mild that the windows were left down, and Jeanne, tired of dreaming, and her stock of happy visions exhausted, was now sleeping. Sometimes the numbness caused by resting too long in one position aroused her, and she looked outside and saw the trees fly past her in the clear night, or some cows, lying in a field, raise their heads at the noise of the carriage. Then she settled herself in a fresh position, and tried to continue an interrupted dream, but the continual rumbling of the carriage sounded in her ears, confusing her thoughts, and she shut her eyes again, her mind feeling as tired as her body.

At last the carriage stopped, and men and women came to the doors with lanterns in their hands. They had arrived, and Jeanne, suddenly awakened, sprang out, while her father and Rosalie, lighted by a farmer, almost carried in the baroness; she was quite worn out, and, catching her breath, she kept saying in a weak little voice: "Ah, my children! what shall I do?" She would have nothing to eat or drink, but went to bed and fell asleep at once.

Jeanne and the baron had supper alone. They smiled when their glances met, and, at every moment, took each other's hands across the table; then, both of them filled with a childish delight, they went over the manor which had just been put in thorough repair.

It was one of those big, high, Normandy houses generally built of white stone which turns gray, and which, large enough to accommodate a regiment, have something of the farm about them as well as the château.

An immense hall, going from end to end, divided the house into two parts, its large doors opening opposite each other. A double staircase bestrode this entrance hall leaving the center empty, and, meeting at the height of the first floor, formed a sort of bridge. On the ground-floor, to the right, was the huge drawing-room hung with tapestry with a design of birds and flowers. All the furniture was in tapestry, the subjects of the designs being taken from La Fontaine's fables. Jeanne was delighted at recognizing a chair she had liked when she was quite a child, and which represented the history of the Fox and the Stork. The library, full of old books, and two other rooms, which were not used, came next to the drawing-room. On the left were the dining-room, which had been newly wainscoted, the linen-press, the pantry, the kitchen, and a little room with a bath in it.

A corridor ran the whole length of the first story, the ten doors of as many rooms opening on to it, and Jeanne's room was quite at the end, on the right. The baron had just had it freshly furnished by simply using some hangings and furniture that had been stored away in a garret. Very old Flemish tapestry peopled the room with strange characters, and when she saw the bed Jeanne gave a cry of delight. At the four corners four birds of carved oak, quite black and polished till they shone, supported the bed, looking as though they were its guardians. The sides were decorated with two large garlands of carved flowers and fruit; and the four bed-posts, finely fluted and crowned with Corinthian capitals, supported a cornice of entwined roses and cupids. It was a monumental couch, and yet was very graceful, despite the somber appearance of the wood darkened by age. The counterpane and canopy, made of old dark blue silk, starred here and there with great *fleurs de lis* embroidered in gold, sparkled like two firmaments.

When she had finished admiring the bed, Jeanne, raising her light, examined the tapestry, trying to discover the subject of the design.

A young nobleman and a young lady, dressed in the strangest way in green, red, and yellow, were talking under a blue tree on which white fruit was ripening. A big rabbit of the same color as the fruit was nibbling a little gray grass. Just above the figures, in a conventional distance, five little round houses with pointed roofs could be seen, and up at the top, nearly in the sky, was a red wind-mill. Great branches of flowers twined in and out over the whole.

The next two panels were very like the first, except that out of the houses came four little men, dressed in Flemish costume, who raised their heads to heaven as if to denote their extreme surprise and anger. But the last set of hangings depicted a drama. Near the rabbit, which was still nibbling, the young man was stretched out, apparently dead. The young lady, with her eyes fixed on him, was thrusting a sword into her breast, and the fruit on the tree had become black.

Jeanne was just giving up trying to understand it when she discovered in a corner a microscopic animal, which the rabbit could have eaten as easily as a blade of grass, and which was meant for a lion. Then she recognized the misfortunes of Pyramis and Thisbe; and, although she smiled at the simplicity of the designs, she felt happy at being surrounded by these pictures which would always accord with her dearest hopes; and at the thought that every night this antique and legendary love would watch over her dreams.

The rest of the furniture was of the most different styles, and bore the traces of many generations. A superb Louis XVI chest of drawers, bound with polished brass, stood between two Louis XV armchairs which were still covered with their original brocaded silk. A rosewood escritoire was opposite the mantelpiece, on which, under a glass shade, was a clock made in the time of the Empire. It was in the form of a bronze bee-hive hanging on four marble columns over a garden of gilded flowers. On a small pendulum, coming out of the hive through a long slit, swung a little bee, with enamel wings, backwards and forwards over the flowers; the dial was of painted china and was let into the side of the hive. It struck eleven, and the baron kissed his daughter and went to his own room.

Then Jeanne regretfully went to bed, giving a last look round her room before she put out her candle. Only the head of the bed was against the wall, and on the left was a window through which a stream of moonlight entered, making a pool of light on the floor, and casting pale reflections on the walls over the motionless loves of Pyramis and Thisbe. Through the other window, opposite the foot of the bed, Jeanne could see a big tree bathed in a soft light. She turned over and closed her eyes, but after a little while opened them again, for she still seemed to feel the jolting of the carriage, and its rumbling was yet in her ears.

For some time she lay quite still, hoping thus to soon fall asleep, but the restlessness of her mind communicated itself to her body, and at last she got out of bed. With her arms and feet bare, in her long chemise, which made her look like a phantom, she crossed the flood of light on the boards, opened her window and looked out.

The night was so clear that everything could be seen as plainly as in broad daylight; and the young girl recognized all the country she had so loved as a child.

First of all, just opposite her, was a big lawn looking as yellow as gold under the light of the night. There were two enormous trees before the château, a plane-tree to the north, a linden to the south, and quite at the end of the grass, a little thicket ended the estate which was protected from the hurricanes by five rows of old elms twisted, torn, and sloped like a roof, by the sea wind which was constantly blowing.

This kind of park was bounded on the right and left by two long avenues of immense poplar-trees (called *peuples* in Normandy) which separated the squire's residence from the two farms adjoining, one of which was occupied by the Couillards, the other by the Martins. These *peuples* had given the names to the château. Beyond this enclosure lay a large piece of uncultivated ground covered with gorse, over which the wind rustled and blew day and night. Then the coast suddenly fell a hundred yards, forming a high, white cliff, the foot of which was washed by the sea; and Jeanne gazed at the vast, watery expanse whose waves seemed to be sleeping under the stars.

In this repose of nature, when the sun was absent, the earth gave out all her perfumes. A jasmine, which had climbed round the lower windows, exhaled its pentrating fragrance which united with the subtler odor of the budding leaves, and the soft breeze brought with it the damp, salt smell of the seaweeds and the beach.

At first the young girl gave herself up to the pleasure of simply breathing, and the peace of the country calmed her as would a cool bath. All the animals which wake at evening-time, and hide their obscure existence in the peacefulness of the night, filled the clear darkness with a silent restlessness. Great birds fled silently through the air like shadows; the humming of invisible insects could be heard, and noiseless races took place across the dewy grass or along the quiet sandy roads. The short monotonous croak of the frogs was the only sound that could be distinguished.

It seemed to Jeanne that her heart was getting bigger, becoming full of whisperings like this clear evening, and of a thousand wandering desires like these nocturnal in-

sects whose quivering life surrounded her.    An unconscious sympathy drew her towards this living poetry
and she felt that joy and happiness were floating towards
her through the soft white night, and she began to dream
of love.

Love!  For two years she had been anxiously awaiting the time when it would come to her, and now she
was free to love, she had only to meet — him!  What
should he be like?  She did not know, and did not
trouble herself even to think about it.  *He* would be
*himself,* that was enough.  She only knew that she
should adore him with her whole heart, and that he
would love her with all his strength, and she pictured
herself walking with him on evenings such as this, under
the luminous glow of the stars.  They would walk hand
in hand, pressing close to one another, listening to the
beating of their hearts, mingling their love with the
sweet clearness of the summer nights, and so united that
by the simple power of their love, they would easily
divine each other's inmost thoughts.  And that would
endure indefinitely, in the serenity of an indestructible
affection.

Suddenly she fancied he was there — close to her;
and a vague feeling of sensuality swept over her from
head to foot.  She unconsciously pressed her arms
against her breast, as if to clasp her dream to her; and
something passed over her mouth, held out towards the
unknown, which almost made her faint, as if the springtide wind had given her a kiss of love.

All at once, on the road behind the château, she heard
someone walking in the night, and in the rapture of her
love-filled soul, in a transport of faith in the impossible,
in providential hazards, in divine presentiment, in the

romantic combinations of Fate, she thought: " If it should be he! " She anxiously listened to the steps of the traveler, sure that he would stop at the gate to demand hospitality. But he had passed by and she felt sad, as though she had experienced a deception; then after a moment she understood the feverish excitement of her hopes, and smiled at her own folly.

A little calmer, she let her thoughts float down the stream of a more reasonable reverie, trying to pierce the shadows of the future and planning out her life.

She would live here with him, in their quiet château overlooking the sea. She would have two children, a son for him, and a daughter for herself, and she pictured them running on the grass between the plane-tree and the linden, while their father and mother followed their movements with proud eyes, sometimes exchanging looks full of love above their heads.

She stayed dreaming until the moon had finished her journey across the sky, and began to descend into the sea. The air became cooler. Towards the east the horizon was getting lighter. A cock crowed in the farm on the right, others answered from the farm on the left, their hoarse notes, coming through the walls of the poultry-houses, seeming to be a long way off, and the stars were disappearing from the immense dome of the sky which had gradually whitened. The little chirp of a bird sounded; warblings, timid at first, came from among the leaves; then, getting bolder, they became vibrating, joyous, and spread from branch to branch, from tree to tree. Jeanne suddenly felt a bright light; and raising her head, which she had buried in her hands, she shut her eyes, dazzled by the splendor of the dawn.

A mountain of crimson clouds, partly hidden by the

avenue of poplars, cast a red glow over the awakened
earth, and, breaking through the bright clouds, bathing
the trees, the plain, the ocean, the whole horizon, in a
fiery light, the blazing orb appeared.

Jeanne felt mad with happiness. A delirious joy, an
infinite tenderness before the splendor of nature filled
her heart. It was her sunrise! her dawn! the beginning
of her life! the rising of her hopes! She stretched out
her arms towards the radiant space, with a longing to
embrace the sun; she wanted to speak, to cry aloud
something divine like this day-break; but she remained
dumb in a state of impotent ecstasy. Then, laying her
forehead on her hands, her eyes filled with tears, and
she cried for joy.

When she again raised her head the glorious colors of
the dawning day had already disappeared. She felt
calmer and a little tired and chilled. Leaving the window open, she threw herself on the bed, mused for a few
minutes longer, then fell into such a sound sleep that she
did not hear her father calling her at eight o'clock, and
only awoke when he came into her room.

He wanted to show her the improvements that had
been made in the château; in *her* château.

The back of the house was separated from the village
road, which half-a-mile further on joined the high road
from Havre to Fécamp, by a large sort of court planted
with apple-trees. A straight path went across it leading from the steps of the house to the wooden fence, and
the low, thatched out-houses, built of flints from the
beach, ran the whole length of two sides of the court,
which was separated from the adjoining farms by two
long ditches.

The roof of the château had been repaired, the woodwork restored, and the walls mended; all the inside of the house had been painted and the rooms had fresh hangings, and on the old decaying gray walls the snowy shutters and the new plaster stood out like white stains. One of Jeanne's windows was in the front of the house, which looked out over the little wood and the wall of wind-torn elms, on to the sea.

Arm in arm Jeanne and the baron went all over the château without missing a single corner, and then they walked slowly along the long poplar avenues which enclosed the park, as it was called. The grass had grown under the trees, making a green carpet, and the grove at the bottom was delightfully pretty with its little winding paths, separated by leafy walls, running in and out.

Jeanne was startled by a hare springing suddenly across their path; it ran down the slope and made off towards the cliff, among the rushes.

After breakfast, Madame Adélaïde went to lie down as she had not yet recovered from the fatigue of the journey, and the baron proposed that he and Jeanne should walk to Yport. They set off, going through the hamlet of Etouvent in which was situated Les Peuples, and three peasants saluted them as if they had known them all their lives.

They entered the sloping woods which go right down to the sea, and soon the village of Yport came in sight. The women, sitting at their doors mending clothes, looked up as they passed. There was a strong smell of brine in the steep street with the gutter in the middle and the heaps of rubbish lying before the doors. The brown nets to which a few shining shells, looking like fragments of silver, had clung, were drying before the doors of huts whence came the odors of several families

V—2

living in the same room, and a few pigeons were looking for food at the side of the gutter. To Jeanne it was all as new and curious as a scene at a theater.

Turning a sharp corner, they suddenly came upon the smooth opaque blue sea, and opposite the beach they stopped to look around.

Boats, with sails looking like the wings of white birds, were in the offing; to the right and left rose the high cliffs; a sort of cape interrupted the view on one side, while on the other the coast-line stretched out till it could no longer be distinguished, and a harbor and some houses could be seen in a bay a little way off. Tiny waves fringing the sea with foam, broke on the beach with a faint noise, and some Normandy boats, hauled up on the shingle, lay on their sides with the sun shining on their tarred planks; a few fishermen were getting them ready to go out with the evening tide.

A sailor came up with some fish to sell, and Jeanne bought a brill that she insisted on carrying home herself. Then the man offered his services if ever they wanted to go sailing, telling them his name, " Lastique, Joséphin Lastique," over and over again so that they should not forget it. The baron promised to remember him, and then they started to go back to the château.

As the large fish was too heavy for Jeanne, she passed her father's stick through its gills, and carrying it between them, they went gaily up the hill, with the wind in their faces, chattering like two children; and as the brill made their arms ache, they let it drop lower and lower till its big tail swept along the grass.

## II

A DELIGHTFUL life of freedom began for Jeanne. She read, dreamed, and wandered about all alone, walking slowly along the road, building castles in the air, or dancing down the little winding valleys whose sloping sides were covered with golden gorse. Its strong, sweet odor, increased by the heat, intoxicated her like a perfumed wine, while she was lulled by the distant sound of the waves breaking on the beach. When she was in an idle mood she would throw herself down on the thick grass of the hill-side, and sometimes when at the turn of a road she suddenly caught a glimpse of the blue sea, sparkling in the light of the sun, with a white sail at the horizon, she felt an inordinate joy, a mysterious presentiment of future happiness.

She loved to be alone with the calm beauty of nature, and would sit motionless for so long on the top of a hill, that the wild rabbits would bound fearlessly up to her; or she would run swiftly along the cliff, exhilarated by the pure air of the hills, and finding an exquisite pleasure in being able to move without fatigue, like the swallows in the air and the fish in the water.

Very fond of bathing, and strong, fearless, and unconscious of danger, she would swim out to sea till she could no longer be perceived from the shore, feeling refreshed by the cool water, and enjoying the rocking of its clear blue waves. When she was a long way out, she floated, and, with her arms crossed on her breast, gazed at the deep, blue sky, against which a swallow or the white outline of a sea-gull could sometimes be seen. No noise could be heard except the far away murmur of the waves breaking on the beach, and the vague, confused, almost imperceptible sound of the pebbles being drawn down by the receding waves. When she went out too far, a boat put off to bring her in and she would return to the château pale with hunger, but not at all tired, with a smile on her lips, and her eyes dancing with joy.

The baron was planning great agricultural improvements; he wanted to make experiments, to try new machines, to acclimatize foreign plants, and he passed part of his time talking to the peasants, who shook their heads and refused to believe in his ideas.

He often went on the sea with the sailors of Yport, and when he had seen the caves, the springs, and the rocks that were of any interest in the neighborhood, he fished like a common seaman. On windy days, when the breeze filled the sails and forced the boat over till its edge touched the water, and the mackerel-nets trailed over the sides, he would hold a slender fishing-line, waiting with anxiety for the bite of a fish. Then he went out in the moonlight to take up the nets set the night before (for he loved to hear the creaking of the masts, and to breathe the fresh night air), and, after a long time spent in tacking about to find the buoys, guided by a ridge of rocks, the spire of a church, or the light-house at Fécamp, he liked to lie still under the first rays of the rising sun, which turned into a glittering mass the slimy rays and the white-bellied turbot which lay on the deck of the boat.

At every meal, he gave a glowing account of his excursions, and the baroness, in her turn, would tell him how many times she had walked up and down the long poplar-avenues on the right next to the Couillards's farm, the other one not having enough sun on it.

She had been advised to "take exercise," and she

walked for hours together. As soon as the sun was high enough for its warmth to be felt she went out, leaning on Rosalie's arm, and enveloped in a cloak and two shawls, with a red scarf on her head and a black hood over that.

Then she began a long, uninteresting walk from the corner of the château to the first shrubs of the wood and back again. Her left foot, which dragged a little, had traced two furrows where the grass had died. At each end of the path she had had a bench placed, and every five minutes she stopped, saying to the poor, patient maid who supported her: " Let us sit down, my girl; I am a little tired."

And at each rest she left on one or other of the benches first the scarf which covered her head, then one shawl, then the other, then the hood, and then the cloak; and all these things made two big bundles of wraps, which Rosalie carried on her free arm, when they went in to lunch.

In the afternoon the baroness recommenced her walk in a feebler way, taking longer rests, and sometimes dozing for an hour at a time on a couch that was wheeled out of doors for her. She called it taking " her exercise," in the same way as she spoke of " my hypertrophy."

A doctor she had consulted ten years before because she suffered from palpitations, had hinted at hypertrophy. Since then she had constantly used this word, though she did not in the least understand what it meant, and she was always making the baron, and Jeanne, and Rosalie put their hands on her heart, though its beatings could not be felt, so buried was it under her bosom. She obstinately refused to be examined by any other doctor in case he should say she had another malady, and she spoke of " her hypertrophy " so often that it seemed as though this affection of the heart were peculiar to her, and belonged to her, like something unique, to which no one else had any right.   The baron and Jeanne said " my wife's " or " mamma's hypertrophy " in the same way as they would have spoken of her dress or her umbrella.

She had been very pretty when she was young, and as slender as a reed.   After flirting with the officers of all the regiments of the Empire, she had read *Corinne,* which had made her cry, and, in a certain measure, altered her character.

As her waist got bigger her mind became more and more poetical, and when, through her size, she had to remain nearly all day in her armchair, she dreamed of love adventures, of which she was always the heroine; always thinking of the sort she liked best, like a hand-organ continually repeating the same air.   The languishing romances, where they talk about captives and swallows, always made her cry; and she even liked some of Béranger's coarse verses, because of the grief they expressed.   She would sit motionless for hours, lost in thought, and she was very fond of Les Peuples, because it served as a scene for her dreams, the surrounding woods, the sea, and the waste land reminding her of Sir Walter Scott's books, which she had lately been reading.

On rainy days she stayed in her room looking over what she called her " relics."   They were all her old letters; those from her father and mother, the baron's when she was engaged to him, and some others besides. She kept them in a mahogany escritoire with copper sphinxes at the corners, and she always used a particular tone when she said: " Rosalie, bring me my souvenir-drawer."

The maid would open the escritoire, take out the drawer, and place it on a chair beside her mistress, who slowly read the letters one by one, occasionally letting fall a tear.

Jeanne sometimes took Rosalie's place and accompanied her mother's walks, and listened to her reminiscences of childhood. The young girl recognized herself in these tales, and was astonished to find that her mother's thoughts and hopes had been the same as hers; for every one imagines that he is the first to experience those feelings which made the hearts of our first parents beat quicker, and which will continue to exist in human hearts till the end of time.

These tales, often interrupted for several seconds by the baroness's want of breath, were told as slowly as she walked, and Jeanne let her thoughts run on to the happy future, without waiting to hear the end of her mother's anecdotes.

One afternoon, as they were resting on the seat at the bottom of the walk, they saw a fat priest coming towards them from the other end of the avenue. He bowed, put on a smiling look, bowed again when he was about three feet off, and cried:

" Well, Madame la baronne, and how are we to-day? "

He was the curé of the parish.

The baroness, born in a philosophical century and brought up in revolutionary times by a father who did not believe very much in anything, did not often go to church, although she liked priests with the sort of religious instinct that most women have. She had forgotten all about the Abbé Picot, her curé, and her face colored when she saw him. She began to make excuses for not having gone to see him, but the good-natured priest did not seem at all put out. He looked at Jeanne, complimented her on her good looks, sat down, put his hat on his knees, and wiped his forehead.

He was a very fat, red-faced man, who perspired very freely. Every minute he drew an enormous, checked handkerchief from his pocket and wiped his face and neck; but he had hardly put it back again when fresh drops appeared on his skin and, falling on his cassock, made the dust on it into little, round spots. He was a true country-priest, lively and tolerant, talkative and honest. He told anecdotes, talked about the peasants, and did not seem to have noticed that his two parishioners had not been to mass; for the baroness always tried to reconcile her vague ideas of religion to her indolence, and Jeanne was too happy at having left the convent, where she had been sickened of holy ceremonies, to think about going to church.

The baron joined them. His pantheistic religion made him indifferent to doctrine, and he asked the abbé, whom he knew by sight, to stay to dinner. The priest had the art of pleasing every one, and thanks to the unconscious tact that is acquired by the most ordinary men called by fate to exercise any moral power over their fellow creatures, and the baroness, attracted perhaps by one of these affinities which draw similar natures together, paid every attention to him, the fat man's sanguine face and short breath agreeing with her gasping obesity. By the time dessert was placed on the table he had begun telling funny stories, with the *laisser-*

*aller* of a man who had had a good dinner in congenial society.

All at once, as though a good idea had just occurred to him, he exclaimed:

" Oh, I have a new parishoner I must introduce to you, M. le Vicomte de Lamare."

The baroness, who had all the heraldy of the province at her finger ends, asked:

" Does he belong to the family of Lamare de l'Eure?"

The priest bowed:

" Yes, madame; he is the son of the Vicomte Jean de Lamare, who died last year."

Then Madame Adélaïde, who loved the aristocracy above everything, asked a great many questions, and learnt that the young man had sold the family château to pay his father's debts, and had come to live on one of the three farms that he owned at Etouvent.

This property only brought in about five or six thousand livres a year, but the vicomte was of a foreseeing, economical disposition and meant to live quietly for two or three years, so that he might save enough to go into society and marry well, without having to get into debt or mortgage his farms.

" He is a charming young fellow," added the curé; " and so steady, so quiet. But he can't find many amusements in the country."

" Bring him to see us, M. l'Abbé," said the baron; " he might like to come here sometimes." And then the conversation turned to other subjects.

When they went into the drawing-room the priest asked if he might go out into the garden, as he was used to a little exercise after meals. The baron went out with him, and they walked backwards and forwards the whole length of the château, while their two shadows, the one thin, and the other quite round and looking as though it had a mushroom on its head, fell sometimes before and sometimes behind them, according as they walked towards the moon or turned their backs on it. The curé chewed a sort of cigarette that he had taken from his pocket; he told the baron why he used it in the plain speech of a countryman:

"It is to help the digestion; my liver is rather sluggish."

Looking at the sky where the bright moon was sailing along, he suddenly said:

"That is a sight one never gets tired of."

Then he went in to say good-bye to the ladies.

## III

THE next Sunday the baroness and Jeanne went to mass out of deference to their curé, and after it was over they waited to ask him to luncheon for the following Thursday. He came out of the vestry with a tall, good-looking, young man who had familiarly taken his arm.

As soon as he saw the two ladies he gave a look of pleased surprise, and exclaimed:

"What a lucky thing! Madame la baronne and Mlle. Jeanne, permit me to present to you your neighbor, M. le Vicomte de Lamare."

The vicomte bowed, expressed the desire he had long felt to make their acquaintance, and began to talk with the ease of a man accustomed to good society. His face was one that women raved about and that all men disliked. His black, curly hair fell over a smooth, bronzed forehead, and long, regular eyebrows gave a depth and tenderness to his dark eyes. Long, thick lashes lent to his glance the passionate eloquence which thrills the heart of the high-born lady in her boudoir, and makes the poor girl, with her basket on her arm, turn round in the street, and the languorous charm of his eyes, with their whites faintly tinged with blue, gave importance to his least word and made people believe in the profoundness of his thought. A thick, silky beard hid a jaw which was a little heavy.

After mutual compliments he said good-bye to the ladies; and two days afterwards made his first call at the château.

He arrived just as they were looking at a rustic-seat, placed only that morning under the big plane-tree opposite the drawing-room windows. The baron wanted to have another one under the linden to make a pair, but the baroness, who disliked things to be exactly symmetrical, said no. The vicomte, on being asked his opinion, sided with the baroness.

Then he talked about the surrounding country, which he thought very " picturesque," and about the charming " bits " he had come across in his solitary walks. From time to time his eyes met Jeanne's, as though by chance; and she felt a strange sensation at these sudden looks which were quickly turned away and which expressed a lively admiration and sympathy.

M. de Lamare's father, who had died the year before, had known an intimate friend of M. des Cultaux, the baroness's father, and the discovery of this mutual acquaintance gave rise to endless conversation about marriages, births, and relationships. The baroness, with prodigious feats of memory, talked about the ancestors and descendants of numerous families, and traversed the complicated labyrinths of different genealogies without ever losing herself.

"Tell me, vicomte, have you ever heard of the Saunoys de Varfleur? Gontran, the elder son, married Mademoiselle de Coursil, one of the Coursil-Courvilles; and the younger married a cousin of mine, Mademoiselle de la Roche-Aubert, who was related to the Crisanges. Now, M. de Crisange was an intimate friend of my father, and no doubt knew yours also."

"Yes, madame; was it not the M. de Crisange who emigrated, and whose son ruined himself?"

"That is the very man. He had proposed for my aunt after the death of her husband, the Comte d'Eretry, but she would not accept him because he took snuff. By the way, do you know what has become of the Viloises? They left Touraine about 1813, after a reverse of fortune, to go and live in Auvergne; and I have never heard anything of them since."

"I believe, madame, that the old marquis was killed by a fall from a horse, leaving one daughter married to an Englishman, and the other to a rich merchant who had seduced her."

Names they had heard their parents mention when they were children returned to their minds, and the marriages of these people seemed as important to them as great public events. They talked about men and women they had never seen as if they knew them well, and these people, living so far away, talked about them in the same manner, and they felt as though they were acquainted with each other, almost as if they were friends, or relations, simply because they belonged to the same class and were of equal rank.

The baron was rather unsociable, his philosophic views disagreeing with the beliefs and prejudices of the people of his own rank, did not know any of the families living near, and asked the vicomte about them.

" Oh, there are very good families around here," answered M. de Lamare, in the same tone as he would have said that there were not many rabbits on the hills, and he entered into details about them.

There were only three families of rank in the neighborhood; the Marquis de Coutelier, the head of the Normandy aristocracy; the Vicomte and Vicomtesse de Briseville, people who were very well-born but held themselves rather aloof; and lastly, the Comte de Fourville, a sort of fire-eater who was said to be worrying his wife to death, and who lived in the Château de la Vrillette,, which was built on a lake, passing his time in hunting and shooting. A few parvenus had bought property in the neighborhood, but the vicomte did not know them.

He rose to go, and his last look was for Jeanne as though he would have made his adieu to her specially friendly and tender.

The baroness thought him charming and very *comme il faut,* and the baron remarked that he was a very well-educated man. He was asked to dinner the following week, and after that he visited the château regularly.

Generally he came about four o'clock, joined the baroness in " her avenue," and insisted on her leaning on his arm to take " her exercise." When Jeanne was at home she supported her mother on the other side and all three walked slowly up and down the long path. He did not talk to the young girl but often his dark, velvety eyes met Jeanne's, which were like blue agate.

Sometimes they walked down to Yport with the baron, and one evening, as they were standing on the beach, old Lastique came up to them, and, without taking his pipe from his mouth, for it would have been stranger to see him without his pipe than without his nose, said:

" With this wind, M'sieu l'baron, you'd be able to go to Etretat and back to-morrow quite easily."

Jeanne clasped her hands together; " Oh, papa! If only you would! "

The baron turned to M. de Lamare.

" Will you go, vicomte? We could have lunch over there." And the excursion was planned for the following day.

The next morning Jeanne was up at daybreak. She waited for her father, who took longer to dress, and then they walked over the dewy plain and through the wood filled with the sweet song of the birds, down to Yport, where they found the vicomte and old Lastique sitting on the capstan of their little vessel.

Two sailors helped to start the boat, by putting their shoulders to the sides and pushing with all their might. It was hard to move over the level part of the beach, and Lastique slipped rollers of greased wood under the keel, then went back to his place and drawled out his long " Heave oh! " which was the signal for them all to push together, and when they came to the slant of the beach, the boat set off all at once, sliding over the round pebbles, and making a grating noise like the tearing of linen. It stopped short at the edge of the waves and they all got in, except the two sailors, who pushed the boat off.

A light, steady breeze blowing towards the land just ruffled the surface of the water. The sail was hoisted, filled out a little, and the boat moved gently along hardly rocked by the waves.

At first they sailed straight out to sea. At the horizon the sky could not be distinguished from the ocean; on land the high steep cliff had a deep shadow at its foot. Behind could be seen the brown sails of the boats leaving the white pier of Fécamp, and before lay a rounded rock with a hole right through it, looking like an elephant thrusting its trunk into the water.

Jeanne, feeling a little dizzied by the rocking of the boat, sat holding one side with her hand, and looking out to sea; light, space and the ocean seemed to her to be the only really beautiful things in creation. No one spoke. From time to time old Lastique, who was steering, drank something out of a bottle placed within his reach under the seat. He smoked his stump of a pipe which seemed unextinguishable, and a small cloud of blue smoke went up from it while another issued from the corner of his mouth; he was never seen to relight the clay bowl, which was colored blacker than ebony, or to refill it with tobacco, and he only removed the pipe from his mouth to eject the brown saliva.

The baron sat in the bows and managed the sail, performing the duties of a sailor, and Jeanne and the vicomte were side by side, both feeling a little agitated. Their glances were continually meeting, a hidden sympathy making them raise their eyes at the same moment, for there was already that vague, subtle fondness between them which springs up so quickly between two young people when the youth is good-looking and the girl is pretty. They felt happy at being close together, perhaps because each was thinking of the other.

The sun rose higher in the sky as if to consider from a better vantage point the vast sea stretched out beneath him, while the latter, like a coquette, enveloped herself in a light mist which veiled her from his rays. It was a transparent golden haze which hid nothing but softened everything. It gradually melted away before the sun's flaming darts, and when the full heat of the day began it disappeared entirely, and the sea, smooth as glass, lay glittering in the sun.

Jeanne murmured enthusiastically, " How lovely it is ! "

The vicomte answered " Yes, it is indeed beautiful." And their hearts felt as bright as the clear morning itself.

Suddenly, looking as if the cliff bestrode part of the sea, appeared the great arcades of Etretat, high enough for a ship to pass underneath him without the point of a sharp white rock rising out of the water before the first one.

When they reached the shore, the vicomte lifted Jeanne out that she should not wet her feet in landing, while the baron held the boat close to the beach with a rope; then they went up the steep, shingly beach side by side, both agitated by this short embrace, and they heard old Lastique say to the baron:

" In my opinion they'd make a very handsome couple."

They had lunch in a little inn near the beach. On

the sea they had been quiet, but at the table they had as much to say as children let out of school.

The most simple things gave rise to endless laughter. Old Lastique carefully put his pipe, which was still alight, into his cap before he sat down to table; and everyone laughed. A fly, attracted, no doubt, by the sailor's red nose, persisted on settling on it, and when moving too slowly to catch it he knocked it away, it went over to a very fly-spotted curtain whence it seemed to eagerly watch the sailor's highly-colored nasal organ, for it soon flew back and settled on it again.

Each time the insect returned a loud laugh burst out, and when the old man, annoyed by its tickling, murmured: " What a confoundly obstinate fly! " Jeanne and the vicomte laughed till they cried, holding their serviettes to their mouths to prevent themselves shrieking out loud.

When the coffee had been served Jeanne said:

" Suppose we go for a walk? "

The vicomte got up to go with her, but the baron preferred going out on the beach to take his nap.

" You two go," he said. " You will find me here in an hour's time."

They walked straight along the road, passed a few cottages and a little château which looked more like a big farm, and then found themselves in an open valley. Jeanne had a singing in her ears, and was thrilled by a strange sensation which she had never before experienced. Overhead was a blazing sun, and on each side of the road lay fields of ripe corn drooping under the heat. The feeble, continuous chirp of the swarms of grasshoppers in the corn and hedges was the only sound

V—3

to be heard, and the sky of dazzling blue, slightly tinged with yellow, looked as though it would suddenly turn red, like brass when it is put into a furnace.

They entered a little wood where the trees were so thick that no sunbeams could penetrate their foliage; the grass had died from want of light and fresh air, but the ground was covered with moss, and all around was a cool dampness which chilled them after the heat of the sun.

" See, we could sit down over there," said Jeanne, looking around her as they walked on.

Two trees had died, and through the break in the foliage fell a flood of light, warming the earth, calling to life the grass and dandelion seeds, and expanding the delicate flowers of the anemone and digitalis. A thousand winged insects — butterflies, bees, hornets, big gnats looking like skeleton-flies, ladybirds with red spots on them, beetles with greenish reflections on their wings, others which were black and horned — peopled this one warm and luminous spot in the midst of the cool shadow of the trees.

Jeanne and the vicomte sat down with their heads in the shadow and their feet in the light. They watched these tiny moving insects that a sunbeam had called forth, and Jeanne said softly:

" How lovely the country is ! Sometimes I wish I were a bee or a butterfly that I might bury myself in the flowers."

They began talking about their own habits and tastes in a low, confidential tone. He declared himself tired of his useless life, disgusted with society; it was always the same, one never found any truth, any sincerity. She would have liked to know what town-life was like but

she was convinced beforehand that society would never
be so pleasant as a country-life.

The nearer their hearts drew to one another the more
studiously did they address each other as " monsieur "
and " mademoiselle "; but they could not help their
eyes smiling and their glances meeting, and it seemed to
them that new and better feelings were entering their
hearts, making them ready to love and take an interest
in things they had before cared nothing about.

When they returned from their walk they found that
the baron had gone to a cave formed in the cliff, called
the Chambre aux Desmoiselles, so they waited for him
at the inn, where he did not appear till five o'clock, and
then they started to go home. The boat glided along
so smoothly that it hardly seemed to be moving; the
wind came in gentle puffs filling the sail one second
only to let it flap loosely against the mast the next; and
the tired sun was slowly approaching the sea. The
stillness around made them all silent for a long while,
but at last Jeanne said:

" How I should like to travel ! "

" Yes, but it would be rather dull traveling alone,"
said the vicomte. " You want a companion to whom
you could confide your impressions."

" That is true," she answered thoughtfully; " still, I
like to go for long walks alone. When there is no one
with me I build such castles in the air."

" But two people can better still plan out a happy
future," he said, looking her full in the face.

Her eyes fell; did he mean anything? She gazed at
the horizon as though she would look beyond it; then
she said slowly:

" I should like to go to Italy — and to Greece — and

to Corsica, it must be so wild and so beautiful there."
He preferred the chalets and lakes of Switzerland.
She said: "No, I should like to go either to a country with little or no history like Corsica, or else to one
with very old associations like Greece. It must be so
interesting to find the traces of those nations whose history one has known from childhood, and to see the
places where such great and noble deeds were done."

"Well, for my part, I should like to go to England;
it is such an instructive country," said the vicomte, who
was more practical than Jeanne.

Then they discussed the beauties of every country from
the poles to the equator, and went into raptures over
the unconventional customs of such nations as the Chi-
nese or the Laplanders; but they came to the conclusion
that the most beautiful land in the world is France, with
her temperate climate — cool in summer and warm in
winter — her fertile fields, her green forests, her great,
calm rivers, and her culture in the fine arts which has
existed nowhere else since the palmy days of Athens.

Silence again fell over the little party. The blood-
red sun was sinking, and a broad pathway of light lay
in the wake of the boat leading right up to the dazzling
globe. The wind died out, there was not a ripple on
the water, and the motionless sail was reddened by the
rays of the setting sun. The air seemed to possess some
soothing influence which silenced everything around this
meeting of the elements. The sea, like some huge bird,
awaited the fiery lover who was approaching her shining, liquid bosom, and the sun hastened his descent, em-
purpled by the desire of their embrace. At length he
joined her, and gradually disappeared. Then a freshness came from the horizon, and a breath of air rippled

the surface of the water as if the vanished sun had given a sigh of satisfaction.

The twilight was very short, and the sky soon became dark and studded with stars. Lastique got out the oars, and Jeanne and the vicomte sat side by side watching the trembling, phosphorescent glimmer behind the boat and feeling a keen enjoyment even in breathing the cool night air. The vicomte's fingers were resting against Jeanne's hand which was lying on the seat, and she did not draw it away, the slight contact making her feel happy and yet confused.

When she went to her room that evening Jeanne felt so moved that the least thing would have made her cry. She looked at the clock and fancied that the little bee throbbed like a friendly heart; she thought of how it would be the silent witness of her whole life, how it would accompany all her joys and sorrows with its quick, regular beat, and she stopped the gilded insect to drop a kiss upon its wings. She could have kissed anything, no matter what, and suddenly remembering an old doll she had hidden away in the bottom of a drawer, she got it out and found as much joy in seeing it again as if it had been an old well-loved friend. Pressing it to her bosom she covered its painted cheeks and flaxen hair with warm kisses, then, still holding it in her arms, she began to think.

Was HE the husband referred to by so many inward voices, and was it by a supremely-kind Providence that he was thus sent into her life? Was he really the being created for her, to whom her whole existence would be devoted? Were he and she really predestined to unite their hearts and so beget Love? She did not yet experience those tumultuous feelings, those wild raptures, that profound stirring of her whole soul, which she believed to be love; still she thought she was beginning to love him, for sometimes she felt her senses fail her when she thought of him and she always was thinking of him. Her heart throbbed in his presence, her color came and went when she met his glance, and the sound of his voice sent a thrill through her. That night she hardly slept at all.

Each day her longing for love became greater. She was always consulting the marguerites, or the clouds, or tossing a coin in the air to see whether she was loved or not.

One evening her father said to her:

" Make yourself look very pretty to-morrow morning, Jeanne."

" Why, papa? " she asked.

" That's a secret," replied the baron.

When she came down the next morning, looking fresh and bright in a light summer dress, she found the drawing-room table covered with bon-bon boxes, and an enormous bouquet on a chair.

A cart turned in at the gateway with " Lérat, Confectioner, Contractor for Wedding-breakfasts " on it, and Ludivine, with the aid of a scullery-maid, took from it a great many flat baskets from which issued an appetizing odor.

The vicomte came in soon after; his trousers were fastened tightly under the varnished boots which showed off his small feet to perfection. His tightly-fitting coat was closely fastened, except on the chest, where it opened to show the lace shirt-frill; and a fine cravat, twisted several times round his neck, forced him to hold up his handsome dark head. His careful toilet

made him look different from usual, and Jeanne stared
at him as though she had never seen him before; she
thought he looked a perfect gentleman from head to
foot.

He bowed, and asked with a smile:

" Well, godmother, are you ready? "

" What do you mean? " stammered out Jeanne.
" What is it all about? "

" Oh, you shall know just now," answered the baron.

The carriage drew up before the door and Madame
Adélaïde, in a handsome dress, came downstairs leaning
on Rosalie, who was struck with such admiration at
the sight of M. de Lamare's elegant appearance, that
the baron murmured:

" I say, vicomte, I think our maid likes the look of
you."

The vicomte blushed up to the roots of his hair, pretended not to hear what the baron said, and, taking up
the big bouquet, presented it to Jeanne. She took it,
feeling still more astonished, and all four got into the
carriage.

" Really, madame, it looks like a wedding! " exclaimed the cook, Ludivine, who had brought some cold
broth for the baroness to have before she started.

When they reached Yport they got out, and, as they
walked through the village, the sailors in new clothes
which still showed where the cloth had been folded,
came out of the houses, touched their hats, shook the
baron by the hand, and followed behind them, forming
a procession, at the head of which walked the vicomte
with Jeanne on his arm.

On arriving at the church a halt was made. A choir-
boy came out carrying a great silver cross, followed by

another pink and white urchin carrying the holy water with the brush in it; behind them came three old choristers, one of whom limped, then the serpent-player, then the curé in a stole with a gold cross embroidered on it. He saluted the baron's party with a smile and a nod, then, with half-closed eyes, his lips moving in prayer, his miter pushed down over his eyes, he followed his surpliced subordinates down to the sea.

On the beach a crowd was waiting round a new boat decorated all over with garlands; its mast, sail, and ropes were covered with long ribbons which fluttered in the breeze, and its name, " Jeanne," was on the stern in gilt letters. Old Lastique was the master of this boat 'that the baron had had built, and he advanced to meet the procession.

At the sight of the cross all the men took off their caps, and a line of nuns, enveloped in their long, straight, black mantles, knelt down. The curé went to one end of the boat with the two choir-boys, while at the other the three old choristers, with their dirty faces and hairy chins shown up by their white surplices, sang at the top of their voices. Each time they paused to take breath, the serpent-player continued his music alone, and he blew out his cheeks till his little gray eyes could not be seen and the very skin of his forehead and neck looked as if it was separated from the flesh.

The calm, transparent sea, its ripples breaking on the shore with a faint, grating noise, seemed to be watching the christening of the tiny boat. Great, white sea-gulls flew by with outstretched wings, and then returned over the heads of the kneeling crowd with a sweeping flight as though they wanted to see what was going on.

The chanting stopped after an " Amen " which was

repeated and sustained for five minutes, and the priest gabbled some Latin words of which only the sonorous terminations could be made out. Then he walked all round the boat sprinkling it with holy water, and commenced to murmur the oremus, stopping opposite the two sponsors, who were standing hand in hand.

The young man's handsome face was quite calm, but the young girl, almost suffocated by the palpitation of her heart, felt as though she should faint, and she trembled so violently that her teeth chattered. The dream that had haunted her for so long seemed all at once to have become a reality. She had heard this ceremony compared to a wedding, the priest was there uttering blessings, and surpliced men were chanting prayers; surely she was being married!

Did the vicomte feel the nervous trembling of her fingers? Did his heart sympathize with hers? Did he understand? did he guess? was he also under the influence of an all-absorbing love-dream? Or was it only the knowledge that women found him irresistible that made him press her hand, gently at first, then harder and harder till he hurt her? Then, without changing the expression of his face, that no one might notice him, he said very distinctly: "Oh, Jeanne, if you liked, this might be our betrothal!"

She slowly bent her head with a movement which perhaps meant "yes"; and some drops of holy water fell on their hands.

The ceremony was over; the women rose from their knees, and everyone began to hurry back. The choir-boy let the cross swing from side to side, or tilt forward till it nearly fell; the curé, no longer praying, hurried behind him; the choristers and the serpent-player

disappeared down a narrow turning to get back and un-
dress quickly, the sailors hastened past in twos and
threes; a good lunch was waiting for them at Les Peuples and the very thought of it quickened their pace and
made their mouths water.

Sixty sailors and peasants sat down to the long table
laid in the courtyard under the apple trees. The baroness sat at the middle of the table with the curé from
Yport on one side of her and the Abbé Picot on the
other; opposite her was the baron between the mayor
and his wife. The mayoress was a thin, elderly country
woman with a nod for everyone; her big Normandy cap
fitted close round her thin face, making her head, with its
round, astonished-looking eyes, look like a white-tufted
fowl's, and she ate in little jerks as if she were pecking
at her plate.

Jeanne was silent, seeing nothing, hearing nothing,
her head turned with joy. At last she asked the vicomte, who was sitting beside her:

" What is your Christian name? "

" Julien," he replied; " did you not know? "

She did not answer him, for she was thinking:
" How often I shall repeat that name to myself."

When lunch was over, the courtyard was left to the
sailors. The baroness began to take her exercise, leaning on the baron and accompanied by the two priests,
and Jeanne and Julien walked down to the wood, and
wandered along its little winding paths. All at once
he took her hands in his.

" Tell me," he said, " will you be my wife? "

She hung her head, and he pleaded:

" Do not keep me in suspense, I implore you."

Then she slowly raised her eyes to his, and in that look he read her answer.

## IV

THE baron went into Jeanne's room before she was up one morning soon after the christening of the boat, and sat down at the foot of the bed.

" M. le Vicomte de Lamare has proposed for you," he said.

Jeanne would have liked to hide her head under the bed-clothes.

" We told him we must think over his proposal before we could give him an answer," continued the baron, who was smiling. " We did not wish to arrange anything without first consulting you; your mother and I made no objection to the marriage, but at the same time we did not make any promise. You are a great deal richer than he is, but when the happiness of a life is at stake the question of money ought not to be considered. He has no relations, so if you married him we should gain a son, whereas if you married anyone else you would have to go among strangers, and we should lose our daughter. We like the young fellow, but the question is, do you like him? "

" I am quite willing to marry him, papa," she stammered out, blushing to the roots of her hair.

The baron looked into her eyes, and said with a smile: " I thought as much, mademoiselle."

Until that evening Jeanne hardly knew what she was doing. She went through everything mechanically, feeling thoroughly worn out with fatigue, although she had done nothing to tire her. The vicomte came about six o'clock and found her sitting with her mother under the plane-tree, and Jeanne's heart beat wildly as the young man came calmly towards them. He kissed the baroness's fingers, then, raising the young girl's trembling hand to his lips, he imprinted on it a long, tender kiss of gratitude.

The happy betrothal time began. The young couple spent their days sitting on the slope leading to the waste land beyond the wood, or walking up and down the baroness's avenue, she with her eyes fixed on the dusty track her mother's foot had made, he talking of the future. Once the marriage agreed to, they wanted it to take place as soon as possible, so it was decided that they should be married in six weeks' time, on the 15th of August, and that they should start on their wedding tour almost immediately afterwards. When Jeanne was asked to what country she should like to go, she chose Corsica, where they would be more alone than in Italy.

They awaited the time of their union without very much impatience, vaguely desiring more passionate embraces, and yet satisfied with a slight caress, a pressure of the hand, a gaze so long that each seemed to read the other's heart through their eyes.

No one was to be asked to the wedding besides Aunt Lison, the baroness's sister, who was a lady-boarder in a convent at Versailles.

After their father's death the baroness wanted her sister to live with her, but the old maid was convinced that she was a nuisance to everybody, and always in the way, and she took apartments in one of the convents which open their doors to the solitary and unhappy, though she occasionally spent a month or two with her relations. She was a small woman with very little to say, and always kept in the background; when she stayed with the baroness she was only seen at meal times, the rest of the day she spent shut up in her room. She had a kind, rather old-looking face, although she was only forty-two, with sad, meek eyes. Her wishes had always been sacrificed to those of everyone else. As a child she had always sat quietly in some corner, never kissed because she was neither pretty nor noisy, and as a young girl no one had ever troubled about her. Her sister, following the example of her parents, always thought of her as of someone of no importance, almost like some object of furniture which she was accustomed to see every day but which never occupied her thoughts.

She seemed ashamed of her name, Lise, because it was so girlish and pretty, and when there seemed no likelihood of her marrying, " Lise " had gradually changed to " Lison." Since the birth of Jeanne she had become " Aunt Lison," a sort of poor relation whom everyone treated with a careless familiarity which hid a good-natured contempt. She was prim and very timid even with her sister and brother-in-law, who liked her as they liked everyone, but whose affection was formed of an indifferent kindness, and an unconscious compassion.

Sometimes when the baroness was speaking of the far-away time of her childhood she would say to fix a date: " It was about the time of Lison's mad attempt." She never said anything more, and there was a certain mystery about this " mad attempt."

One evening, when she was about nineteen years old, Lise had tried to drown herself. No one could under-

stand the reason of this act of folly; there was nothing
in her life or habits to at all account for it. She had
been rescued half-dead, and her parents, shocked at the
deed, had not attempted to discover its cause, but had
only talked about her " mad attempt," in the same way
as they had spoken of the accident to the horse Coco,
when he had broken his leg in a ditch and had to be
killed. Since then Lise had been thought very weak-
minded, and everyone around her gradually came to
look upon her with the mild contempt with which her
relations regarded her; even little Jeanne, perceiving
with the quickness of a child how her parents treated
her aunt, never ran to kiss her or thought of performing any little services for her. No one ever went to
her room, and Rosalie, the maid, alone seemed to know
where it was situated. If anyone wanted to speak to
her a servant was sent to find her, and if she could not
be found no one troubled about her, no one thought of
her, no one would ever have dreamt of saying:

" Dear me! I have not seen Lison this morning."

When she came down to breakfast of a morning, little Jeanne went and held up her face for a kiss, and
that was the only greeting she received. She had no
position in the house and seemed destined never to be
understood even by her relations, never able to gain their
love or confidence, and when she died she would leave
no empty chair, no sense of loss behind her.

When anyone said " Aunt Lison " the words caused
no more feeling of affection in anyone's heart than if the
coffee pot or sugar basin had been mentioned. She always walked with little, quick, noiseless steps, never
making any noise, never stumbling against anything, and
her hands seemed to be made of velvet, so light and

delicate was their handling of anything she touched.

Lison arrived at the château about the middle of July, quite upset by the idea of the marriage; she brought a great many presents which did not receive much attention as she was the giver, and the day after her arrival no one noticed she was there. She could not take her eyes off the sweethearts, and busied herself about the trousseau with a strange energy, a feverish excitement, working in her room, where no one came to see her, like a common seamstress. She was always showing the baroness some handkerchiefs she had hemmed, or some towels on which she had embroidered the monogram, and asking:

" Do you like that, Adélaïde? "

The baroness would carelessly look at the work and answer:

" Don't take so much trouble over it, my dear Lison."

About the end of the month, after a day of sultry heat, the moon rose in one of those warm, clear nights which seem to draw forth all the hidden poetry of the soul. The soft breeze fluttered the hangings of the quiet drawing-room, and the shaded lamp cast a ring of soft light on the table where the baroness and her husband were playing cards. Aunt Lison was sitting by them knitting, and the young people were leaning against the open window, looking out at the garden as it lay bathed in light.

The shadows of the linden and the plane tree fell on the moonlit grass which stretched away to the shadows of the wood.

Irresistibly attracted by the beauty of the sight, Jeanne turned and said:

" Papa, we are going for a walk on the grass."

"Very well, my dear," answered the baron, without looking up from his game.

Jeanne and the vicomte went out and walked slowly down the grass till they reached the little wood at the bottom. They stayed out so long that at last the baroness, feeling tired and wanting to go to her room, said:

"We must call in the lovers."

The baron glanced at the moonlit garden, where the two figures could be seen walking slowly about.

"Leave them alone," he answered, "it is so pleasant out of doors; Lison will wait up for them; won't you, Lison?"

The old maid looked up, and answered in her timid voice: "Oh, yes, certainly."

The baron helped his wife to rise, and, tired himself by the heat of the day,

"I will go to bed, too," he said. And he went upstairs with the baroness.

Then Aunt Lison got up, and, leaving her work on the arm of the easy chair, leant out of the window and looked at the glorious night. The two sweethearts were walking backwards and forwards across the grass, silently pressing each other's hands, as they felt the sweet influence of the visible poetry that surrounded them.

Jeanne saw the old maid's profile in the window, with the lighted lamp behind.

"Look," she said, "Aunt Lison is watching us."

"Yes, so she is," answered the vicomte in the tone of one who speaks without thinking of what he is saying; and they continued their slow walk and their dreams of love. But the dew was falling, and they began to feel chilled.

" We had better go in now," said Jeanne.

They went into the drawing-room, and found Aunt Lison bending over the knitting she had taken up again; her thin fingers were trembling as if they were very tired. Jeanne went up to her.

" Aunt, we will go to bed now," she said.

The old maid raised her eyes; they were red as if she had been crying, but neither of the lovers noticed it. Suddenly the young man saw that Jeanne's thin slippers were quite wet, and fearing she would catch cold:

" Are not your dear little feet cold? " he asked affectionately.

Aunt Lison's fingers trembled so they could no longer hold the work; her ball of wool rolled across the floor, and, hiding her face in her hands, she began to sob convulsively. For a moment Jeanne and the vicomte stood looking at her in mute surprise, then Jeanne, feeling frightened, knelt down beside her, drew away her hands from her face, and asked in dismay:

" What is it, Aunt Lison? What is the matter with you? "

The poor, old maid, trembling all over, stammered out in a broken voice:

" When he asked you — ' Are — are not your dear little feet — cold? ' — I — I thought how no one had — had ever said anything like that to me."

Jeanne felt full of pity for her aunt, but it seemed very funny to think of anyone making love to Lison, and the vicomte turned his head away to hide his laughter. Lison started up, left her wool on the ground and her knitting on the armchair, and abruptly leaving the room, groped her way up the dark staircase to her bedroom.

V—4

The two young people looked at one another, feeling sorry for her, and yet rather amused.

" Poor auntie," murmured Jeanne.

" She must be a little mad this evening," replied Julien.

They were holding each other's hands as if they could not make up their minds to say good-night, and very gently they exchanged their first kiss before Aunt Lison's empty chair. The next day they had forgotten all about the old maid's tears.

The fortnight before her marriage, Jeanne passed calmly and peacefully, as if she were almost exhausted by the number of pleasant hours she had lately had. The morning of the eventful day she had no time to think; she was only conscious of a great sense of nothingness within her, as if beneath her skin, her flesh, and blood, and bones had vanished, and she noticed how her fingers trembled when she touched anything.

She did not regain her self-possession till she was going through the marriage service. Married! She was married! Everything which had happened since dawn seemed a dream, and all around her seemed changed; people's gestures had a new meaning; even the hours of the day did not seem to be in their right places. She felt stunned at the change. The day before nothing had been altered in her life; her dearest hope had only become nearer — almost within her grasp. She had fallen asleep a girl, now she was a woman. She had crossed the barrier which hides the future with all its expected joys and fancied happiness, and she saw before her an open door; she was at last going to realize her dreams.

After the ceremony they went into the vestry, which was nearly empty, for there were no wedding guests; but when they appeared at the door of the church a loud noise made the bride start and the baroness shriek; it was a salvo fired by the peasants, who had arranged to salute the bride, and the shots could be heard all the way to Les Peuples.

Breakfast was served for the family, the curé from Yport, the Abbé Picot, and the witnesses. Then everyone went to walk in the garden till dinner was ready. The baron and the baroness, Aunt Lison, the mayor, and the abbé walked up and down the baroness's path, and the priest from Yport strode along the other avenue reading his breviary.

From the other side of the château came the noisy laughter of the peasants drinking cider under the apple-trees. The whole countryside in its Sunday garb was in the court, and the girls and young men were playing games and chasing each other.

Jeanne and Julien went across the wood, and at the top of the slope stood silently looking at the sea. It was rather chilly, although it was the middle of August; there was a north wind, and the sun was shining in the midst of a cloudless sky, so the young couple crossed the plain to find shelter in the wooded valley leading to Yport. In the coppice no wind could be felt, and they left the straight road and turned into a narrow path running under the trees.

They could hardly walk abreast, and he gently put his arm round her waist; she did not say anything, but her heart throbbed, and her breath came quickly; the branches almost touched their heads, and they often had to bend low to pass under them. She broke off a leaf; underneath it lay two lady-birds looking like delicate, red shells.

" Look, it's a husband and wife," she said, innocently, feeling a little more at ease.

Julien's mouth brushed her ear.

" To-night you will be my little wife," he said.

Although she had learnt a great deal since she had been living among the fields, as yet only the poetical side of love had presented itself to her mind, and she did not understand him. Was she not already his wife?

Then he began to drop little kisses on her forehead, and on her neck just where some soft, stray hairs curled; instinctively she drew her head away from him, startled and yet enraptured by these kisses to which she was not accustomed. Looking up they found they had reached the end of the wood. She stopped, a little confused at finding herself so far from home; what would everyone think?

" Let us go back," she said.

He withdrew his arm from her waist, and as they turned round they came face to face, so close together that she felt his breath on her cheek. They looked into each other's eyes, each seeking to read the other's soul, and trying to learn its secrets by a determined, penetrating gaze. What would each be like? What would be the life they were commencing together? What joys, what disillusions did married life reserve for them? Suddenly Julien placed his hands on his wife's shoulders, and pressed on her lips such a kiss as she had never before received, a kiss which thrilled her whole being, a 'kiss which gave her such a strange shock that she almost fell to the ground. She wildly pushed him from her.

. " Let us go back. Let us go back," she stammered out.

He did not make any answer, but took both her hands and held them in his own, and they walked back to the house in silence.

At dusk a simple dinner was served, but there was a restraint upon the conversation. The two priests, the mayor, and the four farmers, who had been invited as witnesses, alone indulged in a little coarse gayety which generally accompanies a wedding, and when the laughter died away the mayor would try to revive it with a jest. It was about nine o'clock when the coffee was served. Out of doors, under the apple-trees, the open-air ball had just commenced; the tapers which had been hung on the branches made the leaves look the color of verdigris, and through the open windows of the dining-room all the revelry could be seen. The rustics skipped round, howling a dance-tune, accompanied by two violins and a clarionet, the musicians being perched upon a kitchen table. The noisy voices of the peasants sometimes entirely drowned the sound of the instruments, and the thin music sounded as if it was dropping from the sky in little bits, a few notes being scattered every now and then.

Two big barrels, surrounded by flaming torches, provided drink for the crowd, and two servants did nothing but rinse glasses and bowls in a tub, and then hold them, dripping wet, under the taps whence flowed a crimson stream of wine, or a golden stream of cider. The thirsty dancers crowded round, stretched out their hands to get hold of any drinking vessel, and poured the liquid down their dust-filled throats. Bread, butter, cheese, and sausages were laid on a table, and everyone swallowed a mouthful from time to time. As they watched this healthy, noisy fête, the melancholy guests in the dining-room felt that they too would have liked to join the dance, to drink from the great casks, and eat a slice of bread-and-butter and a raw onion.

"By Jove! they are enjoying themselves!" said the mayor, beating time to the music with his knife. "It makes one think of the wedding feast at Ganache."

There was a murmur of suppressed laughter.

"You mean at Cana," replied the Abbé Picot, the natural enemy of every civil authority.

But the mayor held his ground.

"No, M. le curé, I know quite well what I am saying; when I say Ganache, I mean Ganache."

After dinner they went among the peasants for a little while, and then the guests took their leave. The baron and his wife had a little quarrel in a low voice. Madame Adélaïde, more out of breath than ever, seemed to be refusing something her husband was asking her to do; and at last she said almost out loud: "No, my dear, I cannot. I shouldn't know how to begin." The baron abruptly left her, and went up to Jeanne.

"Will you come for a walk with me, my child?" he said.

"If you like, papa," she answered, feeling a little uneasy.

As soon as they were outside the door they felt the wind in their faces — a cold, dry wind which drove the clouds across the sky, and made the summer night feel like autumn. The baron pressed his daughter's arm closely to him, and affectionately pressed her hand. For some minutes they walked on in silence; he could not make up his mind to begin, but, at last, he said:

"My pet, I have to perform a very difficult duty which really belongs to your mother; as she refuses to do what she ought, I am obliged to take her place. I do not know how much you already know of the laws of existence; there are some things which are carefully hidden from children, from girls especially, for girls ought to remain pure-minded and perfectly innocent until the hour their parents place them in the arms of the man who, henceforth, has the care of their happiness; it is his duty to raise the veil drawn over the sweet secret of life. But, if no suspicion of the truth has crossed their minds, girls are often shocked by the somewhat brutal reality which their dreams have not revealed to them. Wounded in mind, and even in body, they refuse to their husband what is accorded to him as an absolute right by both human and natural laws. I cannot tell you any more, my darling; but remember this, only this, that you belong entirely to your husband."

What did she know in reality? What did she guess? She began to tremble, and she felt low-spirited, and overcome by a presentiment of something terrible. When she and her father went in again they stopped in surprise at the drawing-room door. Madame Adélaïde was sobbing on Julien's shoulder. Her noisy tears seemed to be forced from her, and issued at the same time from her nose, mouth and eyes, and the amazed vicomte was awkwardly supporting the huge woman, who had thrown herself in his arms to ask him to be gentle with her darling, her pet, her dear child. The baron hurried forward.

"Oh, pray do not make a scene, do not let us have any tears," he said, taking hold of his wife, and seating her in an armchair while she wiped her face. Then turning towards Jeanne:

"Now then, my dear, kiss your mother and go to bed," he said.

Ready to cry herself, Jeanne quickly kissed her parents and ran away. Aunt Lison had already gone to her room, so the baron and his wife were left alone with Julien. They all three felt very awkward, and could think of nothing to say; the two men, in their evening-dress, remained standing, looking into space, and Madame Adélaïde leant back in her armchair, her breast still heaved by an occasional sob. At last the silence became unbearable, and the baron began to talk about the journey the young couple were going to take in a few days.

Jeanne, in her room, was being undressed by Rosalie, whose tears fell like rain; her trembling hands could not find the strings and pins, and she certainly seemed a great deal more affected than her mistress. But Jeanne did not notice her maid's tears; she felt as though she had entered another world, and was separated from all she had known and loved. Everything in her life seemed turned upside down; the strange idea came to her: "Did she really love her husband?" He suddenly seemed some stranger she hardly knew. Three months before she had not even been aware of his existence, and now she was his wife. How had it happened? Did people always plunge into marriage as they might into some uncovered hole lying in their path? When she was in her night-dress she slipped into bed, and the cold sheets made her shiver, and increased the sensation of cold, and sadness and loneliness which had weighed on her mind for two hours. Rosalie went away still sobbing, and Jeanne lay still, anxiously awaiting the revelation she had partly guessed, and that her father had hinted at in confused words — awaiting the unveiling of love's great secret.

There came three soft knocks at the door, though she had heard no one come upstairs. She started violently, and made no answer; there was another knock, and then the door-handle was turned. She hid her head under the clothes as if a thief had got into her room, and then came a noise of boots on the boards, and all at once some one touched the bed. She started again, and gave a little cry; then, uncovering her head, she saw Julien standing beside the bed, looking at her with a smile.

" Oh, how you frightened me! " she said.

" Did you not expect me, then? " he asked.

She made no answer, feeling horribly ashamed of being seen in bed by this man, who looked so grave and correct in his evening-dress. They did not know what to say or do next; they hardly dared to look at one another, in this decisive hour, on which the intimate happiness of their life depended. Perhaps he vaguely felt what perfect self-possession, what affectionate stratagems are needed not to hurt the modesty, the extreme delicacy of a maiden's heart. He gently took her hand and kissed it; then, kneeling by the bed as he would before an altar, he murmured, in a voice soft as a sigh:

" Will you love me? "

She felt a little reassured, and raised her head, which was covered with a cloud of lace.

" I love you already, dear," she said, with a smile.

He took his wife's little slender fingers in his mouth, and, his voice changed by this living gag, he asked:

" Will you give me a proof of your love? "

The question frightened her again, and, only remembering her father's words, and not quite understanding what she said:

" I am yours, dear," she answered.

He covered her hand with humid kisses, and, slowly rising, he bent towards her face, which she again began to hide. Suddenly he threw one arm across the bed, winding it around his wife over the clothes, and slipped his other arm under the bolster, which he raised with her head upon it; then he asked, in a low whisper:

" Then you will make room for me beside you? "

She had an instinctive fear, and stammered out: " Oh, not yet, I entreat you."

He seemed disappointed and a little hurt; then he went on in a voice that was still pleading, but a little more abrupt:

" Why not now, since we have got to come to it sooner or later? "

She did not like him for saying that, but, perfectly resigned and submissive, she said, for the second time:

" I am yours, dear."

Then he went quickly into his dressing-room, and she could distinctly hear the rustling of his clothes as he took them off, the jingling of the money in his pockets, the noise his boots made as he let them drop on the floor. All at once he ran across the room in his drawers and socks to put his watch on the mantelpiece; then he returned to the other room, where he moved about a little while longer. Jeanne turned quickly over to the other side and shut her eyes when she heard him coming. She nearly started out of bed when she felt a cold, hairy leg slide against hers, and, distractedly hiding her face in her hands, she moved right to the edge of the bed, almost crying with fear and horror. He took her in his arms, although her back was turned to him, and eagerly kissed her neck, the lace of her nightcap, and the embroidered collar of her night-dress. Filled with a horrible dread, she did not move, and then she felt his strong hands caressing her. She gasped for breath at this brutal touch, and felt an intense longing to escape and hide herself somewhere out of this man's reach. Soon he lay still, and she could feel the warmth of his body against her back. She did not feel so frightened then, and all at once the thought flashed across her mind that she had only to turn round and her lips would touch his.

At last he seemed to get impatient, and, in a sorrowful voice, he said:

" Then you will not be my little wife? "

" Am I not your wife already? " she said, through her hands.

" Come now, my dear, don't try to make a fool of me," he answered, with a touch of bad temper in his voice.

She felt very sorry when she heard him speak like that, and with a sudden movement she turned towards him to ask his pardon. He passionately seized her in his arms and imprinted burning kisses all over her face and neck. She had taken her hands from her face and lay still, making no response to his efforts, her thoughts

so confused that she could understand nothing, until
suddenly she felt a sharp pain, and then she began to
moan and writhe in his arms.

What happened next? She did not know, for her
head was in a whirl. She was conscious of nothing
more until she felt him raining grateful kisses on her
lips. Then he spoke to her and she had to answer;
then he made other attempts, which she repelled with
horror, and as she struggled she felt against her chest
the thick hair she had already felt against her leg, and
she drew back in dismay. Tired at last of entreating
her without effect, he lay still on his back; then she
could think. She had expected something so different,
and this destruction of her hopes, this shattering of her
expectations of delight, filled her with despair, and she
could only say to herself: "That, then, is what he
calls being his wife; that is it, that is it."

For a long time she lay thus, feeling very miserable,
her eyes wandering over the tapestry on the walls, with
its tale of love. As Julien did not speak or move, she
slowly turned her head towards him, and then she saw
that he was asleep, with his mouth half opened and his
face quite calm. Asleep! she could hardly believe it,
and it made her feel more indignant, more outraged
than his brutal passion had done. How could he sleep
on such a night? There was no novelty for him, then,
in what had passed between them? She would rather
he had struck her, or bruised her with his odious caresses till she had lost consciousness, than that he should
have slept. She leant on her elbow, and bent towards
him to listen to the breath which sometimes sounded
like a snore as it passed through his lips.

Daylight came, dim at first, then brighter, then pink,

then radiant. Julien opened his eyes, yawned, stretched his arms, looked at his wife, smiled, and asked:

" Have you slept well, dear? "

She noticed with great surprise that he said " thou " to her now, and she replied:

" Oh, yes; have you? "

" I? Oh, very well indeed," he answered, turning and kissing her. Then he began to talk, telling her his plans, and using the word " economy " so often that Jeanne wondered. She listened to him without very well understanding what he said, and, as she looked at him, a thousand thoughts passed rapidly through her mind.

Eight o'clock struck.

" We must get up," he said; " we shall look stupid if we stay in bed late to-day;" and he got up first.

When he had finished dressing, he helped his wife in all the little details of her toilet, and would not hear of her calling Rosalie. As he was going out of the room, he stopped to say:

" You know, when we are by ourselves, we can call each other ' thee ' and ' thou,' but we had better wait a little while before we talk like that before your parents. It will sound quite natural when we come back after our honeymoon." And then he went downstairs.

Jeanne did not go down till lunch-time; and the day passed exactly the same as usual, without anything extraordinary happening. There was only an extra man in the house.

## V

FOUR days after the wedding, the berlin in which they were to travel to Marseilles arrived. After the anguish of that first night, Jeanne soon became accustomed to Julien's kisses and affectionate caresses, though their more intimate relations still revolted her.   When they went away she had quite regained her gayety of heart, and the baroness was the only one who showed any emotion at the parting.   Just as the carriage was going off, she put a heavy purse in her daughter's hand.

"That is for any little thing you may want to buy," she said.

Jeanne dropped it into her pocket and the carriage started.

"How much did your mother give you in that purse?" asked Julien in the evening.

Jeanne had forgotten all about it, so she turned it out on her knees, and found there were two thousand francs in gold.

"What a lot of things I shall be able to buy!" she cried, clapping her hands.

At the end of a week they arrived at Marseilles, where the heat was terrible, and the next day they embarked on the *Roi Louis,* the little packet-boat which calls at Ajaccio on its way to Naples, and started for Corsica.   It seemed to Jeanne as if she were in a trance which yet left her the full possession of all her senses, and she could hardly believe she was really going to Corsica, the birthplace of Napoleon, with its wild undergrowth, its bandits, and its mountains.   She and her husband stood side by side on the deck of the boat watching the cliffs of Provence fly past.   Overhead was a bright blue sky, and the waves seemed to be getting thicker and firmer under the burning heat of the sun.

"Do you remember when we went to Etretat in old

Lastique's boat?" asked Jeanne; and, instead of answering her, Julien dropped a kiss right on her ear.

The steamer's paddles churned up the sea, and behind the boat, as far as the eye could reach, lay a long foaming track where the troubled waves frothed like champagne. All at once an immense dolphin leapt out of the water a few fathoms ahead, and then dived in again head foremost. It startled Jeanne, and she threw herself in Julien's arms with a little cry of fear; then she laughed at her terror, and watched for the reappearance of the enormous fish. In a few seconds up it came again, like a huge mechanical toy; then it dived again, and again disappeared; then came two more, then three, then six, which gamboled round the boat, and seemed to be escorting their large wooden brother with the iron fins. Sometimes they were on the left of the boat, sometimes on the right, and, one following the other in a kind of game, they would leap into the air, describe a curve, and replunge into the sea one after the other. Jeanne clapped her hands, delighted at each reappearance of the big, pliant fish, and felt a childish enjoyment in watching them. Suddenly they disappeared, rose to the surface a long way out to sea, then disappeared for good, and Jeanne felt quite sorry when they went away.

The calm, mild, radiant evening drew on; there was not a breath of air to cause the smallest ripple on the sea; the sun was slowly sinking towards that part of the horizon beyond which lay the land of burning heat, Africa, whose glow could almost be felt across the ocean; then, when the sun had quite disappeared, a cool breath of wind, so faint that it could not be called a

breeze, came over the sea. There were all the horrible smells of a packet-boat in their cabin, so Jeanne and
Julien wrapped themselves in their cloaks and lay down
side by side on deck. Julien went to sleep directly, but
Jeanne lay looking up at the host of stars which sparkled with so bright and clear a light in this soft Southern
sky; then the monotonous noise of the engines made her
drowsy, and at last she fell asleep. In the morning she
was awakened by the voices of the sailors cleaning the
boat, and she aroused her husband and got up. The
sea was still all around them, but straight ahead something gray could be faintly seen in the dawn; it looked
like a bank of strange-shaped clouds, pointed and
jagged, lying on the waves. This vague outline gradually became more distinct, until, standing out against
the brightening sky, a long line of mountain-peaks could
be seen. It was Corsica, hidden behind a light veil of
mist.

The sun rose, throwing black shadows around and
below every prominence, and each peak had a crown
of light, while all the rest of the island remained enveloped in mist.

The captain, a little elderly man, bronzed, withered,
and toughened by the rough salt winds, came up on
deck.

"Can you smell my lady over there?" he asked
Jeanne, in a voice that thirty years of command, and
shouting above the noise of the wind, had made hoarse.

She had indeed noticed a strong, peculiar odor of
herbs and aromatic plants.

"It's Corsica that smells like that, madame," went
on the captain. "She has a perfumed breath, just like
a pretty woman. I am a Corsican, and I should know

that smell five miles off, if I'd been away twenty years. Over there, at St. Helena, I hear he is always speaking of the perfume of his country; he belongs to my family."

And the captain took off his hat and saluted Corsica, and then, looking across the ocean, he saluted the great emperor who was a prisoner on that far-away isle, and Jeanne's heart was touched by this simple action. Then the sailor pointed towards the horizon.

" There are the Sanguinaires," he said.

Julien had his arm round his wife's waist, and they both strained their eyes to see what the captain was pointing out. As last they saw some pointed rocks that the boat rounded before entering a large, calm bay, surrounded by high mountains, whose steep sides looked as though they were covered with moss.

" That is the undergrowth," said the captain, pointing out this verdure.

The circle of mountains seemed to close in behind the boat as she slowly steamed across the azure water which was so transparent that in places the bottom could be seen. Ajaccio came in sight; it was a white town at the foot of the mountains, with a few small Italian boats lying at anchor in the harbor, and four or five row-boats came beside the *Roi Louis* to take off the passengers. Julien, who was looking after the luggage, asked his wife in a low tone:

" A franc is enough, isn't it, to give the steward? "

The whole week he had been constantly asking her this question which she hated.

" When you don't know what is enough, give too much," she answered, a little impatiently.

He haggled with every one, landlords and hotel-

V—5

waiters, cabmen and shopmen, and when he had obtained the reduction he wanted, he would rub his hands, and say to Jeanne: " I don't like to be robbed." She trembled when the bills were brought, for she knew beforehand the remarks he would make on each item, and felt ashamed of his bargaining; and when she saw the scornful look of the servants as her husband left his small fee in their hands, she blushed to the roots of her hair. Of course he had a discussion with the boatmen who took them ashore.

The first tree she saw on landing was a palm, which delighted her. They went to a big empty hotel standing at the corner of a vast square, and ordered lunch. When they had finished dessert, Jeanne got up to go and wander about the town, but Julien, taking her in his arms, whispered tenderly in her ear:

" Shall we go upstairs for a little while, my pet? "

" Go upstairs? " she said, with surprise; " but I am not at all tired."

He pressed her to him: " Don't you understand? For two days —"

She blushed crimson.

" Oh, what would everyone say? what would they think? You could not ask for a bedroom in the middle of the day. Oh, Julien, don't say anything about it now, please don't."

" Do you think I care what the hotel-people say or think? " he interrupted. " You'll see what difference they make to me." And he rang the bell.

She did not say anything more, but sat with downcast eyes, disgusted at her husband's desires, to which she always submitted with a feeling of shame and degradation; her senses were not yet aroused, and her hus-

band treated her as if she shared all his ardors. When
the waiter answered the bell, Julien asked him to show
them to their room; the waiter, a man of true Corsican
type, bearded to the eyes, did not understand, and kept
saying that the room would be quite ready by the evening. Julien got out of patience.

" Get it ready at once," he said. " The journey has
tired us and we want to rest."

A slight smile crept over the waiter's face, and
Jeanne would have liked to run away; when they came
downstairs again, an hour later, she hardly dared pass
the servants, feeling sure that they would whisper and
laugh behind her back. She felt vexed with Julien for
not understanding her feelings, and wondering at his
want of delicacy; it raised a sort of barrier between
them, and, for the first time, she understood that two
people can never be in perfect sympathy; they may pass
through life side by side, seemingly in perfect union,
but neither quite understands the other, and every soul
must of necessity be for ever lonely.

They stayed three days in the little town which was
like a furnace, for every breath of wind was shut out
by the mountains. Then they made out a plan of the
places they should visit, and decided to hire some
horses. They started one morning at daybreak on the
two wiry little Corsican horses they had obtained, and
accompanied by a guide mounted on a mule which also
carried some provisions, for inns are unknown in this
wild country. At first the road ran along the bay, but
soon it turned into a shallow valley leading to the mountains. The uncultivated country seemed perfectly bare,
and the sides of the hills were covered with tall weeds,
turned sere and yellow by the burning heat; they often

crossed ravines where only a narrow stream still ran with
a gurgling sound, and occasionally they met a moun-
taineer, sometimes on foot, sometimes riding his little
horse, or bestriding a donkey no bigger than a dog;
these mountaineers always carried a loaded gun which
might be old and rusty, but which became a very for-
midable weapon in their hands. The air was filled with
the pungent smell of the aromatic plants with which the
isle is covered, and the road sloped gradually upwards,
winding round the mountains.

The peaks of blue and pink granite made the island
look like a fairy palace, and, from the heights, the forests of immense chestnut trees on the lower parts of the
hills looked like green thickets. Sometimes the guide
would point to some steep height, and mention a name;
Jeanne and Julien would look, at first seeing nothing,
but at last discovering the summit of the mountain. It
was a village, a little granite hamlet, hanging and clinging like a bird's nest to the vast mountain. Jeanne got
tired of going at a walking pace for so long.

"Let us gallop a little," she said, whipping up her
horse.

She could not hear her husband behind her, and, turning round to see where he was, she burst out laughing.
Pale with fright, he was holding onto his horse's mane,
almost jolted out of the saddle by the animal's motion.
His awkwardness and fear were all the more funny,
because he was such a grave, handsome man. Then
they trotted gently along the road between two thickets formed of juniper trees, green oaks, arbutus trees,
heaths, bay trees, myrtles, and box trees, whose branches
were formed into a network by the climbing clematis,
and between and around which grew big ferns, honey-

suckles, rosemary, lavender, and briars, forming a perfectly impassable thicket, which covered the hill like a
cloak. The travelers began to get hungry, and the
guide rejoined them and took them to one of those
springs so often met with in a mountainous country,
with the icy water flowing from a little hole in the rock
where some passer-by has left the big chestnut leaf
which conveyed the water to his mouth. Jeanne felt
so happy that she could hardly help shouting aloud; and
they again remounted and began to descend, winding
round the Gulf of Sagone.

As evening was drawing on they went through Car-
gése, the Greek village founded so long ago by fugi-
tives driven from their country. Round a fountain
was a group of tall, handsome and particularly graceful
girls, with well formed hips, long hands, and slender
waists; Julien cried "Good-night" to them, and they
answered him in the musical tongue of their ancestors.
When they got to Piana they had to ask for hospitality
quite in the way of the middle ages, and Jeanne trembled with joy as they waited for the door to open in
answer to Julien's knock. Oh, that was a journey!
There they did indeed meet with adventures!

They had happened to appeal to a young couple who
received them as the patriarch received the messenger
of God, and they slept on a straw mattress in an old
house whose woodwork was so full of worms that it
seemed alive. At sunrise they started off again, and
soon they stopped opposite a regular forest of crimson
rocks; there were peaks, columns, and steeples, all mar-
velously sculptured by time and the sea. Thin, round,
twisted, crooked, and fantastic, these wonderful rocks
nine hundred feet high, looked like trees, plants, ani-

mals, monuments, men, monks in their cassocks, horned demons and huge birds, such as one sees in a nightmare, the whole forming a monstrous tribe which seemed to have been petrified by some eccentric god.

Jeanne could not speak, her heart was too full, but she took Julien's hand and pressed it, feeling that she must love something or some one before all this beauty; and then, leaving this confusion of forms, they came upon another bay surrounded by a wall of blood-red granite, which cast crimson reflections into the blue sea. Jeanne exclaimed, " Oh, Julien! " and that was all she could say; a great lump came in her throat and two tears ran down her cheeks. Julien looked at her in astonishment.

" What is it, my pet? " he asked.

She dried her eyes, smiled, and said in a voice that still trembled a little. " Oh, it's nothing, I suppose I am nervous. I am so happy that the least thing upsets me."

He could not understand this nervousness; he despised the hysterical excitement to which women give way and the joy or despair into which they are cast by a mere sensation, and he thought her tears absurd. He glanced at the bad road.

" You had better look after your horse," he said.

They went down by a nearly impassable road, then turning to the right, proceeded along the gloomy valley of Ota. The path looked very dangerous, and Julien proposed that they should go up on foot. Jeanne was only too delighted to be alone with him after the emotion she had felt, so the guide went on with the mule and horses, and they walked slowly after him. The mountain seemed cleft from top to bottom, and the

path ran between two tremendous walls of rock which
looked nearly black. The air was icy cold, and the little bit of sky that could be seen looked quite strange, it
seemed so far away. A sudden noise made Jeanne
look up. A large bird flew out of a hole in the rock;
it was an eagle, and its open wings seemed to touch the
two sides of the chasm as it mounted towards the sky.
Farther on, the mountain again divided, and the path
wound between the two ravines, taking abrupt turns.
Jeanne went first, walking lightly and easily, sending
the pebbles rolling from under her feet and fearlessly
looking down the precipices. Julien followed her, a
little out of breath, and keeping his eyes on the ground
so that he should not feel giddy and it seemed like coming out of Hades when they suddenly came into the full
sunlight.

They were very thirsty, and, seeing a damp track,
they followed it till they came to a tiny spring flowing
into a hollow stick which some goat-herd had put there;
all around the spring the ground was carpeted with
moss, and Jeanne knelt down to drink. Julien followed her example, and as she was slowly enjoying the
cool water, he put his arm around her and tried to take
her place at the end of the wooden pipe. In the struggle between their lips they would in turns seize the small
end of the tube and hold it in their mouths for a few
seconds; then, as they left it, the stream flowed on again
and splashed their faces and necks, their clothes and
their hands. A few drops shone in their hair like
pearls, and with the water flowed their kisses.

Then Jeanne had an inspiration of love. She filled
her mouth with the clear liquid, and, her cheeks puffed
out like bladders, she made Julien understand that he

was to quench his thirst at her lips. He stretched his
throat, his head thrown backwards and his arms open,
and the deep draught he drank at this living spring en-
flamed him with desire. Jeanne leant on his shoulder
with unusual affection, her heart throbbed, her bosom
heaved, her eyes, filled with tears, looked softer, and
she whispered:

, " Julien, I love you! "

Then, drawing him to her, she threw herself down
and hid her shame-stricken face in her hands. He
threw himself down beside her, and pressed her passionately to him; she gasped for breath as she lay nervously
waiting, and all at once she gave a loud cry as though
thunderstruck by the sensation she had invited. It was
a long time before they reached the top of the mountain, so fluttered and exhausted was Jeanne, and it was
evening when they got to Evisa, and went to the house
of Paoli Palabretti, a relation of the guide's. Paoli
was a tall man with a slight cough, and the melancholy
look of a consumptive; he showed them their room, a
miserable-looking chamber built of stone, but which was
handsome for this country, where no refinement is
known. He was expressing in his Corsican patois (a
mixture of French and Italian) his pleasure at receiving them, when a clear voice interrupted him, and a
dark little woman, with big black eyes, a sun-kissed skin,
and a slender waist, hurried forward, kissed Jeanne,
shook Julien by the hand and said: " Good-day, madame; good-day, monsieur; are you quite well? " She
took their hats and shawls and arranged everything
with one hand, for her other arm was in a sling; then
she turned them all out, saying to her husband: " Take
them for a walk till dinner is ready."

M. Palabretti obeyed at once, and, walking between Jeanne and her husband, he took them round the village. His steps and his words both drawled, and he coughed frequently, saying at each fit, "The cold air has got on my lungs." He led them under some immense chestnut-trees, and, suddenly stopping, he said in his monotonous voice:

"It was here that Mathieu Lori killed my cousin Jean Rinaldi. I was standing near Jean, just there, when we saw Mathieu about three yards off. 'Jean,' he cried; 'don't go to Albertacce; don't you go, Jean, or I'll kill you:' I took Jean's arm. 'Don't go Jean,' I said, 'or he'll do it.' It was about a girl, Paulina Sinacoupi, that they were both after. Then Jean cried out, 'I shall go, Mathieu; and you won't stop me, either.' Then Mathieu raised his gun, and, before I could take aim, he fired. Jean leaped two feet from the ground, monsieur, and then fell right on me, and my gun dropped and rolled down to that chestnut there. Jean's mouth was wide open, but he didn't say a word; he was dead."

The young couple stared in astonishment at this calm witness of such a crime.

"What became of the murderer?" asked Jeanne.

Paoli coughed for some time, then he went on:

"He gained the mountain, and my brother killed him the next year. My brother, Philippi Palabretti, the bandit, you know."

Jeanne shuddered. "Is your brother a bandit?" she asked.

The placid Corsican's eye flashed proudly.

"Yes, madame, he was a celebrated bandit, he was; he put an end to six gendarmes. He died with Nicolas Morali after they had been surrounded for six days, and were almost starved to death."

Then they went in to dinner, and the little woman treated them as if she had known them twenty years. Jeanne was haunted by the fear that she would not again experience the strange shock she had felt in Julien's arms beside the fountain, and when they were alone in their room she was still afraid his kisses would again leave her insensible, but she was soon reassured, and that was her first night of love. The next day she could hardly bear to leave this humble abode, where a new happiness had come to her; she drew her host's little wife into her bedroom, and told her she did not mean it as a present in return for their hospitality but she must absolutely insist on sending her a souvenir from Paris, and to this souvenir she seemed to attach a superstitious importance. For a long time the young Corsican woman refused to accept anything at all, but at last she said:

" Well, send me a little pistol, a very little one."

Jeanne opened her eyes in astonishment, and the woman added in her ear, as though she were confiding some sweet and tender secret to her:

" It's to kill my brother-in-law with."

And with a smile on her face, she quickly un-bandaged the arm she could not use, and showed Jeanne the soft, white flesh which had been pierced right through with a stiletto, though the wound had nearly healed.

" If I had not been as strong as he is," she said, " he would have killed me. My husband is not jealous, for he understands me, and then he is ill, you see, so he is not so hot-blooded; besides, I am an honest woman,

madame. But my brother-in-law believes everything
that is told him about me, and he is jealous for my
husband. I am sure he will make another attempt
upon my life, but if I have a little pistol I shall feel
safe, and I shall be sure of having my revenge."

Jeanne promised to send the weapon, affectionately
kissed her new friend and said good-bye. The rest of
her journey was a dream, an endless embrace, an intoxication of caresses; she no longer saw country or people
or the places where they stopped, she had eyes only for
Julien. When they got to Bastia the guide had to be
paid; Julien felt in his pockets, and not finding what
he wanted, he said to Jeanne:

" Since you don't use the two thousand francs your
mother gave you, I might as well carry them; they
will be safer in my pocket, and, besides, then I shan't
have to change any notes."

They went to Leghorn, Florence, and Genoa, and,
one windy morning, they found themselves again at
Marseilles. It was then the fifteenth of October, and
they had been away from Les Peuples two months.
The cold wind, which seemed to blow from Normandy,
chilled Jeanne and made her feel miserable. There
had lately been a change in Julien's behavior towards
her, he seemed tired, and indifferent, and she had a
vague presentiment of evil. She persuaded him to stay
at Marseilles four days longer, for she could not bear
to leave these warm, sunny lands where she had been
so happy, but at last they had to go. They intended
to buy all the things they wanted for their housekeeping
at Paris, and Jeanne was looking forward to buying
all sorts of things for Les Peuples, thanks to her
mother's present; but the very first thing she meant to

purchase was the pistol she had promised to the young Corsican woman at Evisa.

The day after they reached Paris, she said to Julien:

" Will you give me mamma's money, dear? I want to buy some things."

He looked rather cross.

" How much do you want? " he asked.

" Oh — what you like," she answered in surprise.

" I will give you a hundred francs," he answered; " and whatever you do, don't waste it."

She did not know what to say, she felt so amazed and confused, but at last she said in a hesitating way:

" But — I gave you that money to —"

He interrupted her.

" Yes, exactly. What does it matter whether it's in your pocket or mine now that we share everything? I am not refusing you the money, am I? I am going to give you a hundred francs."

She took the five pieces of gold without another word; she did not dare ask for more, so she bought nothing but the pistol.

A week later they started for Les Peuples.

## VI

WHEN the post-chaise drove up, the baron and baroness and all the servants were standing outside the white railings to give the travelers a hearty welcome home. The baroness cried, Jeanne quietly wiped away two tears, and her father walked backwards and forwards nervously. Then, while the luggage was being brought in, the whole journey was gone over again before the drawing-room fire. The eager words flowed from Jeanne's lips, and in half-an-hour she had related everything, except a few little details she forgot in her haste. Then she went to unpack, with Rosalie, who was in a state of great excitement, to help her; when she had finished and everything had been put away in its proper place Rosalie left her mistress, and Jeanne sat down, feeling a little tired. She wondered what she could do next, and she tried to think of some occupation for her mind, some task for her fingers. She did not want to go down to the drawing-room again to sit by her mother who was dozing, and she thought of going for a walk, but it was so miserable out of doors that only to glance out of the window made her feel melancholy.

Then the thought flashed across her mind that now there never would be anything for her to do. At the convent the future had always given her something to think about, and her dreams had filled the hours, so that their flight had passed unnoticed; but she had hardly left the convent when her love-dreams had been realized. In a few weeks she had met, loved, and married a man who had borne her away in his arms without giving her time to think of anything. But now the sweet reality of the first few weeks of married life was going to become a daily monotony, barring the way to all the hopes and delicious fears of an unknown future. There was nothing more to which she could look forward, nothing more for her to do, to-day, to-morrow, or ever. She felt all that with a vague sensation of disillusion and melancholy. She rose and went to lean her forehead against the cold window-pane, and, after looking for some time at the dull sky and heavy clouds, she made up her mind to go out.

Could it really be the same country, the same grass, the same trees as she had seen with such joy in May? What had become of the sun-bathed leaves, and the flaming dandelions, the blood-red poppies, the pure marguerites that had reared their heads amidst the green grass above which had fluttered innumerable yellow butterflies? They were all gone, and the very air seemed changed, for now it was no longer full of life, and fertilizing germs and intoxicating perfumes. The avenues were soaked by the autumn rains and covered with a thick carpet of dead leaves, and the thin branches of the poplars trembled in the wind which was shaking off the few leaves that still hung on them. All day long these last, golden leaves hovered and whirled in the air for a few seconds and then fell, in an incessant, melancholy rain.

Jeanne walked on down to the wood. It gave her the sad impression of being in the room of a dying man. The leafy walls which had separated the pretty winding paths no longer existed, the branches of the shrubs blew mournfully one against the other, the rustling of the fallen leaves, that the wind was blowing about and piling into heaps, sounded like a dying sigh, and the birds hopped from tree to tree with shivering little chirps, vainly seeking a shelter from the cold. Shielded by the elms which formed a sort of vanguard against the sea-wind, the linden and the plane-tree were still covered with leaves, and the one was clothed in a mantle of scarlet velvet, the other in a cloak of orange silk. Jeanne walked slowly along the baroness's avenue, by the side of Couillard's farm, beginning to realize what a dull, monotonous life lay before her;

then she sat down on the slope where Julien had first
told his love, too sad even to think and only feeling that
she would like to go to bed and sleep, so that she might
escape from this melancholy day. Looking up she saw
a seagull blown along by a gust of wind, and she suddenly thought of the eagle she had seen in Corsica in
the somber valley of Ota. As she sat there she
could see again the island with its sun-ripened oranges,
its strong perfumes, its pink-topped mountains, its azure
bays, its ravines, with their rushing torrents, and it gave
her a sharp pain to think of that happy time that was
past and gone; and the damp, rugged country by which
she was now surrounded, the mournful fall of the leaves,
the gray clouds hurrying before the wind, made her
feel so miserable that she went indoors, feeling that she
should cry if she stayed out any longer. She found
her mother, who was accustomed to these dull days,
dozing over the fire. The baron and Julien had gone
for a walk, and the night was drawing on filling the
vast drawing-room with dark shadows which were
sometimes dispersed by the fitful gleams of the fire; out
of doors the gray sky and muddy fields could just be
seen in the fading light.

The baron and Julien came in soon after Jeanne. As
soon as he came into the gloomy room the baron rang
the bell, exclaiming:

"How miserable you look in here! Let us have
some lights."

He sat down before the fire, putting his feet near
the flame, which made the mud drop off his steaming
boots.

"I think it is going to freeze," he said, rubbing his

hands together cheerfully. "The sky is clearing towards the north, and it's a full moon this evening. We shall have a hard frost to-night."

Then, turning towards his daughter:

"Well, my dear," he asked, "are you glad to get back to your own house and see the old people at home again?"

This simple question quite upset Jeanne. Her eyes filled with tears, and she threw herself into her father's arms, covering his face with kisses as though she would ask him to forgive her discontent. She had thought she should be so pleased to see her parents again, and now, instead of joy, she felt a coldness around her heart, and it seemed as if she could not regain all her former love for them until they had all dropped back into their ordinary ways again.

Dinner seemed very long that evening; no one spoke, and Julien did not pay the least attention to his wife. In the drawing-room after dinner, Jeanne dozed over the fire opposite the baroness who was quite asleep, and, when she was aroused for a moment by the voices of the two men, raised in argument over something, she wondered if she would ever become quite content with a pleasureless, listless life like her mother. The crackling fire burnt clear and bright, and threw sudden gleams on the faded tapestry chairs, on the fox and the stork, on the melancholy-looking heron, on the ant and the grasshopper. The baron came over to the fireplace, and held his hands to the blaze.

"The fire burns well to-night," he said; "there is a frost, I am sure."

He put his hands on Jeanne's shoulder, and, pointing to the fire:

"My child," he said, "the hearth with all one's family around it is the happiest spot on earth; there is no place like it. But don't you think we had better go to bed? You must both be quite worn out with fatigue."

Up in her bedroom Jeanne wondered how this second return to the place she loved so well could be so different from the first. "Why did she feel so miserable?" she asked herself; "why did the château, the fields, everything she had so loved, seem to-day so desolate?" Her eyes fell on the clock. The little bee was swinging from left to right and from right to left over the gilded flowers, with the same quick even movement as of old. She suddenly felt a glow of affection for this little piece of mechanism, which told her the hour in its silvery tones, and beat like a human heart, and the tears came into her eyes as she looked at it; she had not felt so moved when she had kissed her father and mother on her return, but the heart has no rules or logic, to guide it.

Julien had made his fatigue the pretext for not sharing his wife's chamber that night, so, for the first time since her marriage, she slept alone. It had been agreed that henceforth they should have separate rooms, but she was not yet accustomed to sleep alone, and, for a long time she lay awake while the moaning wind swept round the house. In the morning she was aroused by the blood-red light falling on her bed. Through the frozen window-panes it looked as if the whole sky were on fire. Throwing a big dressing-gown round her, Jeanne ran to the window and opened it, and in rushed an icy wind, stinging her skin and bringing the water to her eyes. In the midst of a crimson sky, the great red sun was rising behind the trees, and the white frost had made the ground so hard that it rang under the farm-servant's feet. In this one night all the branches of the poplars had been entirely stripped of their few remaining leaves, and, through the bare trees, beyond the plain, appeared the long, green line of the sea, covered with white-crested waves. The plane-tree and the linden were being rapidly stripped of their bright coverings by the cold wind, and showers of leaves fell to the ground as each gust swept by.

Jeanne dressed herself, and for want of something better to do, went to see the farmers. The Martins were very surprised to see her. Madame Martin kissed her on both cheeks, and she had to drink a little glass of noyau; then she went over to the other farm. The Couillards were also very surprised when she came in; the farmer's wife gave two pecks at her ears and insisted on her drinking a little glass of cassis; then she went in to breakfast. And that day passed like the previous one, only it was cold instead of damp, and the other days of the week were like the first two, and all the weeks of the month were like the first one.

Little by little, Jeanne's regrets for those happy, distant lands vanished; she began to get resigned to her life, to feel an interest in the many unimportant details of the days, and to perform her simple, regular occupations with care. A disenchantment of life, a sort of settled melancholy gradually took possession of her. What did she want? She did not know herself. She had no desire for society, no thirst for the excitement of the world, the pleasures she might have had possessed no attraction for her, but all her dreams and illusions had faded away, leaving her life as colorless as the old tapestry chairs in the château drawing-room.

Her relations with Julien had completely changed, for he became quite a different man when they settled down after their wedding tour, like an actor who becomes himself again as soon as he has finished playing his part. He hardly ever took any notice of his wife, or even spoke to her; all his love seemed to have suddenly disappeared, and it was very seldom that he accompanied her to her room of a night. He had taken the management of the estate and the household into his own hands, and he looked into all the accounts, saw that the peasants paid their arrears of rent, and cut down every expense. No longer the polished, elegant man who had won Jeanne's heart, he looked and dressed like a well-to-do farmer, neglecting his personal appearance with the carelessness of a man who no longer strives to fascinate. He always wore an old velvet shooting-jacket, covered all over with stains, which he had found one day as he was looking over his old clothes; then he left off shaving, and his long, untrimmed beard made him look quite plain, while his hands never received any attention.

After each meal, he drank four or five small glasses of brandy, and when Jeanne affectionately reproached him, he answered so roughly: "Leave me alone, can't you?" that she never tried to reason with him again.

She accepted all this in a calm way that astonished herself, but she looked upon him now as a stranger who was nothing whatever to her. She often thought of it all, and wondered how it was that after having loved and married each other in a delicious passion of affection they should suddenly awake from their dream

of love as utter strangers, as if they had never lain in
each other's arms.    How was it his indifference did
not hurt her more?    Had they been mistaken in each
other?    Would she have been more pained if Julien
had still been handsome, elegant and attractive?

.    .    .    .    .    .    .

It was understood that at the new year the baron
and baroness were to spend a few months in their
Rouen house, leaving Les Peuples to the young people
who would become settled that winter, and so get accustomed to the place where they were to pass their
lives.    Julien wanted to present his wife to the Brisevilles, the Couteliers and the Fourvilles, but they could
not pay these visits yet because they had not been able
to get the painter to change the coat-of-arms on the
carriage; for nothing in the world would have persuaded Julien to go to the neighboring château in the
old family carriage, which the baron had given up to
him, until the arms of the De Lamares had been quar-
tered on it with those of the Leperthius des Vauds.
Now there was only one man in the whole province who
made a speciality of coats-of-arms, a painter ifrom
Bolbec, named Bataille, who was naturally in great request among all the Normandy aristocracy; so Julien
had to wait for some time before he could secure his
services.

At last, one December morning just as they were
finishing lunch at Les Peuples, they saw a man, with a
box on his back, open the gate and come up the path;
it was Bataille.    He was shown into the dining-room,
and lunch was served to him just as if he had been a
gentleman, for his constant intercourse with the provincial aristocracy, his knowledge of the coats-of-arms,

their mottoes and signification, made him a sort of herald with whom no gentleman need be ashamed to shake hands.

Pencils and paper were brought, and while Bataille ate his lunch, the baron and Julien made sketches of their escutcheons with all the quarters. The baroness, always delighted when anything of this sort was discussed, gave her advice, and even Jeanne took part in the conversation, as if it aroused some interest in her. Bataille, without interrupting his lunch, occasionally gave an opinion, took the pencil to make a sketch of his idea, quoted examples, described all the aristocratic carriages in Normandy, and seemed to scatter an atmosphere of nobility all around him. He was a little man with thin gray hair and paint-daubed hands which smelt of oil. It was said that he had once committed a grave offense against public morality, but the esteem in which he was held by all the titled families had long ago effaced this stain on his character.

As soon as the painter had finished his coffee, he was taken to the coach-house and the carriage was uncovered. Bataille looked at it, gave an idea of the size he thought the shield ought to be, and then, after the others had again given their opinions, he began his work. In spite of the cold the baroness ordered a chair and a foot-warmer to be brought out for her that she might sit and watch the painter. Soon she began to talk to him, asking him about the marriages and births and deaths of which she had not yet heard, and adding these fresh details to the genealogical trees which she already knew by heart. Beside her, astride a chair, sat Julien, smoking a pipe and occasionally spitting on the ground as he watched the growth of the colored certificate of his nobility. Soon old Simon on his way to the kitchen garden stopped, with his spade on his shoulder, to look at the painting, and the news of Bataille's arrival having reached the two farms the farmers' wives came hurrying up also. Standing on either side of the baroness, they went into ecstasies over the drawing and kept repeating: "He must be clever to paint like that."

The shields on both carriage-doors were finished the next morning about eleven o'clock. Everyone came to look at the work now it was done, and the carriage was drawn out of the coach-house that they might the better judge of the effect. The design was pronounced perfect, and Bataille received a great many compliments before he strapped his box on his back and went off again; the baron, his wife, Jeanne and Julien all agreed that the painter was a man of great talent, and would, no doubt, have become an artist, if circumstances had permitted.

For the sake of economy, Julien had accomplished some reforms which brought with them the need of fresh arrangements. The old coachman now performed the duties of gardener, the vicomte himself undertaking to drive, and as he was obliged to have someone to hold the horses when the family went to make a visit, he had made a groom of a young cowherd named Marius. The horses had been sold to do away with the expense of their keep, so he had introduced a clause in Couillard's and Martin's leases by which the two farmers bound themselves to each provide a horse once a month, on whatever day the vicomte chose.

When the day came the Couillards produced a big, raw-boned, yellowish horse, and the Martins a little, white, long-haired nag; the two horses were harnessed, and Marius, buried in an old livery of Simon's, brought the carriage round to the door. Julien, who was in his best clothes, would have looked a little like his old, elegant self, if his long beard had not made him look common. He inspected the horses, the carriage, and the little groom, and thought they looked very well, the only thing of any importance in his eyes being the new coat-of-arms. The baroness came downstairs on her husband's arm, got in, and had some cushions put behind her back; then came Jeanne. She laughed first at the strange pair of horses, and her laughter increased when she saw Marius with his face buried under his cockaded hat (which his nose alone prevented from slipping down to his chin), and his hands lost in his ample sleeves, and the skirts of his coat coming right down to his feet, which were encased in enormous boots; but when she saw him obliged to throw his head right back before he could see anything, and raise his knee at each step as though he were going to take a river in his stride, and move like a blind man when he had an order given him, she gave a shout of laughter. The baron turned round, looked for a moment at the little fellow who stood looking so confused in his big clothes, and then he too was overcome with laughter, and, hardly able to speak, called out to his wife:

" Lo-lo-look at Ma-Marius! Does-doesn't he look fun-funny? "

The baroness leaned out of the carriage-window, and, catching sight of Marius, she was shaken by such a fit of laughter that the carriage moved up and down on its springs as if it were jolting over some deep ruts.

" What on earth is there to laugh at like that? " said

Julien, his face pale with anger. " You must be perfect idiots, all of you."

Jeanne sat down on the steps, holding her sides and quite unable to contain herself; the baron followed her example, and, inside the carriage, convulsive sneezes and a sort of continual clucking intimated that the baroness was suffocating with laughter. At last Marius' coat began to shake; no doubt, he understood the cause of all this mirth, and he giggled himself, beneath his big hat. Julien rushed towards him in a rage; he gave him a box on the ear which knocked the boy's hat off and sent it rolling onto the grass; then, turning to the baron, he said, in a voice that trembled with anger:

" I think you ought to be the last one to laugh. Whose fault is it that you are ruined? We should not be like this if you had not squandered your fortune and thrown away your money right and left."

All the laughter stopped abruptly, but no one spoke. Jeanne, ready to cry now, quietly took her place beside her mother. The baron, without a word, sat down opposite, and Julien got up on the box, after lifting up the crying boy whose cheek was beginning to swell. The long drive was performed in silence, for they all felt awkward and unable to converse on ordinary topics. They could only think of the incident that had just happened, and, rather than broach such a painful subject, they preferred to sit in dull silence.

They went past a great many farm-houses startling the black fowls and sending them to the hedges for refuge, and sometimes a yelping dog followed for a little while and then ran back to his kennel with bristling hair, turning round every now and then to send another bark after the carriage. A lad in muddy sabots, was

slouching along with his hands in his pockets, his
blouse blown out by the wind and his long lazy legs
dragging one after the other, and as he stood on one
side for the carriage to pass, he awkwardly pulled off
his cap. Between each farm lay meadows with other
farms dotted here and there in the distance, and it
seemed a long while before they turned up an avenue of
firs which bordered the road. Here the carriage leant
on one side as it passed over the deep ruts, and the
baroness felt frightened and began to give little screams.
At the end of the avenue there was a white gate which
Marius jumped down to open, and then they drove
round an immense lawn and drew up before a high,
gloomy-looking house which had all its shutters closed.

The hall-door opened, and an old, semi-paralyzed
servant (in a red and black striped waistcoat, over
which was tied an apron) limped sideways down the
steps; after asking the visitors' names he showed them
into a large drawing-room, and drew up the closed
Venetian blinds. The furniture was all covered up,
and the clock and candelabra were enveloped in white
cloths; the room smelt moldy, and its damp, cold atmosphere seemed to chill one to the very heart. The
visitors sat down and waited. Footsteps could be heard
on the floor above, hurrying along in an unusual bustle, for the lady of the house had been taken unawares
and was changing her dress as quickly as possible; a
bell rang several times and then they could hear more
footsteps on the stairs. The baroness, feeling thoroughly cold, began to sneeze frequently; Julien walked
up and down the room, Jeanne sat by her mother, and
the baron stood with his back against the marble mantelpiece.

At last a door opened, and the Vicomte and Vicomtesse de Briseville appeared. They were a little, thin couple of an uncertain age, both very formal and rather embarrassed. The vicomtesse wore a flowered silk gown and a cap trimmed with ribbons, and when she spoke it was in a sharp, quick voice. Her husband was in a tight frock-coat; his hair looked as if it had been waxed, and his nose, his eyes, his long teeth and his coat, which was evidently his best one, all shone as if they had been polished with the greatest care. He returned his visitors' bow with a bend of the knees.

When the ordinary complimentary phrases had been exchanged no one knew what to say next, so they all politely expressed their pleasure at making this new acquaintance and hoped it would be a lasting one; for, living as they did in the country all the year round, an occasional visit made an agreable change. The icy air of the drawing-room froze the very marrow of their bones, and the baroness was seized by a fit of coughing, interrupted at intervals by a sneeze. The baron rose to go.

" You are not going to leave us already? Pray, stay a little longer," said the Brisevilles.

But Jeanne followed her father's example in spite of all the signs made her by Julien, who thought they were leaving too soon. The vicomtesse would have rung to order the baron's carriage, but the bell was out of order, so the vicomte went to find a servant. He soon returned, to say that the horses had been taken out, and the carriage would not be ready for some minutes. Everyone tried to find some subject of conversation; the rainy winter was discussed, and Jeanne, who could not prevent herself shivering, try as she would, asked if their hosts did not find it very dull living alone all the year round. Such a question astounded the Brisevilles. Their time was always fully occupied, what with writing long letters to their numerous aristocratic relations and pompously discussing the most trivial matters, for in all their useless, petty occupations, they were as formally polite to each other as they would have been to utter strangers. At last the carriage, with its two ill-matched steeds, drew up before the door, but Marius was nowhere to be seen; he had gone for a walk in the fields, thinking he would not be wanted again until the evening. Julien, in a great rage, left word for him to be sent after them on foot, and, after a great many bows and compliments, they started for Les Peuples again.

As soon as they were fairly off, Jeanne and the baron, in spite of the uncomfortable feeling that Julien's ill-temper had caused, began to laugh and joke about the Brisevilles' ways and tones. The baron imitated the husband and Jeanne the wife, and the baroness, feeling a little hurt in her reverence for the aristocracy, said to them:

"You should not joke in that way. I'm sure the Brisevilles are very well-bred people, and they belong to excellent families."

They stopped laughing for a time, out of respect for the baroness's feelings, but every now and then Jeanne would catch her father's eye, and then they began again. The baron would make a very stiff bow, and say in a solemn voice:

"Your château at Les Peuples must be very cold, madame, with the sea-breeze blowing on it all day long."

Then Jeanne put on a very prim look, and said with a smirk, moving her head all the time like a duck on the water:

"Oh, monsieur, I have plenty to fill up my time. You see we have so many relations to whom letters must be written, and M. de Briseville leaves all correspondence to me, as his time is taken up with the religious history of Normandy that he is writing in collaboration with the Abbé Pelle."

The baroness could not help smiling, but she repeated, in a half-vexed, half-amused tone:

"It isn't right to laugh at people of our own rank like that."

All at once the carriage came to a standstill, and Julien called out to someone on the road behind; Jeanne and the baron leant out of the windows, and saw some singular creature rolling, rather than running, towards them. Hindered by the floating skirts of his coat, unable to see for his hat, which kept slipping over his eyes, his sleeves waving like the sails of a windmill, splashing through the puddles, stumbling over every large stone in his way, hastening, jumping, covered with mud, Marius was running after the carriage as fast as his legs could carry him. As soon as he came up Julien leant down, caught hold of him by the coat collar, and lifted him up on the box seat; then, dropping the reins, he began to pommel the boy's hat, which at once slipped down to his shoulders. Inside the hat, which sounded as if it had been a drum, Marius yelled at the top of his voice, but it was in vain that he struggled and tried to jump down, for his master held him firmly with one hand while he beat him with the other.

" Papa! oh, papa!" gasped Jeanne; and the baroness, filled with indignation, seized her husband's arm,
and exclaimed: " Stop him, Jacques, stop him!"
The baron suddenly let down the front window, and
catching hold of the vicomte's sleeve:

" Are you going to stop beating that child? " he said
in a voice that trembled with anger.

Julien turned round in astonishment.

" But don't you see what a state the little wretch has
got his livery into? "

" What does that matter to me? " exclaimed the
baron, with his head between the two. " You sha'n't
be so rough with him."

Julien got angry.

" Kindly leave me alone," he said; " it's nothing to
do with you;" and he raised his hand to strike the lad
again. The baron caught hold of his son-in-law's wrist,
and flung his uplifted hand heavily down against the
woodwork of the seat, crying:

" If you don't stop that, I'll get out and soon make
you."

He spoke in so determined a tone that the vicomte's
rage suddenly vanished, and, shrugging his shoulders,
he whipped up the horses, and the carriage moved on
again. All this time Jeanne and her mother had sat
still, pale with fright, and the beating of the baroness's
heart could be distinctly heard. At dinner that evening
Julien was more agreeable than usual, and behaved as
if nothing had happened. Jeanne, her father, and Madame Adélaïde easily forgave, and, touched by his good
temper, they joined in his gayety with a feeling of relief.
When Jeanne mentioned the Brisevilles, her husband

even made a joke about them, though he quickly added:
" But one can see directly that they are gentle-
people."

No more visits were paid, as everyone dreaded any
reference to Marius, but they were going to send cards
to their neighbors on New Year's day, and then wait to
call on them until spring came, and the weather was
warmer.

On Christmas day and New Year's day, the curé, the
mayor, and his wife dined at Les Peuples, and their two
visits formed the only break in the monotonous days.
The baron and baroness were to leave the château on
the ninth of January; Jeanne wanted them to stay
longer, but Julien did not second her invitation, so the
baron ordered the post-chaise to be sent from Rouen.
The evening before they went away was clear and
frosty, so Jeanne and her father walked down to Yport,
for they had not been there since Jeanne's return from
Corsica.

They went across the wood where she had walked on
her wedding-day with him whose companion she was
henceforth to be, where she had received his first kiss,
and had caught her first glimpse of that sensual love
which was not fully revealed to her till that day in the
valley of Ota when she had drunk her husband's kisses
with the water.

There were no leaves, no climbing plants, in the copse
now, only the rustling of the branches, and that dry,
crackling noise that seems to fill every wood in winter.

They reached the little village and went along the
empty, silent streets, which smelt of fish and of sea-
weed. The big brown nets were hanging before the
doors, or stretched out on the beach as of old; towards

Fécamp the green rocks at the foot of the cliff could be seen, for the tide was going out, and all along the beach the big boats lay on their sides looking like huge fish.

As night drew on, the fishermen, walking heavily in their big sea-boots, began to come down on the shingle in groups, their necks well wrapped up with woolen scarfs, and carrying a liter of brandy in one hand, and the boat-lantern in the other. They busied themselves round the boats, putting on board, with true Normandy slowness, their nets, their buoys, a big loaf, a jar of butter, and the bottle of brandy and a glass. Then they pushed off the boats, which went down the beach with a harsh noise, then rushed through the surf, balanced themselves on the crest of a wave for a few seconds, and spread their brown wings and disappeared into the night, with their little lights shining at the bottom of the masts. The sailors' wives, their big, bony frames shown off by their thin dresses, stayed until the last fisherman had gone off, and then went back to the hushed village, where their noisy voices roused the sleeping echoes of the gloomy streets.

The baron and Jeanne stood watching these men go off into the darkness, as they went off every night, risking their lives to keep themselves from starving, and yet gaining so little that they could never afford to eat meat.

"What a terrible, beautiful thing is the ocean!" said the baron. "How many lives are at this very moment in danger on it, and yet how exquisite it looks now, with the shadows falling over it! Doesn't it, Jeannette?"

"This is not so pretty as the Mediterranean," she answered with a watery smile.

" The Mediterranean! " exclaimed the baron scornfully. " Why, the Mediterranean's nothing but oil or sugared water, while this sea is terrific with its crests of foam and its wild waves. And think of those men who have just gone off on it, and who are already out of sight."

Jeanne gave in.

" Yes, perhaps you are right," she said with a sigh, for the word " Mediterranean " had sent a pang through her heart, and turned her thoughts to those far-away countries where all her dreams lay buried.

They did not go back through the wood, but walked along the road; they walked in silence, for both were saddened by the thought of the morrow's parting. As they passed the farmhouses, they could smell the crushed apples — that scent of new cider which pervades all Normandy at this time of the year — or the strong odor of cows and the healthy, warm smell of a dunghill. The dwelling houses could be distinguished by their little lighted windows, and these tiny lights, scattered over the country, made Jeanne think of the loneliness of human creatures, and how everything tends to separate and tear them away from those they love, and her heart seemed to grow bigger and more capable of understanding the mysteries of existence.

" Life is not always gay," she said in tones of resignation.

The baron sighed.

" That is true, my child," he replied; " but we cannot help it."

The next day the baron and baroness went away, leaving Jeanne and Julien alone

## VII

THE young couple got into the habit of playing cards; every day after lunch Jeanne played several games of bezique with her husband, while he smoked his pipe and drank six or eight glasses of brandy. When they had finished playing, Jeanne went upstairs to her bedroom, and, sitting by the window, worked at a petticoat flounce she was embroidering, while the wind and rain beat against the panes. When her eyes ached she looked out at the foamy, restless sea, gazed at it for a few minutes, and then took up her work again.

She had nothing else to do, for Julien had taken the entire management of the house into his hands, that he might thoroughly satisfy his longing for authority and his mania for economy. He was exceedingly stingy; he never gave the servants anything beyond their exact wages, never allowed any food that was not strictly necessary. Every morning, ever since she had been at Les Peuples, the baker had made Jeanne a little Normandy cake, but Julien cut off this expense, and Jeanne had to content herself with toast.

Wishing to avoid all arguments and quarrels, she never made any remark, but each fresh proof of her husband's avarice hurt her like the prick of a needle. It seemed so petty, so odious to her, brought up as she had been in a family where money was never thought of any importance. How often she had heard her mother say: " Money is made to be spent "; but now Julien kept saying to her: " Will you never be cured of throwing money away? " Whenever he could manage to reduce a salary or a bill by a few pence he would

V—7

slip the money into his pocket, saying, with a pleased smile:

"Little streams make big rivers."

Jeanne would sometimes find herself dreaming as she used to do before she was married. She would gradually stop working, and with her hands lying idle in her lap and her eyes fixed on space, she built castles in the air as if she were a young girl again. But the voice of Julien, giving an order to old Simon, would call her back to the realities of life, and she would take up her work, thinking, "Ah, that is all over and done with now," and a tear would fall on her fingers as they pushed the needle through the stuff.

Rosalie, who used to be so gay and lively, always singing snatches of songs as she went about her work, gradually changed also. Her plump round cheeks had fallen in and lost their brightened color, and her skin was muddy and dark. Jeanne often asked her if she were ill, but the little maid always answered with a faint blush, "No, madame," and got away as quickly as she could. Instead of tripping along as she had always done, she now dragged herself painfully from room to room, and seemed not even to care how she looked, for the peddlers in vain spread out their ribbons and corsets and bottles of scent before her; she never bought anything from them now.

At the end of January, the heavy clouds came across the sea from the north, and there was a heavy fall of snow. In one night the whole plain was whitened, and, in the morning the trees looked as if a mantle of frozen foam had been cast over them.

Julien put on his high boots, and passed his time in the ditch between the wood and the plain, watching for the migrating birds. Every now and then his shots would break the frozen silence of the fields, and hordes of black crows flew from the trees in terror. Jeanne, tired of staying indoors, would go out on the steps of the house, where, in the stillness of this snow-covered world, she could hear the bustle of the farms, or the far-away murmur of the waves and the soft continual rustle of the falling snow.

On one of these cold, white mornings she was sitting by her bedroom fire, while Rosalie, who looked worse and worse every day, was slowly making the bed. All at once Jeanne heard a sigh of pain behind her. Without turning her head, she asked:

" What is the matter with you, Rosalie? "

The maid answered as she always did:

" Nothing, madame," but her voice seemed to die away as she spoke.

Jeanne had left off thinking about her, when she suddenly noticed that she could not hear the girl moving. She called: " Rosalie."

There was no answer. Then she thought that the maid must have gone quietly out of the room without her hearing her, and she cried in a louder tone: " Rosalie! " Again she received no answer, and she was just stretching out her hand to ring the bell, when she heard a low moan close beside her. She started up in terror.

Rosalie was sitting on the floor with her back against the bed, her legs stretched stiffly out, her face livid, and her eyes staring straight before her. Jeanne rushed to her side.

" Oh, Rosalie! What is the matter? what is it? " she asked in affright.

The maid did not answer a word, but fixed her wild eyes on her mistress and gasped for breath, as if tortured by some excruciating pain. Then, stiffening every muscle in her body, and stifling a cry of anguish between her clenched teeth, she slipped down on her back, and all at once, something stirred underneath her dress, which clung tightly round her legs. Jeanne heard a strange, gushing noise, something like the death-rattle of someone who is suffocating, and then came a long low wail of pain; it was the first cry of suffering of a child entering the world.

The sound came as a revelation to her, and, suddenly losing her head, she rushed to the top of the stairs, crying:

" Julien!   Julien! "

" What do you want? " he answered, from below.

She gasped out, " It's Rosalie who — who —" but before she could say any more Julien was rushing up the stairs two at a time; he dashed into the bedroom, raised the girl's clothes, and there lay a creased, shriveled, hideous, little atom of humanity, feebly whining and trying to move its limbs.   He got up with an evil look on his face, and pushed his distracted wife out of the room, saying:

" This is no place for you.   Go away and send me Ludivine and old Simon."

Jeanne went down to the kitchen trembling all over, to deliver her husband's message, and then afraid to go upstairs again, she went into the drawing-room, where a fire was never lighted, now her parents were away. Soon she saw Simon run out of the house, and come back five minutes after with Widow Dentu, the village midwife.   Next she heard a noise on the stairs which sounded as if they were carrying a body, then Julien came to tell her that she could go back to her room. She went upstairs and sat down again before her bedroom fire, trembling as if she had just witnessed some terrible accident.

" How is she? " she asked.

Julien, apparently in a great rage, was walking about the room in a preoccupied, nervous way. He did not answer his wife for some moments, but at last he asked, stopping in his walk:

" Well, what do you mean to do with this girl? "

Jeanne looked at her husband as if she did not understand his question.

" What do you mean? " she said. " I don't know; how should I? "

" Well, anyhow, we can't keep that child in the house," he cried, angrily.

Jeanne looked very perplexed, and sat in silence for some time. At last she said:

" But, my dear, we could put it out to nurse somewhere? "

He hardly let her finish her sentence.

" And who'll pay for it? Will you? "

" But surely the father will take care of it," she said, after another long silence. " And if he marries Rosalie, everything will be all right."

" The father! " answered Julien, roughly; " the father! Do you know who is the father? Of course you don't. Very well, then! "

Jeanne began to get troubled: " But he certainly will not forsake the girl; it would be such a cowardly thing to do. We will ask her his name, and go and see him and force him to give some account of himself."

Julien had become calmer, and was again walking about the room.

"My dear girl," he replied, "I don't believe she will tell you the man's name, or me either. Besides, suppose he wouldn't marry her? You must see that we can't keep a girl and her illegitimate child in our house."

But Jeanne would only repeat, doggedly:

"Then the man must be a villain; but we will find out who he is, and then he will have us to deal with instead of that poor girl."

Julien got very red.

"But until we know who he is?" he asked.

She did not know what to propose, so she asked Julien what he thought was the best thing to do. He gave his opinion very promptly.

"Oh, I should give her some money, and let her and her brat go to the devil."

That made Jeanne very indignant.

"That shall never be done," she declared; "Rosalie is my foster-sister, and we have grown up together. She has erred, it is true, but I will never turn her out-of-doors for that, and, if there is no other way out of the difficulty, I will bring up the child myself."

"And we should have a nice reputation, shouldn't we, with our name and connections?" burst out Julien. "People would say that we encouraged vice, and sheltered prostitutes, and respectable people would never come near us. Why, what can you be thinking of? You must be mad!"

"I will never have Rosalie turned out," she repeated, quietly. "If you will not keep her here, my mother will take her back again. But we are sure to find out the name of the father."

At that, he went out of the room, too angry to talk to her any longer, and as he banged the door after him he cried:

" Women are fools with their absurd notions! "

In the afternoon Jeanne went up to see the invalid. She was lying in bed, wide awake, and the Widow Dentu was rocking the child in her arms. As soon as she saw her mistress Rosalie began to sob violently, and when Jeanne wanted to kiss her, she turned away and hid her face under the bed-clothes. The nurse interfered and drew down the sheet, and then Rosalie made no further resistance, though the tears still ran down her cheeks.

The room was very cold, for there was only a small fire in the grate, and the child was crying. Jeanne did not dare make any reference to the little one, for fear of causing another burst of tears, but she held Rosalie's hand and kept repeating mechanically:

" It won't matter; it won't matter. "

The poor girl glanced shyly at the nurse from time to time; the child's cries seemed to pierce her heart, and sobs still escaped from her occasionally, though she forced herself to swallow her tears. Jeanne kissed her again, and whispered in her ear: " We'll take good care of it, you may be sure of that," and then ran quickly out of the room, for Rosalie's tears were beginning to flow again.

After that, Jeanne went up every day to see the invalid, and every day Rosalie burst into tears when her mistress came into the room. The child was put out to nurse, and Julien would hardly speak to his wife, for he could not forgive her for refusing to dismiss the maid. One day he returned to the subject, but Jeanne drew out a letter from her mother in which the baroness said that if they would not keep Rosalie at Les Peuples she was to be sent on to Rouen directly.

"Your mother's as great a fool as you are," cried Julien; but he did not say anything more about sending Rosalie away, and a fortnight later the maid was able to get up and perform her duties again.

One morning Jeanne made her sit down, and holding both her hands in hers;

"Now, then, Rosalie, tell me all about it," she said, looking her straight in the face.

Rosalie began to tremble.

"All about what, madame?" she said, timidly.

"Who is the father of your child?" asked Jeanne.

A look of despair came over the maid's face, and she struggled to disengage her hands from her mistress's grasp, but Jeanne kissed her, in spite of her struggles, and tried to console her.

"It is true you have been weak," she said, "but you are not the first to whom such a misfortune has happened, and, if only the father of the child marries you, no one will think anything more about it; we would employ him, and he could live here with you."

Rosalie moaned as if she were being tortured, and tried to get her hands free that she might run away.

"I can quite understand how ashamed you feel," went on Jeanne, "but you see that I am not angry, and that I speak kindly to you. I wish to know this man's name for your own good, for I fear, from your grief, that he means to abandon you, and I want to prevent that. Julien will see him, and we will make him marry you, and we shall employ you both; we will see that he makes you happy."

This time Rosalie made so vigorous an effort that she succeeded in wrenching her hands away from her mistress, and she rushed from the room as if she were mad.

" I have tried to make Rosalie tell me her seducer's name," said Jeanne to her husband at dinner that evening, " but I did not succeed in doing so. Try and see if she will tell you, that we may force the wretch to marry her."

" There, don't let me hear any more about all that," he said, angrily. " You wanted to keep this girl, and you have done so, but don't bother me about her."

He seemed still more irritable since Rosalie's confinement than he had been before. He had got into the habit of shouting at his wife, whenever he spoke to her, as if he were always angry, while she, on the contrary, spoke softly, and did everything to avoid a quarrel; but she often cried when she was alone in her room at night. In spite of his bad temper, Julien had resumed the marital duties he had so neglected since his wedding tour, and it was seldom now that he let three nights pass without accompanying his wife to her room.

Rosalie soon got quite well again, and with better health came better spirits, but she always seemed frightened and haunted by some strange dread. Jeanne tried twice more to make her name her seducer, but each time she ran away, without saying anything. Julien suddenly became better tempered, and his young wife began to cherish vague hopes, and to regain a little of her former gayety; but she often felt very unwell, though she never said anything about it.

For five weeks the crisp, shining snow had lain on the frozen ground; in the daytime there was not a cloud to be seen, and at night the sky was strewn with stars. Standing alone in their square courtyards, behind the great frosted trees, the farms seemed dead beneath their snowy shrouds. Neither men nor cattle could go out, and the only sign of life about the homesteads and cottages was the smoke that went straight up from the chimneys into the frosty air.

The grass, the hedges and the wall of elms seemed killed by the cold. From time to time the trees cracked, as if the fibers of their branches were separating beneath the bark, and sometimes a big branch would break off and fall to the ground, its sap frozen and dried up by the intense cold.

Jeanne thought the severe weather was the cause of her ill-health, and she longed for the warm spring breezes. Sometimes the very idea of food disgusted her, and she could eat nothing; at other times she vomited after every meal, unable to digest the little she did eat. She had violent palpitations of the heart, and she lived in a constant and intolerable state of nervous excitement.

One evening, when the thermometer was sinking still lower, Julien shivered as he left the dinner table (for the dining-room was never sufficiently heated, so careful was he over the wood), and rubbing his hands together:

" It's too cold to sleep alone to-night, isn't it, darling? " he whispered to his wife, with one of his old good-tempered laughs.

Jeanne threw her arms round his neck, but she felt so ill, so nervous, and she had such aching pains that evening, that, with her lips close to his, she begged him to let her sleep alone.

"I feel so ill to-night," she said, "but I am sure to be better to-morrow."

"Just as you please, my dear," he answered. "If you are ill, you must take care of yourself." And he began to talk of something else.

Jeanne went to bed early. Julien, for a wonder, ordered a fire to be lighted in his own room; and when the servant came to tell him that "the fire had burnt up," he kissed his wife on the forehead and said good-night.

The very walls seemed to feel the cold, and made little cracking noises as if they were shivering. Jeanne lay shaking with cold; twice she got up to put more logs on the fire, and to pile her petticoats and dresses on the bed, but nothing seemed to make her any warmer. There were nervous twitchings in her legs, which made her toss and turn restlessly from side to side. Her feet were numbed, her teeth chattered, her hands trembled, her heart beat so slowly that sometimes it seemed to stop altogether; and she gasped for breath as if she could not draw the air into her lungs.

As the cold crept higher and higher up her limbs, she was seized with a terrible fear. She had never felt like this before; life seemed to be gradually slipping away from her, and she thought each breath she drew would be her last.

"I am going to die! I am going to die!" she thought; and, in her terror, she jumped out of bed, and rang for Rosalie.

No one came; she rang again, and again waited for an answer, shuddering and half-frozen; but she waited in vain. Perhaps the maid was sleeping too heavily for the bell to arouse her, and, almost beside herself

with fear, Jeanne rushed out onto the landing without
putting anything around her, and with bare feet. She
went noiselessly up the dark stairs, felt for Rosalie's
door, opened it, and called " Rosalie! " then went into
the room, stumbled against the bed, passed her hands
over it, and found it empty and quite cold, as if no one
had slept in it that night.

" Surely she cannot have gone out in such weather
as this," she thought.

Her heart began to beat so violently that it almost
suffocated her, and she went downstairs to rouse Julien,
her legs giving way under her as she walked. She burst
open her husband's door, and hurried across the room,
spurred on by the idea that she was going to die and
the fear that she would become unconscious before she
could see him again.

Suddenly she stopped with a shriek, for by the light
of the dying fire she saw Rosalie's head on the pillow
beside her husband's. At her cry they both started up,
but she had already recovered from the first shock of her
discovery, and fled to her room, while Julien called after
her, " Jeanne! Jeanne! " She felt she could not see
him or listen to his excuses and his lies, and again rushing out of her room she ran downstairs. The staircase
was in total darkness, but filled with the desire of flight,
of getting away without seeing or hearing any more,
she never stayed to think that she might fall and break
her limbs on the stone stairs.

On the last step she sat down, unable to think, unable to reason, her head in a whirl. Julien had jumped
out of bed, and was hastily dressing himself. She
heard him moving about, and she started up to escape

from him. He came downstairs, crying: "Jeanne, do listen to me!"

No, she would not listen; he should not degrade her by his touch. She dashed into the dining-room as if a murderer were pursuing her, looked round for a hiding-place or some dark corner where she might conceal herself, and then crouched down under the table. The door opened, and Julien came in with a light in his hand, still calling, "Jeanne! Jeanne!" She started off again like a hunted hare, tore into the kitchen, round which she ran twice like some wild animal at bay, then, as he was getting nearer and nearer to her, she suddenly flung open the garden door, and rushed out into the night.

Her bare legs sank into the snow up to her knees, and this icy contact gave her new strength. Although she had nothing on but her chemise she did not feel the bitter cold; her mental anguish was too great for the consciousness of any mere bodily pain to reach her brain, and she ran on and on, looking as white as the snow-covered earth. She did not stop once to take breath, but rushed on across wood and plain without knowing or thinking of what she was doing. Suddenly she found herself at the edge of the cliff. She instinctively stopped short, and then crouched down in the snow and lay there with her mind as powerless to think as her body to move.

All at once she began to tremble, as does a sail when caught by the wind. Her arms, her hands, her feet, shook and twitched convulsively, and consciousness returned to her. Things that had happened a long time before came back to her memory: the sail in Lastique's boat with *him*, their conversation, the dawn of their love; the christening of the boat; then her thoughts went still farther back till they reached the night of her arrival from the convent — the night she had spent in happy dreams. And now, now! Her life was ruined; she had had all her pleasure; there were no joys, no happiness, in store for her; and she could see the terrible future with all its tortures, its deceptions, and despair. Surely it would be better to die now, at once.

She heard a voice in the distance crying:

" This way! this way! Here are her footmarks! "
It was Julien looking for her.

Oh! she could not, she would not, see him again! Never again! From the abyss before her came the faint sound of the waves as they broke on the rocks. She stood up to throw herself over the cliff, and in a despairing farewell to life, she moaned out that last cry of the dying — the word that the soldier gasps out as he lies wounded to death on the battlefield — " Mother! "

Then the thought of how her mother would sob when she heard of her daughter's death, and how her father would kneel in agony beside her mangled corpse, flashed across her mind, and in that one second she realized all the bitterness of their grief. She fell feebly back on the snow, and Julien and old Simon came up, with Marius behind them holding a lantern. They drew her back before they dared attempt to raise her, so near the edge of the cliff was she; and they did with her what they liked, for she could not move a muscle. She knew that they carried her indoors, that she was put to bed,

and rubbed with hot flannels, and then she was conscious
of nothing more.

A nightmare — but was it a nightmare? — haunted
her. She thought she was in bed in her own room; it
was broad daylight, but she could not get up, though
she did not know why she could not. She heard a noise
on the boards — a scratching, rustling noise — and all
at once a little gray mouse ran over the sheet. Then
another one appeared, and another which came running
towards her chest. Jeanne was not frightened; she
wanted to take hold of the little animal, and put out her
hand towards it, but she could not catch it.

Then came more mice — ten, twenty, hundreds,
thousands, sprang up on all sides. They ran up the
bed-posts, and along the tapestry, and covered the whole
bed. They got under the clothes, and Jeanne could
feel them gliding over her skin, tickling her legs, running up and down her body. She could see them coming from the foot of the bed to get inside and creep
close to her breast, but when she struggled and stretched
out her hands to catch one, she always clutched the air.
Then she got angry, and cried out, and wanted to run
away; she fancied someone held her down, and that
strong arms were thrown around her to prevent her
moving, but she could not see anyone. She had no idea
of the time that all this lasted; she only knew that it
seemed a very long while.

At last she became conscious again — conscious that
she was tired and aching, and yet better than she had
been. She felt very, very weak. She looked round,
and did not feel at all surprised to see her mother sitting by her bedside with a stout man whom she did not

know. She had forgotten how old she was, and thought she was a little child again, for her memory was entirely gone.

"See, she is conscious," said the stout man.

The baroness began to cry, and the big man said:

"Come, come, madame le baronne; I assure you there is no longer any danger, but you must not talk to her; just let her sleep."

It seemed to Jeanne that she lay for a long time in a doze, which became a heavy sleep if she tried to think of anything. She had a vague idea that the past contained something dreadful, and she was content to lie still without trying to recall anything to her memory. But one day, when she opened her eyes, she saw Julien standing beside the bed, and the curtain which hid everything from her was suddenly drawn aside, and she remembered what had happened.

She threw back the clothes and sprang out of bed to escape from her husband; but as soon as her feet touched the floor she fell to the ground, for she was too weak to stand. Julien hastened to her assistance, but when he attempted to raise her, she shrieked and rolled from side to side to avoid the contact of his hands. The door opened, and Aunt Lison and the Widow Dentu hurried in, closely followed by the baron and his wife, the latter gasping for breath.

They put Jeanne to bed again, and she closed her eyes and pretended to be asleep that she might think undisturbed. Her mother and aunt busied themselves around her, saying from time to time:

"Do you know us now, Jeanne, dear?"

She pretended not to hear them, and made no answer; and in the evening they went away, leaving her to the care of the nurse. She could not sleep all that night, for she was painfully trying to connect the incidents she could remember, one with the other; but there seemed to be gaps in her memory which she could not bridge over. Little by little, however, all the facts came back to her, and then she tried to decide what she had better do. She must have been very ill, or her mother and Aunt Lison and the baron would not have been sent for; but what had Julien said? Did her parents know everything? And where was Rosalie?

The only thing she could do was to go back to Rouen with her father and mother; they could all live there together as they used to do, and it would be just the same as if she had not been married.

The next day she noticed and listened to all that went on around her, but she did not let anyone see that she understood everything and had recovered her full senses. Towards evening, when no one but the baroness was in her room, Jeanne whispered softly:

" Mother, dear ! "

She was surprised to hear how changed her own voice was, but the baroness took her hands, exclaiming:

" My child! my dear little Jeanne! Do you know me, my pet? "

" Yes, mother. But you mustn't cry; I want to talk to you seriously. Did Julien tell you why I ran out into the snow? "

" Yes, my darling. You have had a very dangerous fever."

" That was not the reason, mamma; I had the fever afterwards. Hasn't he told you why I tried to run away, and what was the cause of the fever? "

" No, dear."

V—8

" It was because I found Rosalie in his bed."

The baroness thought she was still delirious, and tried
to soothe her.

" There, there, my darling; lie down and try to go
to sleep."

But Jeanne would not be quieted.

" I am not talking nonsense now, mamma dear,
though I dare say I have been lately," she said. " I
felt very ill one night, and I got up and went to Julien's
room; there I saw Rosalie lying beside him. My grief
nearly drove me mad, and I ran out into the snow,
meaning to throw myself over the cliff."

" Yes, darling, you have been ill; very ill indeed,"
answered the baroness.

" It wasn't that, mamma. I found Rosalie in Juli-
en's bed, and I will not stay with him any longer. You
shall take me back to Rouen with you."

The doctor had told the baroness to let Jeanne have
her own way in everything, so she answered:

" Very well, my pet."

Jeanne began to lose patience.

" I see you don't believe me," she said pettishly.
" Go and find papa; perhaps he'll manage to understand that I am speaking the truth."

The baroness rose slowly to her feet, dragged herself
out of the room with the aid of two sticks, and came
back in a few minutes with the baron. They sat down
by the bedside, and Jeanne began to speak in her weak
voice. She spoke quite coherently, and she told them
all about Julien's odd ways, his harshness, his avarice,
and, lastly, his infidelity.

The baron could see that her mind was not wandering, but he hardly knew what to say or think. He affectionately took her hand, like he used to do when she was a child and he told her fairy tales to send her to sleep.

"Listen, my dear," he said. "We must not do anything rashly. Don't let us say anything till we have thought it well over. Will you promise me to try and bear with your husband until we have decided what is best to be done?"

"Very well," she answered; "but I will not stay here after I get well."

Then she added, in a whisper: "Where is Rosalie now?"

"You shall not see her any more," replied the baron.

But she persisted: "Where is she? I want to know."

He owned that she was still in the house, but he declared she should go at once.

Directly he left Jeanne's room, his heart full of pity for his child and indignation against her husband, the baron went to find Julien, and said to him sternly:

"Monsieur, I have come to ask for an explanation of your behavior to my daughter. You have not only been false to her, but you have deceived her with your servant, which makes your conduct doubly infamous."

Julien swore he was innocent of such a thing, and called heaven to witness his denial. What proof was there? Jeanne was just recovering from brain fever, and of course her thoughts were still confused. She had rushed out in the snow one night at the beginning of her illness, in a fit of delirium, and how could her statement be believed when, on the very night that she said she had surprised her maid in her husband's bed, she was dashing over the house nearly naked, and quite unconscious of what she was doing!

Julien got very angry, and threatened the baron with an action if he did not withdraw his accusation; and the baron, confused by this indignant denial, began to make excuses and to beg his son-in-law's pardon; but Julien refused to take his outstretched hand.

Jeanne did not seem vexed when she heard what her husband had said.

" He is telling a lie, papa," she said, quietly; " but we will force him to own the truth."

For two days she lay silent, turning over all sorts of things in her mind; on the third morning she asked for Rosalie. The baron refused to let the maid go up and told Jeanne that she had left. But Jeanne insisted on seeing her, and said:

" Send someone to fetch her, then."

When the doctor came she was very excited because they would not let her see the maid, and they told him what was the matter. Jeanne burst into tears and almost shrieked: " I will see her! I will see her! "

The doctor took her hand and said in a low voice:

" Calm yourself, madame. Any violent emotion might have very serious results just now, for you are *enceinte.*"

Jeanne's tears ceased directly; even as the doctor spoke she fancied she could feel a movement within her, and she lay still, paying no attention to what was being said or done around her. She could not sleep that night; it seemed so strange to think that within her was another life, and she felt sorry because it was

Julien's child, and full of fears in case it should resemble its father.

The next morning she sent for the baron.

" Papa, dear," she said, " I have made up my mind to know the whole truth; especially now. You hear, I *will* know it, and you know, you must let me do as I like, because of my condition. Now listen; go and fetch M. le curé; he must be here to make Rosalie tell the truth. Then, as soon as he is here, you must send her up to me, and you and mamma must come too; but, whatever you do, don't let Julien know what is going on."

The priest came about an hour afterwards. He was fatter than ever, and panted quite as much as the baroness. He sat down in an armchair and began joking, while he wiped his forehead with his checked handkerchief from sheer habit.

" Well, Madame la baronne, I don't think we are either of us getting thinner; in my opinion we make a very handsome pair." Then turning to the invalid, he said: " Ah, ah! my young lady, I hear we're soon to have a christening, and that it won't be the christening of a boat either, this time, ha, ha, ha! " Then he went on in a grave voice, " It will be one more defender for the country, or," after a short silence, " another good wife and mother like you, madame," with a bow to the baroness.

The door flew open and there stood Rosalie, crying, struggling, and refusing to move, while the baron tried to push her in. At last he gave her a sudden shake, and threw her into the room with a jerk, and she stood in the middle of the floor, with her face in her hands, sobbing violently. Jeanne started up as white as a sheet, and her heart could be seen beating under her thin nightdress. It was some time before she could speak, but at last she gasped out:

" There — there — is no — need for me to — question you. Your confusion in my presence — is — is quite sufficient — proof — of your guilt."

She stopped for a few moments for want of breath, and then went on again:

" But I wish to know all. You see that M. le curé is here, so you understand you will have to answer as if you were at confession."

Rosalie had not moved from where the baron had pushed her; she made no answer, but her sobs became almost shrieks. The baron, losing all patience with her, seized her hands, drew them roughly from her face and threw her on her knees beside the bed, saying:

" Why don't you say something? Answer your mistress."

She crouched down on the ground in the position in which Mary Magdalene is generally depicted; her cap was on one side, her apron on the floor, and as soon as her hands were free she again buried her face in them.

" Come, come, my girl," said the curé, " we don't want to do you any harm, but we must know exactly what has happened. Now listen to what is asked you and answer truthfully."

Jeanne was leaning over the side of the bed, looking at the girl.

" Is it not true that I found you in Julien's bed? " she asked.

" Yes, madame," moaned out Rosalie through her fingers.

At that the baroness burst into tears also, and the sound of her sobs mingled with the maid's.

"How long had that gone on?" asked Jeanne, her eyes fixed on the maid.

"Ever since he came here," stammered Rosalie.

"Since he came here," repeated Jeanne, hardly understanding what the words meant. "Do you mean since — since the spring?"

"Yes, madame."

"Since he first came to the house?"

"Yes, madame."

"But how did it happen? How did he come to say anything to you about it?" burst out Jeanne, as if she could keep back the questions no longer. "Did he force you, or did you give yourself to him? How could you do such a thing?"

"I don't know," answered Rosalie, taking her hands from her face and speaking as if the words were forced from her by an irresistible desire to talk and to tell all. "The day he dined 'ere for the first time, 'e came up to my room. He 'ad 'idden in the garret and I dursn't cry out for fear of what everyone would say. He got into my bed, and I dunno' how it was or what I did, but he did just as 'e liked with me. I never said nothin' about it because I thought he was nice."

"But your — your child? Is it his?" cried Jeanne.

"Yes, madame," answered Rosalie, between her sobs. Then neither said anything more, and the silence was only broken by the baroness's and Rosalie's sobs.

The tears rose to Jeanne's eyes, and flowed noiselessly down her cheeks. So her maid's child had the same father as her own! All her anger had evaporated and in its place was a dull, gloomy, deep despair.

After a short silence she said in a softer, tearful voice.

" After we returned from — from our wedding tour — when did he begin again? "

" The — the night you came back," answered the maid, who was now almost lying on the floor.

Each word rung Jeanne's heart. He had actually left her for this girl the very night of their return to Les Peuples! That, then, was why he had let her sleep alone. She had heard enough now; she did not want to know anything more, and she cried to the girl:

" Go away! go away! "

As Rosalie, overcome by her emotion, did not move, she called to her father:

" Take her away! Carry her out of the room! "

But the curé, who had said nothing up to now, thought the time had come for a little discourse.

" You have behaved very wickedly," he said to Rosalie, " very wickedly indeed, and the good God will not easily forgive you. Think of the punishment which awaits you if you do not live a better life henceforth. Now you are young is the time to train yourself in good ways. No doubt Madame la baronne will do something for you, and we shall be able to find you a husband —"

He would have gone on like this for a long time had not the baron seized Rosalie by the shoulders, dragged her to the door and thrown her into the passage like a bundle of clothes.

When he came back, looking whiter even than his daughter, the curé began again:

" Well, you know, all the girls round here are the same. It is a very bad state of things, but it can't be helped, and we must make a little allowance for the weakness of human nature. They never marry until they are *enceintes;* never, madame. One might almost call it a local custom," he added, with a smile. Then he went on indignantly: " Even the children are the same. Only last year I found a little boy and girl from my class in the cemetery together. I told their parents, and what do you think they replied: ' Well, M'sieu l'curé, we didn't teach it them; we can't help it.' So you see, monsieur, your maid has only done like the others —"

" The maid!" interrupted the baron, trembling with excitement. " The maid! What do I care about her? It's Julien's conduct which I think so abominable, and I shall certainly take my daughter away with me." He walked up and down the room, getting more and more angry with every step he took. " It is infamous the way he has deceived my daughter, infamous! He's a wretch, a villain, and I will tell him so to his face. I'll horsewhip him within an inch of his life."

The curé was slowly enjoying a pinch of snuff as he sat beside the baroness, and thinking how he could make peace. " Come now, M. le baron, between ourselves he has only done like everyone else. I am quite sure you don't know many husbands who are faithful to their wives, do you now? " And he added in a sly, good-natured way: " I bet you, yourself, have played your little games; you can't say conscientiously that you haven't, I know. Why, of course you have! And who knows but what you have made the acquaintance of some little maid just like Rosalie. I tell you every man is the same. And your escapades didn't make your wife unhappy, or lessen your affection for her; did they? "

The baron stood still in confusion. It was true that he had done the same himself, and not only once or twice, but as often as he had got the chance; his wife's presence in the house had never made any difference, when the servants were pretty. And was he a villain because of that? Then why should he judge Julien's conduct so severely when he had never thought that any fault could be found with his own?

Though her tears were hardly dried, the idea of her husband's pranks brought a slight smile to the baroness's lip, for she was one of those good-natured, tender-hearted, sentimental women to whom love adventures are an essential part of existence.

Jeanne lay back exhausted, thinking, with open unseeing eyes, of all this painful episode. The expression that had wounded her most in Rosalie's confession was: " I never said anything about it because I thought he was nice." She, his wife, had also thought him " nice," and that was the sole reason why she had united herself to him for life, had given up every other hope, every other project to join her destiny to his. She had plunged into marriage, into this pit from which there was no escape, into all this misery, this grief, this despair, simply because, like Rosalie, she had thought him " nice."

The door was flung violently open and Julien came in, looking perfectly wild with rage. He had seen Rosalie moaning on the landing, and guessing that she had been forced to speak, he had come to see what was going on; but at the sight of the priest he was taken thoroughly aback.

" What is it? What is the matter? " he asked, in a

voice which trembled in spite of his efforts to make it sound calm.

The baron, who had been so violent just before, dared say nothing after the curé's argument, in case his son-in-law should quote his own example; the baroness only wept more bitterly than before, and Jeanne raised herself on her hands and looked steadily at this man who was causing her so much sorrow. Her breath came and went quickly, but she managed to answer:

" The matter is that we know all about your shameful conduct ever since — ever since the day you first came here; we know that — that — Rosalie's child is yours — like — like mine, and that they will be — brothers."

Her grief became so poignant at this thought that she hid herself under the bedclothes and sobbed bitterly. Julien stood open-mouthed, not knowing what to say or do. The curé again interposed.

" Come, come, my dear young lady," he said, " you mustn't give way like that. See now, be reasonable."

He rose, went to the bedside, and laid his cool hand on this despairing woman's forehead. His simple touch seemed to soothe her wonderfully; she felt calmer at once, as if the large hand of this country priest, accustomed to gestures of absolution and sympathy, had borne with it some strange, peace-giving power.

" Madame, we must always forgive," said the good-natured priest. " You are borne down by a great grief, but God, in His mercy, has also sent you a great joy, since He has permitted you to have hopes of becoming a mother. This child will console you for all your trouble and it is in its name that I implore, that

I adjure, you to forgive M. Julien. It will be a fresh tie between you, a pledge of your husband's future fidelity. Can you steel your heart against the father of your unborn child?"

Too weak to feel either anger or resentment, and only conscious of a crushed, aching, exhausted sensation, she made no answer. Her nerves were thoroughly unstrung, and she clung to life but by a very slender thread.

The baroness, to whom resentment seemed utterly impossible and whose mind was simply incapable of bearing any prolonged strain, said in a low tone:

" Come, Jeanne! "

The curé drew Julien close to the bed and placed his hand in his wife's, giving it a little tap as if to make the union more complete. Then, dropping his professional pulpit tone, he said, with a satisfied air:

" There! that's done. Believe me, it is better so."

The two hands, united thus for an instant, loosed their clasp directly. Julien, not daring to embrace Jeanne, kissed his mother-in-law, then turned on his heel, took the baron (who, in his heart, was not sorry that everything had finished so quietly) by the arm, and drew him from the room to go and smoke a cigar.

Then the tired invalid went to sleep and the baroness and the priest began to chat in low tones. The abbé talked of what had just occurred and proceeded to explain his ideas on the subject, while the baroness assented to everything he said with a nod.

" Very well, then, it's understood," he said, in conclusion. " You give the girl the farm at Barville and I will undertake to find her a good, honest husband. Oh, you may be sure that with twenty thousand francs we shall not want candidates for her hand. We shall have an *embarras de choix.*"

The baroness was smiling happily now, though two tears still lingered on her cheeks.

"Barville is worth twenty thousand francs, at the very least," she said; "and you understand that it is to be settled on the child though the parents will have it as long as they live."

Then the curé shook hands with the baroness, and rose to go.

"Don't get up, Madame la baronne, don't get up," he exclaimed. "I know the value of a step too well myself."

As he went out he met Aunt Lison coming to see her patient. She did not notice that anything extraordinary had happened. No one had told her anything, and, as usual, she had not the slightest idea of what was going on.

## VIII

ROSALIE had left the house and the time of Jeanne's confinement was drawing near. The sorrow she had gone through had taken away all pleasure from the thought of becoming a mother, and she waited for the child's birth without any impatience or curiosity, her mind entirely filled with her presentiment of coming evils.

Spring was close at hand. The bare trees still trembled in the cold wind, but, in the damp ditches, the yellow primroses were already blossoming among the decaying autumn leaves. The rain-soaked fields, the farm-yards and the commons exhaled a damp odor, as of fermenting liquor, and little green leaves peeped out of the brown earth and glistened in the sun.

A big, strongly-built woman had been engaged in Rosalie's place, and she now supported the baroness in her dreary walks along the avenue, where the track made by her foot was always damp and muddy.

Jeanne, low-spirited and in constant pain, leant on her father's arm when she went out, while on her other side walked Aunt Lison, holding her niece's hand, and thinking nervously, of this mysterious suffering that she would never know. They would all three walk for hours without speaking a word, and, while they were out, Julien went all over the country on horseback, for he had suddenly become very fond of riding.

The baron, his wife, and the vicomte, paid a visit to the Fourvilles (whom Julien seemed to know very well, though no one at the château knew exactly how the acquaintance had begun), and another duty call was paid to the Brisevilles, and those two visits were the only break in their dull, monotonous life.

One afternoon, about four o'clock, two people on horseback trotted up to the château. Julien rushed into his wife's room in great excitement:

" Make haste and go down," he exclaimed. " Here are the Fourvilles. They have come simply to make a neighborly call as they know the condition you are in. Say I am out but that I shall be in soon. I am just going to change my coat."

Jeanne went downstairs and found in the drawing-room a gigantic man with big, red moustaches, and a pale, pretty woman with a sad-looking face, sentimental eyes and hair of a dead gold that looked as if the sun had never caressed it. When the fair-haired woman had introduced the big man as her husband, she said:

"M. de Lamare, whom we have met several times, has told us how unwell you are, so we thought we would not put off coming to see you any longer. You see we have come on horseback, so you must look upon this simply as a neighborly call; besides, I have already had the pleasure of receiving a visit from your mother and the baron."

She spoke easily in a refined, familiar way, and Jeanne fell in love with her at once. "In her I might, indeed, find a friend," she thought.

The Comte de Fourville, unlike his wife, seemed as much out of place in a drawing-room as a bull in a china shop. When he sat down he put his hat on a chair close by him, and then the problem of what he should do with his hands presented itself to him. First he rested them on his knees, then on the arms of his chair, and finally joined them as if in prayer.

Julien came in so changed in appearance that Jeanne stared at him in mute surprise. He had shaved himself and looked as handsome and charming as when he was wooing her. His hair, just now so coarse and dull, had been brushed and sprinkled with perfumed oil till it had recovered its soft shining waves, and his large eyes, which seemed made to express nothing but love, had their old winning look in them. He made himself as amiable and fascinating as he had been before his marriage. He pressed the hairy paw of the comte, who seemed much relieved by his presence, and kissed the hand of the comtesse, whose ivory cheek became just tinged with pink.

When the Fourvilles were going away the comtesse said:

" Will you come for a ride on Thursday, vicomte? " And as Julien bowed and replied, " I shall be very pleased, madame," she turned and took Jeanne's hand, saying to her, affectionately:

" When you are well again we must all three go for long rides together. We could make such delightful excursions if you would."

Then she gracefully caught up the skirt of her riding-habit and sprang into the saddle as lightly as a bird, and her husband, after awkwardly raising his hat, leapt on his huge horse, feeling and looking at his ease as soon as he was mounted.

" What charming people! " cried Julien, as soon as they were out of sight. " We may, indeed, think ourselves lucky to have made their acquaintance."

" The little comtesse is delightful," answered Jeanne, feeling pleased herself though she hardly knew why. " I am sure I shall like her; but the husband seems a bear. How did you get to know them? "

" I met them one day at the Brisevilles," he replied, rubbing his hands together cheerfully. " The husband certainly is a little rough, but he is a true gentleman. He is passionately fond of shooting."

Nothing else happened until the end of July. Then, one Tuesday evening, as they were all sitting under the plane-tree beside a little table, on which stood two liqueur glasses and a decanter of brandy, Jeanne suddenly turned very white and put both her hands to her side with a cry. A sharp pain had shot through her and at once died away. In about ten minutes came another one, hardly so severe but of longer duration than the first. Her father and husband almost carried her indoors, for the short distance between the plane-tree and her room seemed miles to her; she could not stifle her moans, and, overpowered by an intolerable sense of heaviness and weight, she implored them to let her sit down and rest.

The child was not expected until September but, in case of accident, a horse was harnessed and old Simon galloped off after the doctor. He came about midnight and at once recognized the signs of a premature confinement. The actual pain had a little diminished, but Jeanne felt an awful deathly faintness, and she thought she was going to die, for Death is sometimes so close that his icy breath can almost be felt.

The room was full of people. The baroness lay back in an armchair gasping for breath; the baron ran hither and thither, bringing all manner of things and completely losing his head; Julien walked up and down looking very troubled, but really feeling quite calm, and the Widow Dentu, whom nothing could surprise or startle, stood at the foot of the bed with an expression suited to the occasion on her face.

Nurse, mid-wife and watcher of the dead, equally ready to welcome the new-born infant, to receive its first cry, to immerse it in its first bath and to wrap it in its first covering, or to hear the last word, the last death-rattle, the last moan of the dying, to clothe them in their last garment, to sponge their wasted bodies, to draw the sheet about their still faces, the Widow Dentu had become utterly indifferent to any of the chances accompanying a birth or a death.

Every now and then Jeanne gave a low moan. For two hours it seemed as if the child would not be born

V—9

yet, after all; but about daybreak the pains recommenced and soon became almost intolerable.  As the involuntary cries of anguish burst through her clenched teeth, Jeanne thought of Rosalie who had hardly even moaned, and whose bastard child had been born without any of the torture such as she was suffering.  In her wretched, troubled mind she drew comparisons between her maid and herself, and she cursed God Whom, until now, she had believed just.  She thought in angry astonishment of how fate favors the wicked, and of the unpardonable lies of those who hold forth inducements to be upright and good.

Sometimes the agony was so great that she could think of nothing else, her suffering absorbing all her strength, her reason, her consiousness.  In the intervals of relief her eyes were fixed on Julien, and then she was filled with a mental anguish as she thought of the day her maid had fallen at the foot of this very bed with her new-born child — the brother of the infant that was now causing her such terrible pain.  She remembered perfectly every gesture, every look, every word of her husband as he stood beside the maid, and now she could see in his movements the same *ennui*, the same indifference for her suffering as he had felt for Rosalie's; it was the selfish carelessness of a man whom the idea of paternity irritates.

She was seized by an excruciating pain, a spasm so agonizing that she thought, " I am going to die!  I am dying ! "  And her soul was filled with a furious hatred; she felt she must curse this man who was the cause of all her agony, and this child which was killing her.  She strained every muscle in a supreme effort to rid herself of this awful burden, and then it felt as if her whole inside were pouring away from her, and her suffering suddenly became less.

The nurse and the doctor bent over her and took something away; and she heard the choking noise she had heard once before, and then the low cry of pain, the feeble whine of the new-born child filled her ears and seemed to enter her poor, exhausted body till it reached her very soul; and, in an unconsciousness movement she tried to hold out her arms.

With the child was born a new joy, a fresh rapture. In one second she had been delivered from that terrible pain and made happier than she had ever been before, and she revived in mind and body as she realized, for the first time, the pleasure of being a mother.

She wanted to see her child. It had not any hair or nails, for it had come before its time, but when she saw. this human larva move its limbs and open its mouth, and when she touched its wrinkled little face, her heart overflowed with happiness, and she knew that she would never feel weary of life again, for her love for the atom she held in her arms would be so absorbing that it would make her indifferent to every-thing else.

From that time her child was her chief, her only care, and she idolized it more, perhaps, because she had been so deceived in her love and disappointed in her hopes. She insisted on having the cot close to her bed, and, when she could get up, she sat by the window the whole day rocking the cradle with her foot. She was even jealous of the wet-nurse, and when the hungry baby held out its arms and mouth towards the big blue-veined breast, she felt as if she would like to tear her son from this strong, quiet peasant woman's arms, and strike and scratch the bosom to which he clung so eagerly.

She embroidered his fine robes herself, putting into them the most elaborate work; he was always surrounded by a cloud of lace and wore the handsomest caps. The only thing she could talk about was the baby's clothes, and she was always interrupting a conversation to hold up a band, or bib, or some especially pretty ribbon for admiration, for she took no notice of what was being said around her as she turned and twisted some tiny garment about in her hands, and held it up to the light to see better how it looked.

" Don't you think he will look lovely in that? " she was always asking, and her mother and the baron smiled at this all-absorbing affection; but Julien would exclaim, impatiently, " What a nuisance she is with that brat! " for his habits had been upset and his overweening importance diminished by the arrival of this noisy, imperious tyrant, and he was half-jealous of the scrap of humanity who now held the first place in the house. Jeanne could hardly bear to be away from her baby for an instant, and she even sat watching him all night through as he lay sleeping in his cradle. These vigils and this continual anxiety began to tell upon her health. The want of sleep weakened her and she grew thinner and thinner, until, at last, the doctor ordered the child to be separated from her.

It was in vain that she employed tears, commands and entreaties. Each night the baby slept with his nurse, and each night his mother rose from her bed and went, barefooted, to put her ear to the keyhole and listen if he was sleeping quietly. Julien found

her there one night as he was coming in late from din-
ning at the Fourvilles, and after that she was locked into
her room every evening to compel her to stay in bed.

The child was to be named Pierre Simon Paul (they
were going to call him Paul) and at the end of August
he was christened, the baron being godfather, and Aunt
Lison godmother. At the beginning of September
Aunt Lison went away, and her absence was as unnoticed as her presence had been.

One evening, after dinner, the curé called at the
château. There seemed an air of mystery about him,
and, after a few commonplace remarks, he asked the
baron and baroness if he could speak to them in pri-
vate for a few moments. They all three walked
slowly down the avenue talking eagerly as they went,
while Julien, feeling uneasy and irritated at this secrecy,
was left behind with Jeanne. He offered to accompany
the priest when he went away, and they walked off
towards the church where the angelus was ringing. It
was a cool, almost cold, evening, and the others soon
went into the house. They were all beginning to feel
a little drowsy when the drawing-room door was suddenly thrown open and Julien came in looking very
vexed. Without stopping to see whether Jeanne was
there or not, he cried to the baron, as soon as he
entered the room:

"Upon my soul you must be mad to go and give
twenty thousand francs to that girl!"

They were all taken too much by surprise to make
any answer, and he went on, too angry to speak distinctly: "I can't understand how you can be such
fools! But there I suppose you will keep on till we
haven't a sou left!"

The baron, recovering himself, a little, tried to check his son-in-law:

"Be quiet!" he exclaimed. "Don't you see that your wife is in the room?"

"I don't care if she is," answered Julien, stamping his foot. "Besides, she ought to know about it. It is depriving her of her rightful inheritance."

Jeanne had listened to her husband in amazement, utterly at a loss to know what it was all about:

"Whatever is the matter?" she asked.

Then Julien turned to her, expecting her to side with him, as the loss of the money would affect her also. He told her in a few words how her parents were trying to arrange a marriage for Rosalie, and how the maid's child was to have the farm at Barville, which was worth twenty thousand francs at the very least. And he kept on repeating:

"Your parents must be mad, my dear, raving mad! Twenty thousand francs! Twenty thousand francs! They can't be in their right senses! Twenty thousand francs for a bastard!"

Jeanne listened to him quite calmly, astonished herself to find that she felt neither anger nor sorrow at his meanness, but she was perfectly indifferent now to everything which did not concern her child. The baron was choking with anger, and at last he burst out, with a stamp of the foot:

"Really, this is too much! Whose fault is it that this girl has to have a dowry? You seem to forget who is her child's father; but, no doubt, you would abandon her altogether if you had your way!"

Julien gazed at the baron for a few moments in silent surprise. Then he went on more quietly:

" But fifteen hundred francs would have been ample to give her. All the peasant-girls about here have children before they marry, so what does it matter who they have them by? And then, setting aside the injustice you will be doing Jeanne and me, you forget that if you give Rosalie a farm worth twenty thousand francs everybody will see at once that there must be a reason for such a gift. You should think a little of what is due to our name and position."

He spoke in a calm, cool way as if he were sure of his logic and the strength of his argument. The baron, disconcerted by this fresh view of the matter, could find nothing to say in reply, and Julien, feeling his advantage, added:

" But fortunately, nothing is settled. I know the man who is going to marry her and he is an honest fellow with whom everything can yet be satisfactorily arranged. I will see to the matter myself."

With that he went out of the room, wishing to avoid any further discussion, and taking the silence with which his words were received to mean acquiescence.

As soon as the door had closed after his son-in-law, the baron exclaimed:

" Oh, this is more than I can stand! "

Jeanne, catching sight of her father's horrified expression, burst into a clear laugh which rang out as it used to do whenever she had seen something very funny:

" Papa, papa! " she cried. " Did you hear the tone in which he said ' twenty thousand francs! ' "

The baroness, whose smiles lay as near the surface as her tears, quivered with laughter as she saw Jeanne's gayety, and thought of her son-in-law's furious face, and his indignant exclamations and determined attempt to prevent this money, which was not his, being given to the girl he had seduced. Finally the baron caught the contagion and they all three laughed till they ached as in the happy days of old. When they were a little calmer, Jeanne said:

"It is very funny, but really I don't seem to mind in the least what he says or does now. I look upon him quite as a stranger, and I can hardly believe I am his wife. You see I am able to laugh at his — his want of delicacy."

And the parents and child involuntarily kissed each other, with smiles on their lips, though the tears were not very far from their eyes.

Two days after this scene, when Julien had gone out for a ride, a tall, young fellow of about four or five-and-twenty, dressed in a brand-new blue blouse, which hung in stiff folds, climbed stealthily over the fence, as if he had been hiding there all the morning, crept along the Couillards' ditch, and went round to the other side of the château where Jeanne and her father and mother were sitting under the plane-tree. He took off his cap and awkwardly bowed as he came towards them, and, when he was within speaking distance, mumbled:

"Your servant, monsieur le baron, madame and company." Then, as no one said anything to him he introduced himself as "Desiré Lecoq."

This name failing to explain his presence at the château, the baron asked:

"What do you want?"

The peasant was very disconcerted when he found he had to state his business. He hesitated, stammered, cast his eyes from the cap he held in his hands to the château roof and back again, and at last began:

" M'sieu l'curé has said somethin' to me about this business —" then, fearing to say too much and thus injure his own interests, he stopped short.

" What business? " asked the baron. " I don't know what you mean."

" About your maid — what's her name — Rosalie," said the man in a low voice.

Jeanne, guessing what he had come about, got up and went away with her child in her arms.

" Sit down," said the baron, pointing to the chair his daughter had just left.

The peasant took the seat with a " Thank you, kindly," and then waited as if he had nothing whatever to say. After a few moments, during which no one spoke, he thought he had better say something, so he looked up to the blue sky and remarked:

" What fine weather for this time of year to be sure. It'll help on the crops finely." And then he again relapsed into silence.

The baron began to get impatient.

" Then you are going to marry Rosalie? " he said in a dry tone, going straight to the point.

At that all the crafty suspicious nature of the Normandy peasant was on the alert.

" That depends," he answered quickly. " Perhaps I am and perhaps I ain't, that depends."

All this beating about the bush irritated the baron.

" Can't you give a straightforward answer? " he exclaimed. " Have you come to say you will marry the girl or not? "

The man looked at his feet as though he expected to find advice there:

"If it's as M'sieu l'curé says," he replied, "I'll have her; but if it's as M'sieu Julien says, I won't."

"What did M. Julien tell you?"

"M'sieu Julien told me as how I should have fifteen hundred francs; but M'sieu l'curé told me as how I should 'ave twenty thousand. I'll have her for twenty thousand, but I won't for fifteen hundred."

The baroness was tickled by the perplexed look on the yokel's face and began to shake with laughter as she sat in her armchair. Her gayety surprised the peasant, who looked at her suspiciously out of the corner of his eye as he waited for an answer.

The baron cut short all this haggling.

"I have told M. le curé that you shall have the farm at Barville, which is worth twenty thousand francs, for life, and then it is to become the child's. That is all I have to say on the matter, and I always keep my word. Now is your answer yes or no?"

A satisfied smile broke over the man's face, and, with a sudden loquacity:

"Oh, then, I don't say no," he replied. "That was the only thing that pulled me up. When M'sieu l'curé said somethin' to me about it in the first place, I said yes at once, 'specially as it was to oblige M'sieu l'baron who'd be sure to pay me back for it, as I says to myself. Ain't it always the way, and doesn't one good turn always deserve another? But M'sieu Julien comes up and then it was only fifteen 'undred francs. Then I says to myself, ' I must find out the rights o' this and so I came 'ere. In coorse I b'lieved your word, M'sieu l'baron, but I wanted to find out the rights o' the case. Short reck'nings make long friends, don't they, M'sieu l'baron?"

He would have gone on like this till dinner-time if
no one had interrupted him, so the baron broke in
with:

" When will you marry her? "

The question aroused the peasant's suspicions again
directly.

" Couldn't I have it put down in writin' first? " he
asked in a halting way.

" Why bless my soul, isn't the marriage-contract
good enough for you? " exclaimed the baron, angered
by the man's suspicious nature.

" But until I get that I should like it wrote down
on paper," persisted the peasant. " Havin' it down
on paper never does no harm."

" Give a plain answer, now at once," said the baron,
rising to put an end to the interview. " If you don't
choose to marry the girl, say so. I know someone else
who would be glad of the chance."

The idea of twenty thousand francs slipping from
his hands into someone else's, startled the peasant out
of his cautiousness, and he at once decided to say
" yes ":

" Agreed, M'sieu l'baron! " he said, holding out his
hand as if he were concluding the purchase of a cow.
" It's done, and there's no going back from the bar-
gain."

The baron took his hand and cried to the cook:

" Ludivine! Bring a bottle of wine."

The wine was drunk and then the peasant went
away, feeling a great deal lighter-hearted than when he
had come.

Nothing was said about this visit to Julien. The
drawing up of the marriage-contract was kept a great

secret; then the banns were published and Rosalie was married on the Monday morning. At the church a neighbor stood behind the bride and bridegroom with a child in her arms as an omen of good luck, and everyone thought Desiré Lecoq very fortunate. " He was born with a caul," said the peasants with a smile.

When Julien heard of the marriage he had a violent quarrel with the baron and baroness and they decided to shorten their visit at Les Peuples. Jeanne was sorry but she did not grieve as before when her parents went away, for now all her hopes and thoughts were centered on her son.

## IX

Now Jeanne was quite well again she thought she would like to return the Fourville's visit, and also to call on the Couteliers. Julien had just bought another carriage at a sale, a phaeton. It only needed one horse, so they could go out twice a month, now, instead of once, and they used it for the first time one bright December morning.

After driving for two hours across the Normandy plains they began to go down to a little valley, whose sloping sides were covered with trees, while the level ground at the bottom was cultivated. The ploughed fields were followed by meadows, the meadows by a fen covered with tall reeds, which waved in the wind like yellow ribbons, and then the road took a sharp turn and the Château de la Vrillette came in sight. It was built between a wooded slope on the one side and a large lake on the other, the water stretching from the

château wall to the tall fir-trees which covered the opposite acclivity.

The carriage had to pass over an old draw-bridge
and under a vast Louis XIII. archway before it drew up
in front of a handsome building of the same period as
the archway, with brick frames round the windows and
slated turrets. Julien pointed out all the different
beauties of the mansion to Jeanne as if he were
thoroughly acquainted with every nook and corner of it.

" Isn't it a superb place? " he exclaimed. " Just
look at that archway! On the other side of the house,
which looks on to the lake, there is a magnificent flight
of steps leading right down to the water. Four boats
are moored at the bottom of the steps, two for the
comte and two for the comtesse. The lake ends down
there, on the right, where you can see that row of
poplars, and there the river, which runs to Fécamp,
rises. The place abounds in wild-fowl, and the comte
passes all his time shooting. Ah! it is indeed a lordly
residence."

The hall door opened and the fair-haired comtesse
came to meet her visitors with a smile on her face.
She wore a trailing dress like a châtelaine of the middle
ages, and, exactly suited to the place in which she lived,
she looked like some beautiful Lady of the Lake.

Four out of the eight drawing-room windows looked
on to the lake, and the water looked dull and dismal,
overshadowed as it was by the gloomy fir-trees which
covered the opposite slope.

The comtesse took both Jeanne's hands in hers as if
she had known her for ages, placed her in a seat and
then drew a low chair beside her for herself, while

Julien, who had regained all his old refinement during the last five months, smiled and chatted in an easy, familiar way. The comtesse and he talked about the rides they had had together. She laughed a little at his bad horsemanship, and called him " The Tottering Knight," and he too laughed, calling her in return " The Amazon Queen."

A gun went off just under the window, and Jeanne gave a little cry. It was the comte shooting teal, and his wife called him in. There was the splash of oars, the grating of a boat against the stone steps and then the comte came in, followed by two dogs of a reddish hue, which lay down on the carpet before the door, while the water dripped from their shaggy coats.

The comte seemed more at his ease in his own house, and was delighted to see the vicomte and Jeanne. He ordered the fire to be made up, and Madeira and biscuits to be brought.

" Of course you will dine with us," he exclaimed.

Jeanne refused the invitation, thinking of Paul; and as he pressed her to stay and she still persisted in her refusal, Julien made a movement of impatience. Then afraid of arousing her husband's quarrelsome temper, she consented to stay, though the idea of not seeing Paul till the next day was torture to her.

They spent a delightful afternoon. First of all the visitors were taken to see the springs which flowed from the foot of a moss-covered rock into a crystal basin of water which bubbled as if it were boiling, and then they went in a boat among the dry reeds, where paths of water had been formed by cutting down the rushes.

The comte rowed (his two dogs sitting each side of

him with their noses in the air) and each vigorous stroke
of the oars lifted the boat half out of the water and sent
it rapidly on its way.   Jeanne let her hand trail in the
water, enjoying the icy coolness, which seemed to soothe
her, and Julien and the comtesse, well wrapped up in
rugs, sat in smiling silence in the stern of the boat, as
if they were too happy to talk.

The evening drew on, and with it the icy, northerly
wind came over the withered reeds.   The sun had disappeared behind the firs, and it made one cold only to
look at the crimson sky, covered with tiny, red fantasti-
cally-shaped clouds.

They all went in to the big drawing-room where an
enormous fire was blazing.   The room seemed to be
filled with an atmosphere of warmth and comfort, and
the comte gayly took up his wife in his strong arms like
a child, and gave her two hearty kisses on her cheeks.

Jeanne could not help smiling at this good-natured
giant to whom his moustaches gave the appearance of
an ogre.   " What wrong impressions of people one
forms every day," she thought; and, almost involuntarily, she glanced at Julien.   He was standing in the
doorway his eyes fixed on the comte and his face very
pale.   His expression frightened her and, going up to
him, she asked:

" What is the matter? are you ill? "

" There's nothing the matter with me," he answered,
churlishly.   " Leave me alone.   I only feel cold."

Dinner was announced and the comte begged permission for his dogs to come into the dining-room.   They
came and sat one on each side of their master, who every
minute threw them some scrap of food.   The animals

stretched out their heads, and wagged their tails, quivering with pleasure as he drew their long silky ears through his fingers.

After dinner, when Jeanne and Julien began to say good-bye, the comte insisted on their staying to see some fishing by torchlight. They and the comtesse stood on the steps leading down to the lake, while the comte got into his boat with a servant carrying a lighted torch and a net. The torch cast strange trembling reflections over the water, its dancing glimmers even lighting up the firs beyond the reeds; and suddenly, as the boat turned round, an enormous fantastic shadow was thrown on the background of the illumined wood. It was the shadow of a man, but the head rose above the trees and was lost against the dark sky, while the feet seemed to be down in the lake. This huge creature raised its arms as if it would grasp the stars; the movement was a rapid one, and the spectators on the steps heard a little splash.

The boat tacked a little, and the gigantic shadow seemed to run along the wood, which was lighted up as the torch moved with the boat; then it was lost in the darkness, then reappeared on the château wall, smaller, but more distinct; and the loud voice of the comte was heard exclaiming:

"Gilberte, I have caught eight!"

The oars splashed, and the enormous shadow remained standing in the same place on the wall, but gradually it became thinner and shorter; the head seemed to sink lower and the body to get narrower, and when M. de Fourville came up the steps, followed by the servant carrying the torch, it was reduced to his exact proportions, and faithfully copied all his movements. In the net he had eight big fish which were still quivering.

As Jeanne and Julien were driving home, well wrapped up in cloaks and rugs which the Fourvilles had lent them,

"What a good-hearted man that giant is," said Jeanne, almost to herself.

"Yes," answered Julien; "but he makes too much show of his affection, sometimes, before people."

A week after their visit to the Fourvilles, they called on the Couteliers, who were supposed to be the highest family in the province, and whose estate lay near Cany. The new château, built in the reign of Louis XIV, lay in a magnificent park, entirely surrounded by walls, and the ruins of the old château could be seen from the higher parts of the grounds.

A liveried servant showed the visitors into a large, handsome room. In the middle of the floor an enormous Sèvres vase stood on a pedestal, into which a crystal case had been let containing the king's autograph letter, offering this gift to the Marquis Léopold Hervé Joseph Germer de Varneville, de Rollebosc de Coutelier. Jeanne and Julien were looking at this royal present when the marquis and marquise came in, the latter wearing her hair powdered.

The marquise thought her rank constrained her to be amiable, and her desire to appear condescending made her affected. Her husband was a big man, with white hair brushed straight up all over his head, and a haughtiness in his voice, in all his movements, in his every attitude which plainly showed the esteem in which he held himself. They were people who had a strict etiquette for everything, and whose feelings seemed always stilted, like their words.

They both talked on without waiting for an answer, smiled with an air of indifference, and behaved as if they were accomplishing a duty imposed upon them by their superior birth, in receiving the smaller nobles of the province with such politeness. Jeanne and Julien tried to make themselves agreeable, though they felt ill at ease, and when the time came to conclude their visit they hardly knew how to retire, though they did not want to stay any longer. However, the marquise, herself, ended the visit naturally and simply by stopping short the conversation, like a queen ending an audience.

" I don't think we will call on anyone eise, unless you want to," said Julien, as they were going back. " The Fourvilles are quite as many friends as I want."

And Jeanne agreed with him.

Dark, dreary December passed slowly away. Everyone stayed at home like the winter before, but Jeanne's thoughts were too full of Paul for her ever to feel dull. She would hold him in her arms covering him with those passionate kisses which mothers lavish on their children, then offering the baby's face to his father:

" Why don't you kiss him? " she would say. " You hardly seem to love him."

Julien would just touch the infant's smooth forehead with his lips, holding his body as far away as possible, as if he were afraid of the little hands touching him in their aimless movements. Then he would go quickly out of the room, almost as though the child disgusted him.

The mayor, the doctor, and the curé came to dinner

occasionally, and sometimes the Fourvilles, who had become very intimate with Jeanne and her husband. The comte seemed to worship Paul. He nursed the child on his knees from the time he entered Les Peuples to the time he left, sometimes holding him the whole afternoon, and it was marvelous to see how delicately and tenderly he touched him with his huge hands. He would tickle the child's nose with the ends of his long moustaches, and then suddenly cover his face with kisses almost as passionate as Jeanne's. It was the great trouble of his life that he had no children.

March was bright, dry, and almost mild. The Comtesse Gilberte again proposed that they should all four go for some rides together, and Jeanne, a little tired of the long weary evenings and the dull, monotonous days, was only too pleased at the idea and agreed to it at once. It took her a week to make her riding-habit, and then they commenced their rides.

They always rode two and two, the comtesse and Julien leading the way, and the comte and Jeanne about a hundred feet behind. The latter couple talked easily and quietly as they rode along, for, each attracted by the other's straightforward ways and kindly heart, they had become fast friends. Julien and the comtesse talked in whispers alternated by noisy bursts of laughter, and looked in each other's eyes to read there the things their lips did not utter, and often they would break into a gallop, as if impelled by a desire to escape alone to some country far away.

Sometimes it seemed as if something irritated Gilberte. Her sharp tones would be borne on the breeze to the ears of the couple loitering behind, and the comte would say to Jeanne, with a smile:

" I don't think my wife got out of bed the right side
this morning."

One evening, as they were returning home, the comtesse began to spur her mare, and then pull her in with
sudden jerks on the rein.

" Take care, or she'll run away with you," said Julien
two or three times.

" So much the worse for me; it's nothing to do with
you," she replied, in such cold, hard tones that the clear
words rang out over the fields as if they were actually
floating in the air.

The mare reared, kicked, and foamed at the mouth,
and the comte cried out anxiously:

" Do take care what you are doing, Gilberte! "

Then, in a fit of defiance, for she was in one of those
obstinate moods that will brook no word of advice, she
brought her whip heavily down between the animal's
ears. The mare reared, beat the air with her fore legs
for a moment, then, with a tremendous bound, set off
over the plain at the top of her speed. First she crossed
a meadow, then some ploughed fields, kicking up the
wet heavy soil behind her, and going at such a speed
that in a few moments the others could hardly distinguish the comtesse from her horse.

Julien stood stock still, crying: " Madame! Madame! " The comte gave a groan, and, bending down
over his powerful steed, galloped after his wife. He
encouraged his steed with voice and hand, urged it on
with whip and spur, and it seemed as though he carried
the big animal between his legs, and raised it from the
ground at every leap it took. The horse went at an
inconceivable speed, keeping a straight line regardless
of all obstacles; and Jeanne could see the two outlines

of the husband and wife diminish and fade in the distance, till they vanished altogether, like two birds chasing each other till they are lost to sight beyond the
horizon.

Julien walked his horse up to his wife, murmuring
angrily: " She is mad to-day." And they both went
off after their friends, who were hidden in a dip in the
plain. In about a quarter of an hour they saw them
coming back, and soon they came up to them.

The comte, looking red, hot and triumphant, was
leading his wife's horse. The comtesse was very pale;
her features looked drawn and contracted, and she leant
on her husband's shoulder as if she were going to faint.
That day Jeanne understood, for the first time, how
madly the comte loved his wife.

All through the following month the comtesse was
merrier than she had ever been before. She came to
Les Peuples as often as she could, and was always laughing and jumping up to kiss Jeanne. She seemed to have
found some unknown source of happiness, and her husband simply worshiped her now, following her about
with his eyes and seeking every pretext for touching her
hand or her dress.

" We are happier now than we have ever been before," he said, one evening, to Jeanne. " Gilberte has
never been so affectionate as she is now; nothing seems
to vex her or make her angry. Until lately I was never
quite sure that she loved me, but now I know she does."

Julien had changed for the better also; he had become gay and good-tempered, and their friendship
seemed to have brought peace and happiness to both
families.

The spring was exceptionally warm and forward.

The sun cast his warm rays upon the budding trees and
flowers from early morn until the sweet, soft evening.
It was one of those favored years when the world seems
to have grown young again, and nature to delight in
bringing everything to life once more.

Jeanne felt a vague excitement in the presence of this
reawakening of the fields and woods.  She gave way to
a sweet melancholy and spent hours languidly dreaming.  All the tender incidents of her first hours of love
came back to her, not that any renewal of affection for
her husband stirred her heart; *that* had been completely
destroyed; but the soft breeze which fanned her cheek
and the sweet perfume which filled the air seemed to
breathe forth a tender sigh of love which made her
pulse beat quicker.  She liked to be alone, and in the
warm sunshine, to enjoy these vague, peaceful sensations
which aroused no thoughts.

One morning she was lying thus half-dormant, when
suddenly she saw in her mind that sunlit space in the
little wood near Etretat where for the first time she had
felt thrilled by the presence of the man who loved her
then, where he had for the first time timidly hinted
at his hopes, and where she had believed that she was
going to realize the radiant future of her dreams.  She
thought she should like to make a romantic, superstitious pilgrimage to the wood, and she felt as if a visit
to that sunny spot would in some way alter the course
of her life.

Julien had gone out at daybreak, she did not know
whither, so she ordered the Martins' little white horse,
which she sometimes rode, to be saddled, and set off.

It was one of those calm days when there is not a leaf
nor a blade of grass stirring.  The wind seemed dead,

and everything looked as though it would remain motionless until the end of time; even the insects had disappeared. A burning, steady heat descended from the
sun in a golden mist, and Jeanne walked her horse along,
enjoying the stillness, and every now and then looking
up at a tiny white cloud which hung like a snowy fleece
in the midst of the bright blue sky. She went down
into the valley leading to the sea, between the two great
arches which are called the gates of Etretat, and went
slowly towards the wood.

The sunlight poured down through the foliage which,
as yet, was not very thick, and Jeanne wandered along
the little paths unable to find the spot where she had sat
with Julien. She turned into a long alley and, at the
other end of it, saw two saddle-horses fastened to a tree;
she recognized them at once; they were Gilberte's and
Julien's. Tired of being alone and pleased at this unexpected meeting, she trotted quickly up to them, and
when she reached the two animals, which were waiting
quietly as if accustomed to stand like this, she called
aloud. There was no answer.

On the grass, which looked as if someone had rested
there, lay a woman's glove and two whips. Julien and
Gilberte had evidently sat down and then gone farther
on, leaving the horses tied to the tree. Jeanne wondered what they could be doing, and getting off her
horse, she leant against the trunk of a tree and waited
for a quarter of an hour or twenty minutes. She stood
quite motionless, and two little birds flew down onto the
grass close by her. One of them hopped round the
other, fluttering his outstretched wings, and chirping and
nodding his little head; all at once they coupled.
Jeanne watched them, as surprised as if she had never

known of such a thing before; then she thought: "Oh, of course! It is springtime."

Then came another thought — a suspicion. She looked again at the glove, the whips and the two horses standing riderless; then she sprang on her horse with an intense longing to leave this place. She started back to Les Peuples at a gallop. Her brain was busy reasoning, connecting different incidents and thinking it all out.

How was it that she had never noticed anything, had never guessed this before? How was it that Julien's frequent absence from home, his renewed attention to his toilet, his better temper had told her nothing? Now she understood Gilberte's nervous irritability, her exaggerated affection for herself and the bliss in which she had appeared to be living lately, and which had so pleased the comte.

She pulled up her horse for she wanted to think calmly, and the quick movement confused her ideas. After the first shock she became almost indifferent; she felt neither jealousy nor hatred, only contempt. She did not think about Julien at all, for nothing that he could do would have astonished her, but the twofold treachery of the comtesse, who had deceived her friend as well as her husband, hurt her deeply. So everyone was treacherous, and untrue and faithless! Her eyes filled with tears, for sometimes it is as bitter to see an illusion destroyed as to witness the death of a friend. She resolved to say nothing more about her discovery. Her heart would be dead to everyone but Paul and her parents, but she would bear a smiling face.

When she reached home she caught up her son in her arms, carried him to her room and pressed her lips to his face again and again, and for a whole hour she played with and caressed him.

Julien came in to dinner in a very good temper and full of plans for his wife's pleasure.

" Won't your father and mother come and stay with us this year? " he said.

Jeanne almost forgave him his infidelity, so grateful was she to him for making this proposal. She longed to see the two people she loved best after Paul, and she passed the whole evening in writing to them, and urging them to come as soon as possible.

They wrote to say they would come on the twentieth of May; it was then the seventh, and Jeanne awaited their arrival with intense impatience. Besides her natural desire to see her parents, she felt it would be such a relief to have near her two honest hearts, two simple-minded beings whose life and every action, thought and desire had always been upright and pure. She felt she stood alone in her honesty among all this guilt. She had learnt to dissimulate her feelings, to meet the comtesse with an outstretched hand and a smiling face, but her sense of desolation increased with her contempt for her fellow-men.

Every day some village scandal reached her ears which filled her with still greater disgust and scorn for human frailty. The Couillards' daughter had just had a child and was therefore going to be married. The Martins' servant, who was an orphan, a little girl only fifteen years old, who lived near, and a widow, a lame, poverty-stricken woman who was so horribly dirty that she had been nicknamed La Crotte, were all pregnant; and Jeanne was continually hearing of the misconduct of some girl, some married woman with a family, or of some rich farmer who had been held in general respect.

This warm spring seemed to revive the passions of mankind as it revived the plants and the flowers; but to Jeanne, whose senses were dead, and whose wounded heart and romantic soul were alone stirred by the warm springtide breezes, and who only dreamed of the poetic side of love, these bestial desires were revolting and hateful. She was angry with Gilberte, not for having robbed her of her husband, but for having bespattered herself with this filth. The comtesse was not of the same class as the peasants, who could not resist their brutal desires; then how could she have fallen into the same abomination?

The very day that her parents were to arrive, Julien increased his wife's disgust by telling her laughingly, as though it were something quite natural and very funny, that the baker having heard a noise in his oven the day before, which was not baking day, had gone to see what it was, and instead of finding the stray cat he expected to see, had surprised his wife, " who was certainly not putting bread into the oven." " The baker closed the mouth of the oven," went on Julien, " and they would have been suffocated if the baker's little boy, who had seen his mother go into the oven with the blacksmith, had not told the neighbors what was going on." He laughed as he added, " That will give a nice flavor to the bread. It is just like a tale of La Fontaine's."

For some time after that Jeanne could not touch bread.

When the post-chaise drew up before the door with the baron's smiling face looking out of the window,

Jeanne felt fonder of her parents and more pleased to
see them than she had ever been before; but when she
saw her mother she was overcome with surprise and
grief. The baroness looked ten years older than when
she had left Les Peuples six months before. Her huge,
flabby cheeks were suffused with blood, her eyes had a
glazed look, and she could not move a step unless she
was supported on either side; she drew her breath with
so much difficulty that only to hear her made everyone
around her draw theirs painfully also.

The baron, who had lived with her and seen her every
day, had not noticed the gradual change in his wife, and
if she had complained or said her breathing and the
heavy feeling about her heart were getting worse, he
had answered:

" Oh, no, my dear. You have always been like this."

Jeanne went to her own room and cried bitterly when
she had taken her parents upstairs. Then she went to
her father and, throwing herself in his arms, said, with
her eyes still full of tears:

" Oh, how changed mother is! What is the matter
with her? Do tell me what is the matter with her? "

" Do you think she is changed? " asked the baron in
surprise. " It must be your fancy. You know I have
been with her all this time, and to me she seems just the
same as she has always been; she is not any worse."

" Your mother is in a bad way," said Julien to his
wife that evening. " I don't think she's good for much
now."

Jeanne burst into tears.

" Oh, good gracious! " went on Julien irritably. " I
don't say that she is dangerously ill. You always see so

much more than is meant. She is changed, that's all; it's only natural she should begin to break up at her age."

In a week Jeanne had got accustomed to her mother's altered appearance and thought no more about it, thrusting her fears from her, as people always do put aside their fears and cares, with an instinctive and natural, though selfish dislike of anything unpleasant.

The baroness, unable to walk, only went out for about half an hour every day. When she had gone once up and down " her " avenue, she could not move another step and asked to sit down on " her " seat. Some days she could not walk even to the end of the avenue, and would say:

" Let us stop; my hypertrophy is too much for me to-day."

She never laughed as she used to; things which, the year before, would have sent her into fits of laughter, only brought a faint smile to her lips now. Her eyesight was still excellent, and she passed her time in reading *Corinne* and Lamartine's *Meditations* over again, and in going through her " Souvenir-drawer." She would empty on her knees the old letters, which were so dear to her heart, place the drawer on a chair beside her, look slowly over each " relic," and then put it back in its place. When she was quite alone she kissed some of the letters as she might have kissed the hair of some loved one who was dead.

Jeanne, coming into the room suddenly, sometimes found her in tears.

" What is the matter, mamma, dear? " she would ask.

" My souvenirs have upset me," the baroness would

answer, with a long-drawn sigh. " They bring to my mind so vividly the happy times which are all over now, and make me think of people whom I had almost forgotten. I seem to see them, to hear their voices, and it makes me sad. You will feel the same, later on."

If the baron came in and found them talking like this, he would say:

" Jeanne, my dear, if you take my advice, you will burn all your letters — those from your mother, mine, everyone's. There is nothing more painful than to stir up the memories of one's youth when one is old."

But Jeanne, who had inherited her mother's sentimental instincts, though she differed from her in nearly everything else, carefully kept all her old letters to form a " souvenir-box " for her old age, also.

A few days after his arrival, business called the baron away again. The baroness soon began to get better, and Jeanne, forgetting Julien's infidelity and Gilberte's treachery, was almost perfectly happy. The weather was splendid. Mild, starlit nights followed the soft evenings, and dazzling sunrises commenced the glorious days. The fields were covered with bright, sweet-smelling flowers, and the vast calm sea glittered in the sun from morning till night.

One afternoon Jeanne went into the fields with Paul in her arms. She felt an exquisite gladness as she looked now at her son, now at the flowery hedgerows, and every minute she pressed her baby closely to her and kissed him. The earth exhaled a faint perfume, and, as she walked along, she felt as though her happiness were too great for her. Then she thought of her child's future. What would he be? Sometimes she hoped he would become a great and famous man.

Sometimes she felt she would rather he remained with her, passing his life in tender devotion to his mother and unknown to the world. When she listened to the promptings of her mother's heart, she wished him to remain simply her adored son; but when she listened to her reason and her pride she hoped he would make a name and become something of importance in the world.

She sat down at the edge of a ditch and studied the child's face as if she had never really looked at it before. It seemed so strange to think that this little baby would grow up, and walk with manly strides, that these soft cheeks would become bearded, and the feeble murmur change to a deep-toned voice.

Someone called her, and, looking up, she saw Marius running towards her. Thinking he had come to announce some visitor, she got up, feeling vexed at being disturbed. The boy was running as fast as his legs could carry him.

"Madame!" he cried, when he was near enough to be heard. "Madame la baronne is very ill."

Jeanne ran quickly towards the house, feeling as if a douche of cold water had been poured down her spine. There was quite a little crowd standing under the plane tree, which opened to let her through as she rushed forward. There, in the midst, lay the baroness on the ground, her head supported by two pillows, her face black, her eyes closed, and her chest, which for the last twenty years had heaved so tumultuously, motionless. The child's nurse was standing there; she took him from his mother's arms, and carried him away.

"How did it happen? What made her fall?" asked Jeanne, looking up with haggard eyes. "Send for the doctor immediately."

As she turned she saw the curé; he at once offered his
services, and, turning up his sleeves, began to rub the
baroness with Eau de Cologne and vinegar; but she
showed no signs of returning consciousness.

"She ought to be undressed and put to bed," said
the priest; and, with his aid, Joseph Couillard, old
Simon and Ludivine tried to raise the baroness.

As they lifted her, her head fell backwards, and her
dress, which they were grasping, gave way under the
dead weight of her huge body. They were obliged to
lay her down again, and Jeanne shrieked with horror.

At last an armchair was brought from the drawing-
room; the baroness was placed in it, carried slowly indoors, then upstairs, and laid on the bed. The cook
was undressing her as best she could when the Widow
Dentu came in, as if, like the priest, she had "smelt
death," as the servants said. Joseph Couillard hurried
off for the doctor, and the priest was going to fetch the
holy oil, when the nurse whispered in his ear:

"You needn't trouble to go, Monsieur le curé. I
have seen too much of death not to know that she is
gone."

Jeanne, in desperation, begged them to tell her what
she could do, what remedies they had better apply.
The curé thought that anyhow he might pronounce an
absolution, and for two hours they watched beside the
lifeless, livid body, Jeanne, unable to contain her grief,
sobbing aloud as she knelt beside the bed. When the
door opened to admit the doctor, she thought that with
him came safety and consolation and hope, and she
rushed to meet him, trying to tell him, in a voice broken
with sobs, all the details of the catastrophe.

"She was walking — like she does every day — and

she seemed quite well, better even — than usual.  She had eaten some soup and two eggs for lunch, and — quite suddenly, without any warning she fell — and turned black, like she is now; she has not moved since, and we have — tried everything to restore her to consciousness — everything —"

She stopped abruptly for she saw the nurse making a sign to the doctor to intimate that it was all over. Then she refused to understand the gesture, and went on anxiously:

" Is it anything serious?   Do you think there is any danger? "

He answered at last:

" I very much fear that — that life is extinct.   Be brave and try to bear up."

For an answer Jeanne opened her arms, and threw herself on her mother's body.  Julien came in.  He made no sign of grief or pity, but stood looking simply vexed; he had been taken too much by surprise to at once assume an expression of sorrow.

" I expected it," he whispered.   " I knew she could not live long."

He drew out his handkerchief, wiped his eyes, knelt down and crossed himself as he mumbled something, then rose and attempted to raise his wife.  She was clinging to the corpse, almost lying on it as she passionately kissed it; they had to drag her away for she was nearly mad with grief, and she was not allowed to go back for an hour.

Then every shadow of hope had vanished, and the room had been arranged fittingly for its dead occupant. The day was drawing to a close, and Julien and the priest were standing near one of the windows, talking in whispers. The Widow Dentu, thoroughly accustomed to death, was already comfortably dozing in an armchair. The curé went to meet Jeanne as she came into the room, and taking both her hands in his, he exhorted her to be brave under this sorrow, and attempted to comfort her with the consolation of religion. Then he spoke of her dead mother's good life, and offered to pass the night in prayers beside the body.

But Jeanne refused this offer as well as she could for her tears. She wanted to be alone, quite alone, with her mother this last night.

"That cannot be," interposed Julien; "we will watch beside her together."

She shook her head, unable to speak for some moments; then she said:

"She was my mother, and I want to watch beside her alone."

"Let her do as she wants," whispered the doctor; "the nurse can stay in the next room," and Julien and the priest, thinking of their night's rest, gave in.

The Abbé Picot knelt down, prayed for a few moments, then rose and went out of the room, saying, "She was a saintly woman," in the same tone as he always said, "Dominus vobiscum."

"Won't you have some dinner?" asked the vicomte in a perfectly ordinary voice.

Jeanne, not thinking he was speaking to her, made no answer.

"You would feel much better if you would eat something," he went on again.

"Let someone go for papa, directly," she said as if she had not heard what he said; and he went out of the room to dispatch a mounted messenger to Rouen.

Jeanne sank into a sort of stupor, as if she were waiting to give way to her passion of regret until she should
be alone with her mother.  The room became filled
with shadows.  The Widow Dentu moved noiselessly
about, arranging everything for the night, and at last
lighted two candles which she placed at the head of
the bed on a small table covered with a white cloth.
Jeanne seemed unconscious of everything; she was waiting until she should be alone.

When he had dined, Julien came upstairs again and
asked for the second time:

"Won't you have something to eat?"

His wife shook her head, and he sat down looking
more resigned than sad, and did not say anything more.
They all three sat apart from one another; the nurse
dropped off to sleep every now and then, snored for a
little while, then awoke with a start.  After some time
Julien rose and went over to his wife.

"Do you still want to be left alone?" he asked.

She eagerly took his hand in hers:  "Oh, yes; do
leave me," she answered.

He kissed her on the forehead, whispered, "I shall
come and see you during the night," then went away
with the Widow Dentu, who wheeled her armchair into
the next room.

Jeanne closed the door and put both windows wide
open.  A warm breeze, laden with the sweet smell of
the hay, blew into the room, and on the lawn, which
had been mown the day before, she could see the heaps
of dry grass lying in the moonlight.  She turned away
from the window and went back to the bed, for the soft,
beautiful night seemed to mock her grief.

Her mother was no longer swollen as she had been

when she died; she looked simply asleep, only her sleep
was more peaceful than it had ever been before; the
wind made the candles flicker, and the changing shadows made the dead face look as though it moved and
lived again. As Jeanne gazed at it the memories of
her early childhood came crowding into her mind. She
could see again her mother sitting in the convent parlor,
holding out the bag of cakes she had brought for her
little girl; she thought of all her little ways, her affectionate words, the way she used to move, the wrinkles
that came round her eyes when she laughed, the deep
sigh she always heaved when she sat down, and all her
little, daily habits, and as she stood gazing at the dead
body she kept repeating, almost mechanically: "She
is dead; she is dead;" until at last she realized all the
horror of that word.

The woman who was lying there — mamma — little
mother — Madame Adélaïde, was dead! She would
never move, never speak, never laugh, never say,
"Good morning, Jeannette"; never sit opposite her
husband at the dinner table again. She was dead.
She would be enclosed in a coffin, placed beneath the
ground, and that would be the end; they would never
see her again. It could not be possible! What! She,
her daughter, had now no mother! Had she indeed
lost for ever this dear face, the first she had ever looked
upon, the first she had ever loved, this kindly loving
mother, whose place in her heart could never be filled?
And in a few hours even this still, unconscious face
would have vanished, and then there would be nothing
left her but a memory. She fell on her knees in despair,
wringing her hands and pressing her lips to the bed.

"Oh, mother, mother! My darling mother!" she

cried, in a broken voice which was stifled by the bed-
covering.

She felt she was going mad; mad, like the night she
had fled into the snow. She rushed to the window to
breathe the fresh air which had not passed over the
corpse or the bed on which it lay. The new-mown hay,
the trees, the waste land and the distant sea lay peacefully sleeping in the moonlight, and the tears welled up
into Jeanne's eyes as she looked out into the clear, calm
night. She went back to her seat by the bedside and
held her mother's dead hand in hers, as if she were
lying ill instead of dead. Attracted by the lighted candles, a big, winged insect had entered through the open
window and was flying about the room, dashing against
the wall at every moment with a faint thud. It disturbed Jeanne, and she looked up to see where it was,
but she could only see its shadow moving over the white
ceiling.

Its buzzing suddenly ceased, and then, besides the
regular ticking of the clock, Jeanne noticed another
fainter rustling noise. It was the ticking of her mother's watch, which had been forgotten when her dress
had been taken off and thrown at the foot of the bed,
and the idea of this little piece of mechanism still moving while her mother lay dead, sent a fresh pang of anguish through her heart. She looked at the time. It
was hardly half-past ten, and as she thought of the long
night to come, she was seized with a horrible dread,

She began to think of her own life — of Rosalie, of
Gilberte — of all her illusions which had been, one by
one, so cruelly destroyed. Life contained nothing but
misery and pain, misfortune and death; there was nothing true, nothing honest, nothing but what gave rise to

suffering and tears.  Repose and happiness could only
be expected in another existence, when the soul had been
delivered from its early trials.  Her thoughts turned
to the unfathomable mystery of the soul, but, as she
reasoned about it, her poetic theories were invariably
upset by others, just as poetic and just as unreal.
Where was now her mother's soul, the soul which had
forsaken this still, cold body?  Perhaps it was far
away, floating in space.  But had it entirely vanished
like the perfume from a withered flower, or was it wandering like some invisible bird freed from its cage?
Had it returned to God, or was it scattered among the
new germs of creation?  It might be very near; perhaps in this very room, hovering around the inanimate
body it had left, and at this thought Jeanne fancied she
felt a breath, as if a spirit had passed by her.  Her
blood ran cold with terror; she did not dare turn round
to look behind her, and she sat motionless, her heart
beating wildly.

At that moment the invisible insect again commenced
its buzzing, noisy flight, and Jeanne trembled from head
to foot at the sound.  Then, as she recognized the
noise, she felt a little reassured, and rose and looked
around.  Her eyes fell on the escritoire with the
sphinxes' heads, the guardian of the " souvenirs."  As
she looked at it she thought it would be fulfilling a sacred, filial duty, which would please her mother as she
looked down on her from another world, to read these
letters, as she might have done a holy book during this
last watch.

She knew it was the correspondence of her grandfather and grandmother, whom she had never known;
and it seemed as if her hands would join theirs across

her mother's corpse, and so a sacred chain of affection would be formed between those who had died so long ago, their daughter who had but just joined them, and her child who was still on earth.

She opened the escritoire and took out the letters; they had been carefully tied into ten little packets, which were laid side by side in the lowest drawer. A refinement of sentimentality prompted her to place them all on the bed in the baroness's arms; then she began to read.

They were old-fashioned letters with the perfume of another century about them, such as are treasured up in every family. The first commenced " My dearie "; another " My little darling "; then came some beginning " My pet "—" My beloved daughter," then " My dear child "—" My dear Adélaïde "—" My dear daughter," the commencements varying as the letters had been addressed to the child, the young girl, and, later on, to the young wife. They were all full of foolish, loving phrases, and news about a thousand insignificant, homely events, which, to a stranger, would have seemed too trivial to mention: " Father has an influenza; Hortense has burnt her finger; Croquerat, the cat, is dead; the fir tree which stood on the right-hand side of the gate has been cut down; mother lost her mass book as she was coming home from church, she thinks someone must have stolen it," and they talked about people whom Jeanne had never known, but whose names were vaguely familiar to her.

She was touched by these simple details which seemed to reveal all her mother's life and inmost thoughts to her. She looked at the corpse as it lay there, and suddenly she began to read the letters aloud, as though to

console and gladden the dead heart once more; and a
smile of happiness seemed to light up the face.   As she
finished reading them, Jeanne threw the letters on the
foot of the bed, resolving to place them all in her
mother's coffin.

She untied another packet.   These were in another
handwriting, and the first ran thus :

" I cannot live without your kisses.   I love you
madly."

There was nothing more, not even a signature.
Jeanne turned the paper over, unable to understand it.
It was addressed clearly enough to " Madame la bar-
onne Le Perthuis des Vauds."

She opened the next :

" Come to-night as soon as he has gone out.   We
shall have at least one hour together.   I adore you."

A third :

" I have passed a night of longing and anguish.   I
fancied you in my arms, your mouth quivering beneath
mine, your eyes looking into my eyes.   And then I
could have dashed myself from the window, as I
thought that, at that very moment, you were sleeping
beside him, at the mercy of his caresses."

Jeanne stopped in amazement.   What did it all
mean?   To whom were these words of love addressed?
She read on, finding in every letter the same distracted
phrases, the same assignations, the same cautions, and,

at the end, always the five words: "Above all, burn this letter." At last she came to an ordinary note, merely accepting an invitation to dinner; it was signed "Paul d'Ennemare." Why, that was the man of whom the baron still spoke as "Poor old Paul," and whose wife had been the baroness's dearest friend!

Then into Jeanne's mind came a suspicion which at once changed to a certainty — he had been her mother's lover! With a sudden gesture of loathing, she threw from her all these odious letters, as she would have shaken off some venomous reptile, and, running to the window, she wept bitterly. All her strength seemed to have left her; she sank on the ground, and, hiding her face in the curtains to stifle her moans, she sobbed in an agony of despair. She would have crouched there the whole night if the sound of someone moving in the next room had not made her start to her feet. Perhaps it was her father! And all these letters were lying on the bed and on the floor! He had only to come in and open one, and he would know all!

She seized all the old, yellow papers — her grandparents' epistles, the love letters, those she had not unfolded, those that were still lying in the drawer — and threw them all into the fireplace. Then she took one of the candles which were burning on the little table, and set fire to this heap of paper. A bright flame sprang up at once, lighting up the room, the bed and the corpse with a bright, flickering light, and casting on the white bed-curtain a dark, trembling shadow of the rigid face and huge body.

When there was nothing left but a heap of ashes in the bottom of the grate, Jeanne went and sat by the window, as though now she dare not sit by the corpse.

The tears streamed from her eyes, and, hiding her face in her hands, she moaned out in heartbroken tones: "Oh, poor mamma! Poor mamma!"

Then a terrible thought came to her: Suppose her mother, by some strange chance, was not dead; suppose she was only in a trance-like sleep and should suddenly rise and speak! Would not the knowledge of this horrible secret lessen her, Jeanne's, love for her mother? Should she be able to kiss her with the same respect, and regard her with the same esteem as before? No! She knew it would be impossible; and the thought almost broke her heart.

The night wore on; the stars were fading, and a cool breeze sprang up. The moon was slowly sinking towards the sea over which she was shedding her silver light, and the memory of that other night she had passed at the window, the night of her return from the convent, came back to Jeanne. Ah! how far away was that happy time! How changed everything was, and what a different future lay before her from what she had pictured then! Over the sky crept a faint, tender tinge of pink, and the brilliant dawn seemed strange and unnatural to her, as she wondered how such glorious sunrises could illumine a world in which there was no joy or happiness.

A slight sound startled her, and looking round she saw Julien.

"Well, are you not very tired?" he said.

"No," she answered, feeling glad that her lonely vigil had come to an end.

"Now go and rest," said her husband.

She pressed a long sorrowful kiss on her mother's face; then left the room.

That day passed in attending to those melancholy
duties that always surround a death; the baron came
in the evening, and cried a great deal over his wife.
The next day the funeral took place; Jeanne pressed her
lips to the clammy forehead for the last time, drew the
sheet once more over the still face, saw the coffin fastened down, and then went to await the people who
were to attend the funeral.

Gilberte arrived first, and threw herself into Jeanne's
arms, sobbing violently. The carriages began to drive
up, and voices were heard in the hall. The room gradually filled with women with whom Jeanne was not acquainted; then the Marquise de Coutelier and the
Vicomtesse de Briseville arrived, and went up to her
and kissed her. She suddenly perceived that Aunt
Lison was in the room, and she gave her such an affectionate embrace, that the old maid was nearly overcome.
Julien came in dressed in deep mourning; he seemed
very busy, and very pleased that all these people had
come. He whispered some question to his wife about
the arrangements, and added in a low tone:

" It will be a very grand funeral; all the best families are here."

Then he went away again, bowing to the ladies as he
passed down the room.

Aunt Lison and the Comtesse Gilberte stayed with
Jeanne while the burial was taking place. The comtesse repeatedly kissed her, murmuring: " Poor darling, poor darling," and when the Comte de Fourville
came to take his wife home, he wept as if he had lost
his own mother.

## X

THE next few days were very sad, as they always must be directly after a death. The absence of the familiar face from its accustomed place makes the house seem empty, and each time the eye falls on anything the dear, dead one has had in constant use, a fresh pang of sorrow darts through the heart. There is the empty chair, the umbrella still standing in the hall, the glass which the maid has not yet washed. In every room there is something lying just as it was left for the last time; the scissors, an odd glove, the fingered book, the numberless other objects, which, insignificant in themselves, become a source of sharp pain because they recall so vividly the loved one who has passed away. And the voice rings in one's ears till it seems almost a reality, but there is no escape from the house haunted by this presence, for others are suffering also, and all must stay and suffer with each other.

In addition to her natural grief, Jeanne had to bear the pain of her discovery. She was always thinking of it, and the terrible secret increased her former sense of desolation tenfold, for now she felt that she could never put her trust or confidence in anyone again.

The baron soon went away, thinking to find relief from the grief which was deadening all his faculties in change of air and change of scene, and the household at Les Peuples resumed its quiet regular life again.

Then Paul fell ill, and Jeanne passed twelve days in an agony of fear, unable to sleep and scarcely touching food. The boy got well, but there remained the thought that he might die. What should she do if he died? What would become of her? Gradually there came a vague longing for another child, and soon she could think of nothing else; she had always fancied she should like two children, a boy and a girl, and the idea of having a daughter haunted her. But since Rosalie had been sent away, she had lived quite apart from her husband, and at the present moment it seemed utterly impossible to renew their former relations. Julien's affections were centered elsewhere; she knew that; and, on her side, the mere thought of having to submit to his caresses again, made her shudder with disgust.

Still, she would have overcome her repugnance (so tormented was she by the desire of another child) if she could have seen any way to bring about the intimacy she desired; but she would have died rather than let her husband guess what was in her thoughts, and he never seemed to dream of approaching her now. Perhaps she would have given up the idea had not each night the vision of a daughter playing with Paul under the plane tree appeared to her. Sometimes she felt she *must* get up and join her husband in his room; twice, in fact, she did glide to his door, but each time she came back, without having turned the handle, her face burning with shame.

The baron was away, her mother was dead, and she had no one to whom she could confide this delicate secret. She made up her mind, at last, to tell the Abbé Picot her difficulty, under the seal of confession. She went to him one day and found him in his little garden, reading his breviary among the fruit trees. She talked to him for a few minutes about one thing and another, then, " Monsieur l'abbé, I want to confess," she said, with a deep blush.

He put on his spectacles to look at her better, for the

request astonished him. " I don't think you can have any very heavy sins on your conscience," he said, with a smile.

" No, but I want to ask your advice on a subject so — so painful to enter upon, that I dare not talk about it in an ordinary way," she replied, feeling very confused.

He put on his priestly air immediately.

" Very well, my daughter, come to the confessional, and I will hear you there."

But she suddenly felt a scruple at talking of such things in the quietness of an empty church.

" No, Monsieur le curé — after all — if you will let me — I can tell you here what I want to say. See, we will go and sit in your little arbor over there."

As they walked slowly over to the arbor she tried to find the words in which she could best begin her confidence. They sat down, and she commenced, as if she were confessing, " My father," then hesitated, said again, " My father," then stopped altogether, too ashamed to continue.

The priest crossed his hands over his stomach and waited for her to go on. " Well, my daughter," he said, perceiving her embarrassment, " you seem afraid to say what it is; come now, be brave."

" My father, I want to have another child," she said abruptly, like a coward throwing himself headlong into the danger he dreads.

The priest, hardly understanding what she meant, made no answer, and she tried to explain herself, but, in her confusion, her words became more and more difficult to understand.

" I am quite alone in life now; my father and my husband do not agree; my mother is dead, and — and —

the other day I almost lost my son," she whispered with a shudder. "What would have become of me if he had died?"

The priest looked at her in bewilderment. "There, there; come to the point," he said.

"I want to have another child," she repeated.

The abbé was used to the coarse pleasantries of the peasants, who did not mind what they said before him, and he answered, with a sly smile and a knowing shake of the head: "Well, I don't think there need be much difficulty about that."

She raised her clear eyes to his and said, hesitatingly:

"But — but — don't you understand that since — since that trouble with — the — maid — my husband and I live — quite apart."

These words came as a revelation to the priest, accustomed as he was to the promiscuity and easy morals of the peasants. Then he thought he could guess what the young wife really wanted, and he looked at her out of the corner of his eye, pitying her, and sympathizing with her distress.

"Yes, yes, I know exactly what you mean. I can quite understand that you should find your — your widowhood hard to bear. You are young, healthy, and it is only natural; very natural." He began to smile, his lively nature getting the better of him. "Besides, the Church allows these feelings, sometimes," he went on, gently tapping Jeanne's hands. "What are we told? That carnal desires may be satisfied lawfully in wedlock only. Well, you are married, are you not?"

She, in her turn, had not at first understood what his words implied, but when his meaning dawned on her,

her face became crimson, and her eyes filled with tears.

"Oh! Monsieur le curé, what do you mean? What do you think? I assure you — I assure —" and she could not continue for her sobs.

Her emotion surprised the abbé, and he tried to console her.

"There, there," he said; "I did not mean to pain you. I was only joking, and there's no harm in a joke between honest people. But leave it all in my hands, and I will speak to M. Julien."

She did not know what to say. She wished, now, that she could refuse his help, for she feared his want of tact would only increase her difficulties, but she did not dare say anything.

"Thank you, Monsieur le curé," she stammered; and then hurried away.

The next week was passed by Jeanne in an agony of doubts and fears. Then one evening, Julien watched her all through dinner with an amused smile on his lips, and evinced towards her a gallantry which was faintly tinged with irony. After dinner they walked up and down the baroness's avenue, and he whispered in her ear:

"Then we are going to be friends again?"

She made no answer, and kept her eyes fixed on the ground, where there was a straight line, hardly so thickly covered with grass as the rest of the path. It was the line traced by the baroness's foot, which was gradually being effaced, just as her memory was fading, and, as she looked at it, Jeanne's heart felt bursting with grief; she seemed so lonely, so separated from everybody.

"For my part, I am only too pleased," continued Julien. "I should have proposed it before, but I was afraid of displeasing you."

The sun was setting; it was a mild, soft evening, and Jeanne longed to rest her head on some loving heart, and there sob out her sorrows. She threw herself into Julien's arms, her breast heaving, and the tears streaming from her eyes. He looked at her in surprise, thinking this outburst was occasioned by the love she still felt for him, and, unable to see her face, he dropped a condescending kiss upon her hair. Then they went indoors in silence and he followed her to her room.

To him this renewal of their former relations was a duty, though hardly an unpleasant one, while she submitted to his embraces as a disgusting, painful necessity, and resolved to put an end to them for ever, as soon as her object was accomplished. Soon, however, she found that her husband's caresses were not like they used to be; they may have been more refined, they certainly were not so complete. He treated her like a careful lover, instead of being an easy husband.

"Why do you not give yourself up to me as you used to do?" she whispered one night, her lips close to his.

"To keep you out of the family way, of course," he answered, with a chuckle.

She started.

"Don't you wish for any more children, then?" she asked.

His amazement was so great, that, for a moment, he was silent; then:

"Eh? What do you say?" he exclaimed. "Are you in your right senses? Another child? I should think not, indeed! We've already got one too many,

squalling and costing money, and bothering everybody.
Another child! No, thank you!"

She clasped him in her arms, pressed her lips to his
and murmured:

" Oh! I entreat you, make me a mother once more."

" Don't be so foolish," he replied, angrily. " Pray
don't let me hear any more of this nonsense."

She said no more, but she resolved to trick him into
giving her the happiness she desired. She tried to pro-
long her kisses, and threw her arms passionately around
him, pressing him to her, and pretending a delirium of
love she was very far from feeling. She tried every
means to make him lose control over himself, but she
never once succeeded.

Tormented more and more by her desire, driven to
extremities, and ready to do or dare anything to gain
her ends, she went again to the Abbé Picot. She found
him just finishing lunch, with his face crimson from indi-
gestion. He looked up as she came in, and, anxious to
hear the result of his mediation:

" Well? " he exclaimed.

" My husband does not want any more children," she
answered at once without any of the hesitation or
shame-faced timidity she had shown before.

The abbé got very interested, and turned towards her,
ready to hear once more of those secrets of wedded life,
the revelation of which made the task of confessing so
pleasant to him.

" How is that? " he asked.

In spite of her determination to tell him all, Jeanne
hardly knew how to explain herself.

" He — he refuses — to make me a mother."

The priest understood at once; it was not the first

V.—12

time he had heard of such things, but he asked for all the details, and enjoyed them as a hungry man would a feast. When he had heard all, he reflected for a few moments, then said in the calm, matter-of-fact tone he might have used if he had been speaking of the best way to insure a good harvest.

"My dear child, the only thing you can do is to make your husband believe you are pregnant; then he will cease his precautions, and you will become so in reality."

Jeanne blushed to the roots of her hair, but, determined to be ready for every emergency, she argued:

"But — but suppose he should not believe me?"

The curé knew too well the inns and outs of human nature not to have an answer for that.

"Tell everybody you are *enceinte*. When he sees that everyone else believes it, he will soon believe it himself. You will be doing no wrong," he added, to quiet his conscience for advising this deception; "the Church does not permit any connection between man and woman, except for the purpose of procreation."

Jeanne followed the priest's artful device, and, a fortnight later, told Julien she thought she was *enceinte*. He started up.

"It isn't possible! You can't be!"

She gave him her reasons for thinking so.

"Bah!" he answered. "You wait a little while."

Every morning he asked, "Well?" but she always replied: "No, not yet; I am very much mistaken if I am not *enceinte*."

He also began to think so, and his surprise was only equaled by his annoyance.

"Well, I can't understand it," was all he could say. "I'll be hanged if I know how it can have happened."

At the end of a month she began to tell people the news, but she said nothing about it to the Comtesse Gilberte, for she felt an old feeling of delicacy in mentioning it to her. At the very first suspicion of his wife's pregnancy, Julien had ceased to touch her, then, angrily thinking, " Well, at any rate, this brat wasn't wanted," he made up his mind to make the best of it, and recommenced his visits to his wife's room. Everything happened as the priest had predicted, and Jeanne found she would a second time become a mother. Then, in a transport of joy, she took a vow of eternal chastity as a token of her rapturous gratitude to the distant divinity she adored, and thenceforth closed her door to her husband.

She again felt almost happy. She could hardly believe that it was barely two months since her mother had died, and that only such a short time before she had thought herself inconsolable. Now her wounded heart was nearly healed, and her grief had disappeared, while in its place was merely a vague melancholy, like the shadow of a great sorrow resting over her life. It seemed impossible that any other catastrophe could happen now; her children would grow up and surround her old age with their affection, and her husband could go his way while she went hers.

Towards the end of September the Abbé Picot came to the château, in a new cassock which had only one week's stains upon it, to introduce his successor, the Abbé Tolbiac. The latter was small, thin, and very young, with hollow, black-encircled eyes which betokened the depth and violence of his feelings, and a decisive way of speaking as if there could be no appeal from his opinion. The Abbé Picot had been appointed *doyen* of Goderville. Jeanne felt very sad at the thought of his departure; he was connected, in her thoughts, with all the chief events of her life, for he had married her, christened Paul, and buried the baroness. She liked him because he was always good-tempered and unaffected, and she could not imagine Etouvent without the Abbé Picot's fat figure trotting past the farms. He himself did not seem very rejoiced at his advancement.

"I have been here eighteen years, Madame la Comtesse," he said, "and it grieves me to go to another place. Oh! this living is not worth much, I know, and as for the people — well, the men have no more religion than they ought to have, the women are not so moral as they might be, and the girls never dream of being married until it is too late for them to wear a wreath of orange blossoms; still, I love the place."

The new curé had been fidgeting impatiently during this speech, and his face had turned very red.

"I shall soon have all that changed," he said, abruptly, as soon as the other priest had finished speaking; and he looked like an angry child in his worn but spotless cassock, so thin and small was he.

The Abbé Picot looked at him sideways, as he always did when anything amused him.

"Listen, l'abbé," he said. "You will have to chain up your parishioners if you want to prevent that sort of thing; and I don't believe even that would be any good."

"We shall see," answered the little priest in a cutting tone.

The old curé smiled and slowly took a pinch of snuff.

"Age and experience will alter your views, l'abbé;

if they don't you will only estrange the few good
Churchmen you have. When I see a girl come to mass
with a waist bigger than it ought to be, I say to myself
— ' Well, she is going to give me another soul to look
after;'—and I try to marry her. You can't prevent
them going wrong, but you can find out the father of the
child and prevent him forsaking the mother. Marry
them, l'abbé, marry them, and don't trouble yourself
about anything else."

"We will not argue on this point, for we should
never agree," answered the new curé, a little roughly;
and the Abbé Picot again began to express his regret at
leaving the village, and the sea which he could see from
the vicarage windows, and the little funnel-shaped valleys, where he went to read his breviary and where he
could see the boats in the distance. Then the two
priests rose to go, and the Abbé Picot kissed Jeanne,
who nearly cried when she said good-bye.

A week afterwards, the Abbé Tolbiac called again.
He spoke of the reforms he was bringing about as if
he were a prince taking possession of his kingdom.
He begged the vicomtesse to communicate on all the
days appointed by the Church, and to attend mass
regularly on Sundays.

"You and I are at the head of the parish," he said,
" and we ought to rule it, and always set it a good
example; but, if we wish to have any influence, we
must be united. If the Church and the château support each other, the cottage will fear and obey us."

Jeanne's religion was simply a matter of sentiment;
she had merely the dreamy faith that a woman never
quite loses, and if she performed any religious duties
at all it was only because she had been so used to them

at the convent, for the baron's carping philosophy had
long ago overthrown all her convictions.   The Abbé
Picot had always been contented with the little she did
do, and never chid her for not confessing or attending mass oftener; but when the Abbé Tolbiac did not
see her at church on the Sunday, he hastened to the
château to question and reprimand her.   She did not
wish to quarrel with the curé, so she promised to be
more attentive to the services, inwardly resolving to
go regularly only for a few weeks, out of good nature.

Little by little, however, she fell into the habit of
frequenting the church, and, in a short time, she was
entirely under the influence of the delicate-looking,
strong-willed priest.   His zeal and enthusiasm appealed
to her love of everything pertaining to mysticism, and
he seemed to make the chord of religious poetry, which
she possessed in common with every woman, vibrate
within her.   His austerity, his contempt for every
luxury and sensuality, his disdain for the things that
usually occupy the thoughts of men, his love of God,
his youthful, intolerant inexperience, his scathing words,
his inflexible will made Jeanne compare him, in her
mind, to the early martyrs; and she, who had already
suffered so much, whose eyes had been so rudely opened
to the deceptions of life, let herself be completely ruled
by the rigid fanaticism of this boy who was the minister
of Heaven.   He led her to the feet of Christ the
Consoler, teaching her how the holy joys of religion
could alleviate all her sorrows, and, as she knelt in the
confessional she humbled herself and felt little and weak
before this priest, who looked about fifteen years old.

Soon he was detested by the whole country-side.

With no pity for his own weaknesses, he showed a violent intolerance for those of others. The thing above all others that roused his anger and indignation was — love. He denounced it from the pulpit in crude, ecclesiastical terms, thundering out terrible judgments against concupiscence over the heads of his rustic audience; and, as the pictures he portrayed in his fury persistently haunted his mind, he trembled with rage and stamped his foot in anger. The grown-up girls and the young fellows cast side-long glances at each other across the aisle; and the old peasants, who liked to joke about such matters, expressed their disapproval of the little curé's intolerance as they walked back to their farms after service with their wives and sons.

The whole country was in an uproar. The priest's severity and the harsh penances he inflicted at confession were rumored about, and, as he obstinately refused to grant absolution to the girls whose chastity was not immaculate, smiles accompanied the whispers. When, at the holy festivals, several of the youths and girls stayed in their seats instead of going to communicate with the others, most of the congregation laughed outright as they looked at them. He began to watch for lovers like a keeper on the look-out for poachers, and on moonlight nights he hunted up the couples along the ditches, behind the barns and among the long grass on the hill-sides. One night he came upon two who did not cease their love-making even before him; they were strolling along a ditch filled with stones, with their arms round one another, kissing each other as they walked.

"Will you stop that, you vagabonds?" cried the abbé.

" You mind yer own bus'ness, M'sieu l'curé," replied the lad, turning round. " This ain't nothin' to do with you."

The abbé picked up some stones and threw them at the couple as he might have done at stray dogs, and they both ran off, laughing. The next Sunday the priest mentioned them by name before the whole congregation. All the young fellows soon ceased to attend mass.

The curé dined at the château every Thursday, but he very often went there on other days to talk to his *penitente.* Jeanne became as ardent and as enthusiastic as he as she discussed the mysteries of a future existence, and grew familiar with all the old and complicated arguments employed in religious controversy. They would both walk along the baroness's avenue talking of Christ and the Apostles, of the Virgin Mary and of the Fathers of the Church as if they had really known them. Sometimes they stopped their walk to ask each other profound questions, and then Jeanne would wander off into sentimental arguments, and the curé would reason like a lawyer possessed with the mania of proving the possibility of squaring the circle.

Julien treated the new curé with great respect. " That's the sort of a priest I like," he was continually saying. " Half-measures don't do for him," and he zealously set a good example by frequently confessing and communicating. Hardly a day passed now without the vicomte going to the Fourvilles, either to shoot with the comte, who could not do without him, or to ride with the comtesse regardless of rain and bad weather.

" They are riding-mad," remarked the comte; " but the exercise does my wife good."

The baron returned to Les Peuples about the middle
of November. He seemed a different man, he had
aged so much and was so low-spirited; he was fonder
than ever of his daughter, as if the last few months of
melancholy solitude had caused in him an imperative
need of affection and tenderness. Jeanne told him
nothing about her new ideas, her intimacy with the Abbé
Tolbiac, or her religious enthusiasm, but the first time
he saw the priest, he felt an invincible dislike for him,
and when his daughter asked him in the evening:
" Well, what do you think of him? "

" He is like an inquisitor ! " he answered. " He
seems to me a very dangerous man."

When the peasants told him about the young priest's
harshness and bigotry and the sort of war of persecution he waged against natural laws and instincts, his
dislike changed to a violent hatred. He, the baron,
belonged to the school of philosophers who worship
nature; to him it seemed something touching, when he
saw two animals unite, and he was always ready to fall
on his knees before the sort of pantheistic God he worshiped; but he hated the catholic conception of a God,
Who has petty schemes, and gives way to tyrannical
anger and indulges in mean revenge; a God, in fact,
Who seemed less to him than that boundless omnipo-
tent nature, which is at once life, light, earth, thought,
plant, rock, man, air, animal, planet, god and insect,
that nature which produces all things in such bountiful
profusion, fitting each atom to the place it is to occupy
in space, be that position close to or far from the suns
which heat the worlds. Nature contained the germ of
everything, and she brought forth life and thought, as
trees bear flowers and fruit.

To the baron, therefore, reproduction was a great law of Nature, and to be respected as the sacred and divine act which accomplished the constant, though unexpressed will of this Universal Being; and he at once began a campaign against this priest who opposed the laws of creation. It grieved Jeanne to the heart, and she prayed to the Lord, and implored her father not to run counter to the curé, but the baron always answered:

"It is everyone's right and duty to fight against such men, for they are not like human creatures. They are not human," he repeated, shaking his long white hair. "They understand nothing of life, and their conduct is entirely influenced by their harmful dreams, which are contrary to Nature." And he pronounced "contrary to Nature" as if he were uttering a curse.

The priest had at once recognized in him an enemy, and, as he wished to remain master of the château and its young mistress, he temporized, feeling sure of victory in the end. By chance he had discovered the *liaison* between Julien and Gilberte, and his one idea was to break it off by no matter what means. He came to see Jeanne one day towards the end of the wet, mild winter, and, after a long talk on the mystery of life, he asked her to unite with him in fighting against and destroying the wickedness which was in her own family, and so save two souls which were in danger. She asked him what he meant.

"The hour has not come for me to reveal all to you," he replied; "but I will see you again soon," and with that he abruptly left her.

He came again in a few days, and spoke in vague terms of a disgraceful connection between people whose conduct ought to be irreproachable. It was the duty, he said, of those who were aware of what was going on, to use every means to put an end to it. He used all sorts of lofty arguments, and then, taking Jeanne's hand, adjured her to open her eyes, to understand and to help him.

This time Jeanne saw what he meant, but terrified at the thought of all the trouble that might be brought to her home, which was now so peaceful, she pretended not to know to what he was alluding. Then he hesitated no longer, but spoke in terms there could be no misunderstanding.

"I am going to perform a very painful duty, Madame la comtesse, but I cannot leave it undone. The position I hold forbids me to leave you in ignorance of the sin you can prevent. Learn that your husband cherishes a criminal affection for Madame de Fourville."

Jeanne only bent her head in feeble resignation.

"What do you intend to do?" asked the priest.

"What do you wish me to do, Monsieur l'abbé?" she murmured.

"Throw yourself in the way as an obstacle to this guilty love," he answered, violently.

She began to cry, and said in a broken voice:

"But he has deceived me before with a servant; he wouldn't listen to me; he doesn't love me now; he ill-treats me if I manifest any desire that does not please him, so what can I do?"

The curé did not make any direct answer to this appeal.

"Then you bow before this sin! You submit to it!" he exclaimed. "You consent to and tolerate adultery under your own roof! The crime is being perpetrated before your eyes, and you refuse to see it! Are you a Christian woman? Are you a wife and a mother?"

" What would you have me do?" she sobbed.

" Anything rather than allow this sin to continue," he replied. " Anything, I tell you. Leave him. Flee from this house which has been defiled."

" But I have no money, Monsieur l'abbé," she replied. " And I am not brave now like I used to be. Besides, how can I leave without any proofs of what you are saying? I have not the right to do so."

The priest rose to his feet, quivering with indignation.

" You are listening to the dictates of your cowardice, madame. I thought you were a different woman, but you are unworthy of God's mercy."

She fell on her knees:

" Oh! Do not abandon me, I implore you. Advise me what to do."

" Open M. de Fourville's eyes," he said, shortly. " It is his duty to end this *liaison*."

She was seized with terror at this advice.

" But he would kill them, Monsieur l'abbé! And should I be the one to tell him? Oh, not that! Never, never!"

He raised his hand as if to curse her, his whole soul stirred with anger.

" Live on in your shame and in your wickedness, for you are more guilty than they are. You are the wife who condones her husband's sin! My place is no longer here."

He turned to go, trembling all over with wrath. She followed him distractedly, ready to give in, and beginning to promise; but he would not listen to her and

strode rapidly along, furiously shaking his big blue
umbrella which was nearly as high as himself. He saw
Julien standing near the gate superintending the pruning
of some trees, so he turned off to the left to reach the
road by way of the Couillards' farm, and as he
walked he kept saying to Jeanne:

"Leave me, madame. I have nothing further to say
to you."

In the middle of the yard, and right in his path, some
children were standing around the kennel of the dog
Mirza, their attention concentrated on something which
the baron was also carefully considering as he stood in
their midst with his hands behind his back, looking like
a schoolmaster.

"Do come and see me again, Monsieur l'abbé,"
pleaded Jeanne. "If you will return in a few days, I
shall be able to tell you then what I think is the best
course to take, and we can talk it over together."

By that time they had almost reached the group of
children (which the baron had left, to avoid meeting
and speaking to his enemy, the priest) and the curé
went to see what it was that was interesting them so
deeply. It was the dog whelping; five little pups were
already crawling round the mother, who gently licked
them as she lay on her side before the kennel, and just
as the curé looked over the children's heads, a sixth
appeared. When they saw it, all the boys and girls
clapped their hands, crying:

"There's another! There's another!"

To them it was simply a perfectly pure and natural
amusement, and they watched these pups being born as
they might have watched the apples falling from a tree.

The Abbé Tolbiac stood still for a moment in horrified surprise, then, giving way to his passion, he raised his umbrella and began to rain down blows on the children's heads. The startled urchins ran off as fast as they could go, and the abbé found himself left alone with the dog, which was painfully trying to rise. Before she could stand up, he knocked her back again, and began to hit her with all his strength. The animal moaned pitifully as she writhed under these blows from which there was no escape (for she was chained up) and at last the priest's umbrella broke. Then, unable to beat the dog any longer, he jumped on her, and stamped and crushed her under-foot in a perfect frenzy of anger. Another pup was born beneath his feet before he dispatched the mother with a last furious kick, and then the mangled body lay quivering in the midst of the whining pups, which were awkwardly groping for their mother's teats. Jeanne had escaped, but the baron returned and, almost as enraged as the priest, suddenly seized the abbé by the throat, and giving him a blow which knocked his hat off, carried him to the fence and threw him out into the road.

When he turned round, M. le Perthuis saw his daughter kneeling in the midst of the pups, sobbing as she picked them up and put them in her skirt. He strode up to her gesticulating wildly.

" There ! " he exclaimed. " What do you think of that surpliced wretch, now ? "

The noise had brought the farmpeople to the spot, and they all stood round, gazing at the remains of the dog.

" Could one have believed that a man would be so cruel as that ! " said Couillard's wife.

Jeanne picked up the pups, saying she would bring

them up by hand; she tried to give them some milk, but three out of seven died the next day. Then old Simon went all over the neighborhood trying to find a foster-mother for the others; he could not get a dog, but he brought back a cat, asserting that she would do as well. Three more pups were killed, and the seventh was given to the cat, who took to it directly, and lay down on her side to suckle it. That it might not exhaust its foster-mother the pup was weaned a fortnight later, and Jeanne undertook to feed it herself with a feeding-bottle; she had named it Toto, but the baron rechristened it, and called it Massacre.

The priest did not go to see Jeanne again. The next Sunday he hurled curses and threats against the château, denouncing it as a plague-spot which ought to be removed, and going on to anathematize the baron (who laughed at him) and to make veiled, half-timid allusions to Julien's latest amour. The vicomte was very vexed at this, but he did not dare say anything for fear of giving rise to a scandal; and the priest continued to call down vengeance on their heads, and to foretell the downfall of God's enemies in every sermon. At last, Julien wrote a decided, though respectful, letter to the archbishop, and the Abbé Tolbiac, finding himself threatened with disgrace, ceased his denunciations. He began to take long solitary walks; often he was to be met striding along the roads with an ardent, excited look on his face. Gilberte and Julien were always seeing him when they were out riding, sometimes in the distance, on the other side of a common, or on the edge of the cliff, sometimes close at hand, reading his breviary in a narrow valley they were just about to pass through; they always turned another way to avoid

passing him. Spring had come, enflaming their hearts
with fresh desires, and urging them to seek each other's
embraces in any secluded spot to which their rides might
lead them; but the leaves were only budding, the grass
was still damp from the rains of winter, and they could
not, as in the height of summer, hide themselves
amidst the undergrowth of the woods. Lately, they
had generally sheltered their caresses within a movable
shepherd's hut which had been left since autumn, on the
very top of the Vaucotte hill. It stood all alone on the
edge of the precipitous descent to the valley, five hundred yards above the cliff. There they felt quite secure,
for they overlooked the whole of the surrounding
country, and they fastened their horses to the shafts to
wait until their masters were satiated with love.

One evening as they were leaving the hut, they saw
the Abbé Tolbiac sitting on the hill-side, nearly hidden
by the rushes.

"We must leave our horses in that ravine, another
time," said Julien; "in case they should tell our whereabouts," and thenceforth they always tied their horses
up in a kind of recess in the valley, which was hidden
by bushes.

Another evening, they were both returning to La
Vrillette where the comte was expecting Julien to dinner,
when they met the curé coming out of the château. He
bowed, without looking them in the face, and stood on
one side to let them pass. For the moment his visit
made them uneasy, but their anxiety was soon dispelled.

.    .    .    .    .    .    .    .

Jeanne was sitting by the fire reading, one windy
afternoon at the beginning of May, when she suddenly
saw the Comte de Fourville running towards the

château at such a rate as to make her fear he was the bearer of bad news. She hastened downstairs to meet him, and when she saw him close, she thought he must have gone mad. He had on his shooting-jacket and a big fur cap, that he generally only wore on his own grounds, and he was so pale that his red moustaches (which, as a rule, hardly showed against his ruddy face) looked the color of flame. His eyes were haggard and stared vacantly or rolled from side to side.

" My wife is here, isn't she? " he gasped.

" No," answered Jeanne, too frightened to think of what she was saying; " I have not seen her at all to-day."

The comte dropped into a chair, as if his legs had no longer strength to support him, and, taking off his cap, he mechanically passed his handkerchief several times across his forehead; then he started to his feet, and went towards Jeanne with outstretched hands, and mouth opened to speak and tell her of his terrible grief. But suddenly he stopped short, and fixing his eyes on her, murmured, as if he were delirous : " But it is your husband — you also —" and breaking off abruptly, he rushed out towards the sea.

Jeanne ran after him, calling him and imploring him to stop. " He knows all! " she thought, in terror. " What will he do? Oh, pray heaven he may not find them."

He did not listen to her, and evidently knowing whither to direct his steps, ran straight on without any hesitation as to the path he should take. Already he had leapt across the ditch, and was rapidly striding across the reeds towards the cliff. Finding she could not catch him up, Jeanne stood on the slope beyond the

V—13

wood, and watched him as long as he was in sight; then, when she could see him no longer, she went indoors again, tortured with fear and anxiety.

When he reached the edge of the cliff, the comte turned to the right, and again began to run. The sea was very rough, and one after the other the heavy clouds came up and poured their contents on the land. A whistling moaning wind swept over the grass, laying low the young barley, and carrying the great, white sea-gulls inland like sprays of foam. The rain, which came in gusts, beat in the comte's face and drenched his cheeks and moustaches, and the tumult of the elements seemed to fill his heart as well as his ears. There, straight before him in the distance, lay the Vaucotte valley, and between it and him stood a solitary shepherd's hut, with two horses tied to the shafts. (What fear could there be of anyone seeing them on such a day as this?)

As soon as he caught sight of the animals, the comte threw himself flat on the ground, and dragged himself along on his hands and knees, his hairy cap and mud-stained clothes making him look like some monstrous animal. He crawled to the lonely hut, and, in case its occupants should see him through the cracks in the planks he hid himself beneath it. The horses had seen him and were pawing the ground. He slowly cut the reins by which they were fastened with a knife that he held open in his hand, and, as a fresh gust of wind swept by, the two animals cantered off, their backs stung by the hail which lashed against the sloping roof of the shepherd's cot, and made the frail abode tremble on its wheels.

Then the comte rose to his knees, put his eye to the

slit at the bottom of the door, and remained perfectly
motionless while he watched and waited. Some time
passed thus, and then he suddenly leapt to his feet,
covered with mire from head to foot. Furiously he
fastened the bolt, which secured the shelter on the
outside, and seizing the shafts, he shook the hut as
if he would have broken it to atoms. After a moment
he began to drag it along — exerting the strength of a
bull, and bending nearly double in his tremendous effort — and it was towards the almost perpendicular
slope to the valley that he hurried the cottage and its
human occupants who were desperately shouting and
trying to burst open the door, in their ignorance of what
had happened.

At the extreme edge of the slope, the comte let go
of the hut, and it at once begun to run down towards
the valley. At first it moved but slowly, but, its speed
increasing as it went, it moved quicker and quicker, until
soon it was rushing down the hill at a tremendous rate.
Its shafts bumped along the ground and it leaped over
and dashed against the obstacles in its path, as if it had
been endowed with life; it bounded over the head of an
old beggar who was crouching in a ditch, and, as it
passed, the man heard frightful cries issuing from
within it. All at once one of the wheels was torn off,
and the hut turned over on its side. That however,
did not stop it, and now it rolled over and over like a
ball, or like some house uprooted from its foundations
and hurled from the summit of a mountain. It rolled
on and on until it reached the edge of the last ravine;
there it took a final leap, and after describing a curve,
fell to the earth, and smashed like an egg-shell.

Directly it had dashed upon the rocks at the bottom

of the valley, the old beggar, who had seen it falling, began to make his way down through the brambles. He did not go straight to the shattered hut, but, like the cautious rustic that he was, went to announce the accident at the nearest farm-house. The farm people ran to the spot the beggar pointed out, and beneath the fragments of the hut, found two bruised and mangled corpses. The man's forehead was split open, and his face crushed; the woman's jaw was almost separated from her head, and their broken limbs were as soft as if there had not been a bone beneath the flesh. Still the farmers could recognize them, and they began to make all sorts of conjectures as to the cause of the accident.

"What could they have been doin' in the cabin?" said a woman.

The old beggar replied that apparently they had taken refuge from the weather, and that the high wind had overturned the hut, and blown it down the precipice. He added that he himself was going to take shelter in it when he saw the horses fastened to the shafts and concluded that the place was already occupied.

"If it hadn't been for that I should have been where they are now," he said with an air of self-congratulation.

"Perhaps it would have been all the better if you had been," said some one.

"Why would it have been better?" exclaimed the beggar in a great rage. "'Cause I'm poor and they're rich? Look at them now!" he said, pointing to the two corpses with his hooked stick, as he stood trembling and ragged, with the water dripping from him, and his battered hat, his matted beard, his long unkempt hair, making him look terribly dirty and miserable. " We're all equal when we're dead."

The group had grown bigger, and the peasants stood round with a frightened, cowardly look on their faces. After a discussion as to what they had better do, it was finally decided to carry the bodies back to their homes, in the hope of getting a reward. Two carts were got ready, and then a fresh difficulty arose; some thought it would be quite enough to place straw at the bottom of the carts, and others thought it would look better to put mattresses.

" But the mattresses would be soaked with blood," cried the woman who had spoken before. " They'd have to be washed with *eau de javelle*."

" The château people'll pay for that," said a jolly-faced farmer. " They can't expect to get things for nothing."

That decided the matter, and the two carts set off, one to the right, the other to the left, jolting and shaking the remains of these two beings who had so often been clasped in each other's arms, but who would never meet again.

When the comte had seen the hut set off on its terrible journey, he had fled away through the rain and the wind, and had run on and on across the country like a madman. He ran for several hours, heedless of which way his steps were taking him, and, at nightfall, he found himself at his own château. The servants were anxiously awaiting his return, and hastened to tell him that the two horses had just returned riderless, for Julien's had followed the other one.

M. de Fourville staggered back. " Some accident

must have happened to my wife and the vicomte," he said in broken tones. "Let everyone go and look for them."

He started off again, himself, as though he were going to seek them, but, as soon as he was out of sight, he hid behind a bush, and watched the road along which the woman he still loved so dearly would be brought dead or dying, or perhaps maimed and disfigured for life. In a little while a cart passed by, bearing a strange load; it drew up before the château-gates, then passed through them. Yes, he knew it was she; but the dread of hearing the horrible truth forced him to stay in his hiding-place, and he crouched down like a hare, trembling at the faintest rustle.

He waited for an hour—perhaps two—and yet the cart did not come back again. He was persuaded that his wife was dying, and the thought of seeing her, of meeting her eyes was such a torture to him, that, seized with a sudden fear of being discovered and compelled to witness her death, he again set off running, and did not stop till he was hidden in the midst of a wood. Then he thought that perhaps she needed help and that there was no one to take care of her as he could, and he sped back in mad haste.

As he was going into the house, he met his gardener.

"Well?" he cried, excitedly.

The man dared not answer the truth.

"Is she dead?" almost yelled M. de Fourville.

"Yes, Monsieur le comte," stammered the servant.

The comte experienced an intense relief at the answer; all his agitation left him, and he went quietly and firmly up the steps.

In the meantime, the other cart had arrived at Les

Peuples. Jeanne saw it in the distance, and guessing that a corpse lay upon the mattress, understood at once what had happened; the shock was so great that she fell to the ground unconscious. When she came to herself again she found her father supporting her head, and bathing her forehead with vinegar.

" Do you know —? " he asked hesitatingly.

" Yes, father," she whispered, trying to rise; but she was in such pain that she was forced to sink back again.

That evening she gave birth to a dead child — a girl.

She did not see or hear anything of Julien's funeral, for she was delirious when he was buried. In a few days she was conscious of Aunt Lison's presence in her room, and, in the midst of the feverish nightmares by which she was haunted, she strove to recall when, and under what circumstances, the old maid had last left Les Peuples. But even in her lucid moments she could not remember, and she could only feel sure she had seen her since the baroness's death.

## XI

JEANNE was confined to her room for three months and everyone despaired of her life, but very, very gradually health and strength returned to her. Her father and Aunt Lison had come to live at the château, and they nursed her day and night. The shock she had sustained had entirely upset her nervous system; she started at the least noise, and the slightest emotion caused her to go off into long swoons. She had never asked the details of Julien's death. Why should she? Did she not already know enough? Everyone except herself thought it had been an accident,

and she never revealed to anyone the terrible secret of
her husband's adultery, and of the comte's sudden, fearful visit the day of the catastrophe.

Her soul was filled with the sweet, tender memories
of the few, short hours of bliss she owed to her husband, and she always pictured him to herself as he had
been when they were betrothed, and when she had
adored him in the only moments of sensual passion of
her life. She forgot all his faults and harshness; even
his infidelity seemed more pardonable now that death
stood between him and her. She felt a sort of vague
gratitude to this man who had clasped her in his arms,
and she forgave him the sorrows he had caused her,
and dwelt only on the happy moments they had passed
together.

As time wore on and month followed month, covering her grief and memories with the dust of forgetful-
ness, Jeanne devoted herself entirely to her son. The
child became the idol, the one engrossing thought, of
the three beings over whom he ruled like any despot;
there was even a sort of jealousy between his three
slaves, for Jeanne grudged the hearty kisses he gave the
baron when the latter rode him on his knees, and Aunt
Lison, who was neglected by this baby, as she had always been by everyone, and was regarded as a servant
by this master who could not talk yet, would go to her
room and cry as she compared the few kisses, which she
had so much difficulty in obtaining, with the embraces
the child so freely lavished on his mother and grandfather.

Two peaceful, uneventful years were passed thus in
devoted attention to the child; then, at the beginning
of the third winter, it was arranged that they should

all go to Rouen until the spring. But they had hardly
arrived at the damp, old house before Paul had such a
severe attack of bronchitis, that pleurisy was feared.
His distracted mother was convinced that no other air
but that of Les Peuples agreed with him, and they all
went back there as soon as he was well.

Then came a series of quiet, monotonous years.
Jeanne, her father, and Aunt Lison spent all their time
with the child, and were continually going into raptures
over the way he lisped, or with his funny sayings and
doings. Jeanne lovingly called him " Paulet," and,
when he tried to repeat the word, he made them all
laugh by pronouncing it " Poulet," for he could not
speak plainly. The nickname " Poulet " clung to him,
and henceforth, he was never called anything else. He
grew very quickly, and one of the chief amusements of
his " three mothers," as the baron called them, was to
measure his height. On the wainscoting, by the drawing-room door, was a series of marks made with a penknife, showing how much the boy had grown every
month, and these marks, which were called " Poulet's
ladder," were of great importance in everyone's eyes.

Then there came a very unexpected addition to the
important personages of the household — the dog Massacre, which Jeanne had neglected since all her attention had been centered in her son. Ludivine fed him,
and he lived quite alone, and always on the chain, in an
old barrel in front of the stables. Paul noticed him
one morning, and at once wanted to go and kiss him.
The dog made a great fuss over the child, who cried
when he was taken away, so Massacre was unchained,
and henceforth lived in the house. He became Paul's
inseparable friend and companion; they played to-

gether, and lay down side by side on the carpet to go to
sleep, and soon Massacre shared the bed of his playfel-
low, who would not let the dog leave him.   Jeanne
lamented sometimes over the fleas, and Aunt Lison felt
angry with the dog for absorbing so much of the child's
affection, affection for which she longed, and which, it
seemed to her, this animal had stolen.

At long intervals visits were exchanged with the
Brisevilles and the Couteliers, but the mayor and the
doctor were the only regular visitors at the château.

The brutal way in which the priest had killed the
dog, and the suspicions he had instilled into her mind
about the time of Julien's and Gilberte's horrible death,
had roused Jeanne's indignation against the God who
could have such ministers, and she had entirely ceased
to attend church.   From time to time the abbé in-
veighed in outspoken terms against the château, which,
he said, was inhabited by the Spirit of Evil, the Spirit
of Everlasting Rebellion, the Spirit of Errors and of
Lies, the Spirit of Iniquity, the Spirit of Corruption
and Impurity; it was by all these names that he alluded
to the baron.

The church was deserted, and when the curé happened to walk past any fields in which the ploughmen
were at work, the men never ceased their task to speak
to him, or turned to touch their hats.   He acquired the
reputation of being a wizard because he cast out the
devil from a woman who was possessed, and the peasants believed he knew words to dispel charms.   He laid
his hands on cows that gave thin milk, discovered the
whereabouts of things which had been lost by means of
a mysterious incantation, and devoted his narrow mind
to the study of all the ecclesiastical books in which he

could find accounts of the devil's apparitions upon earth, or descriptions of his resources and stratagems, and the various ways in which he manifested his power and exercised his influence.

Believing himself specially called to combat this invisible, harmful Power, the priest had learnt all the forms given in religious manuals to exorcise the devil. He fancied Satan lurked in every shadow, and the phrase *Sicut leo rugiens circuit, quærens quem devoret* was continually on his lips. People began to be afraid of his strange power; even his fellow-clergy (ignorant country priests to whom Beelzebub was an article of their faith, and who, perplexed by the minute directions for the rites to be observed in case of any manifestations of the Evil One's power, at last confounded religion with magic) regarded the Abbé Tolbiac as somewhat of a wizard, and respected him as much for the supernatural power he was supposed to possess as for the irreproachable austerity of his life.

The curé never bowed to Jeanne if he chanced to meet her, and such a state of things worried and grieved Aunt Lison, who could not understand how anyone could systematically stay away from church. Everyone took it for granted that she was religious and confessed and communicated at proper intervals, and no one ever tried to find out what her views on religion really were. Whenever she was quite alone with Paul, Lison talked to him, in whispers, about the good God. The child listened to her with a faint degree of interest when she related the miracles which had been performed in the old times, and, when she told him he must love the good God, very, very dearly, he sometimes asked:

" Where is he, auntie? "

She would point upwards and answer: " Up there,
above the sky, Poulet; but you must not say anything
about it," for she feared the baron would be angry if
he knew what she was teaching the boy. One day,
however, Poulet startled her by asserting: " The good
God is everywhere except in church," and she found he
had been talking to his grandfather about what she had
told him.

Paul was now ten years old; his mother looked forty.
He was strong, noisy, and boldly climbed the trees, but
his education had, so far, been very neglected. He disliked lessons, would never settle down to them, and, if
ever the baron managed to keep him reading a little
longer than usual, Jeanne would interfere, saying:

" Let him go and play, now. He is so young to be
tired with books."

In her eyes he was ·still an infant, and she hardly
noticed that he walked, ran, and talked like a man in
miniature. She lived in constant anxiety lest he should
fall down, or get too cold or too hot, or overload his
stomach, or not eat as much as his growth demanded.

When the boy was twelve years old a great difficulty
arose about his first communion. Lise went to Jeanne's
room one morning, and pointed out to her that the child
could not be permitted to go any longer without religious instruction, and without performing the simplest
sacred duties. She called every argument to her aid,
and gave a thousand reasons for the necessity of what
she was urging, dwelling chiefly upon the danger of
scandal. The idea worried Jeanne, and, unable to give
a decided answer, she replied that Paul could very well
go on as he was for a little longer. A month after this

discussion with Lise, Jeanne called on the Vicomtesse de Briseville.

"I suppose it will be Paul's first communion this year," said the vicomtesse, in the course of conversation.

"Yes, madame," answered Jeanne, taken unawares.

These few words had the effect of deciding her, and, without saying anything about it to her father, she asked Lise to take the child to the catechism class. Everything went on smoothly for a month; then Poulet came back, one evening, with a sore throat, and the next day he began to cough. His frightened mother questioned him as to the cause of his cold and he told her that he had not behaved very well in class, so the curé had sent him to wait at the door of the church, where there was a draught from the porch, until the end of the lesson. After that Jeanne kept him at home, and taught him his catechism herself; but the Abbé Tolbiac refused to admit him to communion, in spite of all Lison's entreaties, alleging, as his reason, that the boy had not been properly prepared.

The following year he refused him again, and the baron was so exasperated that he said plainly there was no need for Paul to believe in such foolery as this absurd symbol of transubstantiation, to become a good and honest man. So it was resolved to bring the boy up in the Christian faith, but not in the Catholic Church, and that he should decide his religion for himself when he reached his majority.

A short time afterwards, Jeanne called on the Brisevilles and received no visit in return. Knowing how punctilious they were in all matters of etiquette, she felt very much surprised at the omission, until the Marquise

de Coutelier haughtily told her the reason of this neglect. Aware that her husband's rank and wealth made
her the queen of the Normandy aristocracy, the marquise ruled in queen-like fashion, showing herself gracious or severe as occasions demanded. She never hesitated to speak as she thought, and reproved, or con-
gratulated, or corrected whenever she thought fit.
When Jeanne called on her she addressed a few icy
words to her visitor, then said in a cold tone: " Society divides itself naturally into two classes: those who
believe in God, and those who do not. The former,
however lowly they may be, are our friends and equals;
with the latter we can have nothing to do."

Jeanne felt that she was being attacked, and replied:
" But cannot one believe in God without constantly
attending church ? "

" No, madame. Believers go to pray to God in his
church, as they would go to visit their friends at their
houses."

" God is everywhere, madame, and not only in the
churches," answered Jeanne, feeling very hurt. " I
believe in his goodness and mercy from the bottom of
my heart, but when there are certain priests between him
and me, I can no longer realize his presence."

" The priest is the standard-bearer of the church,
madame," said the marquise, rising, " and, whoever
does not follow that flag is as much our enemy as the
church's."

Jeanne had risen also. " You believe in the God
of a sect, madame," she replied, quivering with indignation. " *I* believe in the God whom every upright man
reveres," and, with a bow, she left the marquise.

Among themselves the peasants also blamed Jeanne

for not sending Poulet to his first communion. They themselves did not go to mass, and never took the sacrament, or at least, only at Easter when the Church formally commanded it; but when it came to the children, that was a different matter, and not one of them would have dared to bring a child up outside the common faith, for, after all, " Religion is Religion."

Jeanne was quite conscious of the disapproval with which everyone regarded her conduct, but such inconsistency only roused her indignation, and she scorned the people who could thus quiet their consciences so easily, and hide the cowardly fears which lurked at the bottom of their hearts under the mask of righteousness.

The baron undertook to direct Paul's studies, and began to instruct him in Latin. The boy's mother had but one word to say on the subject, " Whatever you do, don't tire him," and, while lessons were going on, she would anxiously hang round the door of the schoolroom, which her father had forbidden her to enter, because, at every moment, she interrupted his teaching to ask: " You're sure your feet are not cold, Poulet? " or " Your head does not ache, does it, Poulet? " or to admonish the master with: " Don't make him talk so much, he will have a sore throat."

As soon as lessons were over the boy went into the garden with his mother and aunt. They were all three very fond of gardening, and took great pleasure and interest in planting and pruning, in watching the seeds they had sown come up and blossom, and in cutting flowers for nosegays. Paul devoted himself chiefly to raising salad plants. He had the entire care of four big beds in the kitchen garden, and there he cultivated lettuce, endive, cos-lettuce, mustardcress, and every other known kind of salad. He dug, watered, weeded, and planted, and made his two mothers work like day laborers, and for hours together they knelt on the borders, soiling their hands and dresses as they planted the seedlings in the holes they made with their forefingers in the mold.

Poulet was almost fifteen; he had grown wonderfully, and the highest mark on the drawing-room wall was over five feet from the ground, but in mind he was still an ignorant, foolish child, for he had no opportunity of expanding his intellect, confined as he was to the society of these two women and the good-tempered old man who was so far behind the times. At last one evening the baron said it was time for the boy to go to college. Aunt Lison withdrew into a dark corner in horror at the idea, and Jeanne began to sob.

"Why does he want to know so much?" she replied. "We will bring him up to be a gentleman farmer, to devote himself to the cultivation of his property, as so many noblemen do, and he will pass his life happily in this house, where we have lived before him and where we shall die. What more can he want?"

The baron shook his head.

"What answer will you make if he comes to you a few years hence, and says: 'I am nothing, and I know nothing through your selfish love. I feel incapable of working or of becoming anyone now, and yet I know I was not intended to lead the dull, pleasureless life to which your short-sighted affection has condemned me.'"

Jeanne turned to her son with the tears rolling down her cheeks.

"Oh, Poulet, you will never reproach me for having loved you too much, will you?"

" No, mamma," promise'd the boy in surprise.

" You swear you will not? "

" Yes, mamma."

" You want to stay here, don't you? "

" Yes, mamma."

" Jeanne, you have no right to dispose of his life in that way," said the baron, sternly. " Such conduct is cowardly — almost criminal. You are sacrificing your child to your own personal happiness."

Jeanne hid her face in her hands, while her sobs came in quick succession.

" I have been so unhappy — so unhappy," she murmured, through her tears. " And now my son has brought peace and rest into my life, you want to take him from me. What will become of me — if I am left — all alone now? "

Her father went and sat down by her side. " And am I no one, Jeanne? " he asked, taking her in his arms. She threw her arms round his neck, and kissed him fondly. Then in a voice still choked with tears and sobs:

" Yes, perhaps you are right papa, dear," she answered; " and I was foolish; but I have had so much sorrow. I am quite willing for him to go to college now."

Then Poulet, who hardly understood what was going to be done with him, began to cry too, and his three mothers kissed and coaxed him and told him to be brave. They all went up to bed with heavy hearts, and even the baron wept when he was alone in his own room, though he had controlled his emotion downstairs. It was resolved to send Paul to the college at Havre at the beginning of the next term, and during the summer he was more spoilt than ever.  His mother moaned as she thought of the approaching separation and she got ready as many clothes for the boy as if he had been about to start on a ten years' journey.

One October morning, after a sleepless night, the baron, Jeanne, and Aunt Lison went away with Poulet in the landau.  They had already paid a visit to fix upon the bed he was to have in the dormitory and the seat he was to occupy in class, and this time Jeanne and Aunt Lison passed the whole day in unpacking his things and arranging them in the little chest of drawers.  As the latter would not contain the quarter of what she had brought, Jeanne went to the head master to ask if the boy could not have another.  The steward was sent for, and he said that so much linen and so many clothes were simply in the way, instead of being of any use, and that the rules of the house forbade him to allow another chest of drawers, so Jeanne made up her mind to hire a room in a little hotel close by, and to ask the landlord himself to take Poulet all he wanted, directly the child found himself in need of anything.

They all went on the pier for the rest of the afternoon and watched the ships entering and leaving the harbor; then, at nightfall, they went to a restaurant for dinner.  But they were too unhappy to eat, and the dishes were placed before them and removed almost untouched as they sat looking at each other with tearful eyes.  After dinner they walked slowly back to the college.  Boys of all ages were arriving on every side, some accompanied by their parents, others by servants. A great many were crying, and the big, dim courtyard was filled with the sound of tears.

When the time came to say good-bye, Jeanne and

Poulet clung to each other as if they could not part,
while Aunt Lison stood, quite forgotten, in the background, with her face buried in her handkerchief. The
baron felt he too was giving way, so he hastened the
farewells, and took his daughter from the college. The
landau was waiting at the door, and they drove back to
Les Peuples in a silence that was only broken by an occasional sob.

Jeanne wept the whole of the following day, and the
next she ordered the phaeton and drove over to Havre.
Poulet seemed to have got over the separation already;
it was the first time he had ever had any companions of
his own age, and, as he sat beside his mother, he fidgeted
on his chair and longed to run out and play. Every
other day Jeanne went to see him, and on Sundays took
him out. She felt as though she had not energy enough
to leave the college between the recreation hours, so she
waited in the *parloir* while the classes were going on
until Poulet could come to her again. At last the head
master asked her to go up and see him, and begged her
not to come so often. She did not take any notice of
his request, and he warned her that if she still persisted
in preventing her son from enjoying his play hours, and
in interrupting his work, he would be obliged to dismiss
him from the college. He also sent a note to the baron,
to the same effect, and thenceforth Jeanne was always
kept in sight at Les Peuples, like a prisoner. She lived
in a constant state of nervous anxiety, and looked forward to the holidays with more impatience than her
son. She began to take long walks about the country,
with Massacre as her only companion, and would stay
out of doors all day long, dreamily musing. Sometimes she sat on the cliff the whole afternoon watching

the sea; sometimes she walked, across the wood, to Yport, thinking, as she went, of how she had walked there when she was young, and of the long, long years which had elapsed since she had bounded along these very paths, a hopeful, happy girl.

Every time she saw her son, it seemed to Jeanne as if ten years had passed since she had seen him last; for every month he became more of a man, and every month she became more aged. Her father looked like her brother, and Aunt Lison (who had been quite faded when she was twenty-five, and had never seemed to get older since) might have been taken for her elder sister.

Poulet did not study very hard; he spent two years in the fourth form, managed to get through the third in one twelvemonth, then spent two more in the second, and was nearly twenty when he reached the rhetoric class. He had grown into a tall, fair youth, with whiskered cheeks and a budding moustache. He came over to Les Peuples every Sunday now, instead of his mother going to see him; and as he had been taking riding lessons for some time past, he hired a horse and accomplished the journey from Havre in two hours.

Every Sunday Jeanne started out early in the morning to go and meet him on the road, and with her went Aunt Lison and the baron, who was beginning to stoop, and who walked like a little old man, with his hands clasped behind his back as if to prevent himself from pitching forward on his face. The three walked slowly along, sometimes sitting down by the wayside to rest, and all the while straining their eyes to catch the first glimpse of the rider. As soon as he appeared, looking like a black speck on the white road, they waved their handkerchiefs, and he at once put his horse at a gallop,

and came up like a whirlwind, frightening his mother
and Aunt Lison, and making his grandfather exclaim,
" Bravo ! " in the admiration of impotent old age.

Although Paul was a head taller than his mother, she
always treated him as if he were a child and still asked
him, as in former years, " Your feet are not cold, are
they, Poulet ? " If he went out of doors, after lunch,
to smoke a cigarette, she opened the window to cry:
" Oh, don't go out without a hat, you will catch cold
in your head "; and when, at night, he mounted his
horse to return, she could hardly contain herself for
nervousness, and entreated her son not to be reckless.

" Do not ride too quickly, Poulet, dear," she would
say. " Think of your poor mother, who would go mad
if anything happened to you, and be careful."

One Saturday morning she received a letter from
Paul to say he should not come to Les Peuples as usual,
the following day, as he had been invited to a party
some of his college friends had got up. The whole of
Sunday Jeanne was tortured by a presentiment of evil,
and when Thursday came, she was unable to bear her
suspense any longer, and went over to Havre.

Paul seemed changed, though she could hardly tell
in what way. He seemed more spirited, and his words
and tones were more manly.

" By the way, mamma, we are going on another excursion and I sha'n't come to Les Peuples next Sunday,
as you have come to see me to-day," he said, all at once,
as if it were the most natural thing in the world.

Jeanne felt as much surprised and stunned as if he
had told her he was going to America; then, when she
was again able to speak :

"Oh, Poulet," she exclaimed, "what is the matter with you? Tell me what is going on."

He laughed and gave her a kiss.

"Why, nothing at all, mamma. I am only going to enjoy myself with some friends, as everyone does at my age."

She made no reply, but when she was alone in the carriage, her head was filled with new and strange ideas. She had not recognized her Poulet, her little Poulet, as of old; she perceived for the first time that he was grown up, that he was no longer hers, that henceforth he was going to live his own life, independently of the old people. To her he seemed to have changed entirely in a day. What! Was this strong, bearded, firm-willed lad her son, her little child who used to make her help him plant his lettuces?

Paul only came to Les Peuples at very long intervals for the next three months, and even when he was there, it was only too plain that he longed to get away again as soon as possible, and that, each evening, he tried to leave an hour earlier. Jeanne imagined all sorts of things, while the baron tried to console her by saying: "There, let him alone, the boy is twenty years old, you know."

One morning, a shabbily dressed old man who spoke with a German accent asked for "Matame la vicom-tesse." He was shown in, and, after a great many ceremonious bows, pulled out a dirty pocketbook, saying:

"I have a leetle paper for you," and then unfolded, and held out a greasy scrap of paper.

Jeanne read it over twice, looked at the Jew, read it over again, then asked:

"What does it mean?"

"I vill tell you," replied the man obsequiously. "Your son wanted a leetle money, and, as I know what a goot mother you are, I lent him joost a leetle to go on vith."

Jeanne was trembling. "But why did he not come to me for it?"

The Jew entered into a long explanation about a gambling debt which had had to be paid on a certain morning before midday, that no one would lend Paul anything as he was not yet of age, and that his "honor would have been compromised," if he, the Jew, had not "rendered this little service" to the young man. Jeanne wanted to send for the baron, but her emotion seemed to have taken all the strength from her limbs, and she could not rise from her seat.

"Would you be kind enough to ring?" she said to the money-lender, at last.

He feared some trick, and hesitated for a moment.

"If I inconvenience you, I vill call again," he stammered.

She answered him by a shake of the head, and when he had rung they waited in silence for the baron. The latter at once understood it all. The bill was for fifteen hundred francs. He paid the Jew a thousand, saying to him:

"Don't let me see you here again," and the man thanked him, bowed, and went away.

Jeanne and the baron at once went over to Havre, but when they arrived at the college they learnt that Paul had not been there for a month. The principal had received four letters, apparently from Jeanne, the first telling him that his pupil was ill, the others to say how he was getting on, and each letter was accompanied by a doctor's certificate; of course they were all forged. Jeanne and her father looked at each other in dismay when they heard this news, and the principal feeling very sorry for them took them to a magistrate that the police might be set to find the young man.

Jeanne and the baron slept at an hotel that night, and the next day Paul was discovered at the house of a fast woman. His mother and grandfather took him back with them to Les Peuples and the whole of the way not a word was exchanged. Jeanne hid her face in her handkerchief and cried, and Paul looked out of the window with an air of indifference.

Before the end of the week they found out that, during the last three months, Paul had contracted debts to the amount of fifteen thousand francs, but the creditors had not gone to his relations about the money, because they knew the boy would soon be of age. Poulet was asked for no explanation and received no reproof, as his relations hoped to reform him by kindness. He was pampered and caressed in every way; the choicest dishes were prepared for him, and, as it was spring-time, a boat was hired for him at Yport, in spite of Jeanne's nervousness, that he might go sailing whenever he liked; the only thing that was denied him was a horse, for fear he should ride to Havre. He became very irritable and passionate and lived a perfectly aimless life. The baron grieved over his neglected studies, and even Jeanne, much as she dreaded to be parted from him again, began to wonder what was to be done with him.

One evening he did not come home. It was found, on inquiry, that he had gone out in a boat with two sailors, and his distracted mother hurried down to Yport, without stopping even to put anything over her head. On the beach she found a few men awaiting the return of the boat, and out on the sea was a little swaying light, which was drawing nearer and nearer to the shore. The boat came in, but Paul was not on board; he had ordered the men to take him to Havre, and had landed there.

The police sought him in vain; he was nowhere to be found, and the woman who had hidden him once before had sold all her furniture, paid her rent, and disappeared also, without leaving any trace behind her. In Paul's room at Les Peuples two letters were found from this creature (who seemed madly in love with him) saying that she had obtained the necessary money for a journey to England. The three inmates of the château lived on, gloomy and despairing, through all this mental torture. Jeanne's hair, which had been gray before, was now quite white, and she sometimes asked herself what she could have done, that Fate should so mercilessly pursue her. One day she received the following letter from the Abbé Tolbiac:

" MADAME: The hand of God has been laid heavily upon you. You refused to give your son to him, and he has delivered him over to a prostitute; will you not profit by this lesson from heaven? God's mercy is infinite, and perhaps he will pardon you if you throw yourself at his feet. I am his humble servant, and I will open his door to you when you come and knock."

Jeanne sat for a long time with this letter lying open on her knees. Perhaps, after all, the priest's words were true; and all her religious doubts and uncertainties returned to harass her mind. Was it possible that God could be vindictive and jealous like men? But if he was not jealous, he would no longer be feared and loved, and, no doubt, it was that we might the better know him, that he manifested himself to men, as influenced by the same feeling as themselves. Then she felt the fear, the cowardly dread, which urges those who hesitate and doubt to seek the safety of the Church, and one evening, when it was dark, she stealthily ran to the vicarage, and knelt at the foot of the fragile-looking priest to solicit absolution. He only promised her a semi-pardon, as God could not shower all his favors on a house which sheltered such a man as the baron. "Still, you will soon receive a proof of the divine mercy," said the priest.

Two days later, Jeanne did indeed receive a letter from her son, and in the excess of her grief, she looked upon it as the forerunner of the consolation promised by the abbé. The letter ran thus:

"MY DEAR MOTHER: Do not be uneasy about me. I am at London, and in good health, but in great need of money. We have not a sou, and some days we have to go without anything to eat. She who is with me, and whom I love with all my heart, has spent all she had (some five thousand francs that she might remain with me, and you will, of course, understand that I am bound in honor to discharge my debt to her at the very first opportunity. I shall soon be of age, but it would be very good of you if you would advance me fifteen thousand francs of what I inherit from papa; it would relieve me from great embarrassments.

" Good-bye, mother dear; I hope soon to see you again, but in the meantime, I send much love to grand-father, Aunt Lison and yourself.   Your son,

" VICOMTE PAUL DE LAMARE."

Then he had not forgotten her, for he had written to her!   She did not stop to think that it was simply to ask her for money; he had not any and some should be sent him; what did money matter?   He had writ-ten to her!

She ran to show the letter to the baron, the tears streaming from her eyes.   Aunt Lison was called, and, word by word, they read over this letter which spoke of their loved one, and lingered over every sentence. Jeanne, transported from the deepest despair to a kind of intoxication of joy, began to take Paul's part.

" Now he has written, he will come back," she said. " I am sure he will come back."

" Still he left us for this creature," said the baron, who was calm enough to reason; " and he must love her better than he does us, since he did not hesitate in his choice between her and his home."

The words sent a pang of anguish through Jeanne's heart, and within her sprang up the fierce, deadly hatred of a jealous mother against the woman who had robbed her of her son.   Until then her every thought had been for Paul, and she had hardly realized that this creature was the cause of all his errors; but the baron's argu-ment had suddenly brought this rival who possessed such fatal influence vividly to her mind, and she felt that between this woman and herself there must be a determined, bitter warfare.   With that thought came

another one as terrible — that she would rather lose
her son than share him with this other; and all her joy
and delight vanished.

The fifteen thousand francs were sent, and for five
months nothing more was heard of Paul. At the end
of that time a lawyer came to the château to see about
his inheritance. Jeanne and the baron acceded to all
his demands without any dispute, even giving up the
money to which the mother had a right for her lifetime,
and when he returned to Paris, Paul found himself the
possessor of a hundred and twenty thousand francs.
During the next six months only four short letters were
received from him, giving news of his doings in a few,
concise sentences, and ending with formal protestations
of affection.

" I am not idle," he said. " I have obtained a post
in connection with the Stock Exchange, and I hope some
day to see my dear relations at Les Peuples."

He never mentioned his mistress, but his silence was
more significant than if he had written four pages about
her; and, in these icy letters, Jeanne could perceive the
influence of this unknown woman who was, by instinct,
the implacable enemy of every mother.

Ponder as they would, the three lonely beings at the
château could think of no means by which they might
rescue Paul from his present life. They would have
gone to Paris, but they knew that would be no good.

" We must let his passion wear itself out," said the
baron; " sooner or later he will return to us of his own
accord." And the mournful days dragged on.

Jeanne and Lison got into the habit of going to
church together without letting the baron know; and a
long time passed without any news from Paul. Then,

one morning they received a desperate letter which terrified them.

"MY DEAR MOTHER: I am lost; I shall have no resource left but to blow out my brains if you do not help me. A speculation which held out every hope of success has turned the wrong way, and I owe eighty-five thousand francs. It means dishonor, ruin, the destruction of all my future if I do not pay, and, I say again, rather than survive the disgrace, I will blow my brains out. I should, perhaps, have done so already, had it not been for the brave and hopeful words of a woman, whose name I never mention to you, but who is the good genius of my life.

"I send you my very best love, dear mother. Goodbye, perhaps for ever.

"PAUL."

Enclosed in the letter was a bundle of business papers giving the details of this unfortunate speculation. The baron answered by return post that they would help as much as they could. Then he went to Havre to get legal advice, mortgaged some property and forwarded the money to Paul. The young man wrote back three letters full of hearty thanks, and said they might expect him almost immediately. But he did not come, and another year passed away.

Jeanne and the baron were on the point of starting for Paris, to find him and make one last effort to persuade him to return, when they received a few lines saying he was again in London, starting a steamboat company which was to trade under the name of " Paul Delamare & Co." "I am sure to get a living out of it," he wrote, " and perhaps it will make my fortune. At any rate I risk nothing, and you must at once see the advantages of the scheme.   When I see you again, I shall be well up in the world; there is nothing like trade for making money, nowadays."

Three months later, the company went into liquidation, and the manager was prosecuted for falsifying the books.   When the news reached Les Peuples, Jeanne had a hysterical fit which lasted several hours.   The baron went to Havre, made every inquiry, saw lawyers and attorneys, and found that the Delamare Company had failed for two hundred and fifty thousand francs. He again mortgaged his property, and borrowed a large sum on Les Peuples and the two adjoining farms.   One evening he was going through some final formalities in a lawyer's office, when he suddenly fell to the ground in an apoplectic fit.   A mounted messenger was at once dispatched to Jeanne, but her father died before she could arrive.   The shock was so great that it seemed to stun Jeanne and she could not realize her loss.   The body was taken back to Les Peuples, but the Abbé Tolbiac refused to allow it to be interred with any sacred rites, in spite of all the entreaties of the two women, so the burial took place at night without any ceremony whatever.   Then Jeanne fell into a state of such utter depression that she took no interest in anything, and seemed unable to comprehend the simplest things.

Paul, who was still in hiding in England, heard of his grandfather's death through the liquidators of the company, and wrote to say he should have come before, but he had only just heard the sad news.   He concluded: " Now you have rescued me from my difficulties, mother dear, I shall return to France, and shall at once come to see you."

Towards the end of that winter Aunt Lison, who was now sixty-eight, had a severe attack of bronchitis. It turned to inflammation of the lungs, and the old maid quietly expired.

" I will ask the good God to take pity on you, my poor little Jeanne," were the last words she uttered.

Jeanne followed her to the grave, saw the earth fall on the coffin, and then sank to the ground, longing for death to take her also that she might cease to think and to suffer. As she fell a big, strong peasant woman caught her in her arms and carried her away as if she had been a child; she took her back to the château, and Jeanne let herself be put to bed by this stranger, who handled her so tenderly and firmly, and at once fell asleep, for she had spent the last five nights watching beside the old maid, and she was thoroughly exhausted by sorrow and fatigue. It was the middle of the night when she again opened her eyes. A night-lamp was burning on the mantelpiece, and, in the armchair, lay a woman asleep. Jeanne did not know who it was, and, leaning over the side of the bed, she tried to make out her features by the glimmering light of the night-lamp. She fancied she had seen this face before, but she could not remember when or where.

The woman was quietly sleeping, her head drooping on one shoulder, her cap lying on the ground and her big hands hanging on each side of the armchair. She was a strong, square-built peasant of about forty or forty-five, with a red face and hair that was turning gray. Jeanne was sure she had seen her before, but she had not the least idea whether it was a long time ago or quite recently, and it worried her to find she could not remember. She softly got out of bed, and went on tiptoe to see the sleeping woman nearer. She recognized her as the peasant who had caught her in her arms in the cemetery, and had afterwards put her to bed; but surely she had known her in former times, under other circumstances. And yet perhaps the face was only familiar to her because she had seen it that day in the cemetery. Still how was it that the woman was sleeping here?

Just then the stranger opened her eyes and saw Jeanne standing beside her. She started up, and they stood face to face, so close together that they touched each other.

" How is it that you're out of bed? " said the peasant; " you'll make yourself ill, getting up at this time of night. Go back to bed again."

" Who are you? " asked Jeanne.

The woman made no answer, but picked Jeanne up and carried her back to bed as easily as if she had been a baby. She gently laid her down, and, as she bent over her, she suddenly began to cover her cheeks, her hair, her eyes with violent kisses, while the tears streamed from her eyes.

" My poor mistress! Mam'zelle Jeanne, my poor mistress! Don't you know me? " she sobbed.

" Rosalie, my lass! " cried Jeanne, throwing her arms round the woman's neck and kissing her; and, clasped in each other's arms they mingled their tears and sobs together.

Rosalie dried her eyes the first. " Come now," she said, " you must be good and not catch cold."

She picked up the clothes, tucked up the bed and put the pillow back under the head of her former mistress, who lay choking with emotion as the memories of days that were past and gone rushed back to her mind.

" How is it you have come back, my poor girl? " she asked.

" Do you think I was going to leave you to live all alone now? " answered Rosalie.

" Light a candle and let me look at you," went on Jeanne.

Rosalie placed a light on the table by the bedside, and for a long time they gazed at each other in silence.

" I should never have known you again," murmured Jeanne, holding out her hand to her old servant. " You have altered very much, though not so much as I have."

" Yes, you have changed, Madame Jeanne, and more than you ought to have done," answered Rosalie, as she looked at this thin, faded, white-haired woman, whom she had left young and beautiful; " but you must remember it's twenty-four years since we have seen one another."

" Well, have you been happy? " asked Jeanne after a long pause.

" Oh, yes — yes, madame. I haven't had much to grumble at; I've been happier than you — that's certain. The only thing that I've always regretted is that I didn't stop here —" She broke off abruptly, finding she had unthinkingly touched upon the very subject she wished to avoid.

" Well, you know, Rosalie, one cannot have everything one wants," replied Jeanne gently; " and now you too are a widow, are you not? " Then her voice trem-

V—15·

bled, as she went on, " Have you any — any other children? "

" No, madame."

" And what is your — your son?   Are you satisfied with him? "

" Yes, madame; he's a good lad, and a hard-working one.   He married about six months ago, and he is going to have the farm now I have come back to you."

" Then you will not leave me again? " murmured Jeanne.

" No fear, madame," answered Rosalie in a rough tone.   " I've arranged all about that."

And for some time nothing more was said.

Jeanne could not help comparing Rosalie's life with her own, but she had become quite resigned to the cruelty and injustice of Fate, and she felt no bitterness as she thought of the difference between her maid's peaceful existence and her own.

" Was your husband kind to you? "

" Oh, yes, madame; he was a good, industrious fellow, and managed to put by a good deal.   He died of consumption."

Jeanne sat up in bed.   " Tell me all about your life, and everything that has happened to you," she said. " I feel as if it would do me good to hear it."

Rosalie drew up a chair, sat down, and began to talk about herself, her house, her friends, entering into all the little details in which country people delight, laughing sometimes over things which made her think of the happy times that were over, and gradually raising her voice as she went on, like a woman accustomed to command, she wound up by saying:

" Oh, I'm well off now; I needn't be afraid of anything. But I owe it all to you," she added in a lower, faltering voice; " and now I've come back I'm not going to take any wages. No! I won't! So, if you don't choose to have me on those terms, I shall go away again."

" But you do not mean to serve me for nothing? " said Jeanne.

" Yes, I do, madame. Money! You give me money! Why, I've almost as much as you have yourself. Do you know how much you will have after all these loans and mortgages have been cleared off, and you have paid all the interest you have let run on and increase? You don't know, do you? Well, then, let me tell you that you haven't ten thousand livres a year; not ten thousand. But I'm going to put everything straight, and pretty soon, too."

She had again raised her voice, for the thought of the ruin which hung over the house, and the way in which the interest money had been neglected and allowed to accumulate roused her anger and indignation. A faint, sad smile which passed over her mistress's face angered her still more, and she cried:

" You ought not to laugh at it, madame. People are good for nothing without money."

Jeanne took both the servant's hands in hers.

" I have never had any luck," she said slowly, as if she could think of nothing else. " Everything has gone the wrong way with me. My whole life has been ruined by a cruel Fate."

" You must not talk like that, madame," said Rosalie, shaking her head. " You made an unhappy marriage, that's all. But people oughtn't to marry before they know anything about their future husbands."

They went on talking about themselves and their past loves like two old friends, and when the day dawned they had not yet told all they had to say.

## XII

In less than a week Rosalie had everything and everybody in the château under her control, and even Jeanne yielded a passive obedience to the servant, who scolded her or soothed her as if she had been a sick child. She was very weak now, and her legs dragged along as the baroness's used to do; the maid supported her when she went out and their conversation was always about bygone times, of which Jeanne talked with tears in her eyes, and Rosalie in the calm quiet way of an impassive peasant.

The old servant returned several times to the question of the interest that was owing, and demanded the papers which Jeanne, ignorant of all business matters, had hidden away that Rosalie might not know of Paul's misdoings. Next Rosalie went over to Fécamp each day for a week to get everything explained to her by a lawyer whom she knew; then one evening after she had put her mistress to bed she sat down beside her and said abruptly:

" Now you're in bed, madame, we will have a little talk."

She told Jeanne exactly how matters stood, and that when every claim had been settled she, Jeanne, would have about seven or eight thousand francs a year; not a penny more.

" Well, Rosalie," answered Jeanne, " I know I shall

not live to be very old, and I shall have enough until
I die."

"Very likely you will, madame," replied Rosalie, getting angry; "but how about M. Paul? Don't you
mean to leave him anything?"

Jeanne shuddered. "Pray, don't ever speak to me
about him; I cannot bear to think of him."

"Yes, but I want to talk to you about him, because
you don't look at things in the right light, Madame
Jeanne. He may be doing all sorts of foolish things
now, but he won't always behave the same. He'll
marry and then he'll want money to educate his children and to bring them up properly. Now listen to
what I am going to say; you must sell Les Peuples —"

But Jeanne started up in bed.

"Sell Les Peuples! How can you think of such a
thing? No! I will never sell the château!"

Rosalie was not in the least put out.

"But I say you will, madame, simply because you
must."

Then she explained her plans and her calculations.
She had already found a purchaser for Les Peuples and
the two adjoining farms, and when they had been sold
Jeanne would still have four farms at Saint Léonard,
which, freed from the mortgages, would bring in about
eight thousand three hundred francs a year. Out of
this income thirteen hundred francs would have to go
for the keeping up and repairing of the property; two
thousand would be put by for unforeseen expenses, and
Jeanne would have five thousand francs to live upon.

"Everything else is gone, so there's an end of it,"
said Rosalie. "But, in future, I shall keep the money.

and M. Paul sha'n't have another penny off you.   He'd
take your last farthing."

"But if he has not anything to eat?" murmured
Jeanne, who was quietly weeping.

"He can come to us if he's hungry; there'll always
be victuals and a bed for him.   He'd never have got
into trouble if you hadn't given him any money the first
time he asked for some."

"But he was in debt; he would have been dishon-
ored."

"And don't you think he'll get into debt just the
same when you've no more money to give him?   You
have paid his debts up to now, so well and good; but
you won't pay any more, I can tell you.   And now,
good-night, madame."

And away she went.

The idea of selling Les Peuples and leaving the house
where she had passed all her life threw Jeanne into a
state of extreme agitation, and she lay awake the whole
night.   "I shall never be able to go away from here,"
she said, when Rosalie came into the room next morning.

"You'll have to, all the same, madame," answered
the maid with rising temper.   "The lawyer is coming
presently with the man who wants to buy the château,
and, if you don't sell it, you won't have a blade of
grass to call your own in four years' time."

"Oh, I cannot!   I cannot!" moaned Jeanne.

But an hour afterwards came a letter from Paul ask-
ing for ten thousand francs.   What was to be done?
Jeanne did not know, and, in her distress, she consulted
Rosalie, who shrugged her shoulders, and observed:

"What did I tell you, madame?   Oh, you'd both of

you have been in a nice muddle if I hadn't come back."

Then, by her advice, Jeanne wrote back:

" My Dear Son:   I cannot help you any more; you have ruined me, and I am even obliged to sell Les Peuples.   But I shall always have a home for you whenever you choose to return to your poor old mother, who has suffered so cruelly through you.          Jeanne."

The lawyer came with M. Jeoffrin, who was a retired sugar baker, and Jeanne herself received them, and invited them to go all over the house and grounds. Then a month after this visit, she signed the deed of sale, and bought, at the same time, a little villa in the hamlet of Batteville, standing on the Montivilliers highroad, near Goderville.

After she had signed the deeds she went out to the baroness's avenue, and walked up and down, heartbroken and miserable while she bade tearful, despairing farewells to the trees, the worm-eaten bench under the plane tree, the wood, the old elm trunk, against which she had leant so many times, and the hillock, where she had so often sat, and whence she had watched the Comte de Fourville running towards the sea on the awful day of Julien's death.   She stayed out until the evening, and at last Rosalie went to look for her and brought her in.   A tall peasant of about twenty-five was waiting at the door.   He greeted Jeanne in a friendly way, as if he had known her a long while:

" Good-day, Madame Jeanne, how are you?  Mother told me I was to come and help with the moving, and I wanted to know what you meant to take with you, so that I could move it a little at a time without it hindering the farm work."

He was Rosalie's son — Julien's son and Paul's brother. Jeanne's heart almost stood still as she looked at him, and yet she would have liked to kiss the young fellow. She gazed at him, trying to find any likeness to her husband or her son. He was robust and ruddy-cheeked and had his mother's fair hair and blue eyes, but there was something in his face which reminded Jeanne of Julien, though she could not discover where the resemblance lay.

" I should be very much obliged if you could show me the things now," continued the lad.

But she did not know herself yet what she should be able to take, her new house was so small, and she asked him to come again in a week's time.

For some time the removal occupied Jeanne's thoughts, and made a change, though a sad one, in her dull, hopeless life. She went from room to room, seeking the pieces of furniture which were associated in her mind with various events in her life, for the furniture among which we live becomes, in time, part of our lives — almost of ourselves — and, as it gets old, and we look at its faded colors, its frayed coverings, its tattered linings, we are reminded of the prominent dates and events of our existence by these time-worn objects which have been the mute companions of our happy and of our sad moments alike.

As agitated as if the decisions she were making had been of the last importance, Jeanne chose, one by one, the things she should take with her, often hesitating and altering her mind at every moment, as she stood unable to decide the respective merits of two armchairs, or of some old escritoire and a still older worktable. She opened and searched every drawer, and tried to con-

nect every object with something that had happened in
bygone days, and when at last she made up her mind
and said: " Yes, I shall take this," the article she had
decided upon was taken downstairs and put into the
dining-room.   She wished to keep the whole of her bedroom furniture, the bed, the tapestry, the clock — everything, and she also took a few of the drawing-room
chairs, choosing those with the designs she had always
liked ever since she could remember — the fox and the
stork, the fox and the crow, the ant and the grasshopper, and the solitary heron.

One day, as she was wandering all over this house
she should so soon have to leave, Jeanne went up into
the garret.   She was amazed when she opened the
door; there lay articles of furniture of every description,
some broken, others only soiled, others again stored
away simply because fresh things had been bought and
put in their places.   She recognized a hundred little
odds and ends which used to be downstairs and had disappeared without her noticing their absence — things of
no value which she had often used, insignificant little
articles, which had stood fifteen years beneath her eyes
and had never attracted her attention, but which now —
suddenly discovered in the lumber-room, lying side by
side with other things older still and which she could
quite distinctly remember seeing when she first returned
from the convent — became as precious in her eyes as
if they had been valued friends that had been a long
time absent from her.   They appeared to her under
a new light, and as she looked at them she felt as she
might have done if any very reserved acquaintances had
suddenly begun to talk and to reveal thoughts and feelings she had never dreamed they possessed.

As she went from one thing to another, and remembered little incidents in connection with them, her heart felt as if it would break. " Why, this is the china cup I cracked a few days before I was married, and here is mamma's little lantern, and the cane papa broke trying to open the wooden gate the rain had swollen."

Besides all these familiar objects there were a great many things she had never seen before, which had belonged to her grandparents or her great-grandparents. Covered with dust they looked like sad, forsaken exiles from another century, their history and adventures for ever lost, for there was no one living now who had known those who had chosen, bought and treasured them, or who had seen the hands which had so often touched them or the eyes which had found such pleasure in looking at them. Jeanne touched them, and turned them about, her fingers leaving their traces on the thick dust; and she stayed for a long, long time amidst these old things, in the garret which was dimly lighted by a little skylight.

She tried to find other things with associations to them, and very carefully she examined some three-legged chairs, a copper warming-pan, a dented foot-warmer (which she thought she remembered) and all the other worn-out household utensils. Then she put all the things she thought she should like to take away together, and going downstairs, sent Rosalie up to fetch them. The latter indignantly refused to bring down " such rubbish," but Jeanne, though she hardly ever showed any will of her own, now would have her own way this time, and the servant had to obey.

One morning young Denis Lecoq (Julien's son) came, with his cart, to take way the first lot of things, and Rosalie went off with him to look after the unloading, and to see that the furniture was put into the right rooms.

When she was alone Jeanne began to visit every room in the château, and to kiss in a transport of passionate sorrow and regret everything that she was forced to leave behind her — the big white birds in the drawing-room tapestry, the old candlesticks, anything and everything that came in her way. She went from room to room, half mad with grief, and the tears streaming from her eyes, and, when she had gone all over the house, she went out to " say good-bye " to the sea. It was the end of September, and the dull yellowish waves stretched away as far as the eye could reach, under the lowering gray sky which hung over the world. For a long, long while, Jeanne stood on the cliff, her thoughts running on all her sorrows and troubles, and it was not till night drew on that she went indoors. In that day she had gone through as much suffering as she had ever passed through in her greatest griefs.

Rosalie had returned enchanted with the new house, " which was much livelier than this big barn of a place that was not even on a main road," but her mistress wept the whole evening.

Now they knew the château was sold the farmers showed Jeanne barely the respect that was due to her, and, though they hardly knew why, among themselves they always spoke of her as " that lunatic." Perhaps, with their brute-like instinct, they perceived her unhealthy and increasing sentimentality, her morbid reveries, and the disordered and pitiful state of her mind which so much sorrow and affliction had unhinged.

Happening to go through the stables the day before

she was to leave Les Peuples, Jeanne came upon Massacre, whose existence she had entirely forgotten. Long past the age at which dogs generally die, he had become blind and paralyzed, and dragged out his life on a bed of straw, whither Ludivine, who never forgot him, brought him his food. Jeanne took him up in her arms, kissed him and carried him into the house; he could hardly creep along, his legs were so stiff, and he barked like a child's wooden toy-dog.

At length the last day dawned. Jeanne had passed the night in Julien's old room, as all the furniture had been moved out of hers, and when she rose she felt as tired and exhausted as if she had just been running a long distance.

In the court-yard stood the gig in which Rosalie and her mistress were to go, and a cart on which the remainder of the furniture and the trunks were already loaded. Ludivine and old Simon were to stay at the château until its new owner arrived, and then, too old to stay in service any longer, they were going to their friends to live on their savings and the pensions Jeanne had given them. Marius had married and left the château long ago.

About eight o'clock a fine, cold rain, which the wind drove in slanting lines, began to fall, and the furniture on the cart had to be covered over with tarpaulins. Some steaming cups of coffee stood on the kitchen-table, and Jeanne sat down and slowly drank hers up; then rising:

" Let us go," she said.

She began to put on her hat and shawl, while Rosalie put on her goloshes. A great lump rose in her throat, and she whispered:

" Rosalie, do you remember how it rained the day we left Rouen to come here? "

She broke off abruptly, pressed her hands to her heart, and fell backwards in a sort of fit. For more than an hour she lay as if she were dead, then, when she at length recovered consciousness, she went into violent hysterics. Gradually she became calmer, but this attack had left her so weak that she could not rise to her feet. Rosalie, fearing another attack if they did not get her away at once, went for her son, and between them, they carried her to the gig, and placed her on the leather-covered seat. Rosalie got up beside her, wrapped up her legs, threw a thick cloak over her shoulders, then, opening an umbrella over her head, cried:

" Make haste, and let's get off, Denis."

The young man climbed up by his mother, sat down with one leg right outside the gig, for want of room, and started off his horse at a quick jerky trot, which shook the two women from side to side. As they turned the corner of the village, they saw someone walking up and down the road; it was the Abbé Tolbiac, apparently waiting to see their departure. He was holding up his cassock with one hand to keep it out of the wet, regardless of showing his thin legs which were encased in black stockings, and his huge, muddy boots. When he saw the carriage coming he stopped, and stood on one side to let it pass. Jeanne looked down to avoid meeting his eyes, while Rosalie, who had heard all about him, furiously muttered: " You brute, you brute! " and seizing her son's hand, " Give him a cut with the whip! " she exclaimed. The young man did not do that, but he urged on his horse and then, just as they were passing the Abbé, suddenly let the wheel of the gig drop into a deep rut. There was a splash, and, in an instant, the priest was covered with mud from head to foot. Rosalie laughed all over her face, and turning round, she shook her fist at the abbé as he stood wiping himself down with his big handkerchief.

"Oh, we have forgotten Massacre!" suddenly cried Jeanne. Denis pulled up, gave Rosalie the reins to hold, and jumped down to run and fetch the dog. Then in a few minutes he came back with the big, shapeless animal in his arms and placed him in the gig between the two women.

## XIII

AFTER a two hours' drive the gig drew up before a little brick house, standing by the high road in the middle of an orchard planted with pear-trees. Four lattice-work arbors covered with honeysuckle and clematis stood at the four corners of the garden, which was planted with vegetables, and laid out in little beds with narrow paths bordered with fruit-trees running between them, and both garden and orchard were entirely surrounded by a thickset hedge which divided them from a field belonging to the next farm. About thirty yards lower down the road was a forge, and that was the only dwelling within a mile. All around lay fields and plains with farms scattered here and there, half-hidden by the four double rows of big trees which surrounded them.

Jeanne wanted to rest as soon as they arrived, but Rosalie, wishing to keep her from thinking, would not let her do so. The carpenter from Goderville had come to help them put the place in order, and they all began to arrange the furniture which was already there without waiting for the last cart-load which was coming on. The arrangement of the rooms took a long time, for everyone's ideas and opinions had to be consulted, and then the cart from Les Peuples arrived, and had to be unloaded in the rain. When night fell the house was in a state of utter disorder, and all the rooms were full of things piled anyhow one on top of the other. Jeanne was tired out and fell asleep as soon as her head touched the pillow.

The next few days there was so much to do that she had no time to fret; in fact, she even found a certain pleasure in making her new home pretty, for all the time she was working she thought that her son would one day come and live there. The tapestry from her bedroom at Les Peuples was hung in the dining-room, which was also to serve as drawing-room, and Jeanne took especial pains over the arrangement of one of the rooms on the first floor, which in her own mind she had already named " Poulet's room; " she was to have the other one on that floor, and Rosalie was to sleep upstairs next to the box-room. The little house thus tastefully arranged, looked pretty when it was all finished, and at first Jeanne was pleased with it though she was haunted by the feeling that there was something missing though she could not tell what.

One morning a clerk came over from the attorney at Fécamp with the three thousand six hundred francs, the price at which an upholsterer had valued the furniture left at Les Peuples. Jeanne felt a thrill of pleasure as she took the money, for she had not expected to get so much, and as soon as the man had gone she put on her hat and hurried off to Goderville to send Paul this un-looked-for sum as quickly as possible. But as she was hastening along the road she met Rosalie coming back from market; the maid suspected that something had happened though she did not at once guess the truth. She soon found it out, however, for Jeanne could not hide anything from her, and placing her basket on the ground to give way to her wrath at her ease, she put her hands on her hips and scolded Jeanne at the top of her voice; then she took hold of her mistress with her right hand and her basket with her left and walked on again towards the house in a great passion. As soon as they were indoors Rosalie ordered the money to be given into her care, and Jeanne gave it her with the exception of the six hundred francs which she said nothing about; but this trick was soon detected and Jeanne had to give it all up. However, Rosalie con-sented to these odd hundreds being sent to the young man, who in a few days wrote to thank his mother for the money. " It was a most welcome present, mother dear," he said, " for we were reduced to utter want."

Time went on but Jeanne could not get accustomed to her new home. It seemed as if she could not breathe freely at Batteville, and she felt more alone and for-saken than ever. She would often walk as far as the village of Verneuil and come back through Trois-Mares, but as soon as she was home she started up to go out again as if she had forgotten to go to the very place to which she had meant to walk. The same thing hap-pened time after time and she could not understand where it was she longed to go; one evening, however, she unconsciously uttered a sentence which at once revealed to her the secret of her restlessness. "Oh! how I long to see the ocean," she said as she sat down to dinner.

The sea! That was what she missed. The sea with its salt breezes, its never-ceasing roar, its tempests, its strong odors; the sea, near which she had lived for five and twenty years, which had always felt near her and which, unconsciously, she had come to love like a human being.

Massacre, too, was very uneasy. The very evening of his arrival at the new house he had installed himself under the kitchen-dresser and no one could get him to move out. There he lay all day long, never stirring, except to turn himself over with a smothered grunt, until it was dark; then he got up and dragged himself towards the garden door, grazing himself against the wall as he went. After he had stayed out of doors a few minutes he came in again and sat down before the stove which was still warm, and as soon as Jeanne and Rosalie had gone to bed he began to howl. The whole night long he howled, in a pitiful, deplorable way, sometimes ceasing for an hour only to recommence in a still more doleful tone. A barrel was put outside the house and he was tied up to it, but he howled just the same out of doors as in, and as he was old and almost dying, he was brought back to the kitchen again.

It was impossible for Jeanne to sleep, for the whole night she could hear the old dog moaning and scratching as he tried to get used to this new house which he found so different from his old home. Nothing would quiet him; his eyes were dim and it seemed as if the knowledge of his infirmity made him keep still while everyone else was awake and downstairs, and at night he wandered restlessly about until daybreak, as if he only dared to move in the darkness which makes all beings sightless for the time. It was an intense relief to everyone when one morning he was found dead.

Winter wore on, and Jeanne gave way more and more to an insuperable hopelessness; it was no longer a keen, heartrending grief that she felt, but a dull, gloomy melancholy. There was nothing to rouse her from it, no one came to see her, and the road which passed before her door was almost deserted. Sometimes a gig passed by driven by a red-faced man whose blouse, blown out by the wind, looked like a blue balloon, and sometimes a cart crawled past, or a peasant and his wife could be seen coming from the distance, growing larger and larger as they approached the house and then diminishing again when they had passed it, till they looked like two insects at the end of the long white line which stretched as far as the eye could reach, rising and falling with the undulation of the earth. When the grass again sprang up a little girl passed the gate every morning with two thin cows which browsed along the side of the road, and in the evening she returned, taking, as in the morning, one step every ten minutes as she followed the animals.

Every night Jeanne dreamt that she was again at Les Peuples. She thought she was there with her father and mother and Aunt Lison as in the old times. Again she accomplished the old, forgotten duties and supported Madame Adélaïde as she walked in her avenue; and each time she awoke she burst into tears.

Paul was continually in her thoughts and she wondered what he was doing, if he were well and if he

ever thought of her. She revolved all these painful
thoughts in her mind as she walked along the low-lying
roads between the farms, and what was more torture
to her than anything else was the fierce jealousy of the
woman who had deprived her of her son. It was this
hatred alone which restrained her from taking any steps
towards finding Paul and trying to see him. She could
imagine her son's mistress confronting her at the door
and asking, " What is your business here, madame? "
and her self-respect would not permit her to run the
risk of such an encounter. In the haughty pride of a
chaste and spotless woman, who had never stooped to
listen to temptation, she became still more bitter against
the base and cowardly actions to which sensual love will
drive a man who is not strong enough to throw off its
degrading chains. The whole of humanity seemed to
her unclean as she thought of the obscene secrets of the
senses, of the caresses which debase as they are given
and received, and of all the mysteries which surround
the attraction of the sexes.

Another spring and summer passed away, and when
the autumn came again with its rainy days, its dull, gray
skies, its heavy clouds, Jeanne felt so weary of the life
she was leading that she determined to make a supreme
attempt to regain possession of her Poulet. Surely the
young man's passion must have cooled by this time, and
she wrote him a touching, pitiful letter:

" MY DEAR CHILD — I am coming to entreat you to
return to me. Think how I am left, lonely, aged and
ill, the whole year with only a servant. I am living now
in a little house by the roadside and it is very miserable
for me, but if you were here everything would seem

different.    You are all I have in the world, and I have
not seen you for seven years.    You will never know
how unhappy I have been and how my every thought
was centered in you.    You were my life, my soul, my
only hope, my only love, and you are away from me,
you have forsaken me.

"Oh! come back, my darling Poulet, come back, and
let me hold you in my arms again; come back to your
old mother who so longs to see you.    JEANNE."

A few days later came the following reply:

"MY DEAR MOTHER — I should only be too glad
to come and see you, but I have not a penny; send me
some money and I will come.    I had myself been thinking of coming to speak to you about a plan which, if
carried out, would permit me to do as you desire.

"I shall never be able to repay the disinterested
affection of the woman who has shared all my troubles,
but I can at least make a public recognition of her faithful love and devotion.    Her behavior is all you could
desire; she is well-educated and well-read and you cannot imagine what a comfort she has been to me.    I
should be a brute if I did not make her some recompense, and I ask your permission to marry her.    Then
we could all live together in your new house, and you
would forgive my follies.    I am convinced that you
would give your consent at once, if you knew her; I
assure you she is very lady-like and quiet, and I know
you would like her.    As for me, I could not live without her.

"I shall await your reply with every impatience, dear
mother.    We both send you much love.— Your son,

"VICOMTE PAUL DE LAMARE."

Jeanne was thunderstruck. As she sat with the letter on her knees, she could see so plainly through the designs of this woman who had not once let Paul return to his friends, but had always kept him at her side while she patiently waited until his mother should give in and consent to anything and everything in the irresistible desire of having her son with her again; and it was with bitter pain that she thought of how Paul obstinately persisted in preferring this creature to herself. "He does not love me, he does not love me," she murmured over and over again.

"He wants to marry her now," she said, when Rosalie came in.

The servant started.

"Oh! madame, you surely will not consent to it. M. Paul can't bring that hussy here."

All the pride in Jeanne's nature rose in revolt at the thought, and though she was bowed down with grief, she replied decidedly:

"No, Rosalie, never. But since he won't come here I will go to him, and we will see which of us two will have the greater influence over him."

She wrote to Paul at once, telling him that she was coming to Paris, and would see him anywhere but at the house where he was living with that wretch. Then while she awaited his reply, she began to make all her preparations for the journey, and Rosalie commenced to pack her mistress's linen and clothes in an old trunk.

"You haven't a single thing to put on," exclaimed the servant, as she was folding up an old, badly-made dress. "I won't have you go with such clothes; you'd be a disgrace to everyone, and the Paris ladies would think you were a servant."

Jeanne let her have her own way, and they both went to Goderville and chose some green, checked stuff, which they left with the dressmaker to be made up.  Then they went to see Me. Roussel the lawyer, who went to Paris for a fortnight every year, to obtain a few directions, for it was twenty-eight years since Jeanne had been to the capital.  He gave them a great deal of advice about crossing the roads and the way to avoid being robbed, saying that the safest plan was to carry only just as much money as was necessary in the pockets and to sew the rest in the lining of the dress; then he talked for a long time about the restaurants where the charges were moderate, and mentioned two or three to which ladies could go, and he recommended Jeanne to stay at the Hôtel de Normandie, which was near the railway station.  He always stayed there himself, and she could say he had sent her.  There had been a railway between Paris and Havre for the last six years, but Jeanne had never seen one of these steam-engines of which everyone was talking, and which were revolutionizing the whole country.

The day passed on, but still there came no answer from Paul.  Every morning, for a fortnight, Jeanne had gone along the road to meet the postman, and had asked, in a voice which she could not keep steady:

"You have nothing for me to-day, Père Malandain?"  And the answer was always the same:  "No nothing yet, *ma bonne dame*."

Fully persuaded that it was that woman who was preventing Paul from answering, Jeanne determined not to wait any longer, but to start at once.  She wanted to take Rosalie with her, but the maid would not go because of increasing the expense of the journey, and she only allowed her mistress to take three hundred francs with her.

" If you want any more money," she said, " write to me, and I'll tell the lawyer to forward you some; but if I give you any more now, Monsieur Paul will have it all."

Then one December morning, Denis Lecoq's gig came to take them both to the railway station, for Rosalie was going to accompany her mistress as far as that. When they reached the station, they found out first how much the tickets were, then, when the trunk had been labeled and the ticket bought, they stood watching the rails, both too much occupied in wondering what the train would be like to think of the sad cause of this journey. At last a distant whistle made them look round, and they saw a large, black machine approaching, which came up with a terrible noise, dragging after it a long chain of little rolling houses. A porter opened the door of one of these little huts, and Jeanne kissed Rosalie and got in.

" *Au revoir*, madame. I hope you will have a pleasant journey, and will soon be back again."

" *Au revoir,* Rosalie."

There was another whistle, and the string of carriages moved slowly off, gradually going faster and faster, till they reached a terrific speed. In Jeanne's compartment there were only two other passengers, who were both asleep, and she sat and watched the fields and farms and villages rush past. She was frightened at the speed at which she was going, and the feeling came over her that she was entering a new phase of life, and was being hurried towards a very different world from that in which she had spent her peaceful girlhood and her monotonous life.

It was evening when she reached Paris. A porter took her trunk, and she followed closely at his heels, sometimes almost running for fear of losing sight of him, and feeling frightened as she was pushed about by the swaying crowd through which she did not know how to pass.

" I was recommended here by Me. Roussel," she hastened to say when she was in the hôtel office.

The landlady, a big, stolid-looking woman, was sitting at the desk.

" Who is Me. Roussel? " she asked.

" The lawyer from Goderville, who stays here every year," replied Jeanne, in surprise.

" Very likely he does," responded the big woman, " but I don't know him. Do you want a room? "

" Yes, madame."

A waiter shouldered the luggage and led the way upstairs.

Jeanne followed, feeling very low-spirited and depressed, and sitting down at a little table, she ordered some soup and the wing of a chicken to be sent up to her, for she had had nothing to eat since day-break. She thought of how she had passed through this same town on her return from her wedding tour, as she ate her supper by the miserable light of one candle, and of how Julien had then first shown himself in his true character. But then she was young and brave and hopeful; now she felt old and timid; and the least thing worried and frightened her.

When she had finished her supper, she went to the

window and watched the crowded street. She would
have liked to go out if she had dared, but she thought
she should be sure to lose herself, so she went to bed.
But she had hardly yet got over the bustle of the journey, and that, and the noise and the sensation of being
in a strange place, kept her awake. The hours passed
on, and the noises outside gradually ceased, but still she
could not sleep, for she was accustomed to the sound,
peaceful sleep of the country, which is so different from
the semi-repose of a great city. Here she was conscious
of a sort of restlessness all around her; the murmur of
voices reached her ears, and every now and then a board
creaked, a door shut, or a bell rang. She was just dozing off, about two o'clock in the morning, when a
woman suddenly began to scream in a neighboring
room. Jeanne started up in bed, and next she thought
she heard a man laughing. As dawn approached she
became more and more anxious to see Paul, and as soon
as it was light, she got up and dressed.

He lived in the Rue du Sauvage, and she meant to
follow Rosalie's advice about spending as little as possible, and walk there. It was a fine day, though the
wind was keen, and there were a great many people hurrying along the pavements. Jeanne walked along the
street as quickly as she could. When she reached the
other end, she was to turn to the right, then to the left;
then she would come to a square, where she was to ask
again. She could not find the square, and a baker from
whom she inquired the way gave her different directions
altogether. She started on again, missed the way, wandered about, and in trying to follow other directions,
lost herself entirely. She walked on and on, and was
just going to hail a cab when she saw the Seine. Then

she decided to walk along the quays, and in about an hour she reached the dark, dirty lane called Rue du Sauvage.

When she came to the number she was seeking, she was so excited that she stood before the door unable to move another step. Poulet was there, in that house! Her hands and knees trembled violently, and it was some moments before she could enter and walk along the passage to the doorkeeper's box.

"Will you go and tell M. Paul de Lamare that an old lady friend of his mother's, is waiting to see him?" she said, slipping a piece of money into the man's hand.

"He does not live here now, madame," answered the doorkeeper.

She started.

"Ah! Where — where is he living now?" she gasped.

"I do not know."

She felt stunned, and it was some time before she could speak again.

"When did he leave?" she asked at last, controlling herself by a violent effort.

The man was quite ready to tell her all he knew.

"About a fortnight ago," he replied. "They just walked out of the house one evening and didn't come back. They owed all over the neighborhood, so you may guess they didn't leave any address."

Tongues of flame were dancing before Jeanne's eyes, as if a gun were being fired off close to her face; but she wanted to find Poulet, and that kept her up and made her stand opposite the doorkeeper, as if she were calmly thinking.

"Then he did not say anything when he left?" .

"No, nothing at all; they went away to get out of paying their debts.

"But he will have to send for his letters."

"He'll send a good many times before he gets them, then; besides, they didn't have ten in a twelvemonth, though I took them up one two days before they left."

That must have been the one she sent.

"Listen," she said, hastily. "I am his mother, and I have come to look for him. Here are ten francs for yourself. If you hear anything from or about him, let me know at once at the Hôtel de Normandie, Rue du Havre, and you shall be well paid for your trouble."

"You may depend upon me, madame," answered the doorkeeper; and Jeanne went away.

She hastened along the streets as if she were bent on an important mission, but she was not looking or caring whither she was going. She walked close to the walls, pushed and buffeted by errand boys and porters; crossed the roads, regardless of the vehicles and the shouts of the drivers; stumbled against the curbstones, which she did not see; and hurried on and on, unconscious of everything and everyone. At last she found herself in some gardens, and, feeling too weary to walk any further, she dropped on a seat. She sat there a long while, apparently unaware that the tears were running down her cheeks, and that passersby stopped to look at her. At last the bitter cold made her rise to go, but her legs would hardly carry her, so weak and exhausted was she. She would have liked some soup, but she dared not go into a restaurant, for she knew people could see she was in trouble, and it made her feel timid and ashamed. When she passed an eating-place she would stop a moment at the door, look inside, and see all the people sitting at the tables eating, and then go on again, saying to herself: " I will go into the next one "; but when she came to the next her courage always failed her again. In the end she went into a baker's shop, and bought a little crescent-shaped roll, which she ate as she went along. She was very thirsty, but she did not know where to go to get anything to drink, so she went without.

She passed under an arch, and found herself in some more gardens with arcades running all round them, and she recognized the Palais Royal. Her walk in the sun had made her warm again, so she sat down for another hour or two. A crowd of people flowed into the gardens — an elegant crowd composed of beautiful women and wealthy men, who only lived for dress and pleasure, and who chatted and smiled and bowed as they sauntered along. Feeling ill at ease amidst this brilliant throng, Jeanne rose to go away; but suddenly the thought struck her that perhaps she might meet Paul here, and she began to walk from end to end of the gardens, with hasty, furtive steps, carefully scanning every face she met.

Soon she saw that people turned to look and laugh at her, and she hurried away, thinking it was her odd appearance and her green-checked dress, which Rosalie had chosen and had made up, that attracted everyone's attention and smiles. She hardly dared ask her way, but she did at last venture, and when she had reached her hotel, she passed the rest of the day sitting on a chair at the foot of the bed. In the evening she dined off some soup and a little meat, like the day before, and then undressed and went to bed, performing all the duties of her toilet quite mechanically, from sheer habit.

The next morning she went to the police office to see if she could get any help there towards the discovery of her son's whereabouts. They told her they could not promise her anything, but that they would attend to the matter. After she had left the police office, she wandered about the streets, in the hopes of meeting her child, and she felt more friendless and forsaken among the busy crowds than she did in the midst of the lovely fields.

When she returned to the hotel in the evening, she was told that a man from M. Paul had asked for her, and was coming again the next day. All the blood in her body seemed to suddenly rush to her heart and she could not close her eyes all night. Perhaps it was Paul himself! Yes, it must be so, although his appearance did not tally with the description the hotel people had given of the man who had called, and when, about nine o'clock in the morning, there came a knock at her door, she cried, " Come in! " expecting her son to rush into her arms held open to receive him.

But it was a stranger who entered — a stranger who began to apologize for disturbing her and to explain that he had come about some money Paul owed him. As he spoke she felt herself beginning to cry, and she tried to hide her tears from the man by wiping them away with the end of her finger as soon as they reached the corners of her eyes. The man had heard of her arrival from the concierge at the Rue du Sauvage, and as he could not find Paul he had come to his mother. He held out a paper which Jeanne mechanically took; she saw " 90 francs " written on it, and she drew out the money and paid the man. She did not go out at all that day, and the next morning more creditors appeared.

She gave them all the money she had left, except twenty francs, and wrote and told Rosalie how she was placed.

Until her servant's answer came she passed the days in wandering aimlessly about the streets. She did not know what to do or how to kill the long, miserable hours; there was no one who knew of her troubles, or to whom she could go for sympathy, and her one desire was to get away from this city and to return to her little house beside the lonely road, where, a few days before, she had felt she could not bear to live because it was so dull and lonely. Now she was sure she could live nowhere else but in that little home where all her mournful habits had taken root.

At last, one evening, she found a letter from Rosalie awaiting her with two hundred francs enclosed.

" Come back as soon as possible, Madame Jeanne," wrote the maid, " for I shall send you nothing more. As for M. Paul, I will go and fetch him myself the next time we hear anything from him.—With best respects, your servant, ROSALIE."

And Jeanne started back to Batteville one bitterly cold, snowy morning.

## XIV

AFTER her return from Paris, Jeanne would not go out or take any interest in anything. She rose at the same hour every morning, looked out of the window to see what sort of day it was, then went downstairs and sat before the fire in the dining-room. She stayed there the whole day, sitting perfectly still with her eyes fixed on the flames while she thought of all the sorrows she had passed through. The little room grew darker and darker, but she never moved, except to put more wood on the fire, and when Rosalie brought in the lamp she cried:

"Come, Madame Jeanne, you must stir about a bit, or you won't be able to eat any dinner again this evening."

Often she was worried by thoughts which she could not dismiss from her mind, and she allowed herself to be tormented by the veriest trifles, for the most insignificant matters appeared of the greatest importance to her diseased mind. She lived in the memories of the past, and she would think for hours together of her girlhood and her wedding tour in Corsica. The wild scenery that she had long forgotten suddenly appeared before her in the fire, and she could recall every detail, every event, every face connected with the island. She could always see the features of Jean Ravoli, the guide, and sometimes she fancied she could even hear his voice.

At other times she thought of the peaceful years of Paul's childhood — of how he used to make her tend the salad plants, and of how she and Aunt Lison used to kneel on the ground, each trying to outdo the other in giving pleasure to the boy, and in rearing the greater number of plants.

Her lips would form the words, "Poulet, my little Poulet," as if she were talking to him, and she would cease to muse, and try for hours to write in the air the letters which formed her son's name, with her outstretched finger. Slowly she traced them before the fire, fancying she could see them, and, thinking she had made a mistake, she began the word over and over again, forcing herself to write the whole name though her arm trembled with fatigue. At last she would become so nervous that she mixed up the letters, and formed other words, and had to give it up.

She had all the manias and fancies which beset those who lead a solitary life, and it irritated her to the last degree to see the slightest change in the arrangement of the furniture. Rosalie often made her go out with her along the road, but after twenty minutes or so Jeanne would say: "I cannot walk any further, Rosalie," and would sit down by the roadside. Soon movement of any kind became distasteful to her, and she stayed in bed as late as she could. Ever since a child she had always been in the habit of jumping out of bed as soon as she had drunk her *cafe au lait.* She was particularly fond of her morning coffee, and she would have missed it more than anything. She always waited for Rosalie to bring it with an impatience that had a touch of sensuality in it, and as soon as the cup was placed on the bedside table she sat up, and emptied it, somewhat greedily. Then she at once drew back the bedclothes and began to dress. But gradually she fell into the habit of dreaming for a few moments after she had placed the empty cup back in the saucer, and from that she soon began to lie down again, and at last she stayed in bed every day until Rosalie came back in a temper and dressed her almost by force.

She had no longer the slightest will of her own. Whenever her servant asked her advice, or put any question to her, or wanted to know her opinion, she always answered: "Do as you like, Rosalie." So firmly did she believe herself pursued by a persistent ill luck that she became as great a fatalist as an Oriental, and she

was so accustomed to seeing her dreams unfulfilled, and
her hopes disappointed, that she did not dare undertake
anything fresh, and hesitated for days before she commenced the simplest task, so persuaded was she that
whatever she touched would be sure to go wrong.

" I don't think anyone could have had more misfortune than I have had all my life," she was always saying.

" How would it be if you had to work for your bread,
and if you were obliged to get up every morning at six
o'clock to go and do a hard day's work?" Rosalie
would exclaim. " That's what a great many people
have to do, and then when they get too old to work, they
die of want."

" But my son has forsaken me, and I am all alone,"
Jeanne would reply.

That enraged Rosalie.

" And what if he has? How about those whose
children enlist, or settle in America?" (America, in
her eyes, was a shadowy country whither people went
to make their fortune, and whence they never returned).
" Children always leave their parents sooner or later;
old and young people aren't meant to stay together.
And then, what if he were dead?" she would finish up
with savagely, and her mistress could say nothing after
that.

Jeanne got a little stronger when the first warm days
of spring came, but she only took advantage of her better health to bury herself still deeper in her gloomy
thoughts.

She went up to the garret one morning to look for
something, and, while she was there, happened to open
a box full of old almanacs. It seemed as if she had

V—17

found the past years themselves, and she was filled with emotion as she looked at the pile of cards. They were of all sizes, big and little, and she took them every one down to the dining-room and began to lay them out on the table in the right order of years. Suddenly she picked up the very first one — the one she had taken with her from the convent to Les Peuples. For a long time she gazed at it with its dates which she had crossed out the day she had left Rouen, and she began to shed slow, bitter tears — the weak, pitiful tears of an aged woman — as she looked at these cards spread out before her on the table, and which represented all her wretched life.

Then the thought struck her that by means of these almanacs she could recall all that she had ever done, and giving way to the idea, she at once devoted herself to the task of retracing the past. She pinned all the cards, which had grown yellow with age, up on the tapestry, and then passed hours before one or other of them, thinking, " What did I do in that month ? "

She had put a mark beside all the important dates in her life, and sometimes, by means of linking together and adding one to the other, all the little circumstances which had preceded and followed a great event, she succeeded in remembering a whole month. By dint of concentrated attention, and efforts of will and of memory, she retraced nearly the whole of her first two years at Les Peuples, recalling without much difficulty this far-away period of her life, for it seemed to stand out in relief. But the following years were shrouded in a sort of mist and seemed to run one into the other, and sometimes she pored over an almanac for hours without being able to remember whether it was even in that

year that such and such a thing had happened. She
would go slowly round the dining-room looking at these
images of past years, which, to her, were as pictures
of an ascent to Calvary, until one of them arrested her
attention and then she would sit gazing at it all the rest
of the day, absorbed in her recollections.

Soon the sap began to rise in the trees; the seeds were
springing up, the leaves were budding and the air was
filled with the faint, sweet smell of the apple blossoms
which made the orchards a glowing mass of pink. As
summer approached Jeanne became very restless. She
could not keep still; she went in and out twenty times a
day, and, as she rambled along past the farms, she
worked herself into a perfect state of fever.

A daisy half hidden in the grass, a sunbeam falling
through the leaves, or the reflection of the sky in a
splash of water in a rut was enough to agitate and affect
her, for their sight brought back a kind of echo of the
emotions she had felt when, as a young girl, she had
wandered dreamily through the fields; and though now
there was nothing to which she could look forward, the
soft yet exhilarating air sent the same thrill through her
as when all her life had lain before her. But this pleasure was not unalloyed with pain, and it seemed as if the
universal joy of the awakening world could now only
impart a delight which was half sorrow to her grief-
crushed soul and withered heart. Everything around
her seemed to have changed. Surely the sun was hardly
so warm as in her youth, the sky so deep a blue, the
grass so fresh a green, and the flowers, paler and less
sweet, could no longer arouse within her the exquisite
ecstasies of delight as of old. Still she could enjoy the
beauty around her, so much that sometimes she found

herself dreaming and hoping again; for, however cruel
Fate may be, is it possible to give way to utter despair
when the sun shines and the sky is blue?

She went for long walks, urged on and on by her
inward excitement, and sometimes she would suddenly
stop and sit down by the roadside to think of her troubles. Why had she not been loved like other women?
Why had even the simple pleasure of an uneventful
existence been refused her?

Sometimes, again forgetting for a moment that she
was old, that there was no longer any pleasure in store
for her, and that, with the exception of a few more
lonely years, her life was over and done, she would build
all sorts of castles in the air and make plans for such a
happy future, just as she had done when she was sixteen.
Then suddenly remembering the bitter reality she would
get up again, feeling as if a heavy load had fallen upon
her, and return home, murmuring:

"Oh, you old fool! You old fool!"

Now Rosalie was always saying to her:

"Do keep still, madame. What on earth makes you
want to run about so?"

"I can't help it," Jeanne would reply sadly. "I am
like Massacre was before he died."

One morning Rosalie went into her mistress's room
earlier than usual.

"Make haste and drink up your coffee," she said as
she placed the cup on the table. "Denis is waiting to
take us to Les Peuples. I have to go over there on
business."

Jeanne was so excited that she thought she would
have fainted, and, as she dressed herself with trembling

fingers, she could hardly believe she was going to see her dear home once more.

Overhead was a bright, blue sky, and, as they went along, Denis's pony would every now and then break into a gallop. When they reached Etouvent, Jeanne could hardly breathe, her heart beat so quickly, and when she saw the brick pillars beside the château gate, she exclaimed, " Oh," two or three times in a low voice, as if she were in the presence of something which stirred her very soul, and she could not help herself.

They put up the horse at the Couillards' farm, and, when Rosalie and her son went to attend to their business, the farmer asked Jeanne if she would like to go over the château, as the owner was away, and gave her the key.

She went off alone, and when she found herself opposite the old manor she stood still to look at it. The outside had not been touched since she had left. All the shutters were closed, and the sunbeams were dancing on the gray walls of the big, weather-beaten building. A little piece of wood fell on her dress, she looked up and saw that it had fallen from the plane tree, and she went up to the big tree and stroked its pale, smooth bark as if it had been alive. Her foot touched a piece of rotten wood lying in the grass; it was the last fragment of the seat on which she had so often sat with her loved ones — the seat which had been put up the very day of Julien's first visit to the château.

Then she went to the hall-door. She had some difficulty in opening it as the key was rusty and would not turn, but at last the lock gave way, and the door itself only required a slight push before it swung back. The

first thing Jeanne did was to run up to her own room.
It had been hung with a light paper and she hardly
knew it again, but when she opened one of the windows
and looked out, she was moved almost to tears as she
saw again the scene she loved so well — the thicket, the
elms, the common, and the sea covered with brown sails
which, at this distance, looked as if they were motionless.

Then she went all over the big, empty house. She
stopped to look at a little hole in the plaster which the
baron had made with his cane, for he used to make a
few thrusts at the wall whenever he passed this spot, in
memory of the fencing bouts he had had in his youth.
In her mother's bedroom she found a small gold-headed
pin stuck in the wall behind the door, in a dark corner
near the bed. She had stuck it there a long while ago
(she remembered it now), and had looked everywhere
for it since, but it had never been found; and she kissed
it and took it with her as a priceless relic.

She went into every room, recognizing the almost invisible spots and marks on the hangings which had not
been changed and again noting the odd forms and faces
which the imagination so often traces in the designs of
the furniture coverings, the carvings of mantelpieces
and the shadows on soiled ceilings. She walked
through the vast, silent château as noiselessly as if she
were in a cemetery; all her life was interred there.

She went down to the drawing-room. The closed
shutters made it very dark, and it was a few moments
before she could distinguish anything; then, as her eyes
became accustomed to the darkness, she gradually made
out the tapestry with the big, white birds on it. Two
armchairs stood before the fireplace, looking as if they
had just been vacated, and the very smell of the room —

a smell that had always been peculiar to it, as each human being has his, a smell which could be perceived at once, and yet was vague like all the faint perfumes of old rooms — brought the memories crowding to Jeanne's mind.

Her breath came quickly as she stood with her eyes fixed on the two chairs, inhaling this perfume of the past; and, all at once, in a sudden hallucination occasioned by her thoughts, she fancied she saw — she did see — her father and mother with their feet on the fender as she had so often seen them before. She drew back in terror, stumbling against the door-frame, and clung to it for support, still keeping her eyes fixed on the armchairs. The vision disappeared and for some minutes she stood horror-stricken; then she slowly regained possession of herself and turned to fly, afraid that she was going mad. Her eyes fell on the wainscoting against which she was leaning and she saw Poulet's ladder. There were all the faint marks traced on the wall at unequal intervals and the figures which had been cut with a penknife to indicate the month, and the child's age and growth. In some places there was the baron's big writing, in others her own, in others again Aunt Lison's, which was a little shaky. She could see the boy standing there now, with his fair hair, and his little forehead pressed against the wall to have his height measured, while the baron exclaimed: "Jeanne, he has grown half an inch in six weeks," and she began to kiss the wainscoting in a frenzy of love for the very wood.

Then she heard Rosalie's voice outside, calling: "Madame Jeanne! Madame Jeanne! lunch is waiting," and she went out with her head in a whirl. She felt unable to understand anything that was said to her. She ate what was placed before her, listened to what was being said without realizing the sense of the words, answered the farmers' wives when they inquired after her health, passively received their kisses and kissed the cheeks which were offered to her, and then got into the chaise again.

When she could no longer see the high roof of the château through the trees, something within her seemed to break, and she felt that she had just said good-bye to her old home for ever.

They went straight back to Batteville, and as she was going indoors Jeanne saw something white under the door; it was a letter which the postman had slipped there during their absence. She at once recognized Paul's handwriting and tore open the envelope in an agony of anxiety. He wrote:

"MY DEAR MOTHER: I have not written before because I did not want to bring you to Paris on a fruitless errand, for I have always been meaning to come and see you myself. At the present moment I am in great trouble and difficulty. My wife gave birth to a little girl three days ago, and now she is dying and I have not a penny. I do not know what to do with the child; the doorkeeper is trying to nourish it with a feeding-bottle as best she can, but I fear I shall lose it. Could not you take it? I cannot send it to a wet nurse as I have not any money, and I do not know which way to turn. Pray answer by return post.

"Your loving son,
"PAUL."

Jeanne dropped on a chair with hardly enough strength left to call Rosalie. The maid came and they read the letter over again together, and then sat looking at each other in silence.

" I'll go and fetch the child myself, madame," said Rosalie at last. " We can't leave it to die."

" Very well, my girl, go," answered Jeanne.

" Put on your hat, madame," said the maid, after a pause, " and we will go and see the lawyer at Goderville. If that woman is going to die, M. Paul must marry her for the sake of the child."

Jeanne put on her hat without a word. Her heart was overflowing with joy, but she would not have allowed anyone to see it for the world, for it was one of those detestable joys in which people can revel in their hearts, but of which they are all the same ashamed; her son's mistress was going to die.

The lawyer gave Rosalie detailed instructions which the servant made him repeat two or three times; then, when she was sure she knew exactly what to do, she said:

" Don't you fear; I'll see it's all right now." And she started for Paris that very night.

Jeanne passed two days in such an agony of mind that she could fix her thoughts on nothing. The third morning she received a line from Rosalie merely saying she was coming back by that evening's train; nothing more; and in the afternoon, about three o'clock, Jeanne sent round to a neighbor to ask him if he would drive her to the Beuzeville railway station to meet her servant.

She stood on the platform looking down the rails (which seemed to get closer together right away as far off as she could see), and turning every now and then to look at the clock.  Ten minutes more — five minutes — two — and at last the train was due, though as yet she could see no signs of it.  Then, all at once, she saw a cloud of white smoke, and underneath it a black speck which got rapidly larger and larger.  The big engine came into the station, snorting and slackening its speed, and Jeanne looked eagerly into every window as the carriages went past her.

The doors opened and several people got out — peasants in blouses, farmers' wives with baskets on their arms, a few *bourgeois* in soft hats — and at last Rosalie appeared, carrying what looked like a bundle of linen in her arms.  Jeanne would have stepped forward to meet her, but all strength seemed to have left her legs and she feared she would fall if she moved.  The maid saw her and came up in her ordinary, calm way.

" Good-day, madame; here I am again, though I've had some bother to get along."

" Well? " gasped Jeanne.

" Well," answered Rosalie, " she died last night. They were married and here's the baby," and she held out the child which could not be seen for its wraps. Jeanne mechanically took it, and they left the station and got into the carriage which was waiting.

" M. Paul is coming directly after the funeral.  I suppose he'll be here to-morrow, by this train."

" Paul —" murmured Jeanne, and then stopped without saying anything more.

The sun was sinking towards the horizon, bathing in a glow of light the green fields which were flecked here and there with golden colewort flowers or blood-red poppies, and over the quiet country fell an infinite peace.

The peasant who was driving the chaise kept clicking his tongue to urge on his horse which trotted swiftly along, and Jeanne looked straight up into the sky which the circling flight of the swallows seemed to cut asunder.

All at once she became conscious of a soft warmth which was making itself felt through her skirts; it was the heat from the tiny being sleeping on her knees, and it moved her strangely.  She suddenly drew back the covering from the child she had not yet seen, that she might look at her son's daughter; as the light fell on its face the little creature opened its blue eyes, and moved its lips, and then Jeanne hugged it closely to her, and, raising it in her arms, began to cover it with passionate kisses.

" Come, come, Madame Jeanne, have done," said Rosalie, in sharp, though good-tempered tones; " you'll make the child cry."

Then she added, as if in reply to her own thoughts:

" After all, life is never so jolly or so miserable as people seem to think."

# HAUTOT SENIOR
### AND
# HAUTOT JUNIOR

## PART I

IN front of the building, half farm-house, half manor-house, one of those rural habitations of a mixed character which were all but seigneurial, and which are at the present time occupied by large cultivators, the dogs lashed beside the apple-trees in the orchard near the house, kept barking and howling at the sight of the shooting-bags carried by the gamekeepers and the boys. In the spacious dining-room kitchen, Hautot Senior and Hautot Junior, M. Bermont, the tax-collector, and M. Mondaru, the notary were taking a pick and drinking a glass before going out to shoot, for it was the opening day.

Hautot Senior, proud of all his possessions, talked boastfully beforehand of the game which his guests were going to find on his lands. He was a big Norman, one of those powerful, sanguineous, bony men, who lift wagon-loads of apples on their shoulders. Half-peasant, half-gentleman, rich, respected, influential, invested with authority he made his son César go as far as the third form at school, so that he might be an educated man, and there he had brought his studies to a stop for fear of his becoming a fine gentleman and paying no attention to the land.

César Hautot, almost as tall as his father, but

thinner, was a good son, docile, content with everything, full of admiration, respect, and deference, for the wishes and opinions of his sire.

M. Bermont, the tax-collector, a stout little man, who showed on his red cheeks a thin network of violet veins resembling the tributaries and the winding courses of rivers on maps, asked:

" And hares — are there any hares on it? "

Hautot Senior answered:

" As much as you like, especially in the Puysatier lands."

" Which direction are we to begin at? " asked the notary, a jolly notary fat and pale, big paunched too, and strapped up in an entirely new hunting-costume bought at Rouen.

" Well, that way, through these grounds.  We will drive the partridges into the plain, and we will beat there again."

And Hautot Senior rose up.  They all followed his example, took their guns out of the corners, examined the locks, stamped with their feet in order to feel themselves firmer in their boots which were rather hard, not having as yet been rendered flexible by the heat of the blood.  Then they went out; and the dogs, standing erect at the ends of their lashes, gave vent to piercing howls while beating the air with their paws.

They set forth for the lands referred to.  They consisted of a little glen, or rather a long undulating stretch of inferior soil, which had on that account remained uncultivated, furrowed with mountain-torrents, covered with ferns, an excellent preserve for game.

The sportsmen took up their positions at some distance from each other, Hautot Senior posting himself

at the right, Hautot Junior at the left, and the two
guests in the middle.   The keeper and those who carried the game-bags followed.   It was the solemn
moment when the first shot it awaited, when the heart
beats a little, while the nervous finger keeps feeling at
the gun-lock every second.

Suddenly the shot went off.   Hautot Senior had
fired.   They all stopped, and saw a partridge breaking
off from a covey which was rushing along at a single
flight to fall down into a ravine under a thick growth
of brushwood.   The sportsman, becoming excited,
rushed forward with rapid strides, thrusting aside the
briers which stood in his path, and he disappeared in
his turn into the thicket, in quest of his game.

Almost at the same instant, a second shot was heard.

" Ha! ha! the rascal! " exclaimed M. Bermont, " he
will unearth a hare down there."

They all waited, with their eyes riveted on the heap
of branches through which their gaze failed to
penetrate.

The notary, making a speaking-trumpet of his hands,
shouted:

" Have you got them? "

Hautot Senior made no response.

Then César, turning towards the keeper, said to him:

" Just go, and assist him, Joseph.   We must keep
walking in a straight line.   We'll wait."

And Joseph, an old stump of a man, lean and knotty,
all whose joints formed protuberances, proceeded at an
easy pace down the ravine, searching at every opening
through which a passage could be effected with the cautiousness of a fox.   Then, suddenly, he cried:

"Oh! come! come! an unfortunate thing has occurred."

They all hurried forward, plunging through the briers.

The elder Hautot, who had fallen on his side, in a fainting condition, kept both his hands over his stomach, from which flowed down upon the grass through the linen vest torn by the lead, long streamlets of blood. As he was laying down his gun, in order to seize the partridge, within reach of him, he had let the firearm fall, and the second discharge going off with the shock, had torn open his entrails. They drew him out of the trench; they removed his clothes, and they saw a frightful wound, through which the intestines came out. Then, after having bandaged him the best way they could, they brought him back to his own house, and they awaited the doctor, who had been sent for, as well as a priest.

When the doctor arrived, he gravely shook his head, and, turning towards young Hautot, who was sobbing on a chair:

"My poor boy," said he, "this has not a good look."

But, when the dressing was finished, the wounded man moved his fingers, opened his mouth, then his eyes, cast around his troubled, haggard glances, then appeared to search about in his memory, to recollect, to understand, and he murmured:

"Ah! good God! this has done for me!"

The doctor held his hand.

"Why no, why no, some days of rest merely — it will be nothing."

Hautot returned:

"It has done for me! My stomach is split! I know it well."

Then, all of a sudden:

" I want to talk to the son, if I have the time."

Hautot Junior, in spite of himself, shed tears, and kept repeating like a little boy.

" P'pa, p'pa, poor p'ps! "

But the father, in a firmer tone:

" Come! stop crying — this is not the time for it. I have to talk to you. Sit down there quite close to me. It will be quickly done, and I will be more calm. As for the rest of you, kindly give me one minute."

They all went out, leaving the father and son face to face.

As soon as they were alone:

" Listen, son! you are twenty-four years; one can say things like this to you. And then there is not such mystery about these matters as we import into them. You know well that your mother is seven years dead, isn't that so? and that I am not more than forty-five years myself, seeing that I got married at nineteen. Is not that true? "

The son faltered:

" Yes, it is true."

" So then your mother is seven years dead, and I have remained a widower. Well! a man like me cannot remain without a wife at thirty-seven isn't that true? "

The son replied:

" Yes, it is true."

The father, out of breath, quite pale, and his face contracted with suffering, went on:

" God! what pain I feel! Well, you understand. Man is not made to live alone, but I did not want to

take a successor to your mother, since I promised her
not to do so. Then — you understand?"

"Yes, father."

"So, I kept a young girl at Rouen, Reu de l'Eperlan
18, in the third story, the second door — I tell you all
this, don't forget — but a young girl, who has been very
nice to me, loving, devoted, a true woman, eh? You
comprehend, my lad?"

"Yes, father."

"So then, if I am carried off, I owe something to her,
but something substantial, that will place her in a safe
position. You understand?"

"Yes, father."

"I tell you that she is an honest girl, and that, but
for you, and the remembrance of your mother, and
again but for the house in which we three lived, I would
have brought her here, and then married her, for certain
— listen — listen, my lad. I might have made a will
— I haven't done so. I did not wish to do so — for
it is not necessary to write down things — things of this
sort — it is too hurtful to the legitimate children — and
then it embroils everything — it ruins everyone! Look
you, the stamped paper, there's no need of it — never
make use of it. If I am rich, it is because I have not
made use of what I have during my own life. You understand, my son?"

"Yes, father."

"Listen again — listen well to me! So then, I have
made no will — I did not desire to do so — and then I
knew what you were; you have a good heart; you are
not niggardly, not too near, in any way, I said to myself
that when my end approached I would tell you all about
it, and that I would beg of you not to forget the girl.

V—18

And then listen again! When I am gone, make your
way to the place at once — and make such arrangements that she may not blame my memory. You have
plenty of means. I leave it to you — I leave you
enough. Listen! You won't find her at home every
day in the week. She works at Madame Moreau's in
the Rue Beauvoisine. Go there on a Thursday. That
is the day she expects me. It has been my day for
the past six years. Poor little thing! she will weep! —
I say all this to you, because I have known you so well,
my son. One does not tell these things in public either
to the notary or to the priest. They happen — everyone knows that — but they are not talked about, save
in case of necessity. Then there is no outsider in the
secret, nobody except the family, because the family con-
sists of one person alone. You understand? "

" Yes, father."

" Do you promise? "

" Yes, father."

" Do you swear it? "

" Yes, father."

" I beg of you, I implore of you, son do not forget.
I bind you to it."

" No, father."

" You will go yourself. I want you to make sure of
everything."

" Yes, father."

" And, then, you will see — you will see what she
will explain to you. As for me, I can say no more to
you. You have vowed to do it."

" Yes, father."

" That's good, my son. Embrace me. Farewell.

I am going to break up, I'm sure.   Tell them  they may come in."

Young Hautot embraced his father, groaning while he did so; then, always docile, he opened the door, and the priest appeared in a white surplice, carrying the holy oils.

But the dying man had closed his eyes, and he refused to open them again, he refused to answer, he refused to show, even by a sign, that he understood.

He had spoken enough, this man; he could speak no more.   Besides he now felt his heart calm; he wanted to die in peace.   What need had he to make a confession to the deputy of God, since he had just done so to his son, who constituted his own family?

He received the last rites, was purified and absolved, in the midst of his friends and his servants on their bended knees, without any movement of his face indicating that he still lived.

He expired about midnight, after four hours' convulsive movements, which showed that he must have suffered dreadfully in his last moments.

## PART II

It was on the following Tuesday that they buried him, the shooting opened on Sunday.   On his return home, after having accompanied his father to the cemetery, César Hautot spent the rest of the day weeping. He scarcely slept at all on the following night, and he felt so sad on awakening that he asked himself how he could go on living.

However, he kept thinking until evening that, in order to obey the last wish of his father, he ought to repair to Rouen next day, and see this girl Catholine Donet, who resided in the Rue d'Eperlan in the third story, second door.   He had repeated to himself in a whisper, just as a little boy repeats a prayer, this name and address, a countless number of times, so that he might not forget them, and he ended by lisping them continually, without being able to stop or to think of what it was, so much were his tongue and his mind possessed by the appellation.

According, on the following day, about eight o'clock, he ordered Graindorge to be yoked to the tilbury, and set forth, at the quick trotting pace of the heavy Norman horse, along the high road from the Ainville to Rouen.   He wore his black frock coat drawn over his shoulders, a tall silk hat on his head, and on his legs his breeches with straps; and he did not wish, on account of the occasion, to dispense with the handsome costume, the blue overall which swelled in the wind, protected the cloth from dust and from stains, and which was to be removed quickly on reaching his destination the moment he had jumped out of the coach.

He entered Rouen accordingly just as it was striking ten o'clock, drew up, as he had usually done at the Hotel des Bon-Enfants, in the Rue des Trois-Mares, submitted to the hugs of the landlord and his wife and their five children, for they had heard the melancholy news; after that, he had to tell them all the particulars about the accident, which caused him to shed tears, to repel all the proffered attentions which they sought to thrust upon him merely because he was wealthy, and to decline even the breakfast they wanted him to partake of, thus wounding their sensibilities.

Then, having wiped the dust off his hat, brushed his
coat and removed the mud stains from his boots, he set
forth in search of the Rue de l'Eperlan, without venturing to make inquiries from anyone, for fear of being
recognized and arousing suspicions.

At length, being unable to find the place, he saw a
priest passing by, and, trusting to the professional dis-
cretion which churchmen possess, he questioned the ec-
clesiastic.

He had only a hundred steps farther to go; it was
exactly the second street to the right.

Then he hesitated. Up to that moment, he had
obeyed, like a mere animal, the expressed wish of the
deceased. Now he felt quite agitated, confused, humiliated, at the idea of finding himself — the son — in
the presence of this woman who had been his father's
mistress. All the morality which lies buried in our
breasts, heaped up at the bottom of our sensuous emotions by centuries of hereditary instruction, all that he
had been taught since he had learned his catechism about
creatures of evil life, to instinctive contempt which
every man entertains towards them, even though he may
marry one of them, all the narrow honesty of the
peasant in his character, was stirred up within him, and
held him back, making him grow red with shame.

But he said to himself:

" I promised the father, I must not break my
promise."

Then he gave a push to the door of the house bearing
the number 18, which stood ajar, discovered a gloomy-
looking staircase, ascended three flights, perceived a
door, then a second door, came upon the string of a bell,
and pulled it. The ringing, which resounded in the

apartment before which he stood, sent a shiver through his frame. The door was opened, and he found himself facing a young lady very well dressed, a brunette with a fresh complexion who gazed at him with eyes of astonishment.

He did not know what to say to her, and she who suspected nothing, and who was waiting for the other, did not invite him to come in. They stood looking thus at one another for nearly half-a-minute, at the end of which she said in a questioning tone:

" You have something to tell me Monsieur? "   He falteringly replied:

" I am M. Hautot's son."

She gave a start, turned pale, and stammered out as if she had known him for a long time:

" Monsieur César? "

" Yes."

" And what next? "

" I have come to speak to you on the part of my father."

She articulated:

" Oh my God! "

She then drew back so that he might enter. He shut the door and followed her into the interior. Then he saw a little boy of four or five years playing with a cat, seated on a floor in front of a stove, from which rose the steam of dishes which were being kept hot.

" Take a seat," she said.

He sat down.

She asked:

" Well? "

He no longer ventured to speak, keeping his eyes fixed on the table which stood in the center of the room,

with three covers laid on it, one of which was for a child.
He glanced at the chair which had its back turned to the
fire. They had been expecting him. That was his
bread which he saw, and which he recognized near the
fork, for the crust had been removed on account of
Hautot's bad teeth. Then, raising his eyes, he noticed
on the wall his father's portrait, the large photograph
taken at Paris the year of the exhibition, the same as
that which hung above the bed in the sleeping apartment at Ainville.

The young woman again asked:

" Well, Monsieur César? "

He kept staring at her. Her face was livid with
anguish; and she waited, her hands trembling with fear.

Then he took courage.

" Well, Mam'zelle, papa died on Sunday last just after he had opened the shooting."

She was so much overwhelmed that she did not move.
After a silence of a few seconds, she faltered in an almost inaudible tone:

" Oh! it is not possible! "

Then, on a sudden, tears showed themselves in her
eyes, and covering her face with her hands, she burst out
sobbing.

At that point the little boy turned round, and, seeing
his mother weeping, began to howl. Then, realizing
that this sudden trouble was brought about by the
stranger, he rushed at César, caught hold of his breeches
with one hand, and with the other hit him with all his
strength on the thigh. And César remained agitated,
deeply affected, with this woman mourning for his
father at one side of him, and the little boy defending
his mother at the other. He felt their emotion taking

possession of himself, and his eyes were beginning to brim over with the same sorrow; so, to recover her self-command, he began to talk:

" Yes," he said, " the accident occurred on Sunday, at eight o'clock —."

And he told, as if she were listening to him, all the facts without forgetting a single detail, mentioning the most trivial matters with the minuteness of a country-man. And the child still kept assailing him, making kicks at his ankles.

When he came to the time at which his father had spoken about her, her attention was caught by hearing her own name, and, uncovering her face she said:

" Pardon me! I was not following you; I would like to know — If you did not mind beginning over again."

He related everything at great length, with stoppages, breaks and reflections of his own from time to time. She listened to him eagerly now perceiving with a woman's keen sensibility all the sudden changes of fortune which his narrative indicated, and trembling with horror, every now and then, exclaiming:

" Oh, my God! "

The little fellow, believing that she had calmed down, ceased beating César, in order to catch his mother's hand, and he listened, too, as if he understood.

When the narrative was finished, young Hautot continued:

" Now we will settle matters together in accordance with his wishes."

" Listen: I am well off he has left me plenty of means. I don't want you to have anything to complain about —"

But she quickly interrupted him.

" Oh, Monsieur César, Monsieur César, not to-day.
I am cut to the heart — another time — another day.
No, not to-day. If I accept, listen! 'Tis not for my-
self — no, no, no, I swear to you. 'Tis for the child.
Besides this provision will be put to his account."

Thereupon, César scared, divined the truth, and
stammering:

" So then —'tis his — the child? "

" Why, yes," she said.

And Hautot, Junior, gazed at his brother with a confused emotion, intense and painful.

After a lengthened silence, for she had begun to weep
afresh, César, quite embarrassed, went on:

" Well, then, Mam'zelle Donet I am going. When
would you wish to talk this over with me? "

She exclaimed:

" Oh! no, don't go! don't go. Don't leave me all
alone with Emile. I would die of grief. I have no
longer anyone, anyone but my child. Oh! what wretchedness, what wretchedness. Mousieur César! Stop!
Sit down again. You will say something more to me.
You will tell me what he was doing over there all the
week."

And César resumed his seat, accustomed to obey.

She drew over another chair for herself in front of
the stove, where the dishes had all this time been sim-
mering, took Emile upon her knees, and asked César a
thousand questions about his father with reference to
matters of an intimate nature, which made him feel
without reasoning on the subject, that she had loved
Hautot with all the strength of her frail woman's heart.

And, by the natural concatenation of his ideas —
which were rather limited in number — he recurred once

more to the accident, and set about telling the story over
again with all the same details.

When he said:

" He had a hole in his stomach — you could put your
two fists into it."

She gave vent to a sort of shriek, and the tears gushed
forth again from her eyes.

Then seized by the contagion of her grief, César began to weep, too, and as tears always soften the fibers
of the heart, he bent over Emile whose forehead was
close to his own mouth, and kissed him.

The mother, recovering her breath, murmured:

" Poor lad, he is an orphan now ! "

" And so am I," said César.

And they ceased to talk.

But suddenly the practical instinct of the housewife,
accustomed to be thoughtful about many things, revived in the young woman's breast.

" You have perhaps taken nothing all the morning,
Monsieur César."

" No, Mam'zelle."

" Oh! you must be hungry.   You will eat a morsel."

" Thanks," he said, " I am not hungry; I have had
too much trouble."

She replied:

" In spite of sorrow, we must live.   You will not refuse to let me get something for you!   And then you
will remain a little longer.   When you are gone, I don't
know what will become of me."

He yielded after some further resistance, and, sitting
down with his back to the fire, facing her, he ate a plate-
ful of tripe, which had been  bubbling in the stove, and
drank a glass of red wine.   But he would not allow

her to uncork the bottle of white wine.  He several
times wiped the mouth of the little boy, who had
smeared all his chin with sauce.

As he was rising up to go, he asked:

" When would you like me to come back to speak
about this business to you, Mam'zelle Donet? "

" If it is all the same to you, say next Thursday,
Monsieur César.  In that way, I would lose none of
my time, as I always have my Thursdays free."

" That will suit me — next Thursday."

" You will come to lunch.  Won't you?

" Oh! On that point I can't give you a promise."

" The reason I suggested is that people can chat better when they are eating.  One has more time too."

" Well, be it so.  About twelve o'clock, then."

And he took his departure, after he had again kissed
little Emile, and pressed Mademoiselle Donet's hand.


## PART III

THE week appeared long to César Hautot.  He had
never before found himself alone, and the isolation
seemed to him insupportable.  Till now, he had lived
at his father's side, just like his shadow, followed him
into the fields, superintended the execution of his orders, and, when they had been a short time separated,
again met him at dinner.  They had spent the evenings
smoking their pipes, face to face with one another,
chatting about horses, cows or sheep, and the grip of
their hands when they rose up in the morning might
have been regarded as a manifestation of deep family
affection on both sides.

Now César was alone, he went vacantly through the

process of dressing the soil of autumn, every moment
expecting to see the tall gesticulating silhouette of his
father rising up at the end of a plain. To kill time,
he entered the houses of his neighbors, told about the
accident to all who had not heard of it, and sometimes
repeated it to the others. Then, after he had finished
his occupations and his reflections, he would sit down at
the side of a road, asking himself whether this kind of
life was going to last for ever.

He frequently thought of Mademoiselle Donet.
He liked her. He considered her thoroughly respectable, a gentle and honest young woman, as his father
had said. Yes, undoubtedly she was an honest girl.
He resolved to act handsomely towards her, and to
give her two thousand francs a year, settling the capital
on the child. He even experienced a certain pleasure
in thinking that he was going to see her on the following
Thursday and arrange this matter with her. And then
the notion of this brother, this little chap of five, who
was his father's son, plagued him, annoyed him a little,
and, at the same time, exhibited him. He had, as it
were, a family in this brat, sprung from a clandestine al-
liance, who would never bear the name of Hautot, a
family which he might take or leave, just as he pleased,
but which would recall his father.

And so, when he saw himself on the road to Rouen on
Thursday morning, carried along by Graindorge
trotting with clattering foot-beats, he felt his heart
lighter, more at peace than he had hitherto felt it since
his bereavement.

On entering Mademoiselle Donet's apartment, he
saw the table laid as on the previous Thursday with the
sole difference that the crust had not been removed from

the bread.   He pressed the young woman's hand, kissed
Emile on the cheeks, and sat down, more at ease than if
he were in his own house, his heart swelling in the same
way.   Mademoiselle Donet seemed to him a little
thinner and paler.   She must have grieved sorely.   She
wore now an air of constraint in his presence, as if she
understood what she had not felt the week before under
the first blow of her misfortune, and she exhibited an
excessive deference towards him, a mournful humility,
and made touching efforts to please him, as if to pay
him back by her attentions for the kindness he had manifested towards her.   They were a long time at lunch
talking over the business, which had brought him there.
She did not want so much money.   It was too much.
She earned enough to live on herself, but she only
wished that Emile might find a few sous awaiting him
when he grew big.   César held out, however, and even
added a gift of a thousand francs for herself for the
expense of mourning.

When he had taken his coffee, she asked:

" Do you smoke? "

" Yes — I have my pipe."

He felt in his pocket.   Good God!   He had forgotten it!   He was becoming quite woebegone about it
when she offered him a pipe of his father that had been
shut up in a cupboard.   He accepted it, took it up in
his hand, recognized it, smelled it, spoke of its quality
in a tone of emotion, filled it with tobacco, and lighted
it.   Then, he set Emile astride on his knee, and made
him play the cavalier, while she removed the table-
cloth, and put the soiled plates at one end of the
sideboard in order to wash them as soon as he was
gone.

About three o'clock, he rose up with regret, quite annoyed at the thought of having to go.

" Well! Mademoiselle Donet," he said, " I wish you good evening, and am delighted to have found you like this."

She remained standing before him, blushing, much affected, and gazed at him while she thought of the other.

" Shall we not see one another again? " she said.

He replied simply:

" Why, yes, mam'zelle, if it gives you pleasure."

" Certainly, Monsieur César.   Will next Thursday suit you then? "

" Yes, Mademoiselle Donet."

" You will come to lunch, of course? "

" Well — if you are so kind as to invite me, I can't refuse."

" It is understood, then, Monsieur César — next Thursday at twelve, the same as to-day."

" Thursday at twelve, Mam'zelle Donet! "

# LITTLE LOUISE ROQUÉ

MEDERIC Rompel, the postman, who was familiarly called by the country people Mederi, started at the usual hour from the posthouse at Rouy-le-Tors. Having passed through the little town with his big strides of an old trooper, he first cut across the meadows of Villaumes in order to reach the bank of the Brindelle, which led him along the water's edge to the village of Carvelin, where his distribution commenced. He went quickly, following the course of the narrow river, which frothed, murmured, and boiled along its bed of grass, under an arch of willow-trees. The big stones, impeding the flow, had around them a cushion of water, a sort of cravat ending in a knot of foam. In some places, there were cascades, a foot wide, often invisible, which made under the leaves, under the tendrils, under a roof of verdure, a big noise at once angry and gentle; then, further on, the banks widened out, and you saw a small, placid lake where trouts were swimming in the midst of all that green vegetation which keeps undulating in the depths of tranquil streams.

Mederic went on without a halt, seeing nothing, and with only this thought in his mind: " My first letter is for the Poivron family, then I have one for M. Renardet; so I must cross the wood."

His blue blouse, fastened round his waist by a black leathern belt moved in a quick, regular fashion above the green hedge of the willow-trees; and his stick of stout

287

holly kept time with the steady movement of his legs.

Then, he crossed the Brindelle over a bridge formed of a single tree thrown lengthwise, with a rope attached to two stakes driven into the river's banks as its only balustrade.

The wood, which belonged to M. Renardet, the Mayor of Carvelin, and the largest landowner in the district, consisted of a number of huge old trees, straight as pillars, and extending for about half a league along the left-bank of the stream which served as a boundary for this immense arch of foliage. Alongside the water there were large shrubs warmed by the sun; but under the trees you found nothing but moss, thick, soft, plastic moss, which exhaled into the stagnant air a light odor of loam with withered branches.

Mederic slackened his pace, took off his black cap adorned with red lace, and wiped his forehead, for it was by this time hot in the meadows, though it was not yet eight o'clock in the morning.

He had just recovered from the effects of the heat, and resumed his accelerated pace when he noticed at the foot of a tree a knife, a child's small knife. When he picked it up, he discovered a thimble and also a needle-case not far away.

Having taken up these objects, he thought: "I'll intrust them to the Mayor," and he resumed his journey, but now he kept his eyes open expecting to find something else.

All of a sudden, he drew up stiffly as if he had knocked himself against a wooden bar; for, ten paces in front of him, lay stretched on her back a little girl, quite naked, on the moss. She was about twelve years old. Her arms were hanging down, her legs parted, and her

face covered with a handkerchief. There were little
spots of blood on her thighs.

Mederic advanced now on tiptoe, as if he were afraid
to make a noise, apprehended some danger, and he
glanced towards the spot uneasily.

What was this? No doubt, she was asleep. Then,
he reflected that a person does not go to sleep thus
naked, at half-past seven in the morning under cool
trees. So then she must be dead; and he must be face
to face with a crime. At this thought, a cold shiver
ran through his frame, although he was an old soldier.
And then a murder was such a rare thing in the country,
and above all the murder of a child, that he could not
believe his eyes. But she had no wound — nothing
save this blood stuck on her leg. How, then, had she
been killed?

He stopped quite near her; and he stared at her, while
he leaned on his stick. Certainly, he knew her, as he
knew all the inhabitants of the district; but, not being
able to get a look at her face, he could not guess her
name. He stooped forward in order to take off the
handkerchief which covered her face, then paused with
outstretched hand, restrained by an idea that occurred
to him.

Had he the right to disarrange anything in the condition of the corpse before the magisterial investigation? He pictured justice to himself as a kind of general whom nothing escapes, and who attaches as much
importance to a lost button as to a stab of a knife in the
stomach. Perhaps under this handkerchief evidence to
support a capital charge could be found; in fact if there
were sufficient proof there to secure a conviction, it
might lost its value, if touched by an awkward hand.

V—19

Then, he raised himself with the intention of hastening towards the Mayor's residence, but again another
thought held him back.   If the little girl was still alive,
by any chance, he could not leave her lying there in
this way.   He sank on his knees very gently, a little bit
away from her through precaution, and extended his
hand towards her feet.   It was icy cold, with the terrible coldness which makes the dead flesh frightful, and
which leaves us no longer in doubt.   The letter-carrier,
as he touched her, felt his heart in his mouth, as he said
to himself afterwards and his lips were parched with dry
spittle.   Rising up abruptly he rushed off under the
trees towards M. Renardet's house.

He walked on in double-quick time, with his stick
under his arm, his hands clenched, and his head thrust
forward, and his leathern bag, filled with letters and
newspapers, kept regularly flapping at his side.

The Mayor's residence was at the end of the wood
which he used as a park, and one side of it was washed
by a little pool formed at this spot by the Brindelle.

It was a big, square house of gray stone, very old,
which had stood many a siege in former days, and at
the end of it was a huge tower, twenty meters high, built
in the water.

From the top of this fortress the entire country
around it could be seen in olden times.   It was called
the Fox's tower, without anyone knowing exactly why;
and from this appellation, no doubt, had come the name
Renardet, borne by the owners of this fief, which had remained in the same family, it was said, for more than
two hundred years.   For the Renardets formed part
of the upper middle class all but noble to be met with
so often in the provinces before the Revolution.

The postman dashed into the kitchen where the servants were taking breakfast, and exclaimed:

" Is the Mayor up?   I   want to speak to him at once."

Mederic was recognized as a man of weight and authority, and it was soon understood that something serious had happened.

As soon as word was brought to M. Renardet, he ordered the postman to be sent up to him.   Pale and out of breath, with his cap in his hand, Mederic found the Mayor seated in front of a long table covered with scattered papers.

He was a big, tall man, heavy and red-faced, strong as an ox and was greatly liked in the district, though of an excessively violent disposition.   Very nearly forty years old, and a widower for the past six months, he lived on his estate like a country gentleman.   His choleric temperament had often brought him into trouble, from which the magistrates of Rouy-le-Tors, like indulgent and prudent friends, had extricated him. Had he not one day thrown the conductor of the diligence from the top of his seat because he was near crushing his retriever, Micmac?   Had he not broken the ribs of a gamekeeper, who abused him for having, with a gun in his hand, passed through a neighbor's property?   Had he not even caught by the collar the sub-prefect, who stopped in the village in the course of an administrative round described by M. Renardet as an electioneering round; for he was against the government, according to his family tradition.

The Mayor asked:

" What's the matter now, Mederic? "

" I found a little girl dead in your wood."

Renardet rose up, with his face the color of brick.

" Do you say — a little girl? "

" Yes, m'sieur, a little girl, quite naked, on her back, with blood on her, dead — quite dead! "

The Mayor gave vent to an oath:

" My God, I'd make a bet 'tis little Louise Roqué! I have just learned that she did not go home to her mother last night.   Where did you find her? "

The postman pointed out where the place was, gave full details, and offered to conduct the Mayor to the spot.

But Renardet became brusque:

" No, I don't need you.   Send the steward, the Mayor's secretary, and the doctor immediately to me, and resume your rounds.   Quick, quick, go and tell them to meet me in the woods."

The letter-carrier, a man used to discipline, obeyed and withdrew, angry and grieved at not being able to be present at the investigation.

The Mayor, in his turn, prepared to go out, took his hat, a big soft hat, and paused for a few seconds on the threshold of his abode.   In front of him stretched a wide sward, in which three large patches were conspicuous — three large beds of flowers in full bloom, one facing the house and the others at either side of it. Further on, rose skyward the principal trees in the wood, while at the left, above the Brindelle widened into a pool, could be seen long meadows, an entirely green flat sweep of the country, cut by dikes and willow edges like monsters, twisted dwarf-trees, always cut short, and having on their thick squat trunks a quivering tuft of thick branches.

At the right, behind the stables, the outhouses, all

the buildings connected with the property, might be seen the village, which was wealthy, being mainly inhabited by rearers of oxen.

Renardet slowly descended the steps in front of his house, and turning to the left, gained the water's edge, which he followed at a slow pace, his hand behind his back. He went on with bent head, and from time to time he glanced round in search of the persons for whom he had sent.

When he stood beneath the trees, he stopped, took off his hat, and wiped his forehead as Mederic had done; for the burning sun was falling in fiery rain upon the ground. Then the Mayor resumed his journey, stopped once more, and retraced his steps. Suddenly, stooping down, he steeped his handkerchief in the stream that glided at his feet, and stretched it round his head, under his hat. Drops of water flowed along his temples over his ears always purple over his strong red neck, and made their way, one after the other, under his white shirt-collar.

As nobody yet appeared he began tapping with his foot, then he called out —

" Hallo! Hallo! "

A voice at his right, answered:

" Hallo! Hallo! "

And the doctor appeared under the trees. He was a thin little man, an ex-military surgeon, who passed in the neighborhood for a very skillful practitioner. He limped, having been wounded while in the service, and had to use a stick to assist him in walking.

Next came the steward and the Mayor's secretary, who, having been sent for at the same time, arrived together. They looked scared, and hurried forward out of breath, walking and trotting in turn in order to hasten their progress, and moving their arms up and down so vigorously that they seemed to do more work with them than with their legs.

Renardet said to the doctor:

" You know what the trouble is about? "

" Yes, a child found dead in the wood by Mederic."

" That's quite correct. Come on."

They walked on side by side, followed by the two men.

Their steps made no noise on the moss, their eyes were gazing downward right in front of them.

The doctor hastened his steps, interested by the discovery. As soon as they were near the corpse, he bent down to examine it without touching it. He had put on a pair of glasses, as when one is looking at some curious object, and turned round very quietly.

He said without rising up:

" Violated and assassinated, as we are going to prove presently. This little girl moreover, is almost a woman — look at her throat."

Her two breasts, already nearly full-developed, fell over her chest, relaxed by death.

The doctor lightly drew away the handkerchief which covered her face. It looked black, frightful, the tongue protruding, the eyes bloodshot. He went on:

" Faith, she was strangled the moment the deed was done."

He felt her neck:

" Strangled with the hands without leaving any special trace, neither the mark of the nails nor the imprint of the fingers. Quite right. It is little Louise Roqué, sure enough! "

He delicately replaced the handkerchief:

"There's nothing for me to do — She's been dead for the last hour at least. We must give notice of the matter to the authorities."

Renardet, standing up, with his hands behind his back, kept staring with a stony look at the little body exposed to view on the grass. He murmured:

"What a wretch! We must find the clothes."

The doctor felt the hands, the arms, the legs. He said:

"She must have been bathing, no doubt. They ought to be at the water's edge."

The Mayor thereupon gave directions:

"Do you, Princépe" (this was his secretary), go and look for those clothes for me along the river. Do you, Maxime" (this was the steward), "hurry on towards Roug-le-Tors, and bring on here to me the examining magistrate with the gendarmes. They must be here within an hour. You understand."

The two men quickly departed, and Renardet said to the doctor:

"What miscreant has been able to do such a deed in this part of the country."

The doctor murmured:

"Who knows? Everyone is capable of that? Everyone in particular and nobody in general. No matter, it must be some prowler, some workman out of employment. As we live under a Republic, we must expect to meet only this kind of person along the roads."

Both of them were Bonapartists.

The Mayor went on:

" Yes, it can only be a stranger, a passer-by, a vaga-
bond without heart or home."

The doctor added with the shadow of a smile on his
face:

" And without a wife.   Having neither a good supper nor a good bed, he procured the rest for himself.
You can't tell how many men there may be in the world
capable of a crime at a given moment.   Did you know
that this little girl had disappeared? "

And with the end of his stick he touched one after
the other the stiffened fingers of the corpse, resting on
them as on the keys of a piano.

" Yes, the mother came last night to look for me
about nine o'clock, the child not having come home
from supper up to seven.   We went to try and find her
along the roads up to midnight, but we did not think
of the wood.   However, we needed daylight to carry
out a search with a practical result."

" Will you have a cigar? " said the doctor.

" Thanks, I don't care to smoke.   It gives me a turn
to look at this."

They both remained standing in front of this corpse
of a young girl, so pale, on the dark moss.   A big fly
with a blue belly that was walking along one of the
thighs, stopped at the bloodstains, went on again, always rising higher, ran along the side with his lively,
jerky movements, climbed up one of the breasts, then
came back again to explore the other, looking out for
something to drink on this dead girl.   The two men
kept watching this wandering black speck.

The doctor said:

" How pretty it is, a fly on the skin!   The ladies of

the last century had good reason to paste them on their faces. Why has this fashion gone out?"

The Mayor seemed not to hear, plunged as he was in deep thought.

But, all of a sudden, he turned round, for he was surprised by a shrill noise. A woman in a cap and a blue apron rushed up under the trees. It was the mother, La Roqué. As soon as she saw Renardet she began to shriek:

"My little girl, where's my little girl?" in such a distracted manner that she did not glance down at the ground. Suddenly, she saw the corpse, stopped short, clasped her hands, and raised both her arms while she uttered a sharp, heartrending cry — the cry of a mutilated animal. Then she rushed towards the body, fell on her knees, and took off, as if she would have snatched it away, the handkerchief that covered the face. When she saw that frightful countenance, black and convulsed, she rose up with a shudder, then pressed her face against the ground, giving vent to terrible and continuous screams with her mouth close to the thick moss.

Her tall, thin frame, to which her clothes were clinging tightly, was palpitating, shaken with convulsions. They could see her bony ankles and her dried up calves covered with thick blue stockings, shivering horribly; and she went digging the soil with her crooked fingers as if in order to make a hole there to hide herself in it.

The doctor moved, said in a low tone:

"Poor old woman!"

Renardet felt a strange rumbling in his stomach; then he gave vent to a sort of loud sneeze that issued at the same time through his nose and through his mouth; and, drawing his handkerchief from his pocket, he began to weep internally, coughing, sobbing, and wiping his face noisily.

He stammered —

" Damn — damn — damned pig to do this! I would like to see him guillotined."

But Princépe reappeared, with his hands empty. He murmured —

" I have found nothing, M'sieu le Maire, nothing at all anywhere."

The doctor, scared, replied in a thick voice, drowned in tears:

" What is that you could not find? "

" The little girl's clothes."

" Well — well — look   again, and find them — or you'll have to answer to me."

The man, knowing that the Mayor would not brook opposition, set forth again with hesitating steps, casting on the corpse indirect and timid glances.

Distant voices arose under the trees, a confused sound, the noise of an approaching crowd; for Mederic had, in the course of his rounds carried the news from door to door.   The people of the neighborhood, stupefied at first, had gone chatting from their own firesides into the street, from one threshold to another.   Then they gathered together.   They talked over, discussed, and commented on the event for some minutes, and they had now come to see it for themselves.

They arrived in groups a little faltering and uneasy through fear of the first impression of such a scene on their minds.   When they saw the body they stopped, not daring to advance, and speaking low.   They grew bold, went on a few steps, stopped again, advanced once

more, and soon they formed around the dead girl, her
mother, the doctor, and Renardet, a thick circle, agitated
and noisy, which crushed forward under the sudden
pushes of the last comers. And now they touched the
corpse. Some of them even bent down to feel it with
their fingers. The doctor kept them back. But the
mayor, waking abruptly out of his torpor, broke into
a rage, and, seizing Dr. Labarbe's stick, flung himself on
his townspeople, stammering:

" Clear out — clear out — you pack of brutes —
clear out! "

And in a second, the crowd of sightseers had fallen
back two hundred meters.

La Roqué was lifted up, turned round, and placed in
a sitting posture, and she now remained weeping with
her hands clasped over her face.

The occurrence was discussed among the crowd;
and young lads' eager eyes curiously scrutinized this
naked body of a girl. Renardet perceived this, and
abruptly taking off his vest, he flung it over the little
girl, who was entirely lost to view under the wide garment.

The spectators drew near quietly. The wood was
filled with people, and a continuous hum of voices rose
up under the tangled foliage of the tall trees.

The Mayor, in his shirt sleeves, remained standing,
with his stick in his hands, in a fighting attitude. He
seemed exasperated by this curiosity on the part of the
people, and kept repeating:

" If one of you come nearer, I'll break his head just
as I would a dog's."

The peasants were greatly afraid of him. They
held back. Dr. Labarbe, who was smoking, sat down

beside La Roqué, and spoke to her in order to distract her attention. The old woman soon removed her hands from her face, and she replied with a flood of tearful words, emptying her grief in copious talk. She told the whole story of her life, her marriage, the death of her man, a bullsticker, who had been gored to death, the infancy of her daughter, her wretched existence as a widow without resources and with a child to support. She had only this one, her little Louise, and the child had been killed — killed in this wood. All of a sudden, she felt anxious to see it again, and dragging herself on her knees towards the corpse, she raised up one corner of the garment that covered her; then she let it fall again, and began wailing once more. The crowd remained silent, eagerly watching all the mother's gestures.

But all of a sudden, a great swaying movement took place, and there was a cry of "the gendarmes! the gendarmes!"

The gendarmes appeared in the distance, coming on at a rapid trot, escorting their captain and a little gentleman with red whiskers, who was bobbing up and down like a monkey on a big white mare.

The steward had just found M. Putoin, the examining magistrate, at the moment when he was mounting his horse to take his daily ride, for he posed as a good horseman to the great amusement of the officers.

He alighted along with the captain, and passed the hands of the Mayor and the Doctor, casting a ferret-like glance on the linen vest which swelled above the body lying underneath.

When he was thoroughly acquainted with the facts, he first gave orders to get rid of the public, whom the gendarmes drove out of the wood, but who soon reappeared in the meadow, and formed a hedge, a big hedge of excited and moving heads all along the Brindelle, on the other side of the stream.

The doctor in his turn, gave explanations, of which Renardet took a note in his memorandum book. All the evidence was given, taken down, and commented on without leading to any discovery. Maxime, too, came back without having found any trace of the clothes.

This disappearance surprised everybody; no one could explain it on the theory of theft, and as these rags were not worth twenty sous, even this theory was inadmissible.

The examining magistrate, the mayor, the captain, and the doctor, set to work by searching in pairs, putting aside the smallest branches along the water.

Renardet said to the judge:

" How does it happen that this wretch has concealed or carried away the clothes, and has thus left the body exposed in the open air and visible to everyone? "

The other, sly and knowing, answered:

" Ha! Ha! Perhaps a dodge? This crime has been committed either by a brute or by a crafty blackguard. In any case we'll easily succeed in finding him."

The rolling of a vehicle made them turn their heads round. It was the deputy magistrate, the doctor and the registrar of the court who had arrived in their turn. They resumed their searches, all chatting in an animated fashion.

Renardet said suddenly:

" Do you know that I am keeping you to lunch with me? "

Everyone smilingly accepted the invitation, and the

examining magistrate, finding that the case of little Louise Roqué was quite enough to bother about for one day, turned towards the Mayor:

" I can have the body brought to your house, can I not?   You have a room in which you can keep it for me till this evening."

The other got confused, and stammered:

" Yes — no —no.  To  tell  the  truth,  I  prefer that it should not come into my house on account of — on account of my servants who are already talking about ghosts in — in my tower, in the Fox's tower.   You know — I could no longer keep a single one.   No — I prefer not to have it in my house."

The magistrate began to smile:

" Good! I am going to get it carried off at once to Roug, for the legal examination."

Turning towards the door:

" I can make use of your trap can I not? "

" Yes, certainly."

Everybody came back to the place where the corpse lay.   La Roqué now, seated beside her daughter, had caught hold of her head, and was staring right before her, with a wandering listless eye.

The two doctors endeavored to lead her away, so that she might not witness the dead girl's removal; but she understood at once what they wanted to do, and, flinging herself on the body, she seized it in both arms. Lying on top of the corpse, she exclaimed:

" You shall not have it —'tis mine —'tis mine now. They have killed her on me, and I want to keep her — you shall not have her —! "

All the men, affected and not knowing how to act,

remained standing around her.    Renardet fell on his
knees, and said to her:

" Listen, La Roqué, it is necessary in order to find
out who killed her.   Without this, it could not be found
out.   We must make a search for him in order to
punish him.   When we have found him, we'll give her
up to you.   I promise you this."

This explanation shook the woman's mind, and a feeling of hatred manifested itself in her distracted glance.

" So then they'll take him? "

" Yes, I promise you that."

She rose up, deciding to let them do as they liked;
but, when the captain remarked:

" 'Tis surprising that her clothes were not found."

A new idea, which she had not previously thought
of, abruptly found an entrance into her brain, and she
asked:

" Where are her clothes.   They're mine.   I want
them.   Where have they been put? "

They explained to her that they had not been found.
Then she called out for them with desperate obstinacy
and with repeated moans.

" They're mine — I want them.   Where are they?
I want them! "

The more they tried to calm her the more she
sobbed, and persisted in her demands.   She no longer
wanted the body, she insisted on having the clothes, as
much perhaps through the unconscious cupidity of a
wretched being to whom a piece of silver represents a
fortune, as through maternal tenderness.

And when the little body rolled up in blankets which
had been brought out from Renardet's house, had disappeared in the vehicle, the old woman standing under

the trees, held up by the Mayor and the Captain, exclaimed:

" I have nothing, nothing, nothing in the world, not
even her little cap — her little cap."

The curé had just arrived, a young priest already
growing stout. He took it on himself to carry off La
Roqué, and they went away together towards the
village. The mother's grief was modified under the
sugary words of the clergyman, who promised her a
thousand compensations. But she incessantly kept repeating:

" If I had only her little cap."

Sticking to this idea which now dominated every
other.

Renardet exclaimed some distance away:

" You lunch with us, Monsieur l'Abbé — in an hour's
time."

The priest turned his head round, and replied:

" With pleasure, Monsieur le Maire. I'll be with
you at twelve."

And they all directed their steps towards the house
whose gray front and large tower built on the edge of
the Brindelle, could be seen through the branches.

The meal lasted a long time. They talked about the
crime. Everybody was of the same opinion. It had
been committed by some tramp passing there by mere
chance while the little girl was bathing.

Then the magistrates returned to Roug, announcing
that they would return next day at an early hour. The
doctor and the curé went to their respective homes, while
Renardet, after a long walk through the meadows, returned to the wood where he remained walking till
nightfall with slow steps, his hands behind his back.

He went to bed early, and was still asleep next morning when the examining magistrate entered his room. He rubbed his hands together with a self-satisfied air. He said:

" Ha! ha! You're still sleeping.    Well, my dear fellow, we have news this morning."

The Mayor sat up on his bed.

" What, pray? "

" Oh!  Something strange.  You remember well how the mother yesterday clamored for some memento of her daughter, especially her little cap?  Well, on opening her door this morning, she found on the threshold, her child's two little wooden shoes.  This proves that the crime was perpetrated by some one from the district, some one who felt pity for her.  Besides, the postman, Mederic comes and brings the thimble, the knife and the needle case of the dead girl.  So then the man in carrying off the clothes in order to hide them, must have let fall the articles which were in the pocket. As for me, I attach special importance about the wooden shoes, as they indicate a certain moral culture and a faculty for tenderness on the part of the assassin.  We will therefore, if I have no objection, pass in review together the principal inhabitants of your district."

The Mayor got up.  He rang for hot water to shave with, and said:

" With pleasure, but it will take rather a long time, and we may begin at once."

M. Putoin had sat astride on a chair, thus pursuing even in a room, his mania for horsemanship.

Renardet now covered his chin with a white lather while he looked at himself in the glass; then he sharpened his razor on the strop and went on:

V—20

" The principal inhabitant of Carvelin bears the name
of Joseph Renardet, Mayor, a rich landowner, a rough
man who beats guards and coachmen —"

The examining magistrate burst out laughing:

" That's enough; let us pass on to the next."

" The second in importance is ill. Pelledent, his
deputy, a rearer of oxen, an equally rich landowner, a
crafty peasant, very sly, very close-fisted on every question of money, but incapable in my opinion, of having
perpetrated such a crime."

M. Putoin said:

" Let us pass on."

Then, while continuing to shave and wash himself,
Renardet went on with the moral inspection of all the
inhabitants of Carvelin.  After two hours' discussion,
their suspicions were fixed on three individuals who had
hitherto borne a shady reputation — a poacher named
Cavalle, a fisher for trails and crayfish named Paquet,
and a bullsticker named Clovis.


## PART II

THE search for the perpetrator of the crime lasted
all the summer, but he was not discovered.  Those who
were suspected and those who were arrested easily
proved their innocence, and the authorities were compelled to abandon the attempt to capture the criminal.

But this murder seemed to have moved the entire
country in a singular fashion.  There redisquietude, a
vague fear, a sensation of mysterious terror, springing
not merely from the impossibility of discovering any
trace of the assassin, but also and above all from that
strange finding of the wooden shoes in front of La

Roqué's door on the day after the crime. The certainty that the murderer had assisted at the investigation, that he was still living in the village without doubt, left a gloomy impression on people's minds, and appeared to brood over the neighborhood like an incessant menace.

The wood besides, had become a dreaded spot, a place to be avoided, and supposed to be haunted.

Formerly, the inhabitants used to come and sit down on the moss at the feet of the huge tall trees, or walk along the water's edge watching the trouts gliding under the green undergrowth. The boys used to play bowls, hide-and-seek and other games in certain places where they had upturned, smoothed out, and leveled the soil, and the girls, in rows of four or five, used to trip along holding one another by the arms, and screaming out with their shrill voices ballads which grated on the ear, and whose false notes disturbed the tranquil air and set the teeth on edge like drops of vinegar. Now nobody went any longer under the wide lofty vault, as if people were afraid of always finding there some corpse lying on the ground.

Autumn arrived, the leaves began to fall. They fell down day and night, descended from the tall trees, round and round whirling to the ground; and the sky could be seen through the bare branches. Sometimes when a gust of wind swept over the tree-tops, the slow, continuous rain suddenly grew heavier, and became a storm with a hoarse roar, which covered the moss with a thick carpet of yellow water that made rather a squashing sound under the feet. And the almost imperceptible murmur, the floating, ceaseless murmur gentle and sad, of this rainfall seemed like a low wail, and those leaves continually falling, seemed like tears, big tears shed by the tall mournful trees which were weeping, as it were, day and night over the close of the year, over the ending of warm dawns and soft twilights, over the ending of hot breezes and bright suns, and also perhaps over the crime which they had seen committed under the shade of their branches, over the girl violated and killed at their feet. They wept in the silence of the desolate empty wood, the abandoned, dreaded wood, where the soul, the childish soul of the dead little girl must be wandering all alone.

The Brindelle, swollen by the storms, rushed on more quickly, yellow and angry, between its dry banks, between two thin, bare willow-hedges.

And here was Renardet suddenly resuming his walks under the trees. Every day, at sunset, he came out of his house decended the front steps slowly, and entered the wood, in a dreamy fashion with his hands in his pockets. For a long time he paced over the damp soft moss, while a legion of rooks, rushing to the spot from all the neighboring haunts in order to rest in the tall summits, unrolled themselves through space, like an immense mourning veil· floating in the wind, uttering violent and sinister screams. Sometimes, they rested, dotting with black spots the tangled branches against the red sky, the sky crimsoned with autumn twilights. Then, all of a sudden, they set again, croaking frightfully and trailing once more above the wood the long dark festoon of their flight.

They swooped down at last, on the highest treetops, and gradually their cawings died away while the advancing night mingled their black plumes with the blackness of space.

Renardet was still strolling slowly under the trees; then, when the thick darkness prevented him from walking any longer, he went back to the house, sank all of a heap into his armchair in front of the glowing hearth, stretching towards the fire his damp feet from which for some time under the flames vapor emanated.

Now, one morning, an important bit of news was circulated around the district; the Mayor was getting his wood cut down.

Twenty woodcutters were already at work. They had commenced at the corner nearest to the house, and they worked rapidly in the master's presence.

At first, the loppers climbed up the trunk. Tied to it by a rope collar, they cling round in the beginning with both arms, then, lifting one leg, they strike it hard with a blow of the edge of a steel instrument attached to each foot. The edge penetrates the wood, and remains stuck in it; and the man rises up as if on a step in order to strike with the steel attached to the other foot, and once more supports himself till he lifts his first foot again.

And with every upward movement he raises higher the rope collar which fastens him to the tree. Over his loins, hangs and glitters the steel hatchet. He keeps continually clinging on in an easy fashion like a parasitic creature attacking a giant; he mounts slowly up the immense trunk, embracing it and spurring it in order to decapitate it.

As soon as he reaches the first branches, he stops, detaches from his side the sharp ax, and strikes. He strikes slowly, methodically, cutting the limb close to the trunk, and, all of a sudden, the branch cracks, gives away, bends, tears itself off, and falls down grazing the neighboring trees in its fall. Then, it crashes down on the ground with a great sound of broken wood, and its slighter branches keep quivering for a long time.

The soil was covered with fragments which other men cut in their turn, bound in bundles, and piled in heaps, while the trees which were still left standing seemed like enormous posts, gigantic forms amputated and shorn by the keen steel of the cutting instruments.

And when the lopper had finished his task, he left at the top of the straight slender shaft of the tree the rope collar which he had brought up with him, and afterwards descends again with spurlike prods along the discrowned trunk, which the woodcutters thereupon attacked at the base, striking it with great blows which resounded through all the rest of the wood.

When the foot seemed pierced deeply enough, some men commenced dragging to the accompaniment of a cry in which they joined harmoniously, at the rope attached to the top; and, all of a sudden, the immense mast cracked and tumbled to the earth with the dull sound and shock of a distant cannon-shot.

And each day the wood grew thinner, losing its trees which fell down one by one, as an army loses its soldiers.

Renardet no longer walked up and down. He remained from morning till night, contemplating, motionless, and with his hands behind his back the slow death of his wood. When a tree fell, he placed his· foot on it as if it were a corpse. Then he raised his eyes to the next with a kind of secret, calm impatience, as if he had expected, hoped for, something at the end of this massacre.

Meanwhile, they were approaching the place where little Louise Roqué had been found.  At length, they came to it one evening, at the hour of twilight.

As it was dark, the sky being overcast, the wood-cutters wanted to stop their work, putting off till next day the fall of an enormous beech-tree, but the master objected to this, and insisted that even at this hour they should lop and cut down this giant, which had over-shadowed the crime.

When the lopper had laid it bare, had finished its toilets for the guillotine, when the woodcutters were about to sap its base, five men commenced hauling at the rope attached to the top.

The tree resisted; its powerful trunk, although notched up to the middle was as rigid as iron.  The workmen, altogether, with a sort of regular jump, strained at the rope, stooping down to the ground, and they gave vent to a cry with throats out of breath, so as to indicate and direct their efforts.

Two woodcutters standing close to the giant, re-mained with axes in their grip, like two executioners ready to strike once more, and Renardet, motionless, with his hand on the bark, awaited the fall with an un-easy, nervous feeling.

One of the men said to him:

"You're too near, Monsieur le Maire.  When it falls, it may hurt you."

He did not reply and did not recoil.  He seemed ready himself to catch the beech-tree in his open arms in order to cast it on the ground like a wrestler.

All at once, at the foot of the tall column of wood there was a rent which seemed to run to the top, like a painful shake; and it bent slightly, ready to fall, but

still resisting. The men, in a state of excitement, stiffened their arms, renewed their efforts with greater vigor,
and, just as the tree, breaking, came crashing down,
Renardet suddenly made forward step, then stopped,
his shoulders raised to receive the irresistible shock, the
mortal shock which would crush him on the earth.

But the beech-tree, having deviated a little, only
rubbed against his loins, throwing him on his face five
meters away.

The workmen dashed forward to lift him up. He
had already risen to his knees, stupefied, with wandering eyes, and passing his hand across his forehead, as
if he were awaking out of an attack of madness.

When he had got to his feet once more, the men,
astonished, questioned him, not being able to understand
what he had done. He replied, in faltering tones, that
he had had for a moment a fit of abstraction, or rather
a return to the days of his childhood, that he imagined
he had to pass his time under a tree, just as street-boys
rush in front of vehicles driving rapidly past, that he
had played at danger, that, for the past eight days, he
felt this desire growing stronger within him, asking
himself whether, every time one was cracking, so as to
be on the point of falling, he could pass beneath it without being touched. It was a piece of stupidity he confessed; but everyone has these moments of insanity, and
these temptations towards boyish folly.

He made this explanation in a slow tone, searching
for his words, and speaking in a stupefied fashion.

Then, he went off, saying:

" Till to-morrow, my friends — till to-morrow."

As soon as he had got back to his room, he sat down

before his table, which his lamp, covered with a shade, lighted up brightly, and, clasping his hands over his forehead, be began to cry.

He remained crying for a long time, then wiped his eyes, raised his head, and looked at the clock.    It was not yet six o'clock.

He thought:

" I have time before dinner."

And he went to the door and locked it.    He then came back, and sat down before his table.    He pulled out a drawer in the middle of it, and taking from it a revolver, laid it down over his papers, under the glare of the sun.    The barrel of the fire-arm glittered and cast reflections which resembled flames.

Renardet gazed at it for some time with the uneasy glance of a drunken man; then he rose by, and began to pace up and down the room.

He walked from one end of the apartment to the other, and stopped from time to time and started to pace up and down again a moment afterwards.    Suddenly, he opened the door of his dressing room, steeped a napkin in a water-jug and moistened his forehead, as he had done on the morning of the crime.

Then he went walking up and down once more. Each time he passed the table the gleaming revolver attracted his glance, tempted his hand; but he kept watching the clock, and reflected:

" I have still time."

It struck half-past six.    Then he took up the revolver, opened his mouth wide with a frightful grimace, and stuck the barrel into it, as if he wanted to swallow it.    He remained in this position for some seconds without moving, his finger on the lock, then, suddenly, seized with a shudder of horror, he dropped the pistol on the carpet.

And he fell back on his arm-chair, sobbing:

" I can't.  I dare not!  My God!  My God! How can I have the courage to kill myself? "

There was a knock at the door.  He rose up in a stupefied condition.  A servant said:

" Monsieur's dinner is ready."

He replied:

" All right.  I'm going down."

Then he picked up the revolver, locked it up again in the drawer, then he looked at himself in the glass over the mantelpiece to see whether his face did not look too much convulsed.  It was as red as usual, a little redder perhaps.  That was all.  He went down, and seated himself before the table.

He ate slowly, like a man who wants to drag on the meal, who does not want to be alone with himself.

Then he smoked several pipes in the hall while the plates were being removed.  After that, he went back to his room.

As soon as he was shut up in it, he looked under his bed, opened all his cupboards, explored every corner, rummaged through all the furniture.  Then he lighted the tapers over the mantelpiece, and, turning round several times, ran his eye all over the apartment with an anguish of terror that made his face lose its color, for he knew well that he was going to see her, as on every night — Little Louise Roqué, the little girl he had violated and afterwards strangled.

Every night the odious vision came back again. First, it sounded in his ears like a kind of snorting such

as is made by a threshing machine or the distant passage of a train over a bridge. Then he commenced
to pant, to feel suffocated, and he had to unbutton
his shirt-collar and his belt. He moved about
to make his blood circulate, he tried to read, he attempted to sing. It was in vain. His thoughts, in
spite of himself, went back to the day of the murder,
and made him begin it all over again in all its most
secret details, with all the violent emotions he had experienced from the first minute to the last.

He had felt on rising up that morning, the morning
of the horrible day, a little stupefaction and dizziness
which he attributed to the heat, so that he remained in
his room till the time came for breakfast.

After the meal he had taken a siesta, then, towards
the close of the afternoon, he had gone out to breathe
the fresh, soothing breeze under the trees in the wood.

But, as soon as they were outside, the heavy, scorch-
ing air of the plain oppressed him more. The sun, still
high in the heavens, poured out on the parched soil,
dry and thirsty, floods of ardent light. Not a breath
of wind stirred the leaves. Every beast and bird, even
the grasshoppers, were silent. Renardet reached the
tall trees, and began to walk over the moss where the
Brindelle sent forth a slight, cool vapor under the immense roof of trees. But he felt ill at ease. It
seemed to him that an unknown, invisible hand, was
squeezing his neck, and he scarcely thought of anything,
having usually few ideas in his head. For the last three
months, only one thought haunted him, the thought of
marrying again. He suffered from living alone, suffered from it morally and physically. Accustomed for
ten years past to feeling a woman near him, habituated

to her presence every moment, to her embrace each successive day, he had need, an imperious and perplexing need of incessant contact with her and the regular touch of her lips. Since Madame Renardet's death, he had suffered continually without knowing why, he had suffered from not feeling her dress brush against his legs every day, and, above all, from no longer being able to grow calm and languid between her arms. He had been scarcely six months a widower, and he had already been looking out through the district for some young girl or some widow he might marry when his period of marrying was at an end.

He had a chaste soul, but it was lodged in a powerful Herculean body, and carnal images began to disturb his sleep and his vigils. He drove them away; they came back again; and he murmured from time to time, smiling at himself:

"Here I am, like St. Antony."

Having had this morning several besetting visions, the desire suddenly came into his breast to bathe in the Brindelle in order to refresh himself and appease the ardor of his heat.

He knew, a little further on, a large deep spot where the people of the neighborhood came sometimes to take a dip in summer. He went there.

Thick willow trees hid this clear volume of water where the current rested and went to sleep for a little while before starting its way again. Renardet, as he appeared, thought he heard a light sound, a faint smell which was not that of the stream on the banks. He softly put aside the leaves and looked. A little girl, quite naked in the transparent water, was beating the waves with both hands, dancing about in them a little and dipping herself with pretty movements. She was not a child nor was she yet a woman. She was plump and formed, while preserving an air of youthful precocity, as of one who had grown rapidly, and who was now almost ripe. He no longer moved, overcome with surprise, with a pang of desire, holding his breath with a strange poignant emotion. He remained there, his heart beating as if one of his sensual dreams had just been realized, as if an impure fairy had conjured up before him this creature so disturbing to his blood, so very young this little rustic Venus, was born in the waves of the sea.

Suddenly the little girl came out of the water, and without seeing came over to where he stood looking for her clothes in order to dress herself. While she was gradually approaching with little hesitating steps, through fear of the sharp pointed stones, he felt himself pushed towards her by an irresistible force, by a bestial transport of passion, which stirred up all his flesh, stupefied his soul, and made him tremble from head to foot.

She remained standing some seconds behind the willow tree which concealed him from view. Then, losing his reason entirely, he opened the branches, rushed on her, and seized her in his arms. She fell, too scared to offer any resistance, too much terror-stricken to cry out, and he possessed her without understanding what he was doing.

He woke up from his crime, as one wakes out of a nightmare. The child burst out weeping.

He said:

"Hold your tongue! Hold your tongue! I'll give you money."

But she did not hear him, she went on sobbing.

He went on:

"Come now, hold your tongue! Do hold your tongue. Keep quiet."

She still kept shrieking, writhing in the effort to get away from him. He suddenly realized that he was ruined, and he caught her by the neck to stop her mouth from uttering these heartrending, dreadful screams. As she continued to struggle with the desperate strength of a being who is seeking to fly from death, he pressed his enormous hands on the little throat swollen with cries, and in a few seconds he had strangled her so furiously did he grip her, without intending to kill her but only to make her keep silent.

Then he rose up overwhelmed with horror.

She lay before him with her face bleeding and blackened. He was going to rush away when there sprang up in his agitated soul the mysterious and undefined instinct that guides all beings in the hour of danger.

It was necessary to throw the body into the water; but another impulse drove him towards the clothes, of which he made a thin parcel. Then as he had a piece of twine in his pocket, he tied it up and hid it in a deep portion of the stream, under the trunk of a tree, the foot of which was steeped in the Brindelle.

Then he went off at a rapid pace, reached the meadows, took a wide turn in order to show himself to some peasants who dwelt some distance away at the opposite side of the district, and he came back to dine at the usual hour, and told his servants all that was supposed to have happened during his walk.

He slept, however, that night; he slept with a heavy brutish sleep, such as the sleep of persons condemned to

death must be occasionally. He only opened his eyes
at the first glimmer of dawn, and he waited, tortured
by the fear of having his crime discovered, for his usual
waking hour.

Then he would have to be present at all the stages
of the inquiry as to the cause of death. He did so
after the fashion of a somnambulist, in a hallucination
which showed him things and human beings in a sort of
dream, in a cloud of intoxication, in that dubious sense
of unreality which perplexes the mind at the time of the
greatest catastrophe.

The only thing that pierced his heart was La Roqué's
cry of anguish. At that moment he felt inclined to cast
himself at the old woman's feet, and to exclaim —

" 'Tis I."

But he restrained himself. He went back, however,
during the night, to fish up the dead girl's wooden shoes,
in order to carry them to her mother's threshold.

As long as the inquiry lasted, as long as it was necessary to guide and aid justice, he was calm, master of
himself, sly and smiling. He discussed quietly with the
magistrates all the suppositions that passed through
their minds, combated their opinions, and demolished
their arguments. He even took a keen and mournful
pleasure in disturbing their investigations, in embroil-
ing their ideas in showing the innocence of those whom
they suspected.

But from the day when the inquiry came to a close he
became gradually nervous, more excitable still than he
had been before, although he mastered his irritability.
Sudden noises made him jump up with fear; he shuddered at the slightest thing, trembled sometimes from
head to foot when a fly alighted on his forehead. Then

he was seized with an imperious desire for movement, which compelled him to keep continually on foot,
and made him remain up whole nights walking to and
fro in his own room.

It was not that he was goaded by remorse. His
brutality did not lend itself to any shade of sentiment or
of moral terror. A man of energy and even of violence,
born to make war, to ravage conquered countries and
to massacre the vanquished, full of the savage instincts
of the hunter and the fighter, he scarcely took count of
human life. Though he respected the church through
policy, he believed neither in God nor in the devil, expecting consequently in another life neither chastisement
nor recompense for his acts. As his sole belief, he re-
tained a vague philosophy composed of all the ideas of
the encyclopedists of the last century; and he regarded
religion as a moral sanction of the law, the one and the
other having been invented by men to regulate social
relations. To kill anyone in a duel, or in war, or in a
quarrel, or by accident, or for the sake of revenge, or
even through bravado, would have seemed to him an
amusing and clever thing, and would not have left more
impression on his mind than a shot fired at a hare; but
he had experienced a profound emotion at the murder
of this child. He had, in the first place, perpetrated
it in the distraction of an irresistible gust of passion, in
a sort of spiritual tempest that had overpowered his
reason. And he had cherished in his heart, cherished
in his flesh, cherished on his lips, cherished even to the
very tips of his murderous fingers, a kind of bestial love,
as well as a feeling of crushing horror, towards this
little girl surprised by him and basely killed. Every
moment his thoughts returned to that horrible scene,

and, though he endeavored to drive away this picture from his mind, though he put it aside with terror, with disgust, he felt it surging through his soul, moving about in him, waiting incessantly for the moment to reappear.

Then, in the night, he was afraid, afraid of the shadow falling around him. He did not yet know why the darkness seemed to seem frightful to him; but he instinctively feared it, he felt that it was peopled with terrors. The bright daylight did not lend itself to fears. Things and beings were seen there, and so there were only to be met there natural things and beings which could exhibit themselves in the light of day. But the night, the unpenetrable night, thicker than walls, and empty, the infinite night, so black, so vast, in which one might brush against frightful things, the night when one feels that mysterious terror is wandering, prowling about, appeared to him to conceal an unknown danger, close and menacing.

What was it?

He knew it ere long. As he sat in his armchair, rather late one evening when he could not sleep, he thought he saw the curtain of his window move. He waited, in an uneasy state of mind, with beating heart. The drapery did not stir; then, all of a sudden it moved once more. He did not venture to rise up; he no longer ventured to breathe, and yet he was brave. He had often fought, and he would have liked to catch thieves in his house.

Was it true that this curtain did move? he asked himself, fearing that his eyes had deceived him. It was, moreover, such a slight thing, a gentle flutter of lace, a kind of trembling in its folds, less than an undulation such as is caused by the wind.

V—21

Renardet sat still, with staring eyes, and outstretched neck; and he sprang to his feet abruptly ashamed of his fear, took four steps, seized the drapery with both hands, and pulled it wide apart. At first, he saw nothing but darkened glass, resembling plates of glittering ink. The night, the vast, impenetrable sketched behind as far as the invisible horizon. He remained standing in front of this illimitable shadow, and suddenly he perceived a light, a moving light, which seemed some distance away.

Then he put his face close to the window-pane, thinking that a person looking for crayfish might be poaching in the Brindelle, for it was past midnight, and this light rose up at the edge of the stream, under the trees. As he was not yet able to see clearly, Renardet placed his hands over his eyes; and suddenly this light became an illumination, and he beheld little Louise Roqué naked and bleeding on the moss. He recoiled frozen with horror, sank into his chair, and fell backward. He remained there some minutes, his soul in distress, then he sat up and began to reflect. He had had a hallucination — that was all; a hallucination due to the fact that a marauder of the night was walking with a lantern in his hand near the water's edge. What was there astonishing, besides, in the circumstance that the recollection of his crime should sometimes bring before him the vision of the dead girl?

He rose up, swallowed a glass of wine and sat down again.

He thought.

" What am I to do if this come back? "

And it did come back; he felt it; he was sure of it.

Already his glance was drawn towards the window; it
called him; it attracted him.    In order to avoid looking
at it, he turned aside his chair.    Then he took a book
and tried to read; but it seemed to him that he
presently heard something stirring behind him, and he
swung round his armchair on one foot.

The curtain still moved — unquestionably, it did
move this time; he could no longer have any doubt
about it.

He rushed forward and seized it in his grasp so
violently that he knocked it down with its fastener.
Then, he eagerly pasted his face against the glass.    He
saw nothing.    All was black without; and he breathed
with the delight of a man whose life has just been saved.

Then, he went back to his chair, and sat down
again; but almost immediately he felt a longing once
more to look out through the window.    Since the curtain had fallen the space in front of him made a sort of
dark patch fascinating and terrible on the obscure landscape.    In order not to yield to this dangerous temptation, he took off his clothes, blew out the light, went to
bed, and shut his eyes.

Lying on his back motionless, his skin hot and moist,
he awaited sleep.    Suddenly a great gleam of light
flashed across his eyelids.    He opened them, believing
that his dwelling was on fire.    All was black as before,
and he leaned on his elbow in order to try to distinguish
his window which had still for him an unconquer-
able attraction.    By dint of straining his eyes, he could
perceive some stars, and he arose, groped his way
across the room, discovered the panes with his outstretched hands, and placed his forehead close to them.

There below, under the trees, the body of the little girl glittered like phosphorus, lighting up the surrounding darkness.

Renardet uttered a cry and rushed towards his bed, where he lay till morning, his head hidden under the pillow.

From that moment, his life became intolerable. He passed his days in apprehension of each succeeding night; and each night the vision came back again. As soon as he had locked himself up in his room, he strove to struggle; but in vain. An irresistible force lifted him up and pushed him against the glass, as if to call the phantom, and ere long he saw it lying at first in the spot where the crime was committed, lying with arms and legs outspread, just in the way the body had been found.

Then the dead girl rose up and came towards him with little steps just as the child had done when she came out of the river. She advanced quietly, passing straight across the grass, and over the border of withered flowers. Then she rose up into the air towards Renardet's window. She came towards him, as she had come on the day of the crime towards the murderer. And the man recoiled before the apparition — he retreated to his bed and sank down upon it, knowing well that the little one had entered the room, and that she now was standing behind the curtain which presently moved. And until daybreak, he kept staring at this curtain, with a fixed glance, ever waiting to see his victim depart.

But she did not show herself any more; she remained there behind the curtain which quivered tremulously now and then.

And Renardet, his fingers clinging to the bedclothes, squeezed them as he had squeezed the throat of little Louise Roqué.

He heard the clock striking the hours; and in the stillness the pendulum kept ticking in time with the loud beatings of his heart. And he suffered, the wretched man, more than any man had ever suffered before.

Then, as soon as a white streak of light on the ceiling announced the approaching day, he felt himself free, alone, at last, alone in his room; and at last he went to sleep. He slept then some hours — a restless, feverish sleep in which he retraced in dreams the horrible vision of the night just past.

When, later on, he went down to breakfast, he felt doubled up as if after prodigious fatigues; and he scarcely ate anything, still haunted as he was by the fear of what he had seen the night before.

He knew well, however, that it was not an apparition, that the dead do not come back, and that his sick soul, his soul possessed by one thought alone, by an indelible remembrance, was the only cause of his punishment, the only evoker of the dead girl brought back by it to life, called up by it and raised by it before his eyes in which the ineffaceable image remained imprinted. But he knew, too, that he could not cure it, that he would never escape from the savage persecution of his memory; and he resolved to die, rather than to endure these tortures any longer.

Then, he thought of how he would kill himself. He wished for something simple and natural, which would preclude the idea of suicide. For he clung to his reputation, to the names bequeathed to him by his ancestors; and if there were any suspicion as the cause of his death, people's thoughts might be perhaps directed towards the mysterious crime, towards the murderer who could not be found, and they would not hesitate to accuse him of the crime.

A strange idea came into his head, that of getting himself crushed by the tree at the foot of which he had assassinated little Louise Roqué. So he determined to have his wood cut down, and to simulate an accident. But the beech-tree refused to smash his ribs.

Returning to his house, a prey to utter despair he had snatched up his revolver, and then he did not dare to fire it.

The dinner bell summoned him. He could eat nothing, and then he went up-stairs again. And he did not know what he was going to do. Now that he had escaped the first time, he felt himself a coward. Presently, he would be ready, fortified, decided, master of his courage and of his resolution; now, he was weak and feared death as much as he did the dead girl.

He faltered:

" I will not venture it again — I will not venture it."

Then he glanced with terror, first at the revolver on the table, and next at the curtain which hid his window. It seemed to him, moreover that something horrible would occur as soon as his life was ended. Something? What? A meeting with her perhaps. She was watching for him; she was waiting for him; she was calling him; and her object was to seize him in her turn, to draw him towards the doom that would avenge her, and to lead him to die so that she might exhibit herself thus every night.

He began to cry like a child, repeating:

" I will not venture it again — I will not venture it."

Then, he fell on his knees, and murmured:

"My God! my God!" without believing, nevertheless, in God.   And he no longer dared, in fact, to look out through his window where he knew the apparition was visible nor at his table where his revolver gleamed.

When he had risen up, he said:

"This cannot last; there must be an end of it."

The sound of his voice in the silent room made a shiver of fear pass through his limbs, but, as he could not bring himself to come to a determination as he felt certain that his finger would always refuse to pull the trigger of his revolver, he turned round to hide his head under the bedclothes, and plunged into reflection.

He would have to find some way in which he could force himself to die, to invent some device against himself, which would not permit of any hesitation on his part, any delay, any possible regrets.   He envied condemned criminals who are led to the scaffold surrounded by soldiers.   Oh! if he could only beg of some one to shoot him; if he could, confessing the state of his soul, confessing his crime to a sure friend who would never divulge it, obtain from him death.

But from whom could he ask this terrible service? From whom?   He cast about in his thoughts among his friends whom he knew intimately.   The doctor? No, he would talk about it afterwards, most certainly. And suddenly a fantastic idea entered his mind.   He would write to the examining magistrate, who was on terms of close friendship with him and would denounce himself as the perpetrator of the crime.   He would in this letter confess everything, revealing how his soul had been tortured, how he had resolved to die, how he had hesitated about carrying out his resolution, and what means he had employed to strengthen his failing courage. And in the name of their old friendship he would implore of the other to destroy the letter as soon as he had ascertained that the culprit had inflicted justice on himself. Renardet might rely on this magistrate, he knew him to be sure, discreet, incapable of even an idle word. He was one of those men who have an inflexible conscience governed, directed, regulated by their reason alone.

Scarcely had he formed this project when a strange feeling of joy took possession of his heart, He was calm now. He would write his letter slowly, then at daybreak he would deposit it in the box nailed to the wall in his office, then he would ascend his tower to watch for the postman's arrival, and when the man in the blue blouse showed himself, he would cast himself head foremost on the rocks on which the foundations rested. He would take care to be seen first by the workmen who had cut down his wood. He could then climb to the step some distance up which bore the flag staff displayed on fête days. He would smash this pole with a shake and precipitate it along with him.

Who would suspect that it was not an accident? And he would be killed completely, having regard to his weight and the height of the tower.

Presently he got out of bed, went over to the table, and began to write. He omitted nothing, not a single detail of the crime, not a single detail of the torments of his heart, and he ended by announcing that he had passed sentence on himself, that he was going to execute the criminal, and begging of his friend, his old friend, to be careful that there should never be any stain on his memory.

When he had finished his letter, he saw that the day had dawned.

He closed and sealed it, wrote the address; then he descended with light steps, hurried towards the little white box fastened to the wall in the corner of the farmhouse, and when he had thrown into it the paper which made his hand tremble, he came back quickly, shut the bolts of the great door, and climbed up to his tower to wait for the passing of the postman, who would convey his death sentence.

He felt self-possessed, now. Liberated! Saved!

A cold dry wind, an icy wind, passed across his face. He inhaled it eagerly, with open mouth, drinking in its chilling kiss. The sky was red, with a burning red, the red of winter, and all the plain whitened with frost glistened under the first rays of the sun, as if it had been powdered with bruised glass.

Renardet, standing up, with his head bare, gazed at the vast tract of country before him, the meadow to the left, and to the right the village whose chimneys were beginning to smoke with the preparations for the morning meal. At his feet he saw the Brindelle flowing towards the rocks, where he would soon be crushed to death. He felt himself reborn on that beautiful frosty morning, full of strength, full of life. The light bathed him, penetrated him like a new-born hope. A thousand recollections assailed him, recollections of similar mornings, of rapid walks on the hard earth which rang under his footsteps, of happy chases on the edges of pools where wild ducks sleep. All the good things that he loved, the good things of existence rushed into memory, penetrated him with fresh desires, awakened all the vigorous appetites of his active, powerful body.

And he was about to die? Why? He was going to kill himself stupidly, because he was afraid of a shadow — afraid of nothing? He was still rich and in the prime of life! What folly! But all he wanted was distraction, absence, a voyage in order to forget.

This night even he had not seen the little girl because his mind was preoccupied, and so had wandered towards some other subject. Perhaps he would not see her any more? And even if she still haunted him in this house, certainly she would not follow him elsewhere! The earth was wide, the future was long.

Why die?

His glance traveled across the meadows, and he perceived a blue spot in the path which wound alongside the Brindelle. It was Mederic coming to bring letters from the town and to carry away those of the village.

Renardet got a start, a sensation of pain shot through his breast, and he rushed towards the winding staircase to get back his letter, to demand it back from the postman. Little did it matter to him now whether he was seen. He hurried across the grass moistened by the light frost of the previous night, and he arrived in front of the box in the corner of the farm-house exactly at the same time as the letter carrier.

The latter had opened the little wooden door, and drew forth the four papers deposited there by the inhabitants of the locality.

Renardet said to him:

"Good morrow, Mederic."

"Good morrow, M'sieu le Maire."

"I say, Mederic, I threw a letter into the box that I want back again. I came to ask you to give it back to me."

"That's all right, M'sieur le Maire — you'll get it."

And the postman raised his eyes. He stood petrified at the sight of Renardet's face. The Mayor's cheeks were purple, his eyes were glaring with black circles round them as if they were sunk in his head, his hair was all tangled, his beard untrimmed, his necktie unfastened. It was evident that he had not gone to bed.

The postman asked:

"Are you ill, M'sieur le Maire?"

The other, suddenly comprehending that his appearance must be unusual, lost countenance, and faltered —

"Oh! no — oh! no. Only I jumped out of bed to ask you for this letter. I was asleep. You understand?"

He said in reply:

"What letter?"

"The one you are going to give back to me."

Mederic now began to hesitate. The Mayor's attitude did not strike him as natural. There was perhaps a secret in that letter, a political secret. He knew Renardet was not a Republican, and he knew all the tricks and chicaneries employed at elections.

He asked:

"To whom is it addressed, this letter of yours?"

"To M. Putoin, the examining magistrate — you know my friend, M. Putoin, well!"

The postman searched through the papers, and found the one asked for. Then he began looking at it, turning it round and round between his fingers, much perplexed, much troubled by the fear of committing a grave offense or of making an enemy for himself of the Mayor.

Seeing his hesitation, Renardet made a movement for the purpose of seizing the letter and snatching it away from him. This abrupt action convinced Mederic that some important secret was at stake and made him resolve to do his duty, cost what it may.

So he flung the letter into his bag and fastened it up, with the reply:

"No, I can't, M'sieur le Maire. From the moment it goes to the magistrate, I can't."

A dreadful pang wrung Renardet's heart, and he murmured:

"Why, you know me well. You are even able to recognize my handwriting. I tell you I want that paper."

"I can't."

"Look here, Mederic, you know that I'm incapable of deceiving you — I tell you I want it."

"No, I can't."

A tremor of rage passed through Renardet's soul.

"Damn it all, take care! You know that I don't go in for chaffing, and that I could get you out of your job, my good fellow, and without much delay either. And then, I am the Mayor of the district, after all; and I now order you to give me back that paper."

The postman answered firmly:

"No, I can't, M'sieur le Maire."

Thereupon, Renardet, losing his head, caught hold of the postman's arms in order to take away his bag; but, freeing himself by a strong effort, and springing backwards, the letter carrier raised his big holly stick. Without losing his temper, he said emphatically:

"Don't touch me, M'sieur le Maire, or I'll strike. Take care, I'm only doing my duty!"

Feeling that he was lost, Renardet suddenly became humble, gentle, appealing to him like a crying child:

"Look here, look here, my friend, give me back that letter, and I'll recompense you — I'll give you money. Stop! Stop! I'll give you a hundred francs, you understand — a hundred francs!"

The postman turned on his heel and started on his journey.

Renardet followed him, out of breath, faltering:

"Mederic, Mederic, listen! I'll give you a thousand francs, you understand — a thousand francs."

The postman still went on without giving any answer.

Renardet went on:

"I'll make your fortune, you understand — whatever you wish — fifty thousand francs — fifty thousand francs for that letter! What does it matter to you? You won't? Well, a hundred thousand — I say — a hundred thousand francs. Do you understand? A hundred thousand francs — a hundred thousand francs."

The postman turned back, his face hard, his eye severe:

"Enough of this, or else I'll repeat to the magistrate everything you have just said to me."

Renardet stopped abruptly. It was all over. He turned back and rushed towards his house, running like a hunted animal.

Then, in his turn, Mederic stopped, and watched this

flight with stupefaction. He saw the Mayor re-entering his own house, and he waited still as if something astonishing was about to happen.

In fact, presently the tall form of Renardet appeared on the summit of the Fox's tower. He ran round the platform, like a madman. Then he seized the flagstaff and shook it furiously without succeeding in breaking it, then, all of a sudden, like a swimmer taking a plunge, he dashed into the air with his two hands in front of him.

Mederic rushed forward to give succor. As he crossed the park, he saw the woodcutters going to work. He called out to them telling them an accident had occurred, and at the foot of the walls they found a bleeding body the head of which was crushed on a rock. The Brindelle surrounded this rock, and over its clear, calm waters, swollen at this point, could be seen a long red stream of mingled brains and blood.

## MOTHER AND DAUGHTER

"THE Comtesse Samoris."

"That lady in black over there?"

"The very one. She's wearing mourning for her daughter, whom she killed."

"Come now! You don't mean that seriously?"

"Oh! it is a very simple story, without any crime in it, any violence."

"Then what really happened?"

"Almost nothing. Many courtesans were born to be virtuous women, they say; and many women called virtuous were born to be courtesans — is that not so? Now, Madame Samoris, who was born a courtesan, had a daughter born a virtuous woman, that's all."

"I don't quite understand you."

"I'll explain what I mean. The Comtesse Samoris is one of those tinsel foreign women hundreds of whom are rained down every year on Paris. A Hungarian or Wallachian countess, or I know not what, she appeared one winter in apartments she had taken in the Champs Elysees, that quarter for adventurers and adventuresses, and opened her drawing-room to the first comer or to anyone that turned up.

"I went there. Why? you will say. I really can't tell you. I went there, as everyone goes to such places because the women are facile and the men are dishonest. You know that set composed of filibusters with varied decorations, all noble, all titled, all unknown at the embassies, with the exception of those who are spies. All talk of their honor without the slightest occasion for doing so, boast of their ancestors, tell you about their lives, braggarts, liars, sharpers, as dangerous as the false cards they have up their sleeves, as delusive as their name — in short, the aristocracy of the bagnio.

" I adore these people. They are interesting to study, interesting to know, amusing to understand, often clever, never commonplace like public functionaries. Their wives are always pretty, with a slight flavor of foreign roguery, with the mystery of their existence, half of it perhaps spent in a house of correction. They have, as a rule, magnificent eyes and incredible hair. I adore them also.

" Madame Samoris is the type of these adventuresses, elegant, mature, and still beautiful. Charming feline creatures, you feel that they are vicious to the marrow of their bones. You find them very amusing when you visit them; they give card-parties; they have dances and suppers; in short, they offer you all the pleasures of social life.

" And she had a daughter — a tall, fine-looking girl, always ready for entertainments, always full of laughter and reckless gayety — a true adventuress's daughter — but, at the same time, an innocent, unsophisticated, artless girl, who saw nothing, knew nothing, understood nothing of all the things that happened in her father's house."

" How do you know about him? "

" How do I know? That's the funniest part of the business! One morning, there was a ring at my door, and my valet came up to tell me that M. Joseph Bonenthal wanted to speak to me. I said directly: ' And who is this gentleman? ' My valet replied: ' I don't

know, monsieur; perhaps 'tis someone that wants employment.' And so it was. The man wanted me to
take him as a servant. I asked him where he had been
last. He answered: 'With the Comtesse Samoris.'
'Ah!' said I, 'but my house is not a bit like hers.'
'I know that well, monsieur,' he said, 'and that's the
very reason I want to take service with monsieur. I've
had enough of these people: a man may stay a little
while with them, but he won't remain long with them.'
I required an additional man servant at the time, and
so I took him.

"A month later, Mademoiselle Yveline Samoris died
mysteriously, and here are all the details of her death I
could gather from Joseph, who got them from his
sweetheart, the Comtesse's chambermaid:

"It was a ball-night, and two newly-arrived guests
were chatting behind a door. Mademoiselle Yveline,
who had just been dancing, leaned against this door to
get a little air.

"They did not see her approaching; but she heard
what they were saying. And this was what they said:

"'But who is the father of the girl?'

"'A Russian, it appears, Count Rouvaloff. He
never comes near the mother now.'

"'And who is the reigning prince to-day?'

"'That English prince standing near the window;
Madame Samoris adores him. But her adoration of
anyone never lasts longer than a month or six weeks.
Nevertheless, as you see, she has a large circle of admirers. All are called — and nearly all are chosen.
That kind of thing costs a good deal, but — hang it,
what can you expect?'

"'And where did she get this name of Samoris?'

V—22

" ' From the only man perhaps that she ever loved — a Jewish banker from Berlin who goes by the name of Samuel Morris.'

" ' Good. Thanks. Now that I know all about her, and see her sort, I'm off ! '

" What a start there was in the brain of the young girl endowed with all the instincts of a virtuous woman ! What despair overwhelmed that simple soul ! What mental tortures quenched her endless gayety, her delightful laughter, her exulting satisfaction with life ! What a conflict took place in that youthful heart up to the moment when the last guest had left ! Those were things that Joseph could not tell me. But, the same night, Yveline abruptly entered her mother's room just as the Comtesse was getting into bed, sent out the waiting-maid, who was close to the door, and, standing erect and pale, and with great staring eyes, she said:

" ' Mamma, listen to what I heard a little while ago during the ball.'

" And she repeated word for word the conversation just as I told it to you.

" The Comtesse was so stupefied that she did not know what to say in reply, at first. When she recovered her self-possession, she denied everything, and called God to witness that there was no truth in the story.

" The young girl went away, distracted but not convinced. And she watched her mother.

" I remember distinctly the strange alteration that then took place in her. She was always grave and melancholy. She used to fix on us her great earnest eyes as if she wanted to read what was at the bottom of our hearts.   We did not know what to think of her, and we used to maintain that she was looking out for a husband.

"One evening her doubts were dispelled.   She caught her mother with a lover.   Thereupon she said coldly, like a man of business laying down the terms of an agreement:

"'Here is what I have determined to do, mamma: We will both go away to some little town — or rather into the country.   We will live there quietly as well as we can.   Your jewelry alone may be called a fortune. If you wish to marry some honest man, so much the better; still better will it be if I can find one.   If you don't consent to do this, I will kill myself.'

"This time, the Comtesse ordered her daughter to go to bed, and never to administer again this lecture so unbecoming in the mouth of a child towards her mother.

"Yveline's answer to this was:   'I give you a month to reflect.   If, at the end of that month, we have not changed our way of living, I will kill myself, since there is no other honorable issue left to my life.'

"Then she took herself off.

"At the end of a month, the Comtesse Samoris was giving balls and suppers just the same as ever.   Yveline then, under the pretext that she had a bad toothache purchased a few drops of chloroform from a neighboring chemist.   The next day she purchased more; and, every time she went out, she managed to procure small doses of the narcotic.   She filled a bottle with it.

"One morning she was found in bed, lifeless, and already quite cold, with a cotton mask over her face.

"Her coffin was covered with flowers, the church was hung in white. There was a large crowd at the funeral ceremony.

"Ah! well, if I had known — but you never can know — I would have married that girl, for she was infernally pretty."

"And what became of the mother?"

"Oh! she shed a lot of tears over it. She has only begun to receive visits again for the past week."

"And what explanation is given of the girl's death?"

"Oh! 'tis pretended that it was an accident caused by a new stove, the mechanism of which got out of order. As a good many such accidents have happened, the thing looks probable enough."

# A PASSION

THE sea was brilliant and unruffled, scarcely stirred, and on the pier the entire town of Havre watched the ships as they came on. They could be seen at a distance, in great numbers; some of them, the steamers, with plumes of smoke; the others, the sailing vessels, drawn by almost invisible tugs, lifting towards the sky their bare masts, like leafless trees.

They hurried from every end of the horizon towards the narrow mouth of the jetty which devoured these monsters; and they groaned, they shrieked, they hissed while they spat out puffs of steam like animals panting for breath.

Two young officers were walking on the landing-stage, where a number of people were waiting, saluting or returning salutes, and sometimes stopping to chat.

Suddenly, one of them, the taller, Paul d'Henricol, pressed the arm of his comrade, Jean Renoldi, then, in a whisper, said:

" Hallo, here's Madame Poincot; give a good look at her. I assure you that she's making eyes at you."

She was moving along on the arm of her husband. She was a woman of about forty, very handsome still, slightly stout, but, owing to her graceful fullness of figure, as fresh as she was at twenty. Among her friends she was known as the Goddess on account of her proud gait, her large black eyes, and the entire air of nobility of her person. She remained irreproach-

341

able; never had the least suspicion cast a breath on her life's purity. She was regarded as the very type of a virtuous, uncorrupted woman. So upright that no man had ever dared to think of her.

And yet for the last month Paul d'Henricol had been assuring his friend Renoldi that Madame Poincot was in love with him, and he maintained that there was no doubt of it.

" Be sure I don't deceive myself. I see it clearly. She loves you — she loves you passionately, like a chaste woman who had never loved. Forty years is a terrible age for virtuous women when they possess senses; they become foolish, and commit utter follies. She is hit, my dear fellow; she is falling like a wounded bird, and is ready to drop into your arms. I say — just look at her ! "

The tall woman, preceded by her two daughters, aged twelve and fifteen years, suddenly turned pale, on her approach, as her eyes lighted on the officer's face. She gave him an ardent glance, concentrating her gaze upon him, and no longer seemed to have any eyes for her children, her husband, or any other person around her. She returned the salutation of the two young men without lowering her eyes, glowing with such a flame that a doubt, at last, forced its way into Lieutenant Renoldi's mind.

His friend said, in the same hushed voice: " I was sure of it. Did you not notice her this time? By Jove, she is a nice tit-bit ! "

.     .     .     .        .     .     .     .

But Jean Renoldi had no desire for a society intrigue. Caring little for love, he longed, above all, for a quiet life, and contented himself with occasional amours such

as a young man can always have.   All the sentimentality, the attentions, and the tenderness which a well-bred
woman exacts bored him.   The chain, however slight it
might be, which is always formed by an adventure of
this sort, filled him with fear.   He said: " At the end
of a month I'll have had enough of it, and I'll be forced
to wait patiently for six months through politeness."

Then, a rupture exasperated him, with the scenes, the
allusions, the clinging attachment, of the abandoned
woman.

He avoided meeting Madame Poincot.

But, one evening he found himself by her side at a
dinner-party, and he felt on his skin, in his eyes, and
even in his heart, the burning glance of his fair neighbor.   Their hands met, and almost involuntarily were
pressed together in a warm clasp.   Already the intrigue was almost begun.

He saw her again, always in spite of himself.   He
realized that he was loved.   He felt himself moved by
a kind of pitying vanity when he saw what a violent
passion for him swayed this woman's breast.   So he
allowed himself to be adored, and merely displayed
gallantry, hoping that the affair would be only sentimental.

But, one day, she made an appointment with him for
the ostensible purpose of seeing him and talking freely
to him.   She fell, swooning, into his arms; and he had
no alternative but to be her lover.

And this lasted six months.   She loved him with an
unbridled, panting love.   Absorbed in this frenzied passion, she no longer bestowed a thought on anything else.
She surrendered herself to it utterly — her body, her
soul, her reputation, her position, her happiness — all

she had cast into that fire of her heart, as one casts, as a sacrifice, every precious object into a funeral pier.

He had for some time grown tired of her, and deeply regretted his easy conquest as a fascinating officer; but he was bound, held prisoner. At every moment she said to him: " I have given you everything. What more would you have?" He felt a desire to answer:

" But I have asked nothing from you, and I beg of you to take back what you gave me."

Without caring about being seen, compromised, ruined, she came to see him every evening, her passion becoming more inflamed each time they met. She flung herself into his arms, strained him in a fierce embrace, fainted under the force of rapturous kisses which to him were now terribly wearisome.

He said in a languid tone: " Look here! be reasonable!"

She replied:

" I love you," and sank on her knees gazing at him for a long time in an attitude of admiration. At length, exasperated by her persistent gaze, he tried to make her rise.

" I say! Sit down. Let us talk."

She murmured:

" No, leave me;" and remained there, her soul in a state of ecstasy.

He said to his friend d'Henricol:

" You know, 'twill end by my beating her. I won't have any more of it! It must end, and that without further delay!" Then he went on:

" What do you advise me to do?"

The other replied:

" Break it off."

And Renoldi added, shrugging his shoulders:

"You speak indifferently about the matter; you believe that it is easy to break with a woman who tortures you with attention, who annoys you with kindnesses, who persecutes you with her affection, whose only care is to please you, and whose only wrong is that she gave herself to you in spite of you."

But suddenly, one morning the news came that the regiment was about to be removed from the garrison; Renoldi began to dance with joy. He was saved! Saved without scenes, without cries! Saved! All he had to do now was to wait patiently for two months more. Saved!

In the evening she came to him more excited than she had ever been before. She had heard the dreadful news, and, without taking off her hat she caught his hands and pressed them nervously, with her eyes fixed on his, and her voice vibrating and resolute.

"You are leaving," she said; "I know it. At first, I felt heart-broken; then, I understood what I had to do. I don't hesitate about doing it. I have come to give you the greatest proof of love that a woman can offer. I follow you. For you I am abandoning my husband, my children, my family. I am ruining myself, but I am happy. It seems to me that I am giving myself to you over again. It is the last and the greatest sacrifice. I am yours for ever!"

He felt a cold sweat down his back, and was seized with a dull and violent rage, the anger of weakness. However, he became calm, and, in a disinterested tone, with a show of kindness, he refused to accept her sacrifice, tried to appease her, to bring her to reason, to make her see her own folly! She listened to him, staring at him with her great black eyes and with a smile of disdain on her lips, and said not a word in reply. He went on talking to her, and when, at length, he stopped, she said merely:

" Can you really be a coward?   Can you be one of those who seduce a woman, and then throw her over, through sheer caprice? "

He became pale, and renewed his arguments; he pointed out to her the inevitable consequences of such an action to both of them as long as they lived — how their lives would be shattered and how the world would shut its doors against them.   She replied obstinately: " What does it matter when we love each other? " Then, all of a sudden, he burst out furiously:

" Well, then, I will not.   No — do you understand? I will not do it, and I forbid you to do it."   Then, carried away by the rancorous feeling which had seethed within him so long, he relieved his heart:

" Ah, damn it all, you have now been sticking on to me for a long time in spite of myself, and the best thing for you now is to take yourself off.   I'll be much obliged if you do so, upon my honor! "

She did not answer him, but her livid countenance began to look shriveled up, as if all her nerves and muscles had been twisted out of shape.   And she went away without saying good-bye.

The same night she poisoned herself.

For a week she was believed to be in a hopeless condition.   And in the city people gossiped about the case, and pitied her, excusing her sin on account of the violence of her passion, for overstrained emotions, becoming heroic through their intensity, always obtain forgiveness for whatever is blameworthy in them.   A

woman who kills herself is, so to speak, not an adul-
teress.' And ere long there was a feeling of general
reprobation against Lieutenant Renoldi for refusing to
see her again — a unanimous sentiment of blame.

It was a matter of common talk that he had deserted
her, betrayed her, ill-treated her. The Colonel, overcome by compassion, brought his officer to book in a
quiet way. Paul d'Henricol called on his friend:
" Deuce take it, Renoldi, it's not good enough to let a
woman die; it's not the right thing anyhow."

The other, enraged, told him to hold his tongue,
whereupon d'Henricol made use of the word " infamy." The result was a duel, Renoldi was wounded,
to the satisfaction of everybody, and was for some time
confined to his bed.

She heard about it, and only loved him the more
for it, believing that it was on her account he had
fought the duel; but, as she was too ill to move, she
was unable to see him again before the departure of
the regiment.

He had been three months in Lille when he received
one morning, a visit from the sister of his former mistress.

After long suffering and a feeling of dejection, which
she could not conquer, Madame Poincot's life was now
despaired of, and she merely asked to see him for a minute, only for a minute, before closing her eyes for ever.

Absence and time had appeased the young man's
satiety and anger; he was touched, moved to tears, and
he started at once for Havre.

She seemed to be in the agonies of death. They
were left alone together; and by the bedside of this
woman whom he now believed to be dying, and whom

he blamed himself for killing, though it was not by
his own hand, he was fairly crushed with grief. He
burst out sobbing, embraced her with tender, passionate
kisses, more lovingly than he had ever done in the past.
He murmured in a broken voice:

"No, no, you shall not die! You shall get better!
We shall love each other for ever — for ever!"

She said in faint tones:

"Then it is true. You do love me, after all?"

And he, in his sorrow for her misfortunes, swore,
promised to wait till she had recovered, and full of
loving pity, kissed again and again the emaciated hands
of the poor woman whose heart was panting with feverish, irregular pulsations.

The next day he returned to the garrison.

Six weeks later she went to meet him, quite old-looking, unrecognizable, and more enamored than ever.

In his condition of mental prostration, he consented
to live with her. Then, when they remained together
as if they had been legally united, the same colonel who
had displayed indignation with him for abandoning
her, objected to this irregular connection as being in-
compatible with the good example officers ought to
give in a regiment. He warned the lieutenant on the
subject, and then furiously denounced his conduct, so
Renoldi retired from the army.

He went to live in a village on the shore of the
Mediterranean, the classic sea of lovers.

And three years passed. Renoldi, bent under the
yoke, was vanquished, and became accustomed to the
woman's persevering devotion. His hair had now
turned white.

He looked upon himself as a man done for, gone under. Henceforth, he had no hope, no ambition, no satisfaction in life, and he looked forward to no pleasure in existence.

But one morning a card was placed in his hand, with the name —"Joseph Poincot, Shipowner, Havre."

The husband! The husband, who had said nothing, realizing that there was no use in struggling against the desperate obstinacy of women. What did he want?

He was waiting in the garden, having refused to come into the house. He bowed politely, but would not sit down, even on a bench in a gravel-path, and he commenced talking clearly and slowly.

"Monsieur, I did not come here to address reproaches to you. I know too well how things happened. I have been the victim of — we have been the victims of — a kind of fatality. I would never have disturbed you in your retreat if the situation had not changed. I have two daughters, Monsieur. One of them, the elder, loves a young man, and is loved by him. But the family of this young man is opposed to the marriage, basing their objection on the situation of — my daughter's mother. I have no feeling of either anger or spite, but I love my children, Monsieur. I have, therefore, come to ask my wife to return home. I hope that to-day she will consent to go back to my house — to her own house. As for me, I will make a show of having forgotten, for — for the sake of my daughters."

Renoldi felt a wild movement in his heart, and he was inundated with a delirium of joy like a condemned man who receives a pardon.

He stammered: "Why, yes — certainly, Monsieur — I myself — be assured of it — no doubt — it is right, it is only quite right."

This time M. Poincot no longer declined to sit down.

Renoldi then rushed up the stairs, and pausing at the door of his mistress's room, to collect his senses, entered gravely.

"There is somebody below waiting to see you," he said. "'Tis to tell you something about your daughters."

She rose up. "My daughters? What about them? They are not dead?"

He replied: "No; but a serious situation has arisen, which you alone can settle."

She did not wait to hear more, but rapidly descended the stairs.

Then, he sank down on a chair, greatly moved, and waited.

He waited a long long time. Then he heard angry voices below stairs, and made up his mind to go down.

Madame Poincot was standing up exasperated, just on the point of going away, while her husband had seized hold of her dress, exclaiming: "But remember that you are destroying our daughters, your daughters, our children!"

She answered stubbornly:

"I will not go back to you!"

Renoldi understood everything, came over to them in a state of great agitation, and gasped:

"What, does she refuse to go?"

She turned towards him, and, with a kind of shame-facedness, addressed him without any familiarity of tone, in the presence of her legitimate husband, said:

" Do you know what he asks me to do? He wants me to go back, and live under one roof with him! "

And she tittered with a profound disdain for this man, who was appealing to her almost on his knees.

Then Renoldi, with the determination of a desperate man playing his last card, began talking to her in his turn, and pleaded the cause of the poor girls, the cause of the husband, his own cause. And when he stopped, trying to find some fresh argument, M. Poincot, at his wits' end, murmured, in the affectionate style in which he used to speak to her in days gone by:

" Look here, Delphine! Think of your daughters! "

Then she turned on both of them a glance of sovereign contempt, and, after that, flying with a bound towards the staircase, she flung at them these scornful words:

" You are a pair of wretches! "

Left alone, they gazed at each other for a moment, both equally crestfallen, equally crushed. M. Poincot picked up his hat, which had fallen down near where he sat, dusted off his knees the signs of kneeling on the floor, then raising both hands sorrowfully, while Renoldi was seeing him to the door, remarked with a parting bow:

" We are very unfortunate, Monsieur."

Then he walked away from the house with a heavy step.

# NO QUARTER

THE broad sunlight threw its burning rays on the fields, and under this shower of flame life burst forth in glowing vegetation from the earth. As far as the eye could see, the soil was green; and the sky was blue to the verge of the horizon. The Norman farms scattered through the plain seemed at a distance like little doors enclosed each in a circle of thin beech trees. Coming closer, on opening the worm-eaten stile, one fancied that he saw a giant garden, for all the old apple-trees, as knotted as the peasants, were in blossom. The weather-beaten black trunks, crooked, twisted, ranged along the enclosure, displayed beneath the sky their glittering domes, rosy and white. The sweet perfume of their blossoms mingled with the heavy odors of the open stables and with the fumes of the steaming dunghill, covered with hens and their chickens. It was midday. The family sat at dinner in the shadow of the pear-tree planted before the door — the father, the mother, the four children, the two maid-servants, and the three farm laborers. They scarcely uttered a word. Their fare consisted of soup and of a stew composed of potatoes mashed up in lard.

From time to time one of the maid-servants rose up and went to the cellar to fetch a pitcher of cider.

The husband, a big fellow of about forty, stared at a vine-tree, quite exposed to view, which stood close to the farm-house twining like a serpent under the shutters the entire length of the wall.

He said, after a long silence:

" The father's vine-tree is blossoming early this year. Perhaps it will bear good fruit."

The peasant's wife also turned round, and gazed at the tree without speaking.

This vine-tree was planted exactly in the place where the father of the peasant had been shot.

.    .    .    .    .    .    .    .

It was during the war of 1870. The Prussians were in occupation of the entire country. General Faidherbe, with the Army of the North, was at their head.

Now the Prussian staff had taken up its quarters in this farm-house. The old peasant who owned it, Pere Milon Pierre, received them, and gave them the best treatment he could.

For a whole month the German vanguard remained on the look-out in the village. The French were posted ten leagues away without moving; and yet each night, some of the Uhlans disappeared.

All the isolated scouts, those who were sent out on patrol, whenever they started in groups of two or three, never came back.

They were picked up dead in the morning in a field, near a farm-yard, in a ditch. Their horses even were found lying on the roads with their throats cut by a saber-stroke. These murders seemed to have been accomplished by the same men, who could not be discovered.

The country was terrorized. Peasants were shot on mere information, women were imprisoned, attempts were made to obtain revelations from children by fear.

But, one morning, Pere Milon was found stretched in his stable, with a gash across his face.

. V—23

Two Uhlans ripped open were seen lying three kilometers away from the farm-house. One of them still grasped in his hand his blood-stained weapon. He had fought and defended himself.

A council of war having been immediately constituted, in the open air, in front of the farm-house, the old man was brought before it.

He was sixty-eight years old. He was small, thin, a little crooked, with long hands resembling the claws of a crab. His faded hair, scanty and slight, like the down on a young duck, allowed his scalp to be plainly seen. The brown, crimpled skin of his neck showed the big veins which sank under his jaws and reappeared at his temples. He was regarded in the district as a miser and a hard man in business transactions.

He was placed standing between four soldiers in front of the kitchen table, which had been carried out of the house for the purpose. Five officers and the Colonel sat facing him. The Colonel was the first to speak.

" Pere Milon," he said, in French, " since we came here, we have had nothing to say of you but praise. You have always been obliging, and even considerate towards us. But to-day a terrible accusation rests on you, and the matter must be cleared up. How did you get the wound on your face? "

The peasant gave no reply.

The Colonel went on:

" Your silence condemns you, Pere Milon. But I want you to answer me, do you understand. Do you know who has killed the two Ublans who were found this morning near the cross-roads? "

The old man said in a clear voice:

" It was I ! "

The Colonel, surprised, remained silent for a second, looking steadfastly at the prisoner. Pere Milon maintained his impassive demeanor, his air of rustic stupidity, with downcast eyes, as if he were talking to his curé. There was only one thing that could reveal his internal agitation, the way in which he slowly swallowed his saliva with a visible effort, as if he were choking.

The old peasant's family — his son Jean, his daughter-in-law, and two little children stood ten paces behind scared and dismayed.

The Colonel continued:

" Do you know also who killed all the scouts of our Army, whom we have found every morning, for the past month, lying here and there in the fields? "

The old man answered with the same brutal impassiveness:

" It was I ! "

" It is you, then, that killed them all? "

" All of them — yes, it was I."

" You alone? "

" I alone."

" Tell me the way you managed to do it? "

This time the peasant appeared to be affected; the necessity of speaking at some length incommoded him.

" I know myself. I did it the way I found easiest."

The Colonel proceeded:

" I warn you, you must tell me everything. You will do well, therefore, to make up your mind about it at once. How did you begin it? "

The peasant cast an uneasy glance towards his family, who remained in a listening attitude behind him. He hesitated for another second or so, then all of a sudden, he came to a resolution on the matter.

"I came home one night about ten o'clock and the next day you were here. You and your soldiers gave me fifty crowns for forage with a cow and two sheep. Said I to myself: 'As long as I get twenty crowns out of them, I'll sell them the value of it.' But then I had other things in my heart, which I'll tell you about now. I came across one of your cavalrymen smoking his pipe near my dike, just behind my barn. I went and took my scythe off the hook, and I came back with short steps from behind, while he lay there without hearing anything. And I cut off his head with one stroke, like a feather, while he only said 'Oof!' You have only to look at the bottom of the pond; you'll find him there in a coal-bag, with a big stone tied to it.

"I got an idea into my head. I took all he had on him from his boots to his cap, and I hid them in the bake-house in the Martin wood behind the farm-yard."

The old man stopped. The officers, speechless, looked at one another. The examination was resumed, and this is what they were told.

.    .    .    .    .    .

Once he had accomplished this murder, the peasant lived with only one thought: "To kill the Prussians!" He hated them with the sly and ferocious hatred of a countryman who was at the same time covetous and patriotic. He had got an idea into his head, as he put it. He waited for a few days.

He was allowed to go and come freely, to go out and return just as he pleased, as long as he displayed humility, submissiveness, and complaisance towards the conquerors.

Now, every evening he saw the cavalrymen bearing dispatches leaving the farmhouse; and he went out one night after discovering the name of the village to which they were going, and after picking up by associating with the soldiers the few words of German he needed.

He made his way through his farm-yard slipped into the wood, reached the bake-house, penetrated to the end of the long passage, and having found the clothes of the soldier which he had hidden there, he put them on. Then, he went prowling about the fields, creeping along, keeping to the slopes so as to avoid observation, listening to the least sounds, restless as a poacher.

When he believed the time had arrived he took up his position at the roadside, and hid himself in a clump of brushwood. He still waited. At length, near midnight, he heard the galloping of a horse's hoofs on the hard soil of the road. The old man put his ear to the ground to make sure that only one cavalryman was approaching; then he got ready.

The Uhlan came on at a very quick pace, carrying some dispatches. He rode forward with watchful eyes and strained ears. As soon as he was no more than ten paces away, Pere Milon dragged himself across the road, groaning: "Hilfe! Hilfe!" ("Help! help!")

The cavalryman drew up, recognized a German soldier dismounted, believed that he was wounded, leaped down from his horse, drew near the prostrate man, never suspecting anything, and, as he stooped over the stranger, he received in the middle of the stomach the long curved blade of the saber. He sank down without any death throes, merely quivering with a few last shudders.

Then, the Norman radiant with the mute joy of an old peasant, rose up, and merely to please himself, cut the dead soldier's throat. After that, he dragged the corpse to the dike and threw it in.

The horse was quietly waiting for its rider. Pere Milon got on the saddle, and started across the plain at the gallop.

At the end of an hour, he perceived two more Uhlans approaching the staff-quarters side by side. He rode straight towards them, crying, "Hilfe! hilfe!" The Prussians let him come on, recognizing the uniform without any distrust.

And like a cannon-ball, the old man shot between the two, bringing both of them to the ground with his saber and a revolver. The next thing he did was to cut the throats of the horses — the German horses! Then, softly he re-entered the bake-house, and hid the horse he had ridden himself in the dark passage. There he took off the uniform, put on once more his own old clothes, and going to his bed, slept till morning.

For four days he did not stir out, awaiting the close of the open inquiry as to the cause of the soldiers' deaths; but, on the fifth day, he started out again, and by a similar stratagem killed two more soldiers.

Thenceforth he never stopped. Each night he wandered about, prowled through the country at random, cutting down some Prussians, sometimes here, sometimes there, galloping through the deserted fields under the moonlight, a lost Uhlan, a hunter of men. Then when he had finished his task, leaving behind the corpses lying along the roads, the old horseman went to the bake-house, where he concealed both the animal and the uniform. About midday he calmly returned to the spot to give the horse a feed of oats and some water, and he took every care of the animal, exacting therefore the hardest work.

But, the night before his arrest, one of the soldiers he attacked put himself on his guard, and cut the old peasant's face with a slash of a saber.

He had, however, killed both of them. He had even managed to go back and hide his horse and put on his everyday garb, but, when he reached the stable, he was overcome by weakness, and was not able to m.ke his way into the house.

He had been found lying on the straw, his face covered with blood.

.     .     .     .     .

When he had finished his story, he suddenly lifted his head, and glanced proudly at the Prussian officers.

The Colonel, tugging at his moustache, asked:

" Have you anything more to say? "

" No, nothing more; we are quits. I killed sixteen, not one more, not one less."

" You know you have to die? "

" I ask for no quarter! "

" Have you been a soldier? "

" Yes, I served at one time. And 'tis you killed my father, who was a soldier of the first Emperor, not to speak of my youngest son, Francois, whom you killed last month near Exreux. I owed this to you, and I've paid you back. 'Tis tit for tat! "

The officers stared at one another.

The old man went on:

" Eight for my father, eight for my son — that pays

it off! I sought for no quarrel with you. I don't know you! I only know where you came from. You came to my house here, and ordered me about as if the house was yours. I have had my revenge, and I'm glad of it!"

And stiffening up his old frame, he folded his arms in the attitude of a humble hero.

The Prussians held a long conference. A captain, who had also lost a son the month before, defended the brave old scoundrel.

Then the Colonel rose up, and, advancing towards Pere Milon, he said, lowering his voice:

"Listen, old man! There is perhaps one way of saving your life — it is —"

But the old peasant was not listening to him, and fixing his eyes directly on the German officer, while the wind made the scanty hair move to and fro on his skull, he made a frightful grimace, which shriveled up his pinched countenance scarred by the saber-stroke, and, puffing out his chest, he spat, with all his strength, right into the Prussian's face.

The Colonel, stupefied, raised his hand, and for the second time the peasant spat in his face.

All the officers sprang to their feet and yelled out orders at the same time.

In less than a minute, the old man, still as impassive as ever, was stuck up against the wall, and shot while he cast a smile at Jean, his eldest son, and then at his daughter-in-law and the two children, who were staring with terror at the scene.

# THE IMPOLITE SEX

Madame de X. to Madame de L.

Etretat, Friday.

MY dear Aunt,— I am going to pay you a visit without making much fuss about it. I shall be at Les Fresnes on the 2nd of September, the day before the hunting season opens, as I do not want to miss it, so that I may tease these gentlemen. You are very obliging, aunt, and I would like you to allow them to dine with you, as you usually do when there are no strange guests, without dressing or shaving for the occasion, on the ground that they are fatigued.

They are delighted, of course, when I am not present. But I shall be there, and I shall hold a review, like a general, at the dinner-hour; and, if I find a single one of them at all careless in dress, no matter how little, I mean to send him down to the kitchen to the servant-maids.

The men of to-day have so little consideration for others and so little good manners that one must be always severe with them. We live indeed in an age of vulgarity. When they quarrel with one another, they attack one another with insults worthy of street-porters, and, in our presence, they do not conduct themselves even as well as our servants. It is at the seaside that you see this most clearly. They are to be found there in battalions, and you can judge them in the lump.

Oh! what coarse beings they are!

Just imagine in a train, one of them, a gentleman

361

who looked well, as I thought, at first sight, thanks
to his tailor, was dainty enough to take off his boots in
order to put on a pair of old shoes! Another, an old
man, who was probably some wealthy upstart (these
are the most ill-bred), while sitting opposite to me, had
the delicacy to place his two feet on the seat quite close
to me. This is a positive fact.

At the water-places, there is an unrestrained out-
pouring of unmannerliness. I must here make one
admission — that my indignation is perhaps due to the
fact that I am not accustomed to associate, as a rule,
with the sort of people one comes across here, for I
should be less shocked by their manners if I had the opportunity of observing them oftener. In the inquiry-
office of the hotel, I was nearly thrown down by a
young man who snatched the key over my head.
Another knocked against me so violently without begging my pardon or lifting his hat, coming away from a
ball at the Casino, that he gave me a pain in the chest.
It is the same way with all of them. Watch them ad-
dressing ladies on the terrace; they scarcely ever bow.
They merely raise their hands to their head-gear. But
indeed, as they are all more or less bald, it is their best
plan.

But what exasperates and disgusts me specially is the
liberty they take of talking publicly without any precaution whatsoever about the most revolting adventures. When two men are together, they relate to each
other, in the broadest language and with the most
abominable comments really horrible stories without
caring in the slightest degree whether a woman's ear is
within reach of their voices. Yesterday, on the beach,

I was forced to go away from the place where I sat in order not to be any longer the involuntary confidante of an obscene anecdote, told in such immodest language that I felt just as much humiliated as indignant at having heard it. Would not the most elementary good-breeding have taught them to speak in a lower tone about such matters when we are near at hand. Etretat is, moreover, the country of gossip and scandal. From five to seven o'clock you can see people wandering about in quest of nasty stories about others which they retail from group to group. As you remarked to me, my dear aunt, tittle-tattle is the mark of petty individuals and petty minds. It is also the consolation of women who are no longer loved or sought after. It is enough for me to observe the women who are fondest of gossiping to be persuaded that you are quite right.

The other day I was present at a musical evening at the Casino, given by a remarkable artist, Madame Masson, who sings in a truly delightful manner. I took the opportunity of applauding the admirable Coquelin, as well as two charming boarders of the Vaudeville, M— and Meillet. I was able, on the occasion, to see all the bathers collected together this year on the beach. There were not many persons of distinction among them.

Next day I went to lunch at Yport. I noticed a tall man with a beard who was coming out of a large house like a castle. It was the painter, Jean Paul Laurens. He is not satisfied apparently with imprisoning the subjects of his pictures he insists on imprisoning himself.

Then, I found myself seated on the shingle close to a man still young, of gentle and refined appearance, who was reading some verses. But he read them with such concentration, with such passion, I may say, that he did not even raise his eyes towards me. I was somewhat astonished, and I asked the conductor of the baths without appearing to be much concerned, the name of this gentleman. I laughed inwardly a little at this reader of rhymes: he seemed behind the age, for a man. This person, I thought, must be a simpleton. Well, aunt, I am now infatuated about this stranger. Just fancy, his name is Sully Prudhomme! I turned round to look at him at my ease, just where I sat. His face possesses the two qualities of calmness and elegance. As somebody came to look for him, I was able to hear his voice, which is sweet and almost timid. He would certainly not tell obscene stories aloud in public, or knock against ladies without apologizing. He is sure to be a man of refinement, but his refinement is of an almost morbid, vibrating character. I will try this winter to get an introduction to him.

I have no more news to tell you, my dear aunt, and I must interrupt this letter in haste, as the post-hour is near. I kiss your hands and your cheeks.— Your devoted niece,

BERTHE DE X.

P. S.— I should add, however, by way of justification of French politeness, that our fellow-countrymen are, when traveling, models of good manners in comparison with the abominable English, who seem to have been brought up by stable-boys, so much do they take care not to incommode themselves in any way, while they always incommode their neighbors.

Madame de L. to Madame de X.

Les Fresnes, Saturday.

My Dear Child,— Many of the things you have said
to me are very reasonable, but that does not prevent
you from being wrong.   Like you, I used formerly to
feel very indignant at the impoliteness of men, who,
as I supposed, constantly treated me with neglect; but,
as I grew older and reflected on everything, putting
aside coquetry, and observing things without taking
any part in them myself, I perceived this much — that
if men are not always polite, women are always inde-
scribably rude.

We imagine that we should be permitted to do anything, my darling, and at the same time we consider
that we have a right to the utmost respect, and in the
most flagrant manner we commit actions devoid of that
elementary good-breeding of which you speak with
passion.

I find, on the contrary, that men have, for us, much
consideration, as compared with our bearing towards
them.   Besides, darling, men must needs be, and are,
what we make them.   In a state of society, where
women are all true gentlewomen, all men would become gentlemen.

Mark my words; just observe and reflect.

Look at two women meeting in the street.   What
an attitude each assumes towards the other!   What
disparaging looks!   What contempt they throw into
each glance!   How they toss their heads while they
inspect each other to find something to condemn!
And, if the footpath is narrow, do you think one
woman would make room for another, or will beg

pardon as she sweeps by? Never! When two men jostle each other by accident in some narrow lane, each of them bows and at the same time gets out of the other's way, while we women press against each other stomach to stomach, face to face, insolently staring each other out of countenance.

Look at two women who are acquaintances meeting on a stair case before the drawing-room door of a friend of theirs to whom one has just paid a visit, and to whom the other is about to pay a visit. They begin to talk to each other, and block up the passage. If anyone happens to be coming up behind them, man or woman, do you imagine that they will put themselves half-an-inch out of their way? Never! never!

I was waiting myself, with my watch in my hands, one day last winter, at a certain drawing-room door. And behind two gentlemen were also waiting without showing any readiness to lose their temper, like me. The reason was that they had long grown accustomed to our unconscionable insolence.

The other day, before leaving Paris, I went to dine with no less a person than your husband in the Champs Elysees in order to enjoy the open air. Every table was occupied. The waiter asked us not to go, and there would soon be a vacant table.

At that moment, I noticed an elderly lady of noble figure, who, having paid the amount of her docket, seemed on the point of going away. She saw me, scanned me from head to foot, and did not budge. For more than a full quarter-of-an-hour she sat there, immovable, putting on her gloves, and calmly staring at those who were waiting like myself. Now, two young men who were just finishing their dinner, having seen

me in their turn, quickly summoned the waiter in order
to pay whatever they owed, and at once offered me their
seats, even insisting on standing while waiting for
their change. And, bear in mind, my fair niece,
that I am no longer pretty, like you, but old and white-
haired.

It is we (do you see?) who should be taught politeness, and the task would be such a difficult one that Her-
cules himself would not be equal to it. You speak to
me about Etretat, and about the people who indulged
in " tittle-tattle " along the beach of that delightful
watering-place. It is a spot now lost to me, a thing of
the past, but I found much amusement there in days
gone by.

There were only a few of us, people in good society,
really good society, and a few artists, and we all fra-
ternized. We paid little attention to gossip in those
days.

Well, as we had no insipid Casino, where people only
gather for show, where they talk in whispers, where
they dance stupidly, where they succeed in thoroughly
boring one another, we sought some other way of passing our evenings pleasantly. Now, just guess what
came into the head of one of our husbandry? Nothing less than to go and dance each night in one of the
farm-houses in the neighborhood.

We started out in a group with a street-organ, generally played by Le Poittevin, the painter, with a cotton
nightcap on his head. Two men carried lanterns.
We followed in procession, laughing and chattering
like a pack of fools.

We woke up the farmer and his servant-maids and
laboring men. We got them to make onion-soup

(horror!), and we danced under the apple-trees, to the sound of the barrel-organ. The cocks waking up began to crow in the darkness of the out-houses; the horses began prancing on the straw of their stables. The cool air of the country caressed our cheeks with the smell of grass and of new-mown hay.

How long ago it is! How long ago it is. It is thirty years since then!

I do not want you, my darling, to come for the opening of the hunting season. Why spoil the pleasure of our friends by inflicting on them fashionable toilets on this day of vigorous exercise in the country? This is the way, child, that men are spoiled. I embrace you.— Your old aunt

GENEVIEVE DE Z.

# WOMAN'S WILES

"**W**OMEN?"

"Well, what do you say about women?"

"Well, there are no conjurors more subtle in taking us in at every available opportunity with or without reason, often for the sole pleasure of playing tricks on us. And they play these tricks with incredible simplicity, astonishing audacity, unparalleled ingenuity. They play tricks from morning till night, and they all do it — the most virtuous, the most upright, the most sensible of them. You may add that sometimes they are to some extent driven to do these things. Man. has always idiotic fits of obstinacy and tyrannical desires. A husband is continually giving ridiculous orders in his own house. He is full of caprices; his wife plays on them even while she makes use of them for the purpose of deception. She persuades him that a thing costs so much because he would kick up a row if its price were higher. And she always extricates herself from the difficulty cunningly by a means so simple and so sly that we gape with amazement when by chance we discover them. We say to ourselves in a stupefied state of mind 'How is it we did not see this till now?'"

. . . . . .

The man who uttered the words was an ex-Minister of the Empire, the Comte de L——, a thorough profligate, it was said, and a very accomplished gentleman. A group of young men were listening to him.

He went on:

" I was outwitted by an ordinary uneducated woman in a comic and thorough-going fashion. I will tell you about it for your instruction.

" I was at the time Minister for Foreign Affairs, and I was in the habit of taking a long walk every morning in the Champs Elysees. It was the month of May; I walked along, sniffing in eagerly that sweet odor of budding leaves.

" Ere long, I noticed, that I used to meet every day a charming little woman, one of those marvelous, graceful creatures, who bear the trade-mark of Paris. Pretty? Well, yes and no. Well-made? No, better than that: her waist was too slight, her shoulders .too narrow, her breast too full, no doubt; but I prefer those exquisite human dolls to that great statuesque corpse, the Venus of Milo.

" And then this sort of woman trots along in an incomparable fashion, and the very rustle of her skirt fills the marrow of your bones with desire. She seemed to give me a side-glance as she passed me. But these women give you all sorts of looks — you never can tell . . .

" One morning, I saw her sitting on a bench with an open book between her hands. I came across, and sat down beside her. Five minutes later, we were friends. Then, each day, after the smiling salutation ' Good day, Madame,' ' Good day, Monsieur,' we began to chat. She told me that she was the wife of a Government clerk, that her life was a sad one, that in it pleasures were few and cares numerous, and a thousand other things.

" I told her who I was, partly through thoughtlessness, and partly perhaps through vanity. She pretended to be much astonished.

" Next day, she called at the Ministry to see me; and she came again there so often that the ushers, having their attention drawn to her appearance, used to whisper to one another, as soon as they saw her, the name with which they had christened her ' Madame Leon' that is my Christian name.

" For three months I saw her every morning without growing tired of her for a second, so well was she able incessantly to give variety and piquancy to her physical attractiveness. But one day I saw that her eyes were bloodshot and glowing with suppressed tears, that she could scarcely speak, so much was she preoccupied with secret troubles.

" I begged of her, I implored of her, to tell me what was the cause of her agitation.

" She faltered out at length with a shudder: ' I am — I am pregnant! '

" And she burst out sobbing. Oh! I made a dreadful grimace, and I have no doubt I turned pale, as men generally do at hearing such a piece of news. You cannot conceive what an unpleasant stab you feel in your breast at the announcement of an unexpected paternity of this kind. But you are sure to know it sooner or later. So, in my turn, I gasped: ' But — but — you are married, are you not? '

" She answered: ' Yes, but my husband has been away in Italy for the last two months, and he will not be back for some time.'

" I was determined at any cost to get out of my responsibility.

" I said: ' You must go and join him immediately.'

" She reddened to her very temples, and with downcast eyes, murmured: ' Yes — but —' She either dared
not or would not finish the sentence.

" I understood, and I prudently enclosed her in an
envelope the expenses of the journey.

. . . . . .

" Eight days later, she sent me a letter from Genoa.
The following week, I received one from Florence.
Then letters reached me from Leghorn, Rome, and
Naples.

" She said to me: ' I am in good health, my dear
love, but I am looking frightful. I would not care to
have you see me till it is all over; you would not love
me. My husband suspects nothing. As his business
in this country will require him to stay there much
longer, I will not return to France till after my confinement.'

" And, at the end of about eight months, I received
from Venice these few words: ' It is a boy.'

" Some time after, she suddenly entered my study
one morning, fresher and prettier than ever, and flung
herself into my arms.

" And our former connection was renewed.

" I left the Ministry, and she came to live in my
house in the Rue de Grenelle. She often spoke to me
about the child, but I scarcely listened to what she said
about it; it did not concern me. Now and then I
placed a rather large sum of money in her hand, saying: ' Put that by for him.'

" Two more years glided by; and she was more
eager to tell me some news about the youngster —
' about Leon.'

" Sometimes she would say in the midst of tears:
' You don't care about him; you don't even wish to see
him.   If you know what grief you cause me ! '

" At last I was so much harassed by her that I
promised, one day, to go, next morning, to the Champs
Elysees, when she took the child there for an airing.

" But at the moment when I was leaving the house,
I was stopped by a sudden apprehension.   Man is
weak and foolish.   What if I were to get fond of this
tiny being of whom I was the father — my son?

" I had my hat on my head, my gloves in my hands.
I flung down the gloves on my desk, and my hat on a
chair:

" No.   Decidedly I will not go; it is wiser not to
go.'

" My door flew open.   My brother entered the
room.   He handed me an anonymous letter he had
received that morning:

" ' Warn the Comte de L——, your brother, that
the little woman of the Rue Casette is impudently
laughing at him.   Let him make some inquiries about
her.'

" I had never told anybody about this intrigue, and
I now told my brother the history of it from the beginning to the end.   I added:

" For my part, I don't want to trouble myself any
further about the matter; but will you, like a good fellow, go and find out what you can about her?

" When my brother had left me, I said to myself:
' In what way can she have deceived me?   She has
other lovers?   What does it matter to me?   She is
young, fresh, and pretty; I ask nothing more from her.

She seems to love me, and as a matter of fact, she does not cost me much. Really, I don't understand this business.'

" My brother speedily returned. He had learned from the police all that was to be known about her husband: 'A clerk in the Home Department, of regular habits and good repute, and, moveover, a thinking man, but married to a very pretty woman, whose expenses seemed somewhat extravagant for her modest position.' That was all.

" Now, my brother having sought for her at her residence, and finding that she was gone out, succeeded, with the assistance of a little gold, in making the doorkeeper chatter: 'Madame D——, a very worthy woman, and her husband a very worthy man, not proud, not rich, but generous.'

" My brother asked for the sake of saying something:

" ' How old is her little boy now? '

" ' Why, she has not got any little boy, monsieur.'

" ' What? Little Leon? '

" ' No, monsieur, you are making a mistake.'

" ' I mean the child she had while she was in Italy, two years ago? '

" ' She has never been in Italy, monsieur; she has not quitted the house she is living in for the last five years.'

" My brother, in astonishment, questioned the doorkeeper anew, and then he pushed his investigation of the matter further. No child, no journey.

" I was prodigiously astonished, but without clearly understanding the final meaning of this comedy.

" ' I want,' said I to him, ' to have my mind perfectly clear about the affair. I will ask her to come here to-morrow. You shall receive her instead of me.

If she has deceived me, you will hand her these ten
thousand francs, and I will never see her again. In
fact, I am beginning to find I have had enough of
her.'

"Would you believe it? I had been grieved the
night before because I had a child by this woman; and
I was now irritated, ashamed, wounded at having no
more of her. I found myself free, released from all
responsibility, from all anxiety, and yet I felt myself
raging at the position in which I was placed.

" Next morning my brother awaited her in my study.
She came in as quickly as usual, rushing towards him
with outstretched arms, but when she saw who it was
she at once drew back.

" He bowed, and excused himself.

" ' I beg your pardon, madame, for being here instead of my brother, but he has authorized me to ask
you for some explanations which he would find it painful to seek from you himself.'

" Then, fixing on her face a searching glance, he
said abruptly:

" ' We know you have not a child by him.'

" After the first moment of stupor, she regained
her composure, took a seat, and gazed with a smile at
this man who was sitting in judgment on her.

" She answered simply:

" ' No; I have no child.'

" ' We know also that you have never been in Italy.'

" This time she burst out laughing in earnest.

" ' No, I have never been in Italy.'

" My brother, quite stunned, went on:

" ' The Comte has requested me to give you this
money, and tell you that it is all broken off.'

" She became serious again, calmly putting the money
into her pocket, and, in an ingenuous tone asked:

" ' And I am not, then, to see the Comte any more? '

" ' No, madame.'

" She appeared to be annoyed, and in a passionless
voice she said:

" ' So much the worse; I was very fond of him.'

" Seeing that she had made up her mind on the subject so resolutely, my brother, smiling in his turn, said
to her:

" ' Look here, now, tell me why you invented all this
tricky yarn, complicating it by bringing in the sham
journey to Italy and the child? '

She gazed at my brother in amazement, as if he had
asked her a stupid question, and replied:

" ' I say! How spiteful you are! Do you believe
a poor little woman of the people such as I am — nothing at all — could have for three years kept on my
hands the Comte de L——, Minister, a great per-
sonage, a man of fashion, wealthy and seductive, if she
had not taken a little trouble about it? Now it is all
over. So much the worse. It couldn't last for ever.
None the less I succeeded in doing it for three years.
You will say many things to him on my behalf.'

" She rose up. My brother continued questioning
her:

" ' But — the child? You had one to show him? '

" ' Certainly — my sister's child. She lent it to me.
I'd bet it was she gave you the information.'

" ' Good! And all those letters from Italy? '

" She sat down again so as to laugh at her ease.

" ' Oh! those letters — well, they were a bit of

poetry.   The Comte was not a Minister of Foreign Affairs for nothing.'

" ' But — another thing? '

" Oh! the other thing is my secret.   I don't want to compromise anyone.'

" And bowing to him with a rather mocking smile, she left the room without any emotion, an actress who had played her part to the end."

And the Comte de L —— added by way of moral:

" So take care about putting your trust in that sort of turtle dove! "

# A NIGHT IN SPRING

JEANNE was going to marry her cousin Jacques.
They had known one another from infancy,
and love could not assume the same ceremonious
forms in their case as it does in fashionable society.
They had been brought up together without suspecting that they were in love with one another.

The young girl, with a touch of coquetry, displayed
towards the young man a kind of innocent seductive-
ness; she found him, moreover, nice and good-natured,
and each time she saw him again she embraced him
with all her heart, but without a shudder, without that
shudder which seems to crimple the flesh from the
tips of the fingers to the soles of the feet.

As for him, he thought, quite simply: "She is
dainty, my little cousin;" and he regarded her with
that sort of instinctive tenderness which a man experi-
ences always for a pretty girl. His reflections did not
go farther.

Then, one day, Jeanne chanced to hear her mother
saying to her aunt (to her Aunt Alberte, for Aunt
Lison had remained an old maid):

"I assure you they will love one another immediately, these young people; you will see. As for me,
Jacques is exactly the son-in-law I dream of."

And immediately Jeanne began to adore her cousin
Jacques. Then she blushed when she saw him; her
hand trembled in that of the young man; she cast down
her eyes, then she met his glance, and she made mod-

378

est advances, so as to encourage him to kiss her, and he saw clearly how she felt towards him. He understood, and in a transport which had in it as much gratified vanity as genuine affection, he clasped his cousin in his arms, whispering in her ear: " I love you! I love you! "

From that time there was nothing between them but billing and cooing, love-making, a display of all the amorous feelings rendered easy and natural by their past intimacy. In the parlor, Jacques kissed his intended bride in the presence of the three old women, the three sisters, his mother, Jeanne's mother, and Aunt Lison. He walked out alone with her often for the whole day in the woods, along the river's bank, through the humid meadows, where the grass was starred with wild flowers. And they looked forward to the day fixed for their marriage without any great impatience, but enveloped, bathed in an exquisite sense of happiness, tasting the unspeakable delight of tender caresses, clinging hand-clasps, impassioned glances, so intense that their very souls seemed to mingle; and vaguely oppressed by the longing as yet undefined for closer embraces, feeling a sort of restlessness on their lips which called to each other, seeming to watch and wait for each other, and to give promise of future bliss.

Sometimes, when they spent the entire day in this tempered fire of passion, in those Platonic exchanges of tenderness, they felt as night came on a sense of exhaustion, and both of them emitted long-drawn sighs without knowing why, without quite understanding — stifled sighs of expectation.

The two mothers and their sister, Aunt Lison, observed the course of this youthful love with sympathetic smiles. Aunt Lison especially seemed deeply affected as she watched their movements.

She was a little woman of very few words, who always kept in the background, made no noise, only put in an appearance at meal-times, and then went upstairs again to her own room, where she remained nearly always shut up. She wore an aspect of homely cleanliness and good nature; her eyes had a soft, melancholy look; and she counted for little in the family.

The two sisters, who were widows, having occupied a position in the world, looked upon her as a rather insignificant person. They treated her with an easy familiarity which only veiled their somewhat contemptuous regard for the old maid. She used to be called Lise, having been born in the days when Beranger ruled France. When it was seen that she was not getting married, and that she was never likely to marry, Lise was changed into Lison. To-day she was " Aunt Lison," an unpretentious, tidy-looking old maid, dreadfully timid even with her own relations, who were attached to her with an affection, which was largely composed of habit mingled with compassion and sort of kindly indifference.

The young people never went up to her room to kiss her. The maid-servant was the only person that entered the apartment. She went to fetch Aunt Lison whenever they wanted to talk to her. It seemed as if they did not know where this room was situated — this room where in solitude all that poor life had ebbed away. They paid little attention to her. When she was not there, they never spoke about her, they never bestowed a thought on her. She was one of those retiring creatures, who remain strangers even to their kinsfolk, as if they belonged to an unexplored region of humanity whose deaths would cause no gap, no void, in a household, one of these beings who cannot share in the existence or the habits or the love of those who live side by side with them.

She always went about with short quick steps rarely opening her lips, never causing the slightest disturbance, or giving annoyance to anyone, and it seemed as if she communicated to inanimate objects the quality of making no sound. Her hands appeared to be made of some species of cotton wool, so lightly and delicately did they handle whatever they touched.

When they pronounced the two words, " Aunt Lison," it might be said that the name awakened no thought in anyone's mind. It was as if one had mentioned " the coffee-pot " or " the sugar-basin."

The dog, Loute, certainly possessed a much more marked personality. She was always patted on the back, and they called her " My dear Loute, my lovely Loute, my little Loute." The canine favorite would have been lamented much more than the old maid.

The marriage of the two cousins was to take place at the end of May. The young couple lived with eyes always fastened on one another, with hands always clasped, with only one thought in their minds, with only one passion in their hearts. The late spring this year, lingering, chilly from the white frosts that came night after night, and the cool haze that followed in the mornings, had suddenly made all things burst out into bloom.

Then, one afternoon, the conquering sun, drying up at last the moist earth, cast its rays on the entire plain.

Its gay brightness filled the whole country-side, and penetrated everywhere, into plants and beasts, and men. The amorous birds fluttered about, flapped their wings, and cooed to each other. Jeanne and Jacques, overpowered by a feeling of unutterable bliss, but more timid even than usual, uneasy under these fresh movements of passion which were generated in their breasts by the fermentation of the woods, remained all day sitting on a bench in front of the house, not venturing any longer to wander very far alone, and gazing with vague glances towards the pond, a short distance away, where stately swans were pursuing each other.

Then, as evening came on, they felt more subdued, more tranquil, and, after dinner, they would lean over the open window in the parlor, talking softly, while the two mothers were playing piquet in the white circle of light thrown by the shade of the lamp, and Aunt Lison was knitting stockings for the poor people of the neighborhood.

A row of tall trees extended for some distance behind the pond, and through the still scanty foliage the moon suddenly appeared. It had gradually risen above the tops of the branches, which intercepted the view of its orb, and climbing the sky, in the midst of the stars, which it threw into the background, it shed over the earth that melancholy light in which float white vapors and dreamlike forms so dear to the tender-hearted, to poets and to lovers.

The young people had first glanced towards the moon, then quite impregnated by the soft loveliness of the night, by that aerial radiance which shone on the grass and the trees, they strolled slowly along, and walked across the wide stretch of green sward glowing in the moonlight till they came to the pond with its glittering water.

As soon as they had finished the four games of piquet which they usually played every night, the two mothers, getting sleepy by degrees, felt a desire to go to bed.

" We must call in the young ones," said one of them.

The other cast a rapid glance towards the pale horizon, where two shadows were slowly moving along.

" Let them alone," she said, " it is such a fine night out.  Lison will sit up and wait for them.  Will you not, Lison? "

The old maid raised her anxious eyes, and in her timid voice replied:

" Certainly, I'll wait for them."

And the two sisters went off to bed.

Then, in her turn, Aunt Lison rose up, and laying down her work by the side of her armchair, the wool which she had been knitting and the long needle, she went over to the window, and, leaning on the window with her elbows, contemplated the lovely night.  The two lovers walked on, without stopping, across the grass and kept pacing from the pond to the doorsteps and from the doorsteps to the pond.  They pressed each other's fingers, and no longer uttered a word, as if they were disembodied, and had become a part of the visible poetry exhaled from the earth.  Jeanne suddenly saw the figure of the old maid distinctly outlined by the lamp-light as if it were framed in the window.

" See here," she said, " Aunt Lison is looking out at us."

Jacques raised his head.  " Yes," he answered, " Aunt Lison is looking out at us."

And they went on slowly, still dreaming and talking words of love.

But the dew was falling thickly on the grass, and the cool air made them shiver a little.

" Let us go in now," she said.

And they re-entered the house.

When they reached the parlor, Aunt Lison had resumed her knitting. Her forehead was bent over her work, and her thin little fingers trembled slightly as if they were very tired.

Jeanne came over to her.

" Aunt, we are going to bed now."

The old maid fixed her eyes on the girl. They were red, as if she had been crying. Jacques and his future bride paid no heed to this. But the young man' noticed that his sweetheart's thin shoes were all splashed with water. He was seized with uneasiness, and asked:

" Don't you feel your dear little feet cold ? "

And, all of a sudden the aunt's fingers were shaking so much that her work slipped out of them; the ball of woolen thread rolled down on the floor; and abruptly covering her face with her hands, the old maid began to weep with great convulsive sobs.

The two young people were by her side immediately.

Jeanne, falling on her knees, stretched out her arms excitedly, repeating:

" What's the matter with you, Aunt Lison ? What's the matter with you, Aunt Lison ? "

Then, the poor old maid, in a faltering voice, broken by her sobs, and with her face shriveled by grief, answered :

" It was — it was when he asked you, ' Don't you feel cold — in — in your dear little feet ? Nobody ever said that to me ! — never ! never ! "

# THE JEWELS

MONSIEUR LANTIN met the young girl at a reception given one night by the assistant chief of his department, and love enveloped him like a net.

She was the daughter of a provincial tax-collector who had been dead for some years. She came to Paris afterward with her mother, who associated with some bourgeois families in her neighborhood in the hope of marrying the young girl. They were poor and honorable, unobtrusive and gentle. She appeared to be the absolute type of the virtuous woman to whom a young man would dream of devoting his life. Her delicate beauty had a charm of angelic modesty, and the imperceptible smile that unceasingly hovered on her lips seemed to be a reflection of her heart.

Everybody sang her praises. All who knew her were never tired of repeating: "It will be a lucky man who gets her. It would be impossible to do better."

Monsieur Lantin, who was then chief clerk at the Ministry of the Interior, with an annual salary of thirty-five hundred francs, asked for her hand and married her.

He was incredibly happy with her. She managed his house with such skilful economy that they seemed to live in luxury. There was not a delicate little attention, nor a playful, kittenish caress, she did not lavish on her husband, and the witchery of her person was such that six years after their meeting he loved her even more than at the beginning.

He could find but one fault with her—a love of the theater and imitation jewelry.

Her friends—she knew some of the wives of modest functionaries—were continually sending her boxes for the plays in vogue, even for first nights, and willing or not, she dragged her husband to these entertainments, which fatigued him terribly after his day's work. He begged her to agree to go to the theater with some lady of her acquaintance who could bring her home afterward. It was a long time before she consented, considering it hardly proper to act in this manner. Finally she decided to humor him, and he was infinitely grateful to her.

This taste for the theater soon awakened the need of adorning herself. It is true, her toilettes were always simple, always in good taste and modest, and her gentle grace, her irresistible grace, unpretentious and radiant, seemed to acquire an added flavor from the simplicity of her dresses; but she fell into the habit of hanging two great rhinestones in her ears to simulate diamonds; she wore necklaces of false pearls, imitation bracelets, and combs ornamented with variegated glass masquerading as precious stones.

Her husband, a little shocked by this love of the tawdry, frequently remonstrated with her. "My dear, when one has not the means to buy real jewelry, one should appear adorned only by one's beauty and grace, which, after all, are the rarest of ornaments."

"I know very well that you are right," she

answered with a sweet smile, "but what would you have me do? I like these things. It's my vice, and I can't make myself over. I should have adored real jewels." And she poured necklaces over her fingers and made crystal facets shimmer as she added: "Do look and see how well it's done. One would swear that it is real."

"You have the tastes of a Bohemian," he observed, smiling.

Sometimes in the evening, as they sat alone at the corner of the fire, she brought out the morocco box which contained the "rubbish," as Lantin had styled it, and placed it on the tea-table. She began to examine the imitation jewelry with passionate attention, as if she were able to relish some deep, secret delight, and she would insist upon putting a necklace around her husband's neck, only to burst into a hearty laugh.

"How funny you look!" she would exclaim, and then throw herself on his neck and kiss him as if distracted.

On a cold winter's night she had been to the opera, and returned shivering from head to foot. The following day she began to cough. Eight days later she died of pneumonia.

Lantin narrowly missed following her to the grave. His despair was such that his hair turned white in a month. He cried from morning till night, his soul racked with intolerable suffering and haunted by the memory of her—her smile, her voice, and her consummate charm.

Time did not relieve his anguish. Frequently during office hours, while his colleagues discussed daily happenings, one could see his cheeks suddenly expand, his nose wrinkle, his eyes fill with tears, and, making a fearful face, he would burst out sobbing.

He had kept the room of his companion intact, and every day locked himself in to think of her; all the furniture, and even her clothes, remained just as they had been left the last day.

But life dealt harshly with him. His salary, which in the hands of his wife had sufficed for all the needs of the household, was at present insufficient for himself alone. And he asked himself, in amazement, how she had managed to provide him with excellent wines and give him delicate food which he could no longer provide with his modest means.

He contracted debts and was obliged to raise money in the manner of people who are reduced to expedients. At last, one morning, an entire week before the end of the month, finding himself without a copper, he thought of selling something, and at once it occurred to him to get rid of some of his wife's "rubbish." In the depths of his heart there still lingered a certain hatred for these "make-believes" which had formerly irritated him. Even the sight of them, every day, tainted the memory of his loved one a little.

He searched for a long time in the heap of tinsel she had left behind, because up to the last days of her life she had obstinately continued to buy them, bringing home some new object almost every evening; and he selected the large necklace which she seemed to prefer. He thought it might possibly be worth six or eight francs, because it was really very careful work for imitation-ware.

He put it in his pocket and set out for the Ministry, following the boulevards and looking for the shop of a jeweler which would inspire him with confidence.

He finally found one, and entered, rather ashamed to reveal his misery in this manner, by attempting to sell something of so little value.

"Monsieur," he began, "I should like to know the value of this article."

The dealer took the necklace, examined it, turned it over, took a magnifying-glass, called a clerk, made some observations to him in a low voice, and placed it on the counter and looked at it from a distance to better judge the effect.

Monsieur Lantin, embarrassed by all these ceremonies, had opened his mouth to exclaim, "Oh, I know very well it's worth nothing," when the jeweler prevented him.

"Monsieur, this is worth from twelve to fifteen thousand francs, but I could not buy it unless you let me know exactly how you got it."

The widower's eyes opened to an enormous size, and he remained gaping, unable to understand. Finally he stammered: "You say . . . Are you sure?"

The other misinterpreted his astonishment, and replied, dryly: "You can look elsewhere and see if they will offer you more. As far as I am concerned, it is worth fifteen thousand at the most. Come back if you have no better offer."

Monsieur Lantin, quite idiotic, picked up his necklace and left, obeying a confused yearning for solitude and reflection.

But as soon as he was in the street he was seized

with laughter. "The imbecile! Oh, the imbecile!" he thought. "What if I had taken him at his word. There's a jeweler who doesn't know the real article from imitation-ware."

And he entered another dealer's, at the head of the Rue de la Paix. As soon as the jeweler saw the article he exclaimed:

"I certainly know that. It came from my store."

"How much is it worth?" asked Lantin, very agitated.

"Monsieur, I sold it for twenty-five thousand. I am ready to take it back for eighteen thousand as soon as you explain, to conform to the legal requirements, how you happen to be in possession of it."

At this Monsieur Lantin sat down, paralyzed with amazement. "But . . . but . . . monsieur," he continued, "examine it carefully. Up to the present I thought it was . . . er . . . an imitation."

"Will you give me your name, monsieur?" the jeweler asked.

"Certainly. My name is Lantin. I'm employed at the Ministry of the Interior, and live at 16 Rue des Martyrs."

The merchant opened his files, searched, and began: "As a matter of fact this necklace was sent to the address of Madame Lantin, 16 Rue des Martyrs, on July 20, 1876."

And the two men looked each other in the eye, the employee dumb with surprise, the goldsmith scenting a thief.

The latter continued: "Will you leave this necklace with me for twenty-four hours and I'll give you a receipt."

"Why, yes, certainly," Monsieur Lantin stammered. And he left, folding up the paper, which he put in his pocket. He crossed the street and walked up it again, only to notice that he had blundered in his direction; then he went down to the Tuileries, crossed the Seine, again saw his mistake, and returned to the Champs-Elysées, without a clear idea in his head. He made an effort to reason, to understand. His wife had not been able to buy a thing of such value—no, certainly not. . . . Why, then it must be a present. A present! A present from whom? Why?

He had stopped and remained standing in the middle of the avenue. A horrible doubt hovered about him. . . . She . . . Could she have been capable? . . . Why, then, all the other jewels were also presents! It seemed to him that the earth had begun to sway, that a tree opposite him was falling. He stretched out his arms and collapsed in a faint.

He regained consciousness in a pharmacy where the passers-by had carried him. He went home in a cab, and locked himself in. He cried desperately till nightfall, biting his handkerchief to smother his sobs, and then went to bed, prostrated with fatigue, and sank into a heavy slumber.

A ray of sunlight wakened him, and he slowly got up to go to the Ministry. It was hard to have to work after such upheavals, and it occurred to him that he might ask his chief to be excused; so he wrote to him. Then he remembered that he would have to return to the jeweler's, and he blushed crimson with shame. He deliberated for a long time. After all, he couldn't leave the necklace with that man. He dressed and went out.

It was a beautiful day, and the blue sky stretched over the city, which seemed to smile. Idlers sauntered along with their hands in their pockets.

"How happy one is when one has money," Lantin thought, as he watched them pass. "With money one can even brush away sorrow; one can go where one likes; one can travel and amuse oneself. Oh, if I were rich!"

He noticed that he was hungry, not having eaten since the night before. But his pockets were empty, and he remembered the necklace. Eighteen thousand francs! Eighteen thousand francs! That was a tidy sum.

He reached the Rue de la Paix and began to walk back and forth on the sidewalk opposite the shop. Eighteen thousand francs! Twenty times he was on the point of entering, but shame always prevented him.

Yet he was hungry, very hungry, and without a copper. He suddenly decided, crossed the street on the run to avoid giving himself time to think, and hurried into the goldsmith's.

As soon as the dealer saw him he was insidiously attentive, and offered him an arm-chair with genial urbanity. The clerks themselves appeared, with eyes and lips unmistakably hilarious, to steal a glance at him.

"I have investigated, monsieur," the dealer began, "and if you are still inclined to sell, I am ready to pay you the sum I offered."

"Why, certainly," the employee stammered.

The goldsmith took eighteen large bills from a drawer, which he counted and handed to Lantin, who signed a little receipt, and with a trembling hand put the money in his pocket. Then as he was about to leave he turned to the dealer, who was still smiling.

"I have . . . er . . . other jewels," he began, with downcast eyes, "that came to me from the same legacy. Would you care to buy them also?"

"Why, certainly, monsieur."

The dealer bowed, and a clerk moved away to laugh at his ease, while another blew his nose noisily.

"I shall bring them to you," Lantin replied, unmoved, but very red and solemn. And he took a carriage to go for the jewelry.

When he returned to the merchant's he had not yet lunched. They began to examine the things, piece by piece, valuing each. Nearly all came from the same shop.

Lantin now quibbled over the valuations, and became angry and insisted upon their showing him the book of sales, and spoke louder and louder as the sum total expanded.

The big diamond ear-rings were worth twenty thousand francs; the bracelets, thirty-five thousand; the brooches, rings, and medallions, sixteen thousand. A necklace of emeralds and sapphires brought fourteen thousand; a solitaire suspended from a fine chain forming a necklace reached forty thousand. Altogether they attained the sum of one hundred and ninety-six thousand francs.

"This comes from a person who put all her savings in jewels," the merchant observed, with sly joviality.

"Well, it's one way like any other of investing one's money," Lantin replied, with dignity. And he left, having got the buyer to agree to have a counter appraisement of the articles on the following day.

When he was in the street he looked at the Vendôme Column and felt like climbing up it, just as if it were the greasy pole in some Utopian tournament. He felt light enough on his feet to have played leapfrog over the statue of the Emperor, perched up there in the sky.

He lunched at Voisin's, and drank wine at twenty francs a bottle. Then he took a cab and made a round of the Bois. He watched the carriages with a certain contempt, oppressed by a desire to call to the passers-by:

"I, too, am rich! I have two hundred thousand francs!"

Memory brought him a vision of the Ministry. He drove there and, entering his chief's office with deliberation, announced:

"I come, monsieur, to tender my resignation. I have just inherited three hundred thousand francs."

He went to shake hands with his old colleagues, and confidentially unfolded his plans for his new existence; then he dined at the Café Anglais.

Finding himself seated near a gentleman who appeared distinguished, he could not resist an itching to confide in him, rather coquettishly, that he had just inherited four hundred thousand francs.

For the first time in his life he was not bored at the theater, and passed the night with women.

Six months later he married. His second wife was very virtuous, but of an exacting character. She made him suffer a great deal.

# A COWARD

IN society they called him "the handsome Signoles." His name was Viscount Gontran
Joseph de Signoles.

An orphan and the possessor of a sufficient fortune, as the saying goes, he cut a dash. He had a
fine figure and bearing, enough conversation to make
people credit him with cleverness, a certain natural
grace, an air of nobility and of pride, a gallant
mustache, and a gentle eye—a thing which pleases
women.

In the drawing-rooms he was in great request,
much sought after as a partner for the waltz; and
he inspired among men that smiling hatred which they
always cherish for others of an energetic figure. He
passed a happy and tranquil life, in a comfort of mind
which was most complete. It was known that he
was a good fencer, and as a pistol-shot even better.

"If ever I fight a duel," said he, "I shall choose
pistols. With that weapon I am sure of killing my
man."

Now, one night, having accompanied two young
ladies, his friends, escorted by their husbands, to the
theatre, he invited them all after the play to take
an ice at Tortoni's. They had been there for several
minutes when he perceived that a gentleman seated
at a neighboring table was staring obstinately at one
of his companions. She seemed put out, uneasy,

lowered her head. At last she said to her husband:

"There is a man who is looking me out of countenance. I do not know him; do you?"

The husband, who had seen nothing, raised his eyes, but declared:

"No, not at all."

The young lady continued, half smiling, half vexed:

"It is very unpleasant; that man is spoiling my ice."

Her husband shrugged his shoulders:

"Bast! don't pay any attention to it. If we had to occupy ourselves about every insolent fellow that we meet we should never have done."

But the viscount had risen brusquely. He could not allow that this stranger should spoil an ice which he had offered. It was to him that this insult was addressed, because it was through him and on his account that his friends had entered this café. So the matter concerned him only.

He advanced towards the man and said to him:

"You have, sir, a manner of looking at those ladies which I cannot tolerate. I beg of you to be so kind as to cease from this insistence."

The other answered:

"You are going to mind your own business, curse you."

The viscount said, with close-pressed teeth:

"Take care, sir, you will force me to pass bounds."

The gentleman answered but one word, a foul word, which rang from one end of the café to the other, and, like a metal spring, caused every guest to execute a sudden movement. All those whose backs were turned wheeled round; all the others raised their heads; three waiters pivoted upon their heels like tops; the two ladies at the desk gave a jump, then turned round their whole bodies from the waists up, as if they had been two automata obedient to the same crank.

A great silence made itself felt. Then, on a sudden, a dry sound cracked in the air. The viscount had slapped his adversary's face. Every one rose to interfere. Cards were exchanged between the two.

When the viscount had reached home he paced his room for several minutes with great, quick strides. He was too much agitated to reflect at all. One single idea was hovering over his mind—"a duel"— without arousing in him as yet an emotion of any sort. He had done that which he ought to have done; he had shown himself to be that which he ought to be. People would talk about it, they would praise him, they would congratulate him. He repeated in a loud voice, speaking as one speaks when one's thoughts are very much troubled:

"What a brute the fellow was!"

Then he sat down and began to reflect. He must find seconds, the first thing in the morning. Whom should he choose? He thought over those men of his acquaintance who had the best positions, who were the most celebrated. He finally selected the Marquis de la Tour-Noire, and the Colonel Bourdin, a nobleman and a soldier. Very good indeed! Their names would sound well in the papers. He perceived that he was thirsty, and he drank, one after another, three glasses of water; then he began again to walk up and down the room. He felt himself full of energy. If he blustered a little, if he showed himself resolute at all points, if he demanded rigorous and dangerous conditions, if he insisted on a serious duel, very serious, terrible, his opponent would probably withdraw and make apologies.

He picked up the card which he had pulled out of his pocket and thrown on the table, and he reread it with a single glance. He had already done so at the café and in the cab, by the glimmer of every street lamp, on his way home. "Georges Lamil, 51 Rue Moncey." Nothing more.

He examined these assembled letters, which seemed to him mysterious, and full of a confused meaning. Georges Lamil? Who was this man? What had he been about? Why had he stared at that woman in such a way? Was it not revolting that a stranger, an unknown, should so come and trouble your life, all on a sudden, simply because he had been pleased to fix his eyes insolently upon a woman that you knew? And the viscount repeated yet again, in a loud voice:

"What a brute!"

Then he remained motionless, upright, thinking, his look ever planted on the card. A rage awoke in him against this piece of paper, an anger full of hate in which was mixed a strange, uneasy feeling. It was stupid, this whole affair! He took a little penknife which lay open to his hand, and pricked it into the middle of the printed name, as if he had poniarded some one.

However, they must fight! He considered himself as indeed the insulted party. And, having thus the right, should he choose the pistol or the sword?

With the sword he risked less; but with the pistol he
had the chance of making his adversary withdraw.
It is very rare that a duel with swords proves mortal,
a mutual prudence preventing the combatants from
engaging near enough for the point of a rapier to
enter very deep.   With the pistol he risked his life
seriously; but he might also come out of the affair
with all the honors of the situation, and without going so far as an actual meeting.

He said:

"I must be firm.   He will be afraid."

The sound of his voice made him tremble, and he
looked about him.   He felt himself very nervous.
He drank another glass of water, then began to un-
dress himself to go to bed.

As soon as he was in bed, he blew out the light
and shut his eyes.

He thought:

"I've got all day to-morrow to attend to my affairs.
I'd better sleep first so as to be calm."

He was very warm under the bedclothes, but he
could not manage to doze off.   He turned and
twisted, remained five minutes on his back, then
placed himself on his left side, then rolled over to
his right.

He was still thirsty.   He got up again to drink.
Then an anxiety seized him:

"Shall I be afraid?"

Why did his heart fall to beating so madly at each
of the well-known noises of his chamber?   When the
clock was about to strike, the little grinding sound
of the spring which stands erect, caused him to give
a start; and for several seconds after that he was

obliged to open his mouth to breathe, he remained so much oppressed

He set himself to reasoning with himself upon the possibility of his thing:

"Shall I be afraid?"

No, certainly not, he would not be afraid, because he was resolute to go to the end, because he had his will firmly fixed to fight and not to tremble. But he felt so deeply troubled that he asked himself:

"Can a man be afraid in spite of him?"

And the doubt invaded him, this uneasiness, this dread. If some force stronger than his will, if some commanding, and irresistible power should conquer him, what would happen? Yes, what could happen? He should certainly appear on the field, since he willed to do it. But if he trembled? But if he fainted? And he thought of his situation, of his reputation, of his name.

And a curious necessity seized him on a sudden to get up again and look at himself in the mirror. He relit his candle. When he perceived his face reflected in the polished glass he hardly recognized himself and it seemed to him that he had never seen this man before. His eyes appeared enormous; and he was pale, surely he was pale, very pale.

He remained upright before the mirror. He put out his tongue as if to test the state of his health, and all on a sudden this thought entered into him after the fashion of a bullet:

"The day after to-morrow, at this time, I shall perhaps be dead."

And his heart began again to beat furiously.

"The day after to-morrow, at this time, I shall

perhaps be dead. This person before me, this 'I' which I see in this glass, will exist no longer. What! here I am, I am looking at myself, I feel myself to live, and in twenty-four hours I shall be laid to rest upon this couch, dead, my eyes shut, cold, inanimate, gone."

He turned towards his bed and he distinctly saw himself extended on the back in the same sheets which he had just left. He had the hollow face which dead men have, and that slackness to the hands which will never stir more.

So he grew afraid of his bed, and, in order not to look at it again, he passed into his smoking-room. He took a cigar mechanically, lit it, and again began to walk the room. He was cold; he went towards the bell to wake his valet; but he stopped, his hand lifted towards the bell-rope:

"That fellow will see that I am afraid."

And he did not ring, he made the fire himself. When his hands touched anything they trembled slightly, with a nervous shaking. His head wandered; his troubled thoughts became fugitive, sudden, melancholy; an intoxication seized on his spirit as if he had been drunk.

And ceaselessly he asked himself:

"What shall I do? What will become of me?"

His whole body vibrated, jerky tremblings ran over it; he got up, and approaching the window, he opened the curtains.

The day was coming, a day of summer. The rosy sky made rosy the city, the roofs, and the walls. A great fall of tenuous light, like a caress from the rising sun, enveloped the awakened world; and, with this glimmer, a hope gay, rapid, brutal, seized on the heart of the viscount! Was he mad to let himself be so struck down by fear, before anything had even been decided, before his seconds had seen those of this Georges Lamil, before he yet knew if he was going to fight at all?

He made his toilet, dressed himself, and left the house with a firm step.

He repeated to himself, while walking:

"I must be decided, very decided. I must prove that I am not afraid."

His seconds, the marquis and the colonel, put themselves at his disposition, and after having pressed his hands energetically, discussed the conditions of the meeting.

The colonel asked:

"You want a serious duel?"

The viscount answered:

"Very serious."

The marquis took up the word.

"You insist on pistols?"

"Yes."

"Do you leave us free to settle the rest?"

The viscount articulated with a dry, jerky voice:

"Twenty paces, firing at the word, lifting the arm instead of lowering it. Exchange of shots until some one is badly wounded."

The colonel declared, in a satisfied tone:

"Those are excellent conditions. You are a good shot; the chances are all in your favor."

And they separated. The viscount returned home to wait for them. His agitation, which had been temporarily calmed, was now increasing with every moment. He felt along his arms, along his legs, in his chest, a kind of quivering, a kind of continuous vibration; he could not stay in one place, neither sitting down nor standing up. He had no longer a trace of moisture in his mouth, and he made at every instant a noisy movement of the tongue as if to un-glue it from his palate.

He tried to take his breakfast, but he could not eat. Then he thought of drinking in order to give himself courage, and had a decanter of rum brought him, from which he gulped down, one after the other, six little glasses.

A warmth, like a burn, seized on him. It was fol-lowed as soon by a giddiness of the soul. He thought: "I know the way. Now it will go all right."

But at the end of an hour he had emptied the de-canter, and his state of agitation was become again intolerable. He felt a wild necessity to roll upon the ground, to cry, to bite. Evening fell.

The sound of the door-bell caused him such a feel-ing of suffocation that he had not the strength to rise to meet his seconds.

He did not even dare to talk to them any longer— to say "How do you do?" to pronounce a single word, for fear lest they divine all from the alteration in his voice.

The colonel said:

"Everything is settled according to the conditions which you fixed. Your opponent at first insisted on the privileges of the offended party, but he yielded almost immediately, and has agreed to everything. His seconds are two officers."

The viscount said:

"Thank you."

The marquis resumed:

"Excuse us if we only just run in and out, but we've still a thousand things to do. We must have a good doctor, because the duel is not to stop till after some one is badly hit, and you know there's no trifling with bullets. A place must be appointed near some house where we can carry the wounded one of the two, if it is necessary, etc.; it will take us quite two or three hours more."

The viscount articulated a second time:

"Thank you."

The colonel asked:

"You're all right? You're calm?"

"Yes, quite calm, thanks."

The two men retired.

When he felt himself alone again, it seemed to him that he was going mad. His servant having lit the lamps, he sat down before his table to write some letters. After tracing at the top of a page, "This is my Will," he got up again and drew off, feeling incapable of putting two ideas together, of taking a single resolution, of deciding anything at all.

And so he was going to fight a duel! He could no longer escape that. What could be passing within him? He wanted to fight, he had that intention and that resolution firmly fixed; and he felt very plainly that, notwithstanding all the effort of his mind and all the tension of his will, he would not be able to retain strength enough to go as far as the place of the encounter. He tried to fancy the combat, his own attitude, and the bearing of his adversary.

From time to time, his teeth struck against one another in his mouth with a little dry noise. He tried to read, and took up de Châteauvillard's duelling code. Then he asked himself:

"My adversary, has he frequented the shooting-galleries? Is he well known? What's his class? How can I find out?"

He remembered the book by Baron de Vaux upon pistol-shooters, and he searched through it from one end to the other. Georges Lamil was not mentioned. But, however, if the man had not been a good shot, he would not have accepted immediately that danger-ous weapon and those conditions, which were mortal.

His pistol-case by Gastinne Renette lay on a little round table. As he passed he opened it and took out one of the pistols, then placed himself as if to shoot, and raised his arm; but he trembled from head to foot, and the barrel shook in all directions.

Then he said:

"It is impossible. I cannot fight like this."

At the end of the barrel he regarded that little hole, black and deep, which spits out death; he thought of dishonor, of the whispers in the clubs, of the laughter in the drawing-rooms, of the disdain of women, of the allusions in the papers, of the in-sults which would be thrown at him by cowards.

He went on staring at the pistol, and raising the hammer, he suddenly saw a priming glitter beneath it like a little red flame. The pistol had been left loaded, by chance, by oversight. And he experienced from that a confused inexplicable joy.

If in the presence of the other he had not the calm and noble bearing which is fit, he would be lost for-

ever.   He would be spotted, marked with a sign of
infamy, hunted from society.   And he should not
have that calm and bold bearing; he knew it, he felt
it.   And yet he was really brave, because he wanted to
fight!  He was brave, because——.   The thought which
just grazed him did not even complete itself in his
spirit, but, opening his mouth wide, he brusquely
thrust the pistol-barrel into the very bottom of his
throat and pressed upon the trigger. . . .

When his valet ran in, attracted by the report, he
found him dead, on his back.   A jet of blood had
spattered the white paper on the table and made a
great red stain below the four words:

"This is my Will."

Printed in the United States
114668LV00003B/115/P